新文京開發出版股份有限公司

NEW WCDP

新世紀・新視野・新文京 ─ 精選教科書・考試用書・專業參考書

New Wun Ching Developmental Publishing Co., Ltd.

New Age · New Choice · The Best Selected Educational Publications — NEW WCDP

4th Edition

第4版

醫護英文

醫療照護會話篇

中央研究院院士
陳建仁
👍 專業推薦

審訂者 李燕晉 徐會棋 胡月娟 釋高上 林清華 鍾國彪

編著者 劉明德 胡月娟 釋高上 蔡玫蕙 甘宜弘 薛承君 鄭群亮 黃偉俐
郭彥志 王惠芳 林郁婷 韓文蕙 馮兆康 張銘峰 Jonathan Chen-Ken Seak
Annie Li 呂維倫 王守玉 黃瑋婷 楊美華

掃描QR Code
附贈朗讀MP3

Medical English for
Healthcare Professionals

The Classification of Clinical Specialties 臨床科別分類

Medicine Specialties 內科專科

Cardiology 心臟內科

Endocrinology & Metabolism
內分泌與代謝內科

General Internal Medicine
一般內科

Geriatric Medicine 老年醫學科

Hematology 血液內科

Hepato-Gastroenterology 肝膽內科

Infectious Disease 感染科

Nephrology 腎臟內科

Oncology 腫瘤內科

Respiratory & Thoracic Medicine
呼吸與胸腔內科

Rheumatology & Immunology 風濕免疫內科

Sleep Disorder Clinic 睡眠障礙門診

Surgery Specialties 外科專科

Cardiovascular Surgery 心臟血管外科

Craniomaxillofacial Surgery 顱顏外科

General Surgery 一般外科

Orthopedic Surgery 骨科

Plastic/Cosmetic Surgery 整形／美容外科

Proctology Surgery 直腸外科

Neurosurgery 神經外科

Thoracic Surgery 胸腔外科

Traumatic Surgery 創傷外科

Urologic Surgery 泌尿外科

Pediatric Specialties 小兒專科

Child & Adolescent Psychiatry
兒童與青少年精神科

Health Baby Clinic 健兒門診

Pediatrics 小兒科

Pediatric Dentistry 小兒牙科

Pediatric Dermatology 小兒皮膚科

Pediatric Neurosurgery 小兒神經外科

Pediatric Ophthalmology 小兒眼科

Pediatric Orthopedic Surgery
小兒骨科

Pediatric Otolaryngology 小兒耳鼻喉科

Pediatric Plastic & Reconstructive Surgery
小兒整形與重建外科

Pediatric Rehabilitation 小兒復健科

Pediatric Surgery 小兒外科

Pediatric Urology 小兒泌尿科

Gynecology and Obstetrics 婦產專科

Assisted Reproductive Medicine
人工生殖醫學

Infertility Clinic
不孕症門診

Gynecology 婦科

Obstetrics 產科

Genetic Counseling 基因諮詢

Other Specialties 其他專科

Anesthesiology 麻醉科

Otolaryngology 耳鼻喉科

Dermatology 皮膚科

Pain Clinic 疼痛門診

Emergency Medicine 急診科

Pathology & Laboratory Medicine
病理與實驗診斷醫學

Family Medicine 家庭醫學科

Neurology 神經科

Physical Therapy & Rehabilitation
物理治療與復健科

Nutrition Clinic 營養諮詢門診

Occupational Medicine 職業醫學科

Psychiatry 身心科（精神科）

Ophthalmology 眼科

Radiology/Medical Imaging 影像醫學部

Smoking Cessation Clinic 戒菸門診

Dentistry 牙醫專科

Craniofacial Dentistry 顱顏牙科

Orthodontic Dentistry 牙型矯正科

Dental Implant Surgery 植牙

Pediatric Dentistry 小兒牙科

Endodontic Dentistry 齒內治療科

Periodontic Dentistry 牙周病科

General Dentistry 一般牙科

Prosthetic Dentistry 義齒補綴科

Geriatric Dentistry 老人牙科

Restoration Dentistry 口腔重建

Oral Surgery 口腔外科

Chinese Medicine 中醫專科

Chinese Acupuncture
中醫針灸

Chinese Obstetrics & Gynecology
中醫婦產科

Chinese Allergy Medicine 中醫過敏科

Chinese Pediatric Medicine 中醫兒科

Chinese Internal Medicine 中醫內科

Chinese Traumatology 中醫創傷科

推薦序

　　「工欲善其事，必先利其器」，正確而實用的教科書，是老師和學生必備的書籍。現有的醫護專用英文書籍，雖然琳瑯滿目，但是內容各有偏重的領域，適用於**護理人員的英文學習**，**而且與臨床護理實務結合的書籍**，相當少見。許多新出版的醫護英文書籍，或是倉促出版而有疏漏，或是未能兼顧實用性和易懂性。隨著醫藥護理科技的日新月異，如果培養專業護理人員英語能力的書籍不夠完備而更新，不但直接影響醫護教學的品質，也間接影響醫護人員的語文能力。

　　明德一向力爭上游，也積極關心國內醫護學生的學習成效。很高興看到由劉明德先生主編，集合醫護及外文跨領域專業人才共同編寫的**醫護英文－醫療照護會話篇**之問世。這本嶄新而質優的教學用書，課程章節編排合宜，不僅讓讀者一目瞭然，更符合實際教學需要。本書內容豐富而條理清晰，可以看出編著者和出版公司的用心，可說是臺灣近年來出版的重要醫護書籍之一。它既符合臨床醫學與生命科學的教學需求，並能增進醫護領域學生的臨床學習，值得醫學、護理、醫管（健康事業管理）等科系學生，以及從事臨床護理或行政工作人員一讀。我很樂意再次推薦本書，希望國內的醫護工作者能學習得更有成效，也給國人更安全更有效的醫療照護。

陳建仁　謹識

陳建仁
- 美國約翰霍普金斯大學流行病學博士
- 中央研究院副院長、院士暨特聘研究員
- 國立臺灣大學流行病學與預防醫學研究所教授
- 曾任行政院衛生署署長
- 曾任行政院國家科學委員會主任委員

▲ 陳建仁院士（右）與劉明德攝於導生會

優秀的英文語文能力是研習現代醫學和拓展國際醫療必備的條件。馬偕紀念醫院小兒科為增進醫師們的英文語文能力，在高信安醫師當主任期間(1986－1990)就邀請美國賓州大學兒童醫院 Irving J Olshin 醫師和其他國際知名外賓來短期教學或演講。梁德城醫師接掌兒科時(1990－1996)實施每週三晨會全程用英文報告和討論，並聘請 Allen Hoekman 小兒科醫師在會末做英文評述。Hoekman 醫師在 2001 年 6 月停止英文教學，專心傳播福音。李宏昌主任指派我接下晨會英文評述和教學的任務。在住院醫師報告後，針對其發音、錯字和文法提出修正建議，並播放一段與醫學有關的英文短片，聆聽道地的美語發音，來增加大家的學習興趣。這些短片取材自 AudioDigest、Discovery、ER、Grey's Anatomy、House MD 和有關醫學的電影。我會預先講解生字、片語和俚語，以提高大家的學習效果。

九年後，陳銘仁主任建議找尋有效提升住院醫師英文病歷寫作能力的教材。幸運地在圖書館發現了「**醫護英文－醫療照護會話篇**」。研讀後，深覺這本書的**內容簡明而且英語朗讀清晰**，適合在英文晨會結束前短暫的片段時間播放，不但有助於英文病歷書寫和報告撰寫，而且可提昇大家在臨床上與外國人溝通的能力。實施後，效果良好，輪調到本科的見實習醫師，甚至要出國進修的同仁都來問我書名，並索取補充教材。

研讀本書和應用於晨會教學後，發現書中有幾個錯字或語意不明之處，立即與新文京開發出版公司和作者劉明德老師聯絡。劉老師專程來訪，並邀請我負責修訂。我因為喜愛學習英文，所以樂意的接下這個任務。

　　在這次修訂中，除了校正錯字和語意不明者外，還盡力使中英對照在文義、語態和時態相互吻合，讓讀者在學習醫學英文時也能增強中英互譯的能力，打下勝任國際醫療的基礎。

　　雖然本書已詳細編撰和校稿，相信仍有不少待改進之處。懇請讀者先進，不吝指教。

李燕晉　謹識

李燕晉
- 馬偕紀念醫院小兒科部小兒內分泌科主治醫師
- 臺北醫學大學兼任教授

▲ 李燕晉醫師（右）與劉明德攝於馬偕醫院

　　時光飛逝，在我數十年從事研究的過程中，回首所受的臨床醫學教育，和我數十年來所教導的學生們，驀然發現，好的教科書絕對是一個課程，甚至是一個學門能夠受到重視並蓬勃發展最重要的因素之一。不久之前已問世的醫護英文用語深受讀者喜愛；此刻，再次由新文京開發出版股份有限公司出版，由<u>劉明德</u>先生與<u>郭彥志</u>醫師等人所編著的**醫護英文－醫療照護會話篇**，看得出都是內容相當實在，且容易上手的好書。

　　<u>劉明德</u>先生曾在<u>榮總</u>跟隨我從事研究、並在<u>陽明大學醫學系</u>擔任了我的研究助理，一路所做的研究相當地踏實，而我發現這樣的性格，同時也反映在這本書的內容裡：內容整理豐富，且條理分明、井然有序。本書的出版，對國內**醫護人員的教學與指導**，可說能夠產生相當大的實用功效。因此，在翻閱過內容之後，我欣然地再次接受此書的審訂工作。我認為這樣內容實在的好書，確實是目前國內醫護教育界所需要的，相當值得推薦。

徐會棋　謹識

徐會棋
- 國立陽明大學醫學系專任教授
- 振興醫院腫瘤醫學部藥物治療科兼任主任
- 曾任臺北市立聯合醫院陽明院區院長

▲ 徐會棋教授（左）與劉明德攝於臺北榮總

審訂者序

　　劉明德先生任教於本校醫務管理系與護理系，也有與教學相關的書籍著作，包括：醫護英文用語、醫護專業術語、觀光英語、管理學競爭優勢（譯著）、基礎統計學（校閱）、普通微生物學、公共衛生概論、病歷閱讀、流行病學（編撰中）等。劉先生畢業於臺灣大學，雖然走入學術路線出道較晚，但他向來教學認真，頗受學生讚賞。最近他又回臺灣大學流行病學研究所參與升等研究，相信以他的毅力與勇氣堅持下去，終究會有所收穫。

　　劉先生在醫護英文用語出版後，並未懈怠，仍積極努力完成屬於護理人員在醫院臨床照護非常實用的**醫護英文－醫療照護會話篇**，可以看出他關心護理系學生將來在**臨床應用的需求與培養英文能力**的用心。有鑑於此，我欣然同意加入審閱行列，提供更多的護理資訊。

胡月娟 謹識

胡月娟
- 英國歐斯特大學護理學博士
- 中臺科技大學護理系講座教授

▲ 胡月娟教授（右）與劉明德攝於臺大校友會

審訂者序

　　由明德與郭彥志醫師等人所編著的**醫護英文－醫療照護會話篇**乃是繼醫護英文用語之後，為目前國內最好的**醫院護理臨床教學**書籍之一。明德和我們是大學同窗好友，畢業後雖然各奔前程，但我們還是會彼此交流學術方面的教學經驗。我們得知明德正規劃著這樣一項龐大又艱鉅的工作，編撰如此實用的**護理人員臨床英文用書**。我們當時便應允了明德邀請，為本書進行審訂。

　　在審訂的過程中，發現這本書的內容完完全全和明德的為人一樣，相當實際且清清楚楚。整理不但詳盡，在編排上也設計得別出心裁。以臨床醫護會話為例，明德等編著群將其敘述得相當活潑而不落俗套，著實有別於坊間其他相關書籍。這的的確確是國內教師和學生的一大福音，值得護理科系及醫護相關科系學生好好一讀。

釋高上、林清華、鍾國彪 謹識

▲ 林清華醫師（右）與劉明德造訪台大
　生命科學系施秀惠教授（中）

釋高上
- 國立臺灣大學醫學工程研究所博士
- 新光醫院骨科主任

林清華
- 高雄醫學大學醫學研究所博士
- 高雄市立凱旋醫院成人精神科主任、主治醫師

鍾國彪
- 美國約翰霍普金斯大學衛生政策與管理博士
- 國立臺灣大學健康政策與管理研究所教授

主編者序

　　筆者曾在弘光科技大學、中臺科技大學、聖母醫護管理專校任教醫管與醫護英文、醫學術語、微生物免疫學、病理學等課程,教學經驗豐富。在醫護英文用語出版後,為使護理科學生的**臨床英文對話**能力提升,筆者與薛承君醫師研擬出版**醫護英文－醫療照護會話篇**、病歷閱讀等書。期待這本與郭彥志醫師等人精撰的**護理英文用書**能造福莘莘學子,並於臨床應用,這是我們最大的欣慰與榮幸。

　　編撰過程中,筆者經統整各方寶貴意見後,隨即邀請教授群、醫護專業群及外語專業群共同編著,以做出有別於坊間相關書籍的實用工具書,使本書更添光采。感謝各位的熱忱參與,在此致上十二萬分的謝意!本次改版特別新增 COVID-19 照護會話,祈能對臨床應用有所助益。

　　此外,特別感謝推薦者:中央研究院陳建仁院士、台南市新樓醫院張銘峰醫師提供參考資料、臺大醫院林昱任醫師、劉卓鷹醫師、淡江大學外語學院院長宋美瑾(前臺大外文系教授、系主任)協助完成一般牙科單元之撰寫,以及多位專業醫師的協助,使得本書更具專業應用價值!最後,更要感謝即將前往美國哈佛大學研究所進修的 Annie Li、臺大學妹黃瑋婷、蔡孟玲,以及新文京開發出版股份有限公司相關人員的大力協助,並期盼任教老師及讀者不吝指正,謝謝!

劉明德 謹識

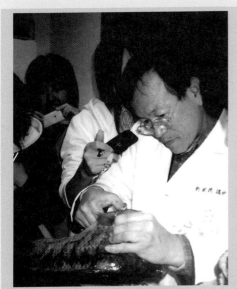

▲ 筆者於聖母醫護管理專校護理科任教生物學實驗

作者簡介

✎ 主編者

▶ **劉明德**

國立臺灣大學流行病學與預防醫學研究所升等研究

國立臺灣大學微生物學研究所碩士（榜首）

國立臺灣大學公共衛生學系學士

國立臺灣大學健康政策與管理研究所演講「婚姻品質及生活品質」講師

現任國立聯合大學健康與生活、環保與生活講師

現任弘光科技大學通識學院微生物與人類文明、健康與生活講師

弘光科技大學健康事業管理系醫學英文及術語講師

中臺科技大學護理系醫護英文及通識教育中心環境教育講師

中臺科技大學醫務管理系醫管英文、醫學術語及護理系健康心理學講師

輔英科技大學應用外語系演講「跨領域醫護英文教學」講師

臺灣首府大學觀光英文、生物技術及健康科學講師

育達科技大學通識教育中心生物醫學、環保與生活、健康管理講師

聖母醫護管理專校護理科醫護英文與術語、病理學、（微）生物學實驗講師

仁德醫護管理專校公共衛生、（微）生物學、解剖生理、微生物科技與生活講師

考試院外語（英語）領隊人員及格

2015年錯過升等助理教授

✎ 醫護專業群

▶ **胡月娟**

英國歐斯特大學護理學博士

國立臺灣大學護理學碩士

中臺科技大學護理系講座教授

▶ **釋高上**

國立臺灣大學醫學工程研究所博士

國立臺灣大學醫學系學士（第一名）

新光醫院骨科主任

輔仁大學醫學系教授

曾任亞東紀念醫院骨科主治醫師、臺大醫院骨科兼任主治醫師（教學診）

▶ **蔡玫蕙**

國立陽明大學醫學院生理學研究所博士

臺北醫學大學呼吸治療學系兼任副教授

▶ **甘宜弘**

臺北醫學大學醫學研究所碩士、醫學系學士

衛生福利部雙和醫院神經外科主治醫師

▶ **薛承君**

國立陽明大學醫學院急重症醫學研究所碩士

國立臺灣大學醫學系學士

新北市土城醫院急診醫學科主任

作者簡介

▶ 鄭群亮
國立臺灣大學醫學系學士
臺南市營新醫院院長
曾任長庚醫院林口總院骨科及外科主
治醫師

▶ 黃偉俐
美國俄亥俄大學心理學碩士、博士候
選人
國立臺灣大學醫學系學士
黃偉俐身心科診所院長
曾任新店耕莘醫院精神科主治醫師、
桃園晨新診所身心科主任

▶ 郭彥志
國立臺灣大學醫學系學士
桃園長庚醫院腎臟科醫師

▶ 王惠芳
國立臺灣大學農業化學研究所微生物
組碩士
高雄醫學大學學士後醫學系學士
羅東聖母醫院新陳代謝科主治醫師
聖母醫護管理專校護理科兼任講師

▶ 林郁婷
國立臺灣大學牙醫學系學士
國立臺灣大學附設醫院牙醫師

▶ 韓文蕙
國立臺灣大學公共衛生學院衛生政策
與管理研究所博士
曾任國立金門大學護理系系主任、副
教授
曾任元培科技大學護理系系主任

▶ 馮兆康
國立陽明大學公共衛生研究所博士
弘光科技大學健康事業管理系副教授

▶ 張銘峰
國立成功大學醫學院醫學士
財團法人臺灣基督長老教會新樓醫院
家庭醫學科主任、主治醫師

▶ Jonathan Chen-Ken Seak
M.B.B.S., International Medical
University, Malaysia
University Malaya Medical Centre
(UMMC)
Sarawak General Hospital

▶ Annie Li
Cornell University, College of
Veterinary Medicine, U.S.A.
National Taiwan University, Center for
Zoonoses Research, Taiwan
美國哈佛大學公共衛生研究所碩士進
修

▶ 王守玉
澳洲昆士蘭科技大學 (Queensland
University of Technology)護理哲學
博士
曾任弘光科技大學護理系副教授

▶ 楊美華
Ulster University (UK)護理碩士
國立成功大學護理系學士
臺北榮民總醫院重粒子及放射腫瘤部
護理師
曾任臺北榮民總醫院血液腫瘤科護理
師
曾任元培科技大學護理系兼任講師

外語專業群

▶ 呂維倫
國立臺灣大學語言學研究所博士
國立臺灣大學外國語文學系學士
捷克馬薩里克大學英美研究系研究員
Discovery 特聘翻譯撰稿人

▶ 黃瑋婷
國立臺灣大學外國語文學系學士
教育部國際文化教育事業處高考及格
曾任國立臺灣大學解剖暨細胞生物學
研究所研究助理

目 錄

Respiratory and Thoracic Unit
呼吸胸腔科

Learning Goals 學習目標 ✏️

1. Assessing patients with respiratory disease
2. Asking for information about the sputum
3. Assessing respiratory function
4. Providing health education to patients

Outline 本章大綱 ✏️

- The Components of the Respiratory System
  呼吸系統的組成
- Case Information: Pulmonary Tuberculosis,
  COVID-19 個案資訊：肺結核、新冠肺炎
- Admission Assessment　入院評估
- Hospitalization　住院療護
- Discharge Instructions　出院衛教

*Medical English for
Healthcare Professionals*

The Components of the Respiratory System 呼吸系統的組成

01

The respiratory system consists of a series of airways conducting air to the alveoli, the final branches of the respiratory tree where air is exchanged. The atmospheric air first enters the **nostrils**[1] and **nasal cavity**[2], where the nasal hairs (**vibrissa**[3]) filter air to get rid of any large foreign substances. Then the air goes through the **pharynx**[4], **larynx**[5], **trachea**[6], **bronchi**[7] and eventually enters the lungs.

Via these airways, the air is humidified and warmed. The air then enters our lungs by travelling through numerous branches of the airway and finally arrives in the **alveoli**[8]. Alveoli are tiny air sacs where air exchange occurs. Oxygen diffuses into capillaries surrounding the alveoli and carbon dioxide leaves the blood stream. Both of these processes depend on partial pressure.

呼吸系統由一連串的呼吸道及其末端專司氣體交換的肺泡組成。大氣中的空氣首先進入鼻孔和鼻腔，在此由鼻毛過濾空氣中大的異物。接著空氣經過咽、喉、氣管、支氣管，最後進入肺臟。

經過這些呼吸通道時，空氣會被溼潤化與增溫。空氣經過無數呼吸道的分支，而進入我們的肺臟，最後到達肺泡。肺泡是微小的氣囊，氣體在此交換。氧氣擴散至環繞肺泡周圍的微血管，而二氧化碳離開血流。兩者的擴散過程取決於各自的分壓。

Terminology 術語

1. nostril [ˈnɑstrɪl] 鼻孔
2. nasal cavity [ˈnezl ˈkævətɪ] 鼻腔
3. vibrissa [vaɪˈbrɪsə] 鼻毛
4. pharynx [ˈfærɪŋks] 咽
5. larynx [ˈlærɪŋks] 喉

6. trachea [ˈtrekɪə] 氣管
7. bronchi [ˈbrɑŋkaɪ] 支氣管（複數）（bronchus 單數）
8. alveoli [ælˈvɪəlaɪ] 肺泡（複數）（alveolus 單數）

Case Information 個案資訊

Pulmonary Tuberculosis [ˈpʌlməˌnɛrɪ t(j)uˌbɜkjəˈlosɪs] **肺結核**

1. **Cause**: Mycobacterium. The most common form is *Mycobacterium tuberculosis*.
2. **Symptoms & Signs**: Fever, chills, prolonged and productive cough, cough with blood, night sweats, weight loss, and chest pain.

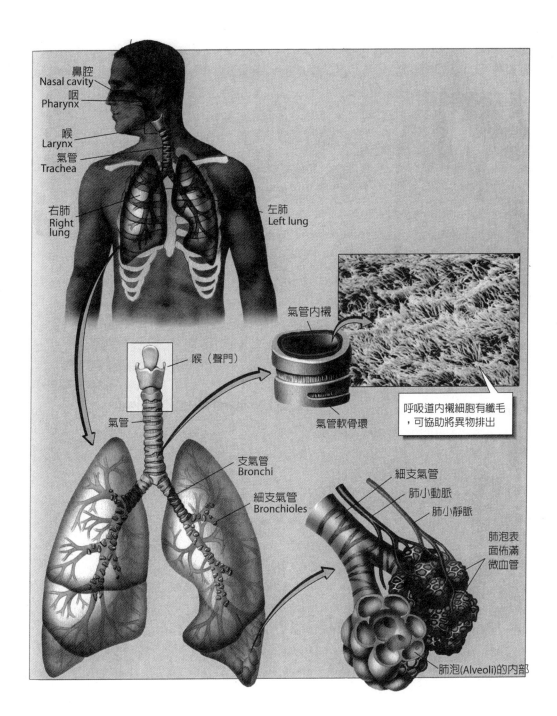

鼻腔
Nasal cavity

咽
Pharynx

喉
Larynx

氣管
Trachea

右肺
Right lung

左肺
Left lung

氣管內襯

喉（聲門）

氣管

氣管軟骨環

呼吸道內襯細胞有纖毛，可協助將異物排出

支氣管
Bronchi

細支氣管
Bronchioles

細支氣管

肺小動脈

肺小靜脈

肺泡表面佈滿微血管

肺泡(Alveoli)的內部

Case Information 個案資訊

3. **Care**:

(1) Remain in isolation if necessary.

(2) Take medications on a regular basis.

(3) Pay attention to any side effects from the medications.

(4) Undergo chest X-ray examinations regularly.

Admission Assessment　入院評估

Mr. Wu, a 65-year-old man, has been coughing for a long time.

N: Nurse　**P:** Patient

N: Good morning, Mr. Wu. What brings you to the hospital today?

P: I have been coughing for about 8 months.

N: Can you please describe your cough? For instance, are you producing **sputum**[1] or experiencing **heartburn**[2]?

P: There's a little sputum sometimes when I cough.

N: What color is your sputum? Is there blood in it?

P: My sputum is yellow with **tiny**[3] **bloody streaks**[4].

N: Are you experiencing any other symptoms, such as fever, sweating at night or weight loss?

P: I haven't had a fever, but I've been sweating at night and recently lost 5 kg within the last 6 months.

N: Did you see a doctor for treatment?

P: Yes, I used to go to a clinic. But the medications didn't resolve any of my problems.

N: *(Places the **stethoscope**[5] on his back)* Please breathe slowly and deeply. *(Moves it)* Once again. *(Moves it again)* Once again. I don't hear any abnormal respiratory sounds. Do you smoke?

P: Yes, I've smoked one pack a day since I was fifteen.

N: What's your **occupation**[6]? Some diseases can be associated with working environments.

P: I used to be a teacher but retired about 4 years ago.

N: Has anyone in your family had symptoms similar to yours?

P: No, none of them have had this kind of condition.

N: OK, the doctor has arranged a chest X-ray to figure out if there is a problem with your lungs. Then we'll take a sputum sample for examination. Please wait for me here.

P: OK, thank you.

65 歲的吳先生咳嗽好久了。

吳先生早安，你今天為何來院呢？

我已經咳嗽 8 個月了。

可以請你描述一下咳嗽症狀嗎？譬如說有痰或是感到心口灼熱？

咳嗽時，有時會有一些痰。

痰的顏色為何？是否有血呢？

痰是黃色的，裡面有一點血絲。

還有其他症狀嗎？譬如發燒、夜間流汗或是體重減輕呢？

我沒有發燒，但最近會在夜間流汗，體重在半年內減輕 5 公斤。

你有就醫診治嗎？

有的，我曾經到診所就醫，但藥物治療無效。

（把聽診器放在他的背上）請慢慢深呼吸。（移動聽診器）再一次。（再次移動）再一次。沒有聽到異常的呼吸音。你吸菸嗎？

有的，15 歲開始，每天一包。

你的職業是什麼？有些疾病與工作環境有關。

我是個老師，約在 4 年前退休。

家中成員有類似你的症狀嗎？

他們沒有任何人有這種情形。

好的，醫師已安排你要照胸部 X 光以了解肺部的問題。接著我們會採集你的痰液檢體做檢查。請在這兒等我。

好的，謝謝。

Nursing Notes　護理記錄

C/O coughing up yellowish sputum with tiny bloody streaks for 8 months. Went to the clinic for treatment but failed to resolve the problem. Has smoked one pack a day for the last 50 years.

主訴咳嗽 8 個月未止且咳出黃色帶有血絲的痰液。前往診所診治無效。吸菸習慣為每天一包，持續最近 50 年。

 Tips on Writing

主訴的寫法及用法：C/O(C/C)＋名詞(N.)／動名詞(Ving)

C/O＝Complaint of　個案主訴（抱怨）

C/C＝Chief Complaint　主訴

例：C/O chest pain.

　　No C/O discomfort.

　　C/O coughing up yellow sputum for two weeks.

 Vocabulary and Sentence Examples　字彙與例句

1. sputum [ˋspjutəm]
   (n.) 痰液

   It's crucial to collect his sputum sample if you suspect pneumonia.　若懷疑他有肺炎，則採集痰液檢體便攸關重要。

2. heartburn [ˋhɑrt͵bɝn]
   (n.) 胃灼熱；心口灼熱

   Patients with GERD (gastroesophageal reflux disease) may experience heartburn, especially after meals.
   胃食道逆流症患者會感覺到心口灼熱，特別在餐後。

3. tiny [ˋtaɪnɪ]
   (adj.) 微（細）小的

   Viruses are a group of tiny pathogens capable of causing diseases.　病毒是一群足以致病的微小病原體。

4. bloody streak　血絲
   [ˋblʌdɪ strik]

   There're bloody streaks on the bowel movement.
   糞便裡有血絲。

5. stethoscope (n.) 聽診器
   [ˋstɛθə͵skop]

   A stethoscope is a tool which can amplify sounds from within the body.　聽診器是一種可以放大來自體內的聲音的工具。

6. occupation (n.) 職業
   [͵ɑkjəˋpeʃən]

   May I ask what your occupation is?
   我可以詢問您的職業嗎？

Hospitalization　住院療護

Mr. Wu rested on the bed, while the nurse explained his condition to him.

N: The doctor said that the chest X-ray **revealed**[1] a nodule on your right lung, so he suggested that you receive another examination. However, this procedure is somewhat **invasive**[2].

P: What kind of examination is this? Is it very scary?

N: This procedure is called a **bronchoscopy**. The doctor will use a tube, **insert**[3] it into your airway and take samples from your nodule.

P: I can't visualize what this the procedure will be like. It makes me feel nervous.

N: The process may cause some discomfort. The doctor will use local **anesthetics** to relieve any pain.

(Suddenly, Mr. Wu starts to cough vigorously)

N: Are you alright?

P: *(Still coughing)* No, I'm having difficulty breathing.

N: Sitting up straight may help you breathe easier.

P: Oh, much better now. Thank you very much.

N: Now I have to check your **vital signs**. *(Later)* Your body temperature is 37.5 degrees Celsius, pulse rate 85 beats/min and respiratory rate 24 breaths/min. That means you're a little warm and breathing a bit quickly.

N: Please breathe deeply and slowly. I'll use the stethoscope to check if your respiratory sounds are normal. *(After the checkup)* You have some abnormal respiratory sounds. I'll be sure to tell the doctor.

P: What should I do if I begin having difficulty breathing again?

N: I'll place a **nasal cannula** over your nose so that you receive more oxygen. Also, smoking will worsen the condition of your lungs.

P: I see. I'll try my best to **quit**[4] smoking.

N: OK. The doctor will come to visit you in a few minutes.

吳先生在病床上休息，護理師正在向他解釋一些事情。

醫師說胸部 X 光顯示您的右肺有一個小結節，因此他建議你再做檢查。然而，這個檢查稍有侵入性。

是什麼樣的檢查？它很可怕嗎？

那是支氣管鏡檢查。醫師會放一條管子進入你的呼吸道，然後對你的小結節進行取樣。

我無法想像檢查過程。我感到緊張。

過程中會有些不適，但醫師會用局部麻醉劑來減輕疼痛。

（吳先生忽然劇烈地咳嗽）

你還好嗎？

（仍在咳嗽）我感到呼吸困難。

坐直能協助你呼吸順暢些。

好多了。多謝你。

我現在必須檢查你的生命徵象。（一會兒後）你的體溫是攝氏 37.5 度，脈搏每分鐘 85 下，呼吸每分鐘 24 下。表示你有點發燒以及稍微呼吸急促。

現在請慢慢深呼吸，我將用聽診器檢查你的呼吸音是否正常。（檢查後）你有些異常的呼吸音。我會告知醫師。

如果我又開始呼吸困難該怎麼辦？

我會在你的鼻子放入鼻套管，使你獲得較多的氧氣。對了，吸菸會讓肺部狀況惡化。

我明白。我會盡力戒菸。

好的。醫師一會兒會來看你。

Nursing Notes 護理記錄

C/O dyspnea. TPR: 37.5℃, 85 /min, 24 /min. Crackles over both lower lung fields. O_2 nasal cannula 2 L/min administered stat as instructed.

主訴呼吸困難。體溫、脈搏及呼吸數值分別為攝氏 37.5 度、85 下／分、24 次／分。兩肺下區出現囉音。依醫囑立即經由鼻套管每分鐘給予 2 升氧氣。

Tips on Writing

1. **as instructed** 的用法：為 the doctor instructed 之合併省略主詞的用法
   若為醫囑給藥，則寫 (Drug was) given as instructed
   若為處置，則寫 (Procedure was) started as instructed.
   例：Aspirin given as instructed.

2. 服藥／給藥的時間頻率副詞：於句尾呈現

   BID＝twice a day
   　　（未必需要規律時間）
   TID＝three times a day（同上）
   QID＝four times a day（同上）
   QD＝once a day
   例：heparin 2000u IV QD.

   Q4H＝every four hours
   PRN＝if necessary, as needed
   　　（需要時給予）
   STAT＝immediately/at once/right away，
   　　　表示立即給藥或進行處置
   例：Normal saline 500 c.c. given stat.

Vocabulary and Sentence Examples 字彙與例句

1. reveal [rɪˋvil] (v.) 顯示	The X-ray refraction revealed the complex struction of this protein.　X 光繞射顯示了這蛋白質的複雜結構。
2. invasive [ɪnˋvesɪv] (adj.) 侵入性的	In addition to surgery, endoscopy is also an invasive procedure for patients. 除了手術之外，內視鏡檢查對病人來說也具有侵入性。
3. insert [ɪnˋsɝt] (v.) 插入；放置	The nurse inserted a nasogastric tube to feed the patient. 護理師為病人放置鼻胃管以便灌食。
4. quit [kwɪt] (v.) 戒除；停止	Please quit smoking for the benefit of your health and your family's health.　請為你自己和你家人的健康戒菸。

1. bronchoscopy [braŋˈkaskəpɪ] 支氣管鏡檢查
2. anesthetic [ˌænəsˈθɛtɪk] 麻醉劑
3. vital signs [ˈvaɪtl̩ saɪns] 生命徵象
4. nasal cannula [ˈnezl̩ ˈkænjələ] 鼻套管（供氧用）

Discharge Instructions 出院衛教

04

Before discharge, the nurse reminded Mr. Wu about some important details.

N: Before you go back home, I'd like to remind you of some important details.

P: What should I be careful about?

N: Pulmonary tuberculosis is only controllable and curable disease if you follow the **instructions**[1] **strictly**[2] and take your medicine regularly. It's also possible that the course of treatment will be **prolonged**[3] if the disease is still detected.

P: I see. How long should I take these medications for?

N: You must take them **continuously**[4] for at least 6 months. During this period, you will have to come back for **follow-up**[5] and pulmonary examinations.

P: I'm afraid that I will sometimes forget to take these medications.

N: Don't worry. We'll contact the health center near your home. If you can't comply with taking your meds, the center will send someone over to remind you everyday.

P: It sounds as if I'll be strictly **monitored**[6]. Doesn't it?

N: I'm sorry you feel that way. We just want you to recover as soon as possible.

P: Alright. Is there anything else?

N: These medications may have variable side effects. If you feel any discomfort, please come back for a **consultation**[7]. Don't stop or adjust any of the dosages by yourself.

出院之前，護理師提醒吳先生重要的事情。

在你回家之前我想提醒你一些重要的事情。

我需要注意什麼事呢？

只有你嚴格地遵守指引並按時服藥時，肺結核才是可以良好控制及治癒的疾病。如果疾病仍在，療程也有可能會延長。

我知道了。那我要吃多久的藥？

你至少需連續服用 6 個月，在此期間你要回診追蹤病情及做肺部檢查。

我擔心我可能有時會忘記吃藥。

別擔心，我們會聯繫你住家附近的健康中心。倘若你的服藥順從性不佳，他們會派人每天提醒你吃藥。

聽起來我將被嚴密監控著，對吧？

抱歉。我們只是希望你早日康復。

好的。還有什麼要注意的？

這些藥物各有不同的副作用，如果你感到任何不適，請務必回診諮詢。千萬不要自行停藥或調整劑量。

P: OK, thank you. I'll be sure to take note of these instructions. | 好的,謝謝你。我會謹記在心。

Nursing Notes 護理記錄

Told the patient the disease is well-controllable if medications are taken and follow-up examinations are done periodically for at least 6 months. Told not to stop medicine or change dosages without consultation.

告知規律服用至少 6 個月的藥物和返診能有效控制病情。告知不可未經諮詢就自行停藥或改變劑量。

Tips on Writing

衛教內容的書寫:病人應當如何做或不應該如何做時,通常會省略主詞(護理師)和受詞(病人),並將子句簡化。例:
The nurse told the patient to exercise regularly. → Told to exercise regularly.

Vocabulary and Sentence Examples 字彙與例句

1. instruction
[ɪnˋstrʌkʃən]
(n.) 指示;說明

Please read the instructions before using this machine.
在使用這台機器前,先閱讀說明書。

2. strictly [ˋstrɪktlɪ]
(adv.) 嚴格地

The ER is strictly for treating patients in urgent need.
急診僅供急症病人之診治。

3. prolong [prəˋlɔŋ]
(v.) 延長

This work day has been prolonged due to his laziness.
因為他懶惰的緣故,工作期被延長了。

4. follow-up [ˋfalo ʌp]
(n.) 追蹤

Please return for a follow-up exam two weeks later.
兩星期後請回來追蹤檢查。

5. continuously
[kənˋtɪnjuəslɪ]
(adv.) 連續地

She worked continuously for 36 hours without resting.
她持續工作 36 小時沒休息。

6. monitor [ˋmanətə]
(v.) 監視;監控
(n.) 監測器

Patients in the intensive care unit have many types of equipment attached monitoring their body systems.
在加護病房的病人身上有很多儀器監測其身體狀況。

7. consultation (n.) 諮詢
[͵kansʌlˋteʃən]

They went to the psychologist for a mental health consultation. 他們去心理師那邊做心理健康諮詢。

More Information

1. 有關咳嗽的各種敘述
   (1) Dry cough/non-productive cough：乾咳，無痰的咳嗽
   (2) Productive cough：有痰的咳嗽
   (3) Mild cough：輕微咳嗽
   (4) Persistent cough：持續咳嗽
   (5) Whooping cough：百日咳

2. 痰液特徵的問診重點
   (1) What was the _color_ of your sputum?　你的痰是什麼顏色的？
   (2) How did it _smell_?　它聞起來如何？
   (3) When was it _produced_?　它何時會產生？
   (4) How much sputum was produced?　有多少痰？
   (5) What else was in the sputum?　痰中還有其他東西嗎？

Exercise 小試身手

● Choose the Correct Answer

( ) 1. The characteristics of _____ can tell us something about the pathogen.   (A) blood   (B) sputum   (C) urine   (D) pus
痰液的特徵可以告訴我們一些關於病原體的資訊。

( ) 2. _____ may be a typical manifestation of GERD.   (A) Heartburn   (B) Handle   (C) Tick   (D) Needle   心口灼熱可能是一種胃食道逆流的典型表現。

( ) 3. We can observe these _____ organisms using a microscope.   (A) huge   (B) tricky   (C) tiny   (D) gross   我們可以用顯微鏡觀察到這些微小的生物。

( ) 4. He is a teacher by _____ .   (A) occupation   (B) situation   (C) occasion   (D) business   他的職業是老師。

( ) 5. The doctor used a _____ to listen to his heart sounds.   (A) endoscope   (B) colonoscopy   (C) laparoscopy   (D) stethoscope
醫師用聽診器檢查他的心音。

( ) 6. It will be beneficial for your health if you _____ smoking.   (A) quit   (B) continue   (C) try   (D) keep   戒菸有益健康。

( ) 7. They brought the baby to the hospital for a health _____ .   (A) mission   (B) consultation   (C) dimissable   (D) discover
他們帶寶寶到醫院進行健康諮詢。

( ) 8. His research _____ that strenuous exercise could be harmful for our bodies.   (A) concealed   (B) revised   (C) revolved   (D) revealed
他的研究顯示劇烈運動可能對身體有害。

( ) 9. These days, the trend is to go with the least _____ surgery.   (A) invade   (B) invasion   (C) invasive   (D) invaded   微創手術已成為趨勢。

( ) 10. Drug addiction isn't just _____ by our own will.   (A) conquered   (B) controllable   (C) cooperative   (D) coordinated
藥物成癮不是只有意志就可以控制的。

● Fill in the Blanks

1. Please turn _____ and go _____ . Then you'll see the Department of _____ _____ . 請右轉直走，就會看到檢驗醫學部。

2. If you discover _____ _____ on your _____ _____ , please let us know. 如果你發現糞便裡有血絲，請告訴我們。

3. Have you ever experienced _____ or acid _____ before? 你先前是否感覺過胸口灼熱或胃酸逆流？

4. _____ can invade your body through your _____ , even if it is very _____ . 即使是微小的傷口，細菌都可能入侵。

5. Please _____ _____ and _____ , I'll check your _____ _____ . 請慢慢深呼吸，我將要檢查你的呼吸音。

● Simplify Nursing Notes

1. One million IU of penicillin was given immediately.
   立即給予盤尼西林 1 百萬國際單位。
   _____

2. The patient's sample was sent to the laboratory right away.
   立即將病人的檢體送往實驗室。
   _____

3. The patient said that she is prone to asthma attacks when jogging.
   病人說她在跑步時特別容易氣喘。
   _____

4. The patient stated that he lost consciousness after falling.
   病人表示他倒下後就失去意識。
   _____

5. The nurse told the patient to take one tablet of antibiotics every six hours.
   告知每 6 小時服用一顆抗生素。
   _____

6. The doctor instructed antacids three times a day. 依醫囑每天給予 3 次制酸劑。
   _____

○ Translation

1. 可以請你描述一下咳嗽症狀嗎？

_____

2. 你的職業是什麼？有些疾病與工作環境有關。

_____

3. 我會在你的鼻子放入鼻套管，使你獲得較多的氧氣。

_____

4. 只有你嚴格地遵守指引並按時服藥時，肺結核才是可以良好控制及治癒的疾病。

_____

5. 不要自行停藥或調整劑量。

_____

Case Information 個案資訊

Coronavirus disease 2019 [kəˈrəʊnəˌvaɪrəs dɪˈziz] **嚴重特殊傳染性肺炎**(COVID-19)

1. **Cause**: Coronavirus disease is an infectious disease caused by the SARS-CoV-2 virus.

2. **Symptoms & Signs**: Fever or chills, cough, cough with sputum, chest pain, shortness of breath or difficulty breathing, fatigue or weakness, feeling very unwell, muscle or body pain, headache, a loss of taste or smell, sore throat. Congestion or runny nose, nausea or vomiting, abdominal pain, diarrhea.

3. **Care**:

   (1) Stay in isolation room until symtoms areimproving and PCR test is negative.
   (2) Take medications as prescribed or instructed.
   (3) Pay attention to any side effects from the medications.
   (4) To provide oxygen delivery devices with a prescription.
   (5) Closely monitoring vital signs.
   (6) Monitoring signs and symptoms of infection, such as: fever, chills, cough and so on.
   (7) Undergo chest X-ray examinations regularly if needed.

Admission Assessment 入院評估

 05

*Mr. Lee, a 68-year-old man, has been suffering from **shortness of breath**[1] for three days.*

N: Good morning, Mr. Lee. Why are you in the hospital today? Can you describe your symptoms for me?

P: I have been having a fever, shortness of breath, a **sore throat**[2] and cough for 3 days.

N: Could you please describe your cough? For example, are you producing **sputum**[3] or experiencing a **dry cough**[4]?

P: There's a little sputum sometimes when I cough.

N: What color is your sputum? Is there blood in it?

68 歲的李先生已經呼吸急促三天了。

李先生早安，你今天為什麼來醫院呢？可以請你描述一下症狀嗎？

我已經發燒、呼吸急促、喉嚨痛跟咳嗽 3 天了。

可以請你描述一下咳嗽症狀嗎？譬如說有痰或是乾咳？

咳嗽時，有時會有一些痰。

痰的顏色為何？是否有血呢？

P: My sputum color is light yellow with tiny bloody streaks.

我的痰是淡黃色的，裡面有一點血絲。

N: Do you have other discomfort today? Such as muscle aches or **loss of smell**[5]?

你還有其他症狀嗎？譬如肌肉疼痛或喪失嗅覺？

P: Yes, I have been having muscle aches these days.

是的，我這幾天有肌肉疼痛。

N: Did you visit to the clinic for treatment before you were admitted to our hospital?

你住院之前有先到診所看診過嗎？

P: Yes, I used to go to a clinic once. But the medications didn't seem to be effective.

有的，我曾經到診所就醫一次，但藥物治療似乎沒有效果。

N: I see. I am going to take your temperature first. In addition, can I ask you a few questions? Have you been vaccinated? How many times have you been vaccinated?

我了解了。我先幫你測量體溫。另外，我可以請問你幾個問題嗎？你打過疫苗嗎？你打過幾次疫苗？

P: Yes, I've got one **vaccination**[6] shot.

有的，我打過一劑疫苗。

N: I am going to check your blood oxygen concentration now.

我現在要幫你測量血氧濃度。

P: Yes, please.

好的，請。

N: Has anyone in your family had symptoms similar to yours?

家中成員有類似你的症狀嗎？

P: No, none of them have had any symptoms like me.

他們沒有出現任何像我一樣的症狀。

N: I understand. Also, the doctor has arranged a chest X-ray and regular blood tests for you. A radiologist will come to here and take an X-ray for you later. After that, I will draw blood samples for examination.

我了解了。另外醫師已經幫你安排照胸部 X 光和血液常規檢查。待會有一位放射師會到這來幫你照 X 光，接著我會再幫你抽血做檢查。

P: OK, thank you.

好的，謝謝。

Nursing Notes　護理記錄

C/O fever, shortness of breath, sore throat, loss of smell and coughing up light yellowish sputum with tiny bloody streaks for 3 days. Visited to the clinic for treatment but failed to resolve problems. COVID-19 tests showed positive results.

主訴發燒、呼吸急促、喉嚨痛、嗅覺喪失、咳嗽三天且咳出淡黃色帶有少量血絲的痰液。前往診所診治無效。新冠肺炎檢驗結果為陽性。

Vocabulary and Sentence Examples　字彙與例句

1. shortness of breath [ˈʃɔrt əv brɛθ] 呼吸急促

   She experiences shortness of breath from time to time.
   她偶爾會呼吸急促。

2. sore throat [sor θrot] (n.) 喉嚨痛

   This medicine should soothe your sore throat.
   這種藥會緩解你的喉嚨痛。

3. sputum [ˈspjutəm] (n.) 痰液

   Please collect your suptum sample in this sputum cup before you have breakfast.　請你在早餐前將痰液收集在痰盒裡。

4. dry cough [draɪ kɔf] (n.) 乾咳

   He has a bad, dry cough, especially at night. He can't sleep well recently. Sometimes, he has vomited after coughing.
   他晚上咳得厲害，他最近睡不好，有時候咳完之後還會嘔吐。

5. loss of smell [luz əv smel] 喪失嗅覺

   One of the symtoms of COVID-19 is loss of smell or taste.
   喪失嗅覺或味覺是新冠肺炎染疫的症狀之一。

6. vaccination [væksəˈneɪʃən] (n.) 接種疫苗

   This is the newest COVID-19 vaccination schedule for adolescent.
   這是關於青少年最新新冠肺炎接種疫苗的排程。

Hospitalization 住院療護

Mr. Lee is lying on the bed while the nurse explained his condition to him.

N: What's your name? The doctor prescribed medicines for you and this is your **antiviral**[1] drugs for COVID-19 treatment. Let me explain how to take this medicine.

P: Okay.

N: The doctor said that the chest X-ray showed a 2 square cm pneumonia patch on your left lower lung field, so he highly recommends that you take the antiviral drugs two times a day for five consecutive days.

P: What are the side **effects**[2] of the antiviral drugs?

N: Most people who take the antiviral pill should not experience serious side effects. Still, there are some possible side effects as follows: diarrhea, increased blood pressure, feeling sick, an **altered**[3] or **impaired**[4] sense of taste.

P: Thank you for the careful instructions.

N: Please let me know if you don't feel well.

P: Yes, I will. Thank you.

N: Now I have to check your vital signs. Your body temperature is 38.5 degrees Celsius, pulse rate 100 beats/min and respiratory rate 24 breaths/min. That means you have a fever now and respiration rate is a bit fast.

N: Next, I am going to check your blood oxygen level.

P: Is my blood oxygen level normal? Actually, I am experiencing shortness of breath now.

N: Your blood oxygen level is 92%. 95 to 100% of blood oxygen level is considered normal. I am going to place a nasal cannula over your nostrils and then you will get more oxygen.

李先生在病床上休息，護理師正在向他解釋一些事情。

請問你的名字？這是醫師為你開立的治療新冠肺炎的藥。我來解釋一下服藥的方式。

好的。

醫師說胸部 X 光顯示有一個肺炎塊在您的左下肺葉，因此他強烈建議你連續五天、每天服用兩次抗病毒藥。

請問藥物副作用是？

多數人服用這種抗病毒藥不會有嚴重的副作用，然而還是有一些可能的副作用產生：腹瀉、血壓高、覺得不舒服、味覺改變或味覺受損。

謝謝你詳細的說明。

身體有不舒服時請告訴我。

好的，我會。謝謝你。

我現在必須檢查你的生命徵象，你的體溫是攝氏 38.5 度，脈搏每分鐘 100 下，呼吸每分鐘 24 下。表示你有發燒且呼吸些微急促。

接下來我要測量你身體的血氧濃度。

我的血氧濃度正常嗎？事實上我現在覺得呼吸急促。

你的血氧濃度是百分之 92，正常的血氧濃度是在百分之 95 到 100。我現在會在你的鼻孔放入鼻套管，讓你獲得較多的氧氣。

I'll be sure to tell the doctor about your conditions soon.

P: Thank you very much.

N: I need to draw your blood for tests. Roll up your right sleeve and make fist, please. Take a deep breath. Don't move please.

P: I see.

N: OK. The doctor will be coming to see you in a minute.

我也會盡快力將你的病況告訴醫師。

非常謝謝你。

我要幫你抽血做檢查，請你右手袖子捲起來手握拳頭。深呼吸，請不要動。

好的。

醫生一會兒就會過來看你。

Nursing Notes　護理記錄

C/O shortness of breath. TPR: 38.5℃, 100/min, 24/min. SpO$_2$ 92%. X-ray showed a 2 square cm pneumonia patch on left lower lung fields. COVID-19 RT-PCR: Detected, Rapid Antigen Test: Positive, O$_2$ nasal cannula 3 L/min administered STAT as instructed.

主訴呼吸急促。體溫、脈搏及呼吸數值分別為攝氏 38.5 度、100 下／分、24 次／分、SpO$_2$ 92%。X 光顯示：左側下肺葉有一塊 2x2 公分肺炎塊。COVID-19 RT-PCR：檢測出病毒（陽性），Antigen Rapid Test（快速抗原檢測）：陽性。依醫囑立即經由鼻套管每分鐘給予 3 公升氧氣。

Vocabulary and Sentence Examples　字彙與例句

1. antiviral [ˌæntɪˈvaɪrəl]
   (adj.) 抗病毒

   Antiviral drugs are not sold over the drugstore and you can only get them if you have prescription from doctor.
   抗病毒藥必須要有醫師處方，無法直接在藥局購買。

2. side effect [ˈsaɪd ɪˌfekt]
   (n.) 副作用

   Abdomial pain and diarrhea are well-known side effects of this drugs.　腹痛和腹瀉是這個藥最常見的副作用。

3. altered [ˈɔltər]
   (adj.) 改變的

   Her life was drastically altered after a badly car accident.
   她的人生在一場嚴重的車禍後徹底改變。

4. impaired [ɪmˈpɛrd]
   (adj.) 損傷；不全

   Her mother has been suffering from hearing-impaired for a couple of years.　她母親身受聽力損傷之苦已經許多年了。

Terminology 術語

1. pneumonia patch 肺炎塊
   [njuˊmonjə pætʃ]
2. blood oxygen concentration 血氧濃度
   [blʌdˊaksədʒən ˌkansɛnˊtreʃən]
3. draw blood 抽血
   [drɔ blʌd]

4. RT-PCR (real-time polymerase chain reaction) 及時反轉錄聚合酶連鎖反應
   [ˊriəl taɪm pəˊlɪməreɪs tʃeɪn rɪˋækʃən]
5. Rapid Antigen Test 快速抗原檢測
   [ˊræpɪd ˊæntədʒən tɛst]

Discharge Instructions 出院衛教

07

Before discharge, the nurse reminded Mr. Lee about some important details.

N: Good morning. Did you sleep well?

P: Good morning. I slept well. Thank you.

N: There's good news for you. You've recovered well. The doctor said you don't need to be in **isolation**[1] today and can leave the hospital this afternoon.

P: That's good.

N: I would like to remind you a few of important things before you leave the hospital.

P: Is there anything I should be **aware**[2] of ?

N: I will provide home care instructions for you.

P: OK.

N: First of all, take your medicine reguﾗy. Besides, monitor your COVID-19 symptoms, such as fever, cough, sore throat, shortness of breath and loss of smell.

P: I see.

N: Your blood oxygen level is around 95 to 98% and it is within the normal range. You may buy a **fingertip**[3] pulse **oximeter**[4] to monitor your oxygen saturation at home if you like. Please go to the emergency room immediately if your blood oxygen level is under 90%, or you develop a fever.

出院之前，護理師提醒李先生重要的事情。

早安。你睡得好嗎？

早安。我睡得很好。謝謝你。

有一個好消息喔，你恢復得很好，醫生說你今天可以解隔離，下午就可以出院了。

太好了。

在你回家之前我想提醒你一些重要的事情。

我需要注意什麼事呢？

我會為您提供居家護理指導。

好的。

首先，請您按時服藥，另外監測新冠肺炎相關症狀，例如：發燒、咳嗽、喉嚨痛、呼吸急促或味覺喪失。

了解。

您的血氧飽和濃度大約在百分之 95 至 98 左右，是在正常範圍內。您可以購買指尖脈搏血氧計在家使用。如果您的血氧濃度在百分之 90 以下或有發燒情形請立刻至急診室就醫。

P: I see. Can I buy the fingertip oximeter from the drugstore?

N: Yes, you can.

N: This is your medicine. The doctor has prescribed a week's supply. Please come back to the **outpatient department**[5] for a visit in one week. I've made an appointment with Dr. Lee for you; this is your appointment form.

P: Alright. Is there anything else?

N: Please follow the nutritionist's instructions as well. Maintaining a balanced diet is a one of the best ways to support your **immune system**[6].

P: OK, thank you. I'll keep it in mind.

我知道了。我可以在藥局買到指尖脈搏血氧計嗎？

可以的。

這是你的出院用藥。請一週後回李醫師的門診追蹤。我幫你預約好李醫師的門診，這張是掛號單。

好的。還有什麼要注意的？

也請您請遵照營養師的飲食指導。維持均衡飲食是支持您免疫系統最好的方式之一。

好的，謝謝你。我會謹記在心。

Nursing Notes 護理記錄

Told to the patients about the symtopms of COVID-19. If family member is experiencing any of COVID-19 related symptoms, please do the rapid antigen test at home first. If the result of test is poitive and the symptoms get worse, please make an appointment of remote telemedicine consultations or go to the emergency room for further treatment.

告訴病人新冠肺炎可能出現的症狀。如果有家屬出現新冠肺炎可能的症狀，建議在家自行先做抗原快篩。快篩結果陽性且症狀變得嚴重，則可預約遠距看診或直接到急診室就診。

Vocabulary and Sentence Examples 字彙與例句

1. isolation [ˌaɪsəˈleʃən]
   (n.) 隔離

   Aysmptomatic patients don't need to be in isolation 5 days after their PCR test showed negative.
   無症狀的病人可以在 PCR test 5 天後解除隔離。

2. aware [əˈwɛr]
   (adj.) 察覺的；知道的

   I was not aware of that she was ill and unconscious.
   我沒有察覺她生病而且意識不清了。

3. fingertip [ˈfɪŋɚˌtɪp]
   (n.) 指尖

   You can open this small box with your fingertips.
   你可以用指尖打開這個小盒子。

4. pulse oximeter
[pʌls ɔkˈsɪmɪtə]
(n.) 脈搏血氧計

Pulse oximeter is a device that is use to measure the oxygen saturation level of body.
脈搏血氧計是用來測量體內氧氣飽和濃度的一種設備。

5. outpatient department
[ˈaʊtˌpeʃənt dɪˈpartmənt]
(n.) 門診

The minor surgeries and treatments can be easily conducted in the outpatient departments.
小手術和簡單的治療可以在門診輕易完成。

6. immune system
[ɪˈmjun ˈsɪstəm]
(n.) 免疫系統

Your immune system can be weakened by infection, smoking, alcohol and malnutrition.
你的免疫系統可能因為感染、吸菸、喝幾或營養不良而減弱。

More Information

COVID-19 的常見症狀

1. Fever or chill：發燒，寒顫

2. Continuous cough：持續性咳嗽

3. A loss or change smell or taste：嗅覺、味覺改變或喪失

4. Shortness of breath：呼吸急促

5. Feeling tired or exhausted：感覺疲憊或筋疲力盡

6. A headache：頭痛

7. A sore throat：喉嚨痛

8. Stuffy or runny nose：鼻塞或流鼻水

9. Loss of appetite：沒有食慾

10. Diarrhea：腹瀉

11. Feeling ill or unwell：覺得不舒服

12. Muscle or body aches：肌肉或全身痛

Exercise 小試身手

● Choose the Correct Answer

( ) 1. Use this _____ to clean the table, please.　(A) cleaner　(B) insecticide
(C) herbicide　(D) disinfectant　請使用這瓶消毒劑清潔桌子。

( ) 2. _____ is one of the typical symptoms of pneumonia.　(A) Headache
(B) Fever　(C) Skin rush　(D) Tremor　發燒是肺炎典型症狀之一。

( ) 3. Here is your _____. Please pick up your medicine at the pharmacy.　(A)
prescription　(B) sheet　(C) paper　(D) order
這是你的處方籤，請到藥局領藥。

( ) 4. You are going to receiving an operation. Please make sure you've _____
everything you need to.　(A) wear　(B) put on　(C) taken off　(D) get on
你將要去開刀房做手術，請確定是否取下所有東西。

( ) 5. As a professional nurse, you should _____ the thoughts of your
patients.　(A) judge　(B) involve　(C) interfere　(D) respect
身為一位專業的護理師，你應該尊重病人的想法。

● Fill in the Blanks

1. How many _____ did you have yesterday? Does your abdominal
feel swollen?　你昨天解了幾次大便？肚子會不會覺得脹？

2. Aysmptomatic patients can be _____ 5 days after their PCR test showed
negitive.　無症狀的病人可以在 PCR test 5 天後解除隔離。

3. Maintaing _____ diet is a one of the best ways to support
your _____.　維持均衡飲食是支持您免疫系統最好的方式之一。

4. Have you _____ or _____ weight recently?　最近體重減輕還是增加？

5. Please take a deep breath and _____, I'll check your _____.
請慢慢深呼吸，吐氣、我將要檢查你的呼吸音。

◉ Simplify Nursing Notes

1. Packed RBC 2U was given immediately.　立即輸注濃縮紅血球 2 單位。

_____

2. The patient complained about chest tightness.　病人抱怨胸悶。

_____

3. Broncoscopy has been arranged.　已經安排支氣管鏡檢查。

_____

4. Health instructions was given.　已經給予病人護理指導。

_____

5. The nurse told the patient to take one tablet of painkiller after each meal.
護理師告知病人每三餐飯後服用一顆止痛藥。

_____

◉ Translation

1. 可以請你描述一下不舒服症狀嗎？

_____

2. 抗病毒藥的副作用是什麼？

_____

3. 我要幫你抽血做檢查，請你右手袖子捲起來，手握拳頭。

_____

4. 你的免疫系統可能因為感染、吸菸、喝酒或營養不良而減弱。

_____

5. 你打過疫苗嗎？

_____

Cardiovascular Unit
心血管科

Medical English for Healthcare Professionals

The Components of the Cardiovascular System 心血管系統的組成

The cardiovascular system consists of the heart (the organ that pumps blood), vessels (the conducting passage way for blood) and blood. The heart has four chambers: the right **atrium**[1], the right **ventricle**[2], the left atrium and the left ventricle. These four chambers, along with the vascular network in the lungs and other organs, combine to form major and minor circulatory systems.

The major circulatory system begins at the left ventricle, where the powerful ventricular **myocardium**[3] pumps blood to the **aorta**[4]. The aorta is the largest artery of the body where branches of **arteries**[5] originate and supply blood to organs. When blood reaches the organs oxygen, carbon dioxide, nutrients and waste are exchanged with the blood. Blood continuously leaves the organs and capillary system via numerous **venules**[6]. Venules converge into large **veins**[7] and the eventually combine to form the **vena cava**[8]. Blood pours into the right atrium and then flows into the right ventricle where the minor circulatory system begins. Blood is next pumped into the pulmonary artery to the lungs. In the alveoli of the lungs, carbon dioxide is exchanged in return for oxygen. The oxygenated blood then travels back to the left atrium.

Circulation of blood within the cardiovascular system is important for the maintenance of life. The **coronary arteries**[9] supply the heart with blood and nutrients. The coronary arteries include the right coronary artery, the **anterior descending branch**[10] and **circumflex branch**[11] of the left coronary artery.

心血管系統由心臟（推動血液的幫浦）、血管（血液的疏導管）及血液組成。心臟的四個腔室－右心房、右心室、左心房及左心室－與肺部及其他器官的血管網絡形成大循環與小循環。

大循環從血液被左心室有力的心肌壓出開始，經過體內最大的動脈－主動脈，以及它無數的分支，到達許多器官。各器官內的細胞開始與動脈來的血液交換氧氣跟二氧化碳，養分和廢物。血液隨後經由小靜脈離開器官，小靜脈匯集成靜脈，最後會合成上下腔大靜脈並注入右心房，接著啟動小循環。它從右心室開始，血液被壓出，經由肺動脈到達肺臟。在肺泡中，二氧化碳和氧氣開始交換，而充分氧合過的血液便匯流回左心房。

心血管系統的循環作用維持了我們的生命。冠狀動脈供應心臟所需的血液及營養，譬如説右冠狀動脈、左冠狀動脈前降枝及迴旋枝。

Terminology 術語

1. atrium [ˈetrɪəm] 心房
2. ventricle [ˈvɛntrɪkl̩] 心室
3. myocardium [ˌmaɪəˈkardɪəm] 心肌
4. aorta [eˈɔrtə] 主動脈
5. artery [ˈartɪrɪ] 動脈
6. venule [ˈvɛnjul] 小靜脈
7. vein [ven] 靜脈
8. vena cava [ˈvænə kevə] 腔靜脈
9. coronary artery 冠狀動脈 [ˈkɔroˌnɛrɪ ˈartərɪ]
10. anterior descending branch 前降枝 [ænˈtɪrɪə dɪˈsɛndɪŋ bræntʃ]
11. circumflex branch 迴旋枝 [ˈsɜkəmˌflɛks bræntʃ]

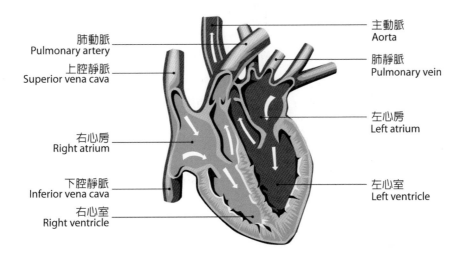

肺動脈
Pulmonary artery

上腔靜脈
Superior vena cava

右心房
Right atrium

下腔靜脈
Inferior vena cava

右心室
Right ventricle

主動脈
Aorta

肺靜脈
Pulmonary vein

左心房
Left atrium

左心室
Left ventricle

Case Information 個案資訊

Angina Pectoris [ænˈdʒaɪnə ˈpɛktərɪs] **心絞痛**

1. **Causes**: Inadequate blood perfusion to the myocardium.
2. **Symptoms & Signs**:
   (1) Chest pain radiating to the neck, jaw or medial arm
   (2) Upper abdominal pain
   (3) Shortness of breath
   (4) Syncope
3. **Care**:
   (1) Avoid refined, salty, and fatty food products.
   (2) Keep fit.
   (3) Take appropriate medications as recommended by the doctor.

Admission Assessment 入院評估

Mr. Lee, a 65-year-old man, experienced sudden chest pain during exercise

65 歲的李先生在運動時忽然感到胸痛。

N: Nurse **P:** Patient

N: Good morning, Mr. Lee. What's your major **concern**[1] today?

李先生早安。你今天主要是為什麼來呢？

P: I was jogging in the park yesterday. Suddenly, I felt pain in my chest. Then I felt a little bit dizzy.

昨天我在公園跑步時，忽然感到胸痛。接著覺得有點頭暈。

N: Has this ever happened before?

以前有發生過嗎？

P: Yes. It started 2 months ago when I came back from a jog. It's been pretty frequent after every jog but is always relieved after I rest for a while.

有的，2 個月前，在我跑完步後通常會發生。但休息一會兒就好了。

N: What did it feel like? Sharp or **dull**[2] pain?

你覺得是銳痛還是隱隱作痛？

P: Well, I think it was a dull pain.

嗯，我想是隱隱作痛吧。

N: Do you or any of your relatives have **hypertension**, **diabetes** or other systemic diseases?

你或你的家人有高血壓、糖尿病或其他全身性疾病嗎？

P: I have hypertension and diabetes. Also, my father died of coronary artery disease.

我有高血壓和糖尿病。我父親又死於冠狀動脈疾病。

N: Have you or any of your family members ever **suffered from**[3] a stroke?

你或你的家人曾經中風過嗎？

P: No, none of us have.

我們都沒有。

N: The doctor said you are likely to have angina pectoris, which usually occurs when there isn't enough blood supplying the heart, especially during exercise.

醫師說你的情形類似心絞痛。它通常發生於心臟血液供應不足時，尤其是運動的時候。

P: Is this serious? Is it going to get worse?

嚴重嗎？情況會惡化嗎？

N: If it worsens, you may develop **myocardial infarction**. This condition can cause your heart to stop beating and function properly. The doctor has arranged for an **electrocardiography** and some lab work to determine your condition.

如果情形惡化，可能會變成心肌梗塞，心臟將無法跳動及運作。醫師要安排心電圖及一些實驗室檢查以確認之。

P: I see. Thank you very much.

我了解了，多謝你。

N: You're welcome. Please feel free to make yourself comfortable on the bed. If you need any assistance, please press the **call button**[4] for help.

不客氣。請在床上休息。若你需要任何協助，請按下叫人鈴。

Nursing Notes　護理記錄

C/O usually has dull chest pain during jogging. Has diabetes and hypertension. Father died of CAD. ECG (EKG) and labwork arranged.

主訴經常在慢跑時感覺胸部鈍痛。他有糖尿病和高血壓。父親死於冠狀動脈疾病。已安排心電圖與實驗室檢查。

Tips on Writing

描述主訴的頻率副詞：usually, often, sometimes, rarely, seldom
例：He usually has shortness of breath after exercise.

Vocabulary and Sentence Examples　字彙與例句

1. concern [kənˈsɜn] (n.) 關心的事 (v.) 關係到	The president expressed his concern about the scandal. 總統對這件醜聞表示他的關切。
2. dull [dʌl] (adj.) 隱約的；模糊的	He felt a sense of dull pain within his abdomen. 他的腹部隱隱作痛。
3. suffer from [ˈsʌfə frɑm] 罹患	John has suffered from diabetes since he was eight. 約翰自 8 歲起便罹患糖尿病。
4. call button (n.) 叫人鈴 [kɔl ˈbʌtn̩]	If you press this call button, the nurse will come here and help you.　如果你按叫人鈴，護理師便會過來協助你。

Terminology 術語

1. hypertension 高血壓
   [haɪpəˈtɛnʃən]

2. diabetes 糖尿病
   [ˌdaɪəˈbitɪs]

3. myocardial infarction 心肌梗塞
   [ˌmaɪəˈkardɪəl ɪnˈfarkʃən]

4. electrocardiography 心電圖(ECG/EKG)
   [ɪˌlɛktrəkardɪˈagrəfɪ]

Hospitalization 住院療護

The nurse returned to see Mr. Lee again.	護理師再次來看李先生的狀況。
N: How do you feel now?	你現在覺得怎樣？
P: Pretty good, thank you.	還不錯，謝謝你。
N: Has the doctor explained the procedure you will be receiving?	醫師有向你解釋你即將做的檢查程序嗎？
P: Yes. He said I would have to receive **catheterization** to check the condition of my coronary arteries.	是的，他說我必須做心導管手術以檢查冠狀動脈的情況。
N: That's right. In addition to your check-up, I'll have to measure your **intakes**[1] and **outputs**[2].	沒錯。此外，我將測量你的飲食攝入量和排出量。
P: Here's the sheet recording what I eat and drink. I wrote everything down.	這是記錄我飲食的單子。我全都寫下來了。
N: This looks quite good. Please keep filling out the sheet. No **greasy**[3] and **salty**[4] foods……	看起來不錯。請持續記錄。不要吃油膩和太鹹的食物……
P: I also eat regularly.	我也有規律飲食。
N: Very good. Strictly obeying these rules is more important than remembering them.	非常好，能嚴格遵守這些原則比記住更為重要。
P: Yeah, but eating foods without much salt or **flavor**[5] makes me feel **miserable**[6].	呃，要我吃不含高鹽和調味料的食物實在有點痛苦。
N: I know, but these foods can be bad for your health.	我明白。但他們有損你的健康。
P: OK, I'll try my best to avoid them.	好吧，我會努力避免的。
N: Here's your medication. This is a **nitroglycerin tablet**[7]. Please place it under your tongue but don't swallow it. This will help relieve some of your discomfort. Are you still feeling any chest pain, discomfort or **tightness**[8] in your chest?	這是你的藥－硝化甘油藥錠。請放在舌下含服而不要吞服。它能協助緩解你的不適。你仍然感到胸痛、胸悶或任何不適嗎？
P: No, none of these. Thanks for all your help.	都沒有，謝謝你的幫忙。

Nursing Notes 護理記錄

Doctor explained the results from the examination. Told to record I/O of fluid and food. Told to follow diet rules. Nitroglycerin tablet given as instructed. No C/O discomfort.

醫師已解釋過檢查結果。告知要記錄食物和飲水的攝入量和排出量及遵守飲食規則。依醫囑給予硝化甘油片。未有不適之主訴。

Vocabulary and Sentence Examples 字彙與例句

1. intake [ˈɪnˌtek]
   (n.) 攝入

   Patients with liver cirrhosis should restrict their salt intake.
   肝硬化患者必須限制鹽分的攝取。

2. output [ˈaʊtˌpʊt]
   (n.) 排出

   Urine output is an indirect parameter for measuring and determining body fluid status.
   排尿量是一種身體水分狀態的間接指標。

3. greasy [ˈgrizɪ]
   (adj.) 油膩的

   After eating this greasy meal, he felt uncomfortable.
   吃完這頓油膩的大餐後他感到不舒服。

4. salty [ˈsɔltɪ]
   (adj.) 鹹的

   The sea water tastes salty. 海水嚐起來鹹鹹的。

5. flavor [flevə]
   (n.) 調味料

   Appropriate use of different flavors can make food more appetizing. 恰當地使用調味料能讓食物更美味。

6. miserable [ˈmɪzərəbl̩]
   (adj.) 痛苦的

   Being bedridden all day is quite miserable.
   長期臥床是一件痛苦的事情。

7. tablet [ˈtæblɪt]
   (n.) 藥錠

   Chew these tablets into small pieces and then swallow them with water. 將這些藥錠嚼碎並以水吞服。

8. tightness [ˈtaɪtnɪs]
   (n.) 緊壓感

   I feel tightness in my chest. 我感到胸悶。

Terminology 術語

1. nitroglycerin [ˌnaɪtrəˈglɪsərɪn] 硝化甘油(NTG)
2. catheterization [ˌkæθətərɪˈzeʃən] 心導管手術

Discharge Instructions　出院衛教

Mr. Lee is reading a newspaper in bed.

N: Congratulations! The doctor said you can go home tomorrow.

P: Great! Thanks for all your help.

N: You're welcome. I have to make sure that you remember all the important details before leaving the hospital.

P: I think I can remember most of them.

N: All right. Let's review your instructions briefly. How are you supposed to take your nitroglycerin tablets?

P: Whenever I have chest pain, I should take one tablet by placing it under my tongue. My medications should be carried with me at all times.

N: That's right. Do you know what to do if your pain is not relieved?

P: Well, I can take another tablet.

N: If the pain **persists**[1]?

P: Then I have to go to the **ER** right away.

N: Good. Where should you **store**[2] these nitroglycerin tablets?

P: In a **tightly**[3] sealed **bottle**[4] made of dark glass. It should be placed in a cool and dry place, out of the reach of children.

N: Well done. How do you know if these tablets are still fresh?

P: They're fresh if I feel a slight **burning**[5] sensation within my mouth. If the color or taste changes, the pill is no longer **effective**[6].

N: Very good. The last and most important thing is that you restrict the salt and oil intake within your diet. Stay fit, and you'll remain healthier.

P: I see. Thank you very much.

李先生正在床上看報紙。

恭喜你，醫生說你明天就可以回家了。

太好了！謝謝你們的協助。

不客氣。在你離開醫院之前，我必須確定你記住了所有重要事項。

我想我幾乎都記得。

好的，那我們複習一下。你應該如何服用硝化甘油藥錠？

不論何時感到胸痛，我應該把藥錠放在舌頭下方含服。我也必須隨身攜帶它們。

沒錯。那麼，如果胸痛情形沒有減輕怎麼辦？

嗯，我可以再服用一片。

如果疼痛持續呢？

那麼我必須立即趕到急診室。

好的，你應該把硝化甘油藥錠存放在何處呢？

放在一個瓶蓋緊閉的黑色玻璃瓶內，並置於乾燥和陰涼之處、兒童拿不到的地方。

很好。那你怎麼知道藥錠是否仍新鮮呢？

新鮮時嘴巴會嚐到燒灼感。如果藥錠顏色或味道改變了，那意謂著藥錠已失效。

非常好。最後也是最重要的是限制飲食中的鹽分及油脂攝取量。維持健康身材會讓你更健康的。

我明白。非常謝謝你。

Nursing Notes　護理記錄

Will be discharged. Discharge instructions given. Told to keep fit and not to eat greasy and salty foods. Told to go to ER if two nitroglycerin tablets cannot relieve chest pain.

病人即將出院。給予出院衛教。告知維持體重且不可食用太過油膩和高鹽分的食物。告知倘若兩片硝化甘油藥錠無法緩解胸痛時應至急診室就醫。

Vocabulary and Sentence Examples　字彙與例句

1. persist [pəˈsɪst] (v.) 持續	The hot weather will persist for three days. 炎熱的天氣將持續三天。
2. store [stɔr] (v.) 貯藏；貯存	This medicine should be stored in the refrigerator. 這種藥物必須貯存在冰箱內。
3. tightly [ˈtaɪtlɪ] (adv.) 緊密地	You should hold the ball tightly before touchdown. 在達陣之前你要緊緊地抱住球。
4. bottle [batḷ] (n.) 瓶子	She found a bottle on the beach with a letter inside. 她在海灘上找到一個裝有信箋的瓶子。
5. burning [ˈbɜnɪŋ] (adj.) 灼熱的	He suddenly felt a burning sensation within his mouth after drinking the water. 在他喝了水之後，突然感到嘴裡有股燒灼感。
6. effective [əˈfɛktɪv] (adj.) 有效的	The most effective way to treat this disease is with surgery. 對這個疾病最有效的治療方式是手術。

Terminology 術語

1. ER＝emergency room [ɪˈmɜʤənsɪ rum] 急診室

More Information

1. **疼痛的問診重點**：當病人表示身上有疼痛時，你必須同時了解 *Where*（疼痛於何處發生？位置會移動嗎？）、*When*（何時開始痛？）、*What*（疼痛的感覺像什麼？）、*How*（疼痛如何發生？如何緩解或加速疼痛？）。

2. **病人對疼痛位置的表達**

   headache [ˈhɛdˌek] 頭痛　　　　　　　stomachache [ˈstʌməkˌek] 胃痛

   toothache [ˈtuθˌek] 牙痛　　　　　　　abdominal pain [æbˈdɑmɪnḷ pen] 腹痛

   neck pain [ˈnɛk pen] 脖子痛　　　　　　back pain [ˈbæk pen] 背痛

   chest pain [ˈtʃɛst pen] 胸痛　　　　　　backache [ˈbækˌek] 背痛

3. **了解病人是否具有冠狀動脈疾病的危險因子**

   (1) Has anyone in *your family* had a similar condition?
   家族裡的人有類似於你的情況的嗎？

   (2) Do you suffer from *hypertension* or *diabetes*?　你有罹患高血壓或糖尿病嗎？
   Do you *smoke* heavily?　你吸菸吸得兇嗎？
   Do you usually eat *greasy foods*?　你經常吃油膩的食物嗎？

4. **教導病人服藥及存放事項**

   (1) Take the medicine with water/meals.　與水／食物一起服用。
   Take the medicine after meals.　餐後服用。
   Take the medicine before you sleep.　睡前服用。
   Take the medicine twice a day.　一天服用兩次。

   (2) Take the whole tablet without chewing it.　整顆吞服，勿嚼（磨）碎。

   (3) Place it under your tongue and don't swallow it.　置於舌下，勿吞服。

   (4) Store it in a cold and dry place.　置於陰涼與乾燥處。
   Store it in the refrigerator.　置於冰箱冷藏。

   (5) Keep it under 4 degrees Celsius (℃).　保存於 4℃ 以下。
   Keep it away from the sun.　避開陽光。
   Keep it out of the reach of children.　勿讓孩童觸及到。

Exercise 小試身手

● Choose the Correct Answer

( ) 1. He was very _____ about his grandfather being admitted to the hospital. (A)concrete (B)concerned (C)constricted (D)conform
他為住院的爺爺感到擔心。

( ) 2. I had a sense of _____ pain in my stomach. (A)dull (B)doll (C)dally (D)dullish 我的胃部隱隱作痛。

( ) 3. When he suffered from a heart attack, he felt _____ within his chest. (A)dullness (B)tightness (C)lose (D)pain 心臟病發作時他感到胸悶。

( ) 4. Some medications should be _____ in the refrigerator. (A)inserted (B)taken (C)stored (D)placed 有些藥物必須貯存在冰箱內。

( ) 5. He was hospitalized because of _____. (A)hypotension (B)hypertension (C) tension (D)high tension 他因為高血壓而住院。

( ) 6. Fried food tastes _____. (A)greasy (B)sweet (C)light (D)greased 油炸的食物吃起來十分油膩。

( ) 7. The new regulations were _____ in relieving heavy traffic. (A)effect (B)affect (C)affective (D)effective 紓解交通的新規定是有效的。

( ) 8. The rain _____ and resulted in serious floods. (A)insisted (B)persisted (C)resisted (D)consisted 持續的大雨造成洪水。

( ) 9. A life without love is quite _____. (A)measurable (B)misery (C)miserable (D)miscible 沒有愛的人生是悲哀的。

( ) 10. Pepper is a sort of spice to add _____. (A)tastes (B)flavor (C)smelling (D)sensation 胡椒是一種調味料。

● Fill in the Blanks

1. _____ patients should follow up _____ with the outpatient department. 糖尿病患者需要定期在門診追蹤治療。

2. _____ _____ is a disease caused by _____ _____ . 心肌梗塞是一種因為心肌缺氧而死所引起的疾病。

3. _____ can help _____ the coronary _____ and help recover the _____ supply to the myocardium. 硝化甘油能幫助放鬆冠狀動脈，使心肌的血液供應恢復。

4. _____ _____ is a predisposition to _____ _____ _____ . 心絞痛是冠狀動脈疾病的警訊。

5. The _____ in the left ventricle is more powerful than the myocardium in the right _____ . 左心室的心肌比右心室的更有力。

● Simplify Nursing Notes

1. The nurse told the patient never to drink too much water.
告知病人不要飲用過多水分。

_____

2. He usually feels abdominal pain after a meal. 他經常在飽食後感覺腹痛。

_____

3. He seldom feels chest pain during exercise. 他鮮少在運動時感覺胸痛。

_____

4. The nurse told the patient to come back to the clinic regularly.
告知病人需定期回診。

_____

5. The doctor instructed an intravenous drip. 根據醫囑給予靜脈輸液。

_____

6. The doctor started the use of an antacid. 根據醫囑開始使用制酸劑。

_____

◉ Translation

1. 你覺得是銳痛還是隱隱作痛？
   _____

2. 你或你的家人有高血壓、糖尿病或其他全身性疾病嗎？
   _____

3. 若你需要任何協助，請按下叫人鈴。
   _____

4. 我將測量你的飲食攝入量和排出量。
   _____

5. 你仍然感到胸痛、胸悶或任何不適嗎？
   _____

Gastrointestinal Unit
胃腸科

Learning Goals 學習目標

1. Assessing patients with black stools
2. Collecting information about abdominal pain
3. Assessing gastrointestinal condition
4. Providing health education to patients

Outline 本章大綱

- The Components of the Gastrointestinal System　胃腸系統的組成
- Case Information: Peptic Ulcer (PU)　個案資訊：消化性潰瘍
- Admission Assessment　入院評估
- Hospitalization　住院療護
- Discharge Instructions　出院衛教

Medical English for Healthcare Professionals

The Components of the Gastrointestinal System 胃腸系統的組成

12

The gastrointestinal system comprised of the digestive tract and several organs which assist with food processing. The digestive tract begins at the mouth and continues to the **esophagus**[1], **stomach**[2], **small intestine**[3], **large intestine**[4], and **rectum**[5].

The organs associated with the digestive tract include the **salivary glands**[6], which secrete **saliva**[7]; the **liver**[8], which handles nutrients absorbed by the small intestine; the **gallbladder**[9], which stores **bile**[10]; the **pancreas**[11], which secretes digestive enzymes and hormones which regulate metabolism.

From the microscopic level, the digestive tract is approximately divided into four layers: the **mucosa**[12], **submucosa**[13], **muscular layer**[14] and **serosa**[15]. The mucosa is where nutrients are absorbed, and is the first barrier for numerous pathogens and noxious substances. If only the mucosa is damaged, this is called **erosion**[16]. However, if the injury is serious enough to also damage the muscular layer, we call this an **ulcer**[17] (or ulceration).

胃腸系統由消化道以及數種協助處理食物的器官。消化道由口開始,經過食道、胃、小腸、大腸到直腸。

與消化道相關的器官包括:唾腺(分泌唾液)、肝臟(處理腸子吸收的養分)、膽囊(貯存膽汁)、胰臟(分泌消化酵素和調節代謝狀態的激素)。

從裡面開始,消化道約略分為四層:黏膜層、黏膜下層、肌肉層及漿膜層。黏膜是吸收營養之處,也是眾多有害物質和病原體首先傷害之處。如果只有黏膜受損,稱為糜爛;如果受損嚴重且延伸到肌肉層,我們便稱之為潰瘍。

Terminology 術語

1. esophagus [ɪˈsafəgəs] 食道
2. stomach [ˈstʌmək] 胃
3. small intestine [smɔl ɪnˈtɛstɪn] 小腸
4. large intestine [lardʒ ɪnˈtɛstɪn] 大腸
5. rectum [ˈrɛktəm] 直腸
6. salivary gland [ˈsælə͵vɛrɪ ˈglænd] 唾腺
7. saliva [səˈlaɪvə] 唾液
8. liver [ˈlɪvə] 肝臟
9. gallbladder [ˈgɔl͵blædə] 膽囊
10. bile [baɪl] 膽汁
11. pancreas [ˈpænkrɪəs] 胰臟
12. mucosa [mjuˈkosə] 黏膜(層)
13. submucosa [͵sʌbmjəˈkosə] 黏膜下層
14. muscular layer [ˈmʌskjələ ˈleə] 肌肉層
15. serosa [sɪˈrosə] 漿膜層
16. erosion [ɪˈroʒən] 糜爛
17. ulcer [ˈʌlsə] 潰瘍

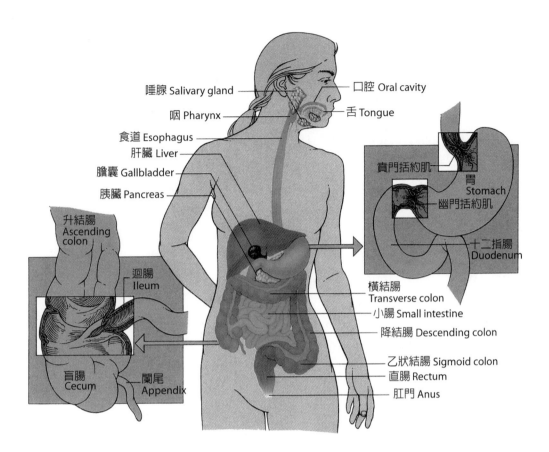

唾腺 Salivary gland
咽 Pharynx
食道 Esophagus
肝臟 Liver
膽囊 Gallbladder
胰臟 Pancreas
口腔 Oral cavity
舌 Tongue
賁門括約肌
胃 Stomach
幽門括約肌
十二指腸 Duodenum
升結腸 Ascending colon
迴腸 Ileum
盲腸 Cecum
闌尾 Appendix
橫結腸 Transverse colon
小腸 Small intestine
降結腸 Descending colon
乙狀結腸 Sigmoid colon
直腸 Rectum
肛門 Anus

Case Information 個案資訊

Peptic Ulcer (PU) [ˈpɛptɪk ˈʌlsə] 消化性潰瘍

1. **Causes**: *Helicobacter pylori* infection, excess gastric acid production, reduced mucosal protection or use of NSAID.

2. **Symptoms & Signs**: Abdominal pain, tarry stools/black stools, and delayed gastric emptying.

3. **Care**:
   (1) Eat meals on time and chew food slowly.
   (2) Avoid spicy foods.
   (3) Maintain a good mood.
   (4) Quit smoking.
   (5) Do not take over-the-counter medications without consultation.
   (6) Go to the hospital right away if symptoms reoccur.

Admission Assessment　入院評估

13

Mr. Liu, a 70-year-old man, passed black stools.

劉先生，70 歲男性，解出黑便。

N: Nurse　**P:** Patient

N: When did you pass black stools? How did you feel after this?

你何時解出黑便呢？解便後的感覺為何？

P: Last night, I felt dizzy and my heart started beating faster after I went to defecate.

昨晚解便後我感到頭暈，而且心跳加速。

N: Have you ever passed black stools before?

你以前有解黑便的情形嗎？

P: No, this was my first time.

沒有，這是第一次。

N: Alright. What other clinical symptoms did you have?

好的，還有其他症狀嗎？

P: Well, I felt like I had abdominal pain.

呢，我感覺肚子痛。

N: When did this begin? Did it come **suddenly**¹ or **gradually**²?

何時開始痛的呢？是忽然發作還是緩緩而來？

P: 2 weeks ago. It came gradually. I felt some discomfort, followed by some pain.

兩週前。它總是緩緩發作，先有些不適，接著就感到疼痛。

N: When did you feel pain? In the morning or in the evening? Before meals or after meals?

你何時會感到疼痛？是早上還是晚上？飯前還是飯後？

P: Right after meals. It continued even when I was hungry.

進食後感到特別痛。即使飢餓時，不適感依然持續著。

N: What did it feel like? Burning, **tearing**³, or **cramping**⁴? Did it extend to other areas?

疼痛感覺像是燒灼的、撕裂的還是痙攣的？是否會往他處蔓延？

P: It felt like burning pain but didn't spread much.

我感到燒灼痛，但不會蔓延。

N: What did you do to relieve the pain?

你如何緩解疼痛呢？

P: I went to the **pharmacy**⁵ and got some **antacids**. The pain was relieved after taking these **medications**⁶.

我去藥局買了制酸劑，服藥之後疼痛就會減緩。

N: Did you feel distended after meals?

你吃飽後會覺得肚子很脹嗎？

P: Yes, even 4 or 5 hours after meals, I still feel like there was a lot of food in my stomach.

是的，飯後約 4~5 小時我仍可感覺到胃裡面有很多食物。

N: Are you currently taking any medications regularly, for example, **Aspirin**?

你有沒有規律服用什麼藥物，譬如說阿斯匹靈？

P: I take Statin to lower my blood lipid levels.

我服用 Statin 降低血脂肪指數。

N: Do you smoke? If so, how long have you smoked and how many cigarettes do you smoke a day? | 你有吸菸嗎？如果有，抽多久？一天抽多少支？

P: Yes, I've smoked 2 packs a day for the past 40 years. | 有的，40 年來我每天抽 2 包。

N: OK. Please lie down and rest. I'll be back in a bit. | 好的。請躺下休息。我待會回來。

Nursing Notes　護理記錄

C/O abdominal pain after passing tarry stools. Took Statin to lower blood lipid level. Took antacid to relieve abdominal pain. Has smoked 2 packs per day for 40 years. Has peptic ulcer with active bleeding. Doctor checked and admitted him.

主訴解黑便後感到腹痛。曾服用制酸劑緩解腹痛、服用 Statin 降低血脂。吸菸習慣為每天 2 包，持續 40 年。病人有消化性潰瘍並且正在出血。醫師檢查後准予住院。

Vocabulary and Sentence Examples　字彙與例句

1. suddenly [ˈsʌdn̩lɪ]
   (adv.) 忽然地
   Suddenly it began raining cats and dogs.
   忽然間下起傾盆大雨。

2. gradually [ˈgrædʒʊəlɪ]
   (adv.) 逐漸地
   They gradually began to know each other better.
   他們開始逐漸地了解對方。

3. tearing [ˈtɛrɪŋ]
   (adj.) 撕裂的
   Aortic dissection usually manifests as a typical tearing pain.　主動脈剝離經常表現出一種典型的撕裂痛。

4. cramp [kræmp]
   (v.) 抽筋；痙攣
   Her calf cramped, making her unable to continue competing in the contest.　她的小腿痙攣，使她無法繼續比賽。

5. pharmacy [ˈfɑrməsɪ]
   (n.) 藥局
   You can buy those over-the-counter medications at the pharmacy.　你可以在藥局買到非處方藥。

6. medication [mɛdɪˈkeʃən]
   (n.) 藥物；藥物治療
   If you have taken certain medications regularly, please tell your doctor.
   如果你有規律服用某些藥物，請告訴你的醫師做為參考。

Terminology 術語

1. antacid [æntˈæsɪd] 制酸劑
2. Aspirin [ˈæspərɪn] 阿斯匹靈

Hospitalization 住院療護

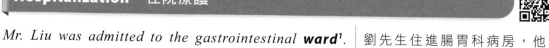

14

Mr. Liu was admitted to the gastrointestinal **ward**[1]. *His* **hemoglobin** *level was low.*

N: Mr. Liu, was your last **bowel movement**[2] black?

P: Yes, it was black.

N: OK. I need to check your heart rate and **blood pressure**[3]. *(Later)* Your heart rate is 110 beats/min and blood pressure is 92/54 mmHg. These numbers may be caused by internal bleeding.

P: This sounds bad. What should I do?

N: We'll put you on an **intravenous drip** to supply fluids and give you a **blood transfusion** if your hemoglobin level remains too low.

P: I'm still weak and dizzy. What has the doctor done to deal with this?

N: The doctor has arranged an **endoscopy** to check your esophagus, stomach and small intestine. If there's a bleeding site found, the doctor will try to stop it directly.

P: I see. Is there anything I have to do before this examination?

N: First, you have to sign a **consent**[4] form in regards to understanding the purpose, process and complications of this procedure. Second, you have to be **NPO** from now on.

P: What does NPO mean?

N: It means you can't eat or drink anything by mouth, including water and medicine.

P: I'll keep this in mind.

N: The doctor has already ordered an **acid reducer** which will be given via an intravenous drip to stop the bleeding.

P: Alright. Will I feel better later?

劉先生住進腸胃科病房，他的血紅素值很低。

劉先生，你上次還是解黑便嗎？

是的，它是黑色的。

好的。我要確認你的心跳及血壓狀況。（稍後）你的心跳為 110 下／分，血壓為 92/54 mmHg。皆可能是內出血所致。

聽起來不太好。我該怎麼辦？

我們會用靜脈點滴給你補充水分，如果血紅素還是過低時也會給你輸血。

我仍然有些虛弱和頭暈。醫師會怎麼處理呢？

醫師已為你安排內視鏡檢查來檢查你的食道、胃及小腸，如果發現出血點，醫師會試著直接止住它。

我了解了，那我在檢查之前需要做什麼呢？

首先，在你了解檢查的目的、過程及併發症之後，我們需要請你簽署知情同意書；第二，從現在開始你必須禁食。

禁食是什麼意思？

禁食意指你不能經口吃任何食物、飲水或服用藥物。

我會謹記在心。

醫師已開立靜脈滴注制酸劑以止血。

好的，那我稍後會感覺好些嗎？

N: Yes, you'll feel better if the bleeding stops. Please call us if you feel worse or want to get out of the bed.

P: I will, thank you.

是的，如果已止血的話，你會感覺好些。若你感覺變糟或想下床時，請告訴我們。

我會的，謝謝你。

 Nursing Notes　護理記錄

Conscious, C/O dizziness. HR: 110/min, BP: 92/54 mmHg. Still has tarry stools. Preparing IV drip and blood transfusion PRN. Signed informed consent form. Waiting for endoscopy. Told to be NPO from now on.

病人意識清楚，主訴頭暈。心跳 110 次／分，血壓 92/54 mmHg。持續解出黑便。準備靜脈點滴注射，必要時輸血。已簽署知情同意書，待做內視鏡檢查。告知病人開始禁食。

 Tips on Writing

1. 主詞為 patient 或 nurse 時，可以省略不寫；若上下句主詞不同，則不可省略。
   例：The patient fell in the morning.　→　Fell in the morning.
2. 主詞明確時，可省略 be 動詞，留下 V-ing 或 V-ed。例：
   She is receiving cardiac catheterization.　→　Receiving cardiac catheterization.

 Vocabulary and Sentence Examples　字彙與例句

1. ward [wɔrd]
   (n.) 病房

   Patients with active pulmonary tuberculosis should be put in the isolation ward.　活動性肺結核病人應住進隔離病房。

2. bowel movement
   [ˈbauəl muvmənt]
   排便；腸蠕動

   May I ask, what is the color of your bowel movement?　我可以請問你排便的顏色嗎？

3. blood pressure
   [blʌd ˈprɛʃə] 血壓

   Epinephrine can help keep blood pressure within an acceptable range.　腎上腺素可將血壓維持在可接受的範圍內。

4. consent [kənˈsɛnt]
   (n.) 同意；同意書

   The patient must sign an informed consent form before the operation.　在手術之前病人必須簽署知情同意書。

Terminology 術語

1. hemoglobin [ˌhiməˈglobɪn] 血紅素
2. intravenous drip [ˌɪntrəˈvinəs drɪp] 靜脈點滴注射
3. blood transfusion [blʌd ˌtrænsˈfjuʒən] 輸血
4. endoscopy [ɛnˈdaskəpɪ] 內視鏡檢查
5. NPO 禁食（*nulla per os*，意指 nothing by mouth）
6. acid reducer [ˈæsɪd rɪˈdjusə] 制酸劑

Discharge Instructions　出院衛教

15

N: Mr. Liu, your condition is **stable**[1] now, and the doctor said you're ready to go home.

P: Great! But I'm worried about what I need to do if I pass another black stool again.

N: Come to the ER immediately if you have black stools, abdominal pain, dizziness or feel **faint**[2].

P: I see. Thank you.

N: You're welcome. The doctor has **prescribed**[3] some medications for you to take home. Please remember to take them as instructed.

P: Don't worry. I'll keep this in mind. Anything else I should work on?

N: Yes. Relax more and maintain a regular **lifestyle**[4]. This means maintaining a good mood, not smoking and not staying up too late.

P: OK, I'll try my best.

N: Also, try to eat a healthy diet. This means maintaining a balanced diet with nutrition, low-salt and avoiding **preserved**[5], **canned**[6] and stimulative foods.

P: Wow, I have to remember a lot!

N: Yes. All of this can help you improve on your health Furthermore, always check your stool color, and don't take other **painkillers**[7] within the next 2 weeks. The doctor has already prescribed meds for you.

劉先生，你現在狀況已穩定，醫師說你可以準備回家了。

太好了，但我擔心萬一回家後再度解出黑便時該怎麼辦。

如果有解黑便、腹痛、頭暈或昏厥的情形，立刻來急診室。

我知道了，謝謝你。

不客氣，醫師開了一些藥物讓你回家服用，請記得按時服藥。

好的。別擔心，我會記得。我還需要注意什麼事情呢？

是的。你必須試著放鬆並且保有規律的生活作息。意即保持心情愉快、不菸酒、不熬夜。

嗯，我盡量。

此外，維持健康飲食。意即營養均衡、低鹽飲食、避免醃製食物、罐頭食品及刺激性食物。

哇，我得記住這麼多的事情！

是的，這些全都有益健康。此外，經常檢查你的糞便顏色，而且兩週內勿服用其他止痛藥，因為醫師已經開給你了。

P: I'll pay more attention to these instructions.

N: Good, then **congratulations**[8] to you!

我會多加留意這些指示的。

很好，那麼恭喜你囉！

Nursing Notes 護理記錄

Will be discharged. Discharge Instructions given. Told to return to the ER if tarry stools, abdominal pain, dizziness, or feel faint.

病人即將出院。給予出院衛教。告知病人如果發生解黑便、腹痛、頭暈或昏厥時應至急診求治。

Vocabulary and Sentence Examples 字彙與例句

1. stable [ˈstebḷ]
   (adj.) 穩定的

   Her vital signs are stable.　她的生命徵象穩定。

2. faint [fent] (adj.)
   昏厥的；即將暈倒的

   He felt faint after severely vomiting.
   他在大量嘔吐後覺得快要暈倒了。

3. prescribe [prɪˈskraɪb]
   (v.) 開（藥方）

   I will prescribe an antacid to relieve your stomachache.
   我將會開一些制酸劑來緩解你的胃痛。

4. lifestyle [ˈlaɪfˌstaɪl]
   (n.) 生活型態

   Maintaining a good lifestyle is important for one's health.
   保有良好的生活型態對個體健康而言是很重要的。

5. canned [kænd]
   (adj.) 罐裝的

   I don't like canned foods.　我不喜歡罐裝食品。

6. preserved [prɪˈzɜvd]
   (adj.) 醃製的

   There is a lot of salt in preserved foods.
   醃製食品的含鹽量很多。

7. painkiller [ˈpenˌkɪlə]
   (n.) 止痛藥

   When you experience a headache, please take one painkiller pill.　當你感到頭痛時，請服用一錠止痛藥。

8. congratulations
   [kənˌgrætʃəˈleʃənz]
   (n.) 恭喜

   Congratulations! You've received a promotion.
   恭喜！你剛剛得到了升遷。

More Information

1. 詢問病人疼痛的狀況

   (1) How do you *feel* now?
       你現在覺得如何？

   (2) Can you *describe* the pain?
       你能對疼痛加以描述嗎？

   (3) *When* did you feel pain?
       你何時感到疼痛過？

   (4) *Where* is it painful? / Where does it hurt?
       哪裡痛？

   (5) *What* does the pain feel like?
       這種疼痛感像什麼？

   (6) *What kind of* pain is it?
       這是什麼樣的痛？

2. 病人對疼痛性質的敘述

   tearing [ˈtɛrɪŋ] 撕裂痛   dull [dʌl] 悶痛

   cramp [kræmp] 絞痛   sharp [ʃɑrp] （如刀割般的）尖銳痛

   burning [ˈbɜnɪŋ] 燒灼痛   stabbing [ˈstæbɪŋ] 刺痛

Exercise 小試身手

● Choose the Correct Answer

( ) 1. The old wanderer yelled out and then collapsed _____ . (A)suddenly
(B)gradually (C)stepwise (D)deliberate
這名老流浪漢忽然間大叫然後倒下。

( ) 2. The _____ pain occurring between your scapulae indicates the possibility of an aortic dissection. (A)bearing (B)tearing (C)burning
(D)cramping 出現在肩胛骨中間的撕裂痛暗示著主動脈剝離的可能性。

( ) 3. Due to strenuous exercise, her leg muscles _____ up. (A)constrict
(B)shorten (C)cramped (D)injures 因為劇烈運動，使她的大腿肌肉痙攣。

( ) 4. Take this prescription and go to the _____ to get your medications.
(A)pharmacy (B)pharmacist (C)pharmacology (D)pharmaceutics
拿著這張處方箋到藥局領藥。

( ) 5. She receives _____ to control her diabetes. (A)meditation
(B)medievalism (C)medication (D)mediocre
她的糖尿病病情正接受藥物控制。

( ) 6. He was admitted to the gastrointestinal _____ due to GI bleeding.
(A)ward (B)bed (C)room (D)hospice
他因為腸胃出血而住進腸胃科病房。

( ) 7. The patient's vital signs were _____ , so he was transferred to the general ward. (A)status (B)steady (C)stable (D)stupor
病人的生命徵象穩定，可以轉到普通病房。

( ) 8. He was sent to the _____ room right after the car accident.
(A)emergent (B)emergency (C)urgent (D)hesitant
他發生車禍後很快地被送到急診室。

● Fill in the Blanks

1. If your _____ _____ becomes tarry in color, please notify your doctors and nurses.　如果你的排便呈現瀝青色，請務必告知醫護人員。

2. An _____ is a kind of basic substance, which can neutralize _____ _____.　制酸劑是一種鹼性物質，可以中和胃酸。

3. _____ can cause _____ _____ via inhibition of normal _____ mechanisms.　阿斯匹靈藉由抑制正常的保護機制而導致胃潰瘍。

4. A lot of _____ can negatively affect your own _____.　很多疾病會在不知不覺間影響你的健康。

5. A _____ may not only be coming from your _____ but also from other areas.　胃痛不僅暗示胃的問題，還可能是其他部位。

● Simplify Nursing Notes

1. The patient complained about chest pain.　病人抱怨胸痛。
_____

2. The patient passed bloody stools.　病人排出血便。
_____

3. The nurse is preparing an IV drip.　護理師正準備靜脈點滴注射。
_____

4. The nurse is checking his vital signs.　護理師正檢查生命徵象。
_____

5. A barium enema was given.　已給予含銀之灌腸劑。
_____

6. Health education was given.　已給予衛教。
_____

7. Endoscopy has been arranged.　已安排內視鏡檢查。
_____

● Translation

1. 你何時解出黑便呢？解便後的感覺為何？

   _____

2. 何時開始痛的呢？是忽然發作還是緩緩而來？

   _____

3. 我們會用靜脈點滴給你補充水分，如果血紅素還是過低時也會給你輸血。

   _____

4. 禁食意指你不能經口吃任何食物、飲水或服用藥物。

   _____

5. 如果有解黑便、腹痛、頭暈或昏厥的情形，立刻來急診室。

   _____

Hepatobiliary Unit
肝膽科

Learning Goals 學習目標

1. Assessing patients with liver cancer
2. Explaining liver cancer treatment methods
3. Providing health education to patients

Outline 本章大綱

- About the Liver and Gallbladder
  關於肝臟與膽囊
- Case Information: Hepatocellular
  Carcinoma (HCC) / Liver Cancer
  個案資訊：肝細胞癌；肝癌
- Admission Assessment　入院評估
- Pre-Operative Care　術前照護
- Post-Operative Care　術後照護

Medical English for
Healthcare Professionals

About the Liver and Gallbladder　關於肝臟與膽囊

The liver and gallbladder are part of the gastrointestinal system. The liver has the ability to metabolize various nutrients and chemicals. It also serves as a target organ for the endocrine system and responds to hormones.

For example, **insulin**[1] secreted by the pancreas, facilitates the conversion of glucose into **glycogen**[2] for storage in the liver. On the other hand, **glucagon**[3], which is also secreted by the pancreas, stimulates the liver to release glucose from its glycogen stores. **Growth hormone**[4], which is secreted by the **anterior pituitary gland**[5], acts on the liver and stimulates the production of **insulin-like growth factors**[6].

Also, when chemicals from the environment pass through the liver, some are metabolized by **hepatocytes**[7]. The liver is such a powerful organ that is indispensable for humans.

The gallbladder, an accessory organ of the liver, stores and concentrates bile. The epithelial cells lining the inside of the gallbladder wall absorb water from bile, secrete **electrolytes**[8] and alter the ingredients of bile.

When we have a meal, gastrointestinal hormones are also released due to stimulation by food contents. These hormones act on smooth muscles in the gallbladder wall causing forceful contractions to squeeze out stored bile. Bile then sufficiently helps digest and absorb fat in food through fat emulsification.

肝臟與膽囊是胃腸系統的一部分，肝臟擁有代謝許多營養和化學物質的能力，它也是內分泌系統的標的器官，對許多激素產生反應。

例如，胰臟分泌的胰島素會促進葡萄糖轉變成肝醣，並貯存於肝臟中。另一方面，胰臟分泌的升糖素會刺激肝臟釋出內貯的肝醣。腦下垂體前葉分泌的生長激素作用在肝臟上，刺激類胰島素生長因子的製造。

環境中的化學物質經過肝臟時，有些會被肝細胞代謝掉。對人類來說，肝臟是個作用強大且不可或缺的器官。

膽囊是肝臟的輔助器官，是貯存及濃縮膽汁之處。襯於膽囊內壁上的上皮細胞可從膽汁中吸收水分、分泌電解質並且改變膽汁的成分。

飲食時，胃腸激素經由食物的刺激而釋放，這些激素作用在膽囊壁的平滑肌上且促進其強力收縮以將膽汁擠壓而出。此外，由於膽汁參與脂肪乳化作用，使我們能充分消化並吸收食物中的脂肪。

Terminology 術語

1. insulin [ˈɪnsəlɪn] 胰島素

2. glycogen [ˈglaɪkədʒən] 肝醣

3. glucagon [ˈglukəgən] 升糖素
4. growth hormone [groθ ˈhɔrmon] 生長激素
5. anterior pituitary gland 腦下垂體前葉 [ænˈtɪrɪɚ pɪˈtjutærɪ glænd]

6. insulin-like growth factor [ˈɪnsəlɪn laɪk groθ ˈfæktɚ] 類胰島素生長因子
7. hepatocyte [ˈhɛpətosaɪt] 肝細胞
8. electrolyte [ɪˈlɛktrəˌlaɪt] 電解質

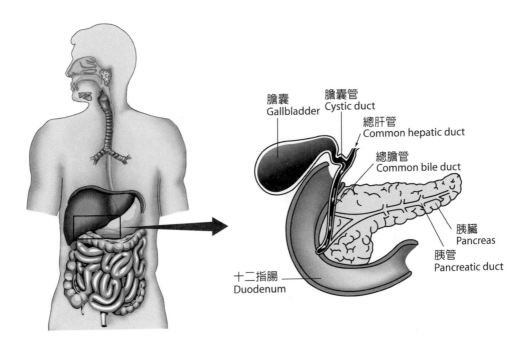

膽囊 Gallbladder
膽囊管 Cystic duct
總肝管 Common hepatic duct
總膽管 Common bile duct
胰臟 Pancreas
胰管 Pancreatic duct
十二指腸 Duodenum

Case Information 個案資訊

Hepatocellular Carcinoma (HCC) / Liver Cancer 肝細胞癌；肝癌
[ˌhɛpətəˈsɛljulɚ ˌkarsɪˈnomə]　　　　[ˈlɪvɚ ˈkænsɚ]

1. **Causes**: Chronic hepatitis B/C infection or alcohol abuse.
2. **Symptoms & Signs**: Abdominal pain, abdominal distension, jaundice, ascites, unexplainable weight loss, and general malaise.
3. **Care**:
   (1) High-fiber and low-fat diet.
   (2) Avoid refined foods.
   (3) Quit drinking.
   (4) Liver cancer treatment.
   (5) Post-operative care: Bed rest, measure blood pressure regularly and give symptomatic treatment.

Mr. Lee, a 57-year-old man, has hepatocellular carcinoma.

李先生，57 歲男性，罹患肝細胞癌。

N: Nurse　**D:** Doctor　**P:** Patient

N: Good morning, Mr. Lee. How are you doing today?

李先生早安。你現在覺得如何？

P: Quite well. I'm just worried about liver tumors.

還不錯，我只是在擔心肝腫瘤。

N: Have you felt any discomfort around your abdomen before?

你肚子以前曾有不舒服嗎？

P: Well, I feel like there's always a little **fluid¹** in my **abdomen**. Sometimes I feel **distended²**.

我覺得肚子裡經常會有一些液體，有時我會感覺漲漲的。

N: How about abdominal pain?

你有腹痛嗎？

P: No.

沒有。

N: Have you had jaundice or **tea-colored urine**?

你有黃疸或是茶色尿嗎？

P: I had jaundice last time I was admitted. But I was fine after discharge.

上次住院時我有黃疸，但是當時我出院後人很好。

N: When's the last time you were admitted?

你上次住院是什麼時候？

P: About one and half years ago.

大約一年半之前。

N: What was your major symptom at that time?

那時主要的症狀為何？

P: I had lots of fluid within my abdomen, and my face and body were very yellow in color.

我的肚子裡有很多水，而且身體和臉色都很黃。

N: The doctor found liver tumors and told you that you had liver cancer. Is that right?

那時醫師已發現肝腫瘤並告知你罹患肝癌。是嗎？

P: That's right.

是的。

N: What was your liver enzyme level like over the last one and half years?

一年半以來你的肝酵素指數如何呢？

P: Around 80.

大約 80。

N: That's high. Have you regularly taken the **anti-viral agents**?

肝酵素指數偏高。你有規律服用抗病毒藥物嗎？

P: Yes, I have followed all instructions from my doctors.

有，我都有按照醫師的囑咐服藥。

N: OK. The blood test shows your **residual liver function** is not good. The doctor will evaluate your condition and **establish**³ a new therapeutic plan with you. Please rest here for now.

P: Alright, I'll wait here.

好的。血液檢查顯示你的肝臟殘餘功能不好，醫師等會兒會來評估狀況並且建立新的治療計畫。請在這裡休息一下。

好的，我會在這兒等候醫生。

Nursing Notes　護理記錄

Admitted for liver cancer treatment. No tea-colored urine or jaundice. Blood biochemistry test performed and showed bad residual liver function.

病人因為進行肝癌治療而住院。沒有茶色尿或黃疸。血液生化檢查已施行並顯示肝臟殘餘功能差。

Vocabulary and Sentence Examples　字彙與例句

1. fluid [ˈfluɪd]
   (n.) 液體

   He studied fluid mechanics in the United Kingdom.
   他在英國修習流體力學。

2. distend [dɪsˈtɛnd]
   (v.) 撐開；使⋯漲起

   Her abdomen was distended from eating too much food.
   她吃太多食物導致腹脹。

3. establish [əˈstæblɪʃ]
   (v.) 建立

   The doctor needs to establish a good relationship with his patients.　醫師需與病患建立良好的關係。

Terminology 術語

1. abdomen 腹部
   [ˈæbdomən]

2. tea-colored urine 茶色尿
   [tiˈkʌləd ˈjurɪn]

3. anti-viral agent 抗病毒藥物
   [æntɪˈvaɪrəl ˈedʒənt]

4. residual liver function 肝臟殘餘功能
   [rɪˈzɪdʒuəl lɪvə ˈfʌŋkʃən]

Pre-Operative Care 術前照護

*The results of his residual liver function were **satisfying**[1]. Mr. Lee was NPO for 6 hours prior to treatment.*

肝殘餘功能檢查結果令人滿意。李先生已空腹 6 小時以備治療。

N: Hello, Mr. Lee, the procedure has been scheduled at 2 p.m. today. Do you have any questions?

李先生好，手術安排在今天下午 2 點。你有什麼問題嗎？

P: I'm curious about other methods used to treat liver cancer.

我對肝癌的其他療法感到好奇。

D: Other than **liver transplantation**, surgical resection is the most direct treatment and more suitable for **solitary**[2] tumors or the tumors that reside within one liver lobe.

撇開肝臟移植，手術切除腫瘤是最直接的方式且適於單顆肝腫瘤或是肝腫瘤較集中於某肝葉時。

P: Is this a feasible procedure for me?

對我而言是否可行呢？

D: No, your tumors are too far apart to be resected together. If we do this, you'll hardly have any normal liver left. That's why I suggest you receive the **trans-arterial chemo-embolization**.

你的肝腫瘤距離太遠以致於無法一起切除。如果這麼做，你幾乎會沒有正常的肝臟。因此建議接受經動脈化療栓塞術。

P: I see. What is this procedure?

我了解了。那程序為何？

D: We'll use a catheter to **pierce**[3] the skin around your **inguinal region** and ascend the vessels supplying blood and nutrients to the tumors. Then we'll inject a medication to block and kill tumor cells.

我們以導管穿刺鼠蹊部的皮膚再上行到供應血液與養分給肝腫瘤的血管中。接著注入藥劑，使癌細胞壞死。

P: I see. What are the risks associated with this surgery?

我懂了。那手術的風險是什麼？

D: You may catch a fever or experience abdominal pain that lasts for 1~2 weeks after surgery. This is caused by tumor necrosis. However, it's possible that your tumor may not be **destroyed**[4] permanently. You may have to receive this procedure again if the tumors return.

術後常有為期 1~2 週的發燒及腹痛，乃因腫瘤壞死所致。但此法不能永遠摧毀腫瘤。你可能在腫瘤復發時還得做一次栓塞術。

P: Alright. Thanks for your explanation.

好的。謝謝你的說明。

D: You're welcome. The nurse will bring you to the Radiology Department later. If you still have any questions, please feel free to call me.

不客氣。護理師稍後會帶你到放射醫學部門去。如果你還有任何問題，請再告訴我。

P: I will. What should I do for now?

N: Please shave around your inguinal region and change your clothes. The radiologist will then come and inject local anesthetic into this site where he will create a **puncture**[5]. Are you and your wife ready?

P: Yes, we're ready.

我會的。我現在應該做什麼？

請剃除鼠蹊部的體毛並換衣服。然後，放射科醫師會在穿刺前於穿刺部位注入局部麻醉劑。你和太太準備好了嗎？

是的，我們已經準備好了。

Nursing Notes　護理記錄

The doctor explained TACE to the patient. Well accepted. Preparation for TACE completed.

醫師向病人解釋經動脈化療栓塞術。病人能夠接受。術前準備完成。

Vocabulary and Sentence Examples　字彙與例句

1. satisfying [ˈsætɪsˌfaɪɪŋ]
   (adj.) 令人滿意的；符合要求的

   He received a satisfying grade in his final exam in bio-chemistry.
   他在生物化學的期末考中得到令人滿意的分數。

2. solitary [ˈsɑləˌtɛrɪ]
   (adj.) 單獨的

   She usually takes long solitary walks along the riverside.
   她通常會在河岸長時間獨自步行。

3. pierce [pɪrs]
   (v.) 穿刺

   Be careful of the needle, or it'll pierce you.
   小心針頭，否則你會被刺到。

4. destroy [dɪˈstrɔɪ]
   (v.) 摧毀

   These viruses destroyed his immune system.
   病毒摧毀了他的免疫系統。

5. puncture [ˈpʌŋktʃə]
   (n.) 刺孔
   (v.) 穿刺

   The radiologist will inject a local anesthetic into this site before creating a puncture.
   放射科醫師會在穿刺前於穿刺部位注入局部麻醉劑。

Terminology 術語

1. liver transplantation [lɪvə ˌtrænsplænˈteʃən] 肝臟移植
2. trans-arterial chemo-embolization [træns ɑrˈtɪrɪəl kimə ˌɛmbəlɪˈzeʃən]
   經動脈化療栓塞術(TACE)
3. inguinal region [ˈɪŋgwɪn̩ ˈridʒən] 鼠蹊部

Post-Operative Care　術後照護

19

The TACE has been completed and Mr. Lee returned to the general ward.

N: Good afternoon, Mr. Lee. How are you feeling now?

P: I feel pain around my inguinal area.

N: This is common after puncturing this site. You might feel pain or burning around the right abdomen. I'll give you a painkiller later.

P: OK, thank you very much.

N: You're welcome. Please place the sandbag over your **thigh**[1] and inguinal region.

P: What is the sandbag for?

N: It is used to **compress**[2] the vessels and to stop the bleeding after the artery has been punctured.

P: How long should I compress it for?

N: 6 hours. For now, you must remain in bed for the next 24 hours, and cannot take a bath or go to the toilet.

P: Well, that sounds inconvenient.

N: I understand. But it's **absolutely**[3] necessary after a procedure like this. You can use this bath **towel**[4] and **chamber pot**[5] for toileting purposes.

P: Alright, I'll try using it.

N: If you feel something wet or warm around your puncture site, please call us so we can check on it.

P: OK, I will.

N: To check if your blood pressure is down or you're bleeding from your puncture site, I'll take your blood pressure and pulse rate every 15 minutes over the next hour and then every 30 minutes over the second hour. After that, I'll come check on you every 2 hours.

P: I see. Thank you very much.

N: By the way, if you feel any discomfort, please call right away.

P: Definitely.

經動脈化療栓塞術已畢，李先生回到一般病房。

李先生你好，現在覺得如何？

我感到鼠蹊部疼痛。

這在穿刺後很常見的，你可能會感到右側腹痛或燒灼感，稍後會給你止痛劑的。

好，非常感謝你。

不客氣。請將砂袋置於大腿及鼠蹊部上。

它有何用途？

砂袋乃於動脈穿刺後，壓迫血管止血用。

我需要壓多久？

6 小時。此外，你必須臥床休息至少 24 小時，包括沐浴及如廁在內。

呃，這樣很不方便。

我懂。不過這對於術後是絕對必要的。你可以在床上用毛巾擦澡或使用便盆如廁。

好吧。我會試試看。

若你覺得穿刺部位溼溼的或暖暖的，請通知我們來檢查。

好，我會的。

為確認血壓是否下降或者傷口出血，我會在第一個小時內每 15 分鐘量一次你的血壓，第二個小時內會每半小時量血壓，之後我會每兩小時來一次。

我明白，非常感謝你。

對了，如果你有不舒服，請立刻告訴我們。

一定。

Nursing Notes 護理記錄

Sandbag placed on the thigh and inguinal region. No active bleeding or decrease in blood pressure. Told to rest in bed for at least 24 hours.

砂袋置於大腿及鼠蹊部，目前沒有傷口出血或血壓下降的情形。告知採絕對臥床休息至少 24 小時。

Tips on Writing

主動改被動／被動改主動的用法

Diet instructions and restrictions were given.＝Taught diet and diet restrictions.

The nurse removed intravenous catheter.＝Intravenous catheter was removed.

The patient will be discharged in two days.＝The doctor will discharge patient in two days.

Vocabulary and Sentence Examples 字彙與例句

1. thigh [θaɪ] (n.) 大腿	His thighs were sore after running in the marathon. 馬拉松比賽以後，他感到大腿痠痛。
2. compress [kəmˋprɛs] (v.) 壓緊	After withdrawing blood, please compress the punctured site to stop the bleeding.　抽血後，請壓住穿刺點以止血。
3. absolutely [ˋæbsəˌlutlɪ] (adv.) 絕對地	Providing confidential patient information to others is absolutely prohibited. 向他人洩漏病人的隱私資訊是絕對禁止的。
4. towel [taul] (n.) 毛巾；浴巾	Please use a towel to wipe the table after you finish eating dinner.　你吃完晚餐後，請用毛巾將桌子擦乾淨。
5. chamber pot 便盆 [ˋtʃembɚ pat]	Patients can use a chamber pot for their bowel movements if necessary.　必要時，可以使用便盆如廁。

More Information

1. 肝膽疾病的問診重點

(1) Have you had any abdominal pain?
你有腹痛的情形嗎？

(2) Can you describe the pain?
你能描述出這種疼痛嗎？

(3) When did you feel pain? Did it happen after meals?
你何時會痛？飯後會感到疼痛嗎？

(4) Has the pain persisted? How long has it persisted?
疼痛是否持續？持續多久？

(5) Where is the pain most prominent?
最痛的地方在哪裡？

(6) Have you felt distension in the abdomen?
你會感到腹脹嗎？

(7) Has your face appeared yellow?
你的臉色看起來黃黃的嗎？

(8) Have you had tea-colored urine?
你有茶色尿嗎？

(9) Have you felt extremely tired within the last 2 months?
你最近 2 個月會感到特別疲倦嗎？

(10) Have you seen any edema within your body?
你身上任何一處有水腫嗎？

(11) Have your legs become swollen?
你小腿有腫脹嗎？

(12) Have you bruised easily?
你容易瘀血嗎？

(13) Are you a hepatitis B or C carrier?
你是 B 型肝炎或 C 型肝炎帶原者嗎？

(14) Have you ever had liver cirrhosis?
你曾有肝硬化的情形嗎？

Exercise 小試身手

● Choose the Correct Answer

( ) 1. The balloon is _____ with nitrogen. (A)dismissed (B)dispute (C)inflated (D)dismute 這氣球因為氮氣而漲大。

( ) 2. It's not easy to _____ a good relationship with strangers. (A)establish (B)accomplish (C)cherish (D)build
要與陌生人建立良好關係是不容易的。

( ) 3. She got a _____ grade on her examination. (A)satisfied (B)satisfactory (C)saturate (D)sad 她在此次考試取得令人滿意的成績。

( ) 4. The earth has a _____ satellite. (A)soltatory (B)solitary (C)solitude (D)solution 地球有一個單獨的衛星。

( ) 5. The government was able to _____ smallpox. (A)clean (B)emit (C)eradicate (D)decorate。 政府有能力可以根治天花。

● Fill in the Blanks

1. A _____ _____ is the most direct way to cure _____ _____ .
肝臟移植是治癒肝癌最直接的方法。

2. _____-_____ _____-_____ cannot cure you from liver cancer but can help control it.
經動脈化療栓塞術無法完全治癒肝癌，只能控制它。

3. When he is unable to _____ from the bed to the bathroom, he can use a _____ _____ for his bowel movements and urine.
當他無法下床行走至浴室時，可以使用便盆如廁。

4. There was a lot of _____ _____ in his abdomen due to his _____ _____ . 他的腹部因為肝硬化的緣故有很多液體累積。

5. Use a _____ _____ to apply pressure on the _____ _____ for six hours after the surgery. 手術過後要用砂袋壓在鼠蹊部六小時。

● Simplify Nursing Notes

1. Taught patient how to clean wound.（改寫成被動用法）

_____

2. Taught patient self-care skills.（改寫成被動用法）

_____

3. Arranged a visit to day care center.（改寫成被動用法）

_____

4. Foley catheter removed.（改寫成主動用法）

_____

5. CT scan arranged.（改寫成主動用法）

_____

● Translation

1. 你有黃疸或是茶色尿嗎？

_____

2. 你有規律服用抗病毒藥物嗎？

_____

3. 手術安排在今天下午 1 點。

_____

4. 你必須臥床休息至少 24 小時。

_____

5. 為確認血壓是否下降或者傷口出血，我會在第一個小時內每 15 分鐘量一次你的血壓。

_____

Endocrinology Unit
內分泌科

Learning Goals 學習目標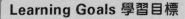

1. Assessing patients with possible DM
2. Assessing patient's blood sugar level
3. Approaching patient with fluctuating glucose level
4. Providing health education to patients

Outline 本章大綱

- The Components of the Endocrine System
  內分泌系統的組成
- Case Information: Diabetes Mellitus (DM)
  個案資訊：糖尿病
- Admission Assessment　入院評估
- Hospitalization　住院療護
- Discharge Instructions　出院衛教

Medical English for
Healthcare Professionals

The Components of the Endocrine System 內分泌系統的組成

20

The endocrine system consists of various endocrine organs and tissues, including the **hypothalamus**[1], **pituitary gland**[2], **thyroid gland**[3], pancreas, **adrenal glands**[4], **testis**[5] (in male) and **ovary**[6] (in female).

The endocrine gland can secrete hormones to the whole body's circulatory system. These hormones exert their functions by acting on target cells.

The endocrine system regulates the body function via a delicate way, affecting metabolism, growth and development, water and electrolyte balance, mental status and immunity.

內分泌系統由許多內分泌器官和組織組成，包括下視丘、腦下垂體、甲狀腺、胰臟、腎上腺、男性睪丸和女性卵巢。

內分泌腺能製造激素並釋放到全身循環。這些激素作用在標的細胞上並發揮其機能。

內分泌系統精巧地調控著身體功能，影響範圍廣泛，從代謝、生長與發育、水分和電解質平衡、心理狀態直到免疫力都有。

Terminology 術語

1. hypothalamus [ˌhaɪpoˈθæləməs] 下視丘
2. pituitary gland [pɪˈtjuɪtærɪ glænd] 腦下垂體
3. thyroid gland [ˈθaɪrɔɪd glænd] 甲狀腺
4. adrenal gland [əˈdrinəl glænd] 腎上腺
5. testis [ˈtɛstɪs] 睪丸
6. ovary [ˈovərɪ] 卵巢

Case Information 個案資訊

Diabetes Mellitus (DM) [ˌdaɪəˈbitiz ˈmɛlətəs] 糖尿病

1. **Causes**: Heredity, unhealthy diet habit (high fat, sugar, etc.), or autoimmunity.
2. **Symptoms & Signs**:
   (1) Polydipsia＝drink a lot
   (2) Polyphagia＝eat a lot
   (3) Polyuria＝urinate a lot
   (4) Loss of body weight
   (5) Disorders involving retina, kidneys, nerves, vessels

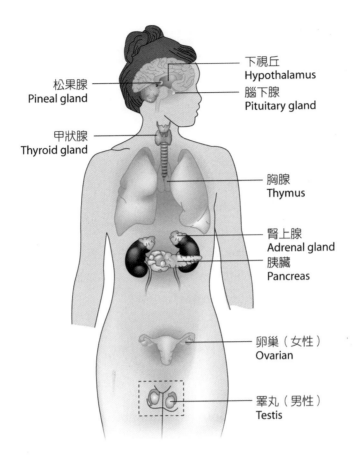

松果腺
Pineal gland

下視丘
Hypothalamus

腦下腺
Pituitary gland

甲狀腺
Thyroid gland

胸腺
Thymus

腎上腺
Adrenal gland

胰臟
Pancreas

卵巢（女性）
Ovarian

睪丸（男性）
Testis

Case Information 個案資訊

3. **Care**:

(1) Monitor blood sugar index.

(2) Maintain a balanced, regular diet.

(3) Maintain a low-sugar, low-salt, low-fat, and high-fiber diet.

(4) Avoid refined, canned or preserved foods.

(5) Exercise regularly and keep fit.

(6) Take medications on time.

(7) Maintain foot hygiene.

(8) Return for follow-up exams regularly.

Admission Assessment 入院評估

21

Mr. Chang, a 50-year-old man, was admitted for hyperglycemia.

張先生是 50 歲男性，因高血糖而住院。

N: Nurse   **P:** patient

N: Good evening, Mr. Chang. Have you felt any discomfort prior to this admission?

晚安，張先生，在這次住院之前你有任何不適嗎？

P: No, but my last regular **health check-up**[1] showed my blood sugar was higher than normal.

沒有。但最近的例行性健康檢查指出我的血糖值高於正常值。

N: Do you always feel thirsty and drink a lot of water?

你常會感到口渴並喝很多水嗎？

P: Yes, I drink about 6 liters of water everyday.

是的，我每天都喝六公升的水。

N: How many times do you go to the **toilet**[2] a day?

你一天上幾次廁所呢？

P: Well, **approximately**[3] 15 times a day.

嗯，大約 15 次。

N: Do you always feel hungry or have you had an increased appetite lately?

你經常會感到飢餓或者感覺胃口比以前好嗎？

P: Yes, I eat a lot but never gain any weight.

是的。我吃很多但體重未增加。

N: I see, the doctor said these symptoms might be associated with diabetes. Has anyone from your family ever suffered from this before?

好的。醫師說這些症狀可能和糖尿病有關，你的家人有誰罹患糖尿病嗎？

P: No, they are all healthy and well.

沒有，他們相當健康。

N: I see. It's time to check your **post-meal**[4] blood sugar. Which finger should I use?

我知道了。檢測飯後血糖的時間到了，我該用哪一隻手指？

P: Please use my left forefinger.

請用我的左手食指。

N: I'll **sterilize**[5] it first, and then stab it with a tiny needle. It will hurt a little.

我會先消毒，接著戳入一枚小針，這會有些疼痛。

P: OK. What is my blood sugar?

好的。我的血糖值如何？

N: 300. It's high for your condition. It should be controlled to less than 180 after meals.

300，對你而言是偏高的。飯後血糖應該低於 180。

P: I see, so how can I control it?

我了解。那我要如何控制它呢？

N: It can be controlled by diet, exercise and medications. The doctor will first **administer**[6] insulin which will decrease and stabilize your blood sugar for now.

血糖可藉由飲食、運動及藥物治療來控制。醫師會先用胰島素來降低並穩定你的血糖。

P: I don't understand how diet and exercise can help.

我不懂飲食與運動有何助益。

N: You'll find out during **diabetic⁷** patient education lessons. Are you interested in joining?

P: Sure, thank you.

你在糖尿病病人衛教課程中便能明白的。您有興趣參加嗎？
當然，非常感謝。

Nursing Notes 護理記錄

Hyperglycemia incidentally found via regular health check-up. Has symptoms of polyphagia, polydipsia and polyuria. No C/O discomfort. PC sugar 300. Explained the treatment plan. Informed patient about education lessons. Interested in joining.

病人偶然經由例行性健康檢查得知高血糖的狀況。有吃多、喝多及尿多的症狀。無不適之主訴。飯後血糖 300 (mg/dL)。解釋治療計畫。介紹病人衛教課程。病人想要參加。

Vocabulary and Sentence Examples 字彙與例句

1. health check-up
   [hɛlθ ˈtʃɛk ʌp]
   健康檢查

   The national health insurance plan provides free health check-ups for citizens over 50 years of age.
   國家健康保險提供 50 歲以上的國民免費健康檢查。

2. toilet [ˈtɔɪlɪt]
   (n.) 廁所

   Please flush the toilet after using it.
   使用過廁所後請沖水。

3. approximately
   [əˈpraksəmɪtlɪ]
   (adv.) 大約地；概略地

   The highway is approximately 500 kilometers in length.
   這條高速公路大約有 500 公里長。

4. post-meal [ˈpostˌmil]
   (adj.) 飯後的

   Post-meal blood sugar help indicate the level of insulin resistance.　飯後血糖值指出胰島素阻抗性的程度。

5. sterilize [ˈstɛrəˌlaɪz]
   (v.) 消毒；無菌

   The surgical instruments should be sterilized before their use.　手術器材在使用前應該要消毒殺菌。

6. administer [ədˈmɪnəstə]
   (v.) 給予（藥物）

   He administered beta-blocker agents to the hypertensive patient.　他給予那位高血壓患者乙型阻斷劑。

7. diabetic [ˌdaɪəˈbɛtɪk]
   (adj.) 糖尿病的

   Diabetic patients who are not treated will have high blood sugar.　未經治療的糖尿病患者有高血糖的情形。

Terminology 術語

1. hyperglycemia [ˌhaɪpəglaɪˈsimɪə] 高血糖

Hospitalization 住院療護

22

Mr. Chang became dizzy, so his family called the nurse.

N: May I help you?

P: Yes, I felt really dizzy after getting out of bed.

N: Do you feel very thirsty, and have you **urinated**[1] a large amount recently?

P: Yes. Are these common symptoms for diabetic patients?

N: Blood sugar can cause different symptoms. Higher blood sugar can make your symptoms more **severe**[2]. Let's check your blood sugar. *(Later)* It's 400!

N: Have you eaten your meals on time?

P: Yes, but I ate more because I felt really hungry.

N: You must have frequent, small meals in order to control your blood sugar. What did you have for lunch?

P: The diabetic diet provided by the **nutrition**[3] department of the hospital. This should be healthy.

N: That's right. Did you eat or drink something after lunch?

P: Uh, I drank a large glass of milk tea.

N: Milk tea? Milk tea is not **suitable**[4] for diabetic patients. There's a lot of sugar and fat in milk tea, which can drastically increase your blood sugar.

P: What kind of dietary rules must I obey then?

N: First, maintain a balanced, regular diet. Second, eat a low-sugar, low-salt, low-fat and high-fiber diet. Third, avoid **refined**[5], canned or preserved foods.

P: This sounds like a strict diet, but I'll try to follow these rules.

N: Very good. You can ask the **nutritionist**[6] for more details later, such as how to eat without **affecting**[7] your blood sugar.

P: OK, I'll take note. Thank you.

張先生變得頭暈，家人找來護士。

我可以幫助你嗎？

是的，我在起床時感到頭很暈。

你會感到很口渴嗎？或者你剛剛有排過很多尿液？

是的，我有。這對糖尿病病患來說常見嗎？

血糖能引發不同的症狀。高血糖使症狀加重。來檢測你的血糖吧。（稍後）血糖值為 400。

你有按時進餐嗎？

有，因為很餓所以我吃很多。

為了控制血糖，你必須少量多餐。你午餐吃什麼？

由醫院營養部提供的糖尿病飲食應該對我有益。

沒錯。那午餐過後你有吃或喝什麼？

呃，我喝了大杯奶茶。

奶茶？它不適合糖尿病患者飲用。奶茶含有許多糖分和油脂，會讓你的血糖大大升高。

那我必須遵守何種飲食規則呢？

第一，定時地均衡飲食；第二，要採低糖、低鹽、低油及較高纖維的飲食；第三，避免精製、罐裝或醃漬食品。

聽起來雖然嚴苛，但我會謹記在心。

非常好。你稍後可以向營養師詢問細節。譬如說要怎麼吃才不影響血糖之類的問題。

好的，我會做筆記。謝謝！

Nursing Notes　護理記錄

C/O dizzy, thirsty and drank a lot of water in the afternoon. One-touch sugar 400. Had milk tea after lunch. Provided diet instructions. Encouraged to ask nutritionist about dietary questions. Keep observing for symptoms of hyperglycemia.

主訴下午感覺頭暈、異常口渴並且大量飲水。手指採血測得血糖為 400 (mg/dL)。於飯後飲用奶茶。給予飲食衛教。鼓勵病人詢問營養師食物問題。續觀察高血糖症狀。

Tips on Writing

1. 症狀觀察的寫法：要觀察尚未發生的 A 症狀是否會發生，使用 **Observe for A** 的句型；要繼續觀察已經發生的 A 症狀時，使用 **Observe A** 的句型。例：
Will keep observing for symptoms of hyperglycemia.
（實情是：The patient **does not have** any symptoms of hyperglycemia yet.）
Will keep observing blood sugar index.
（實情是：The patient **has already** had an elevated blood sugar index.）
2. 主訴的寫法：complain of＋feeling＋形容詞＝complain of 名詞／名詞子句
例：Complain of feeling dizzy＝complain of dizziness

Vocabulary and Sentence Examples　字彙與例句

1. urinate [ˈjurəˌnet]
(v.) 排尿
Patients with urinary tract obstruction have difficulty urinating.　泌尿道阻塞患者有排尿困難的情形。

2. severe [səˈvɪr]
(adj.) 嚴重的；劇烈的
He has a severe cough.
他咳嗽劇烈。

3. nutrition [njuˈtrɪʃən]
(n.) 營養
His poor nutrition caused him to be weak.
營養缺乏讓他變得虛弱。

4. suitable [ˈsjutəbl̩]
(adj.) 適合的
This dress is suitable for you.
這件洋裝很適合妳。

5. refined [rɪˈfaɪnd]
(adj.) 精製的；提煉的
Before petroleum is used, it must be refined.
石油在使用前必須經過提煉。

6. nutritionist [njuˈtrɪʃənɪst]
(n.) 營養師
The nutritionists can teach you how to eat an enjoyable, healthy diet.　營養師能教你如何吃得健康又美味。

7. affect [əˈfɛkt]
(v.) 影響
Hepatitis affected the function of his liver.
肝炎影響了他的肝功能。

Discharge Instructions　出院衛教

23

Mr. Chang showed improvement in his blood sugar control.

張先生的血糖控制進步很多。

N: Good morning, Mr. Chang. Here is your after-meal medication.

張先生午安。這是你的飯後藥物。

P: I understand that this can **inhibit**[1] the **absorption**[2] of glucose and can keep my blood sugar from rising too quickly.

我知道它會抑制葡萄糖的吸收，維持血糖不要上升得太快。

N: Good, do you remember how to control your blood sugar?

很好，那你記得應該如何控制血糖嗎？

P: Yes. First, maintain a balanced and regular diet. Second, avoid foods containing too much sugar, salt or fat. Third, exercise regularly and try to **reduce**[3] my weight.

是的。第一，飲食要均衡及規律；第二，勿攝食過多的糖分、鹽分及油脂；第三，規律地運動並減重。

N: What's the minimum **requirement**[4] for your exercise regime?

如何達到運動的最低要求呢？

P: At least 3 times a week, 30 minutes each time. My heart rate must also reach about 130 beats per minute right after exercising.

每週至少三次運動，每次 30 分鐘。此外，我的心跳速率在運動過後要達到每分鐘 130 下。

N: Very good. Are you forgetting anything else?

很好。有沒有忘了什麼呢？

P: Yes, I have to take my medications regularly and come back here for follow-up exams.

是的，我必須規律地服藥並且回診追蹤檢查。

N: It's great to see that you remember all of this.

看到你全都記得真好。

P: Thank you very much.

非常謝謝你。

N: I know it's not easy to have to follow such strict rules. You will have to self-**motivate**[5] yourself pretty often.

我知道需要遵守如此嚴苛的規則並不容易。你必須常常激勵自己來執行。

P: Don't worry. For my own health, I'll try my best.

別擔心，為了自身健康，我會盡最大的努力的。

N: One more thing, you should try to **prevent**[6] yourself from getting injured. High blood sugar will make you more **susceptible**[7] to infections, especially from wounds on your feet. Keep you feet clean and check yourself if you have any injuries.

還有，你應該要避免受傷。因為高血糖會讓你容易受到感染。特別是腳上的傷口。保持腳部清潔並注意是否有任何的受傷。

P: I'll remember. Thanks.　　　　　　　我會記得。多謝。

Nursing Notes　護理記錄

Blood sugar well controlled. Told to exercise and take medications regularly. Told never to eat food with lots of sugar, salt and fat. Instructed on importance of foot hygiene.

血糖控制良好。告知規律運動與定時服藥。告知不可攝食過多的糖分、鹽分及油脂。告知足部衛生的重要性。

Vocabulary and Sentence Examples　字彙與例句

1. inhibit [ɪnˋhɪbɪt]
   (v.) 抑制
   Some antibiotics can inhibit the growth of bacteria while some can kill them.
   有些抗生素能抑制細菌生長，有些則能殺死他們。

2. absorption [əbˋsɔrpʃən]
   (n.) 吸收
   Absorption of nutrients mainly occurs in the small intestine. 營養的吸收主要發生在小腸。

3. reduce [rɪˋdjus]
   (v.) 減少；降低
   This is designed for reducing the concentration of cholesterol in the blood.
   它是為降低血液中的膽固醇含量而設計的。

4. requirement [rɪˋkwaɪrmənt]
   (n.) 要求；需求
   We must eat fruit and vegetables to meet our basic nutritional requirements.
   我們必須要攝取水果和蔬菜來達到某些維生素的基本需求。

5. motivate [ˋmotəˏvet]
   (v.) 激發
   What motivated you to organize this campaign for environmental conservation?
   什麼事情激發你組織這個環保運動？

6. prevent [prɪˋvɛnt]
   (v.) 避免
   The river embankment prevented the flood from invading this village. 河堤避免洪水入侵這座村莊。

7. susceptible [səˋsɛptəbl̩]
   (adj.) 易感的
   I'm susceptible to colds.
   我容易罹患感冒。

More Information

1. 糖尿病的問診要點：吃多、喝多、尿多、體重減輕

   (1) Have you ever felt excessively thirsty?
      你曾經感到非常口渴嗎？

   (2) Have you ever felt excessively hungry?
      你曾經感到飢餓嗎？

   (3) Do you have to frequently urinate?
      你有頻尿情形嗎？

   (4) Have you experienced unusual weight loss?
      你有體重不尋常地下降的情形嗎？

   (5) Have you ever had blurred vision?
      你的視力模糊嗎？

2. 血糖控制的衛教重點

   (1) Exercise regularly.
      規律運動。

   (2) Sleep adequately.
      睡眠充足。

   (3) Check your feet for possible cuts/injuries.
      檢視雙腳可能有的受傷。

   (4) Have meals at regular intervals daily.
      每天定時進食。

   (5) Take medications as instructed. Do not skip or adjust dosages by yourself.
      遵從指示服藥，不漏掉任何一次，也不自行調整劑量。

   (6) Record your blood sugar index everyday.
      每天記錄血糖指數。

   (7) Stay away from high-sugar and high-lipid diets.
      避免高糖及高脂飲食。

Exercise 小試身手

● Choose the Correct Answer

( ) 1. From holding this activity, we made _____ ten thousand dollars.
(A)appropriately (B)approximately (C)appreciate
舉辦這次活動，我們大約獲利一萬元。

( ) 2. Hyperglycemia is a typical symptom seen in _____ patients.
(A)diabolic (B)diabetic (C)depression (D)elder
高血糖是糖尿病患者的典型症狀。

( ) 3. Surgical instruments used in patients with infectious diseases should be _____ . (A)stirred (B)steamed (C)sterilized (D)cleaned
使用於感染性疾病患者的手術器械必須消毒。

( ) 4. It's beneficial to _____ weight for health reasons. (A)lose (B)increase (C)introduce (D)produce 減重對健康有益。

( ) 5. The doctor _____ a bronchodilator to relieve her symptoms.
(A)adjusted (B)administered (C)adjuncted (D)adjoined
醫師給予她氣管擴張劑來減輕症狀。

● Fill in the Blanks

1. Because he had difficulty _____ , the doctor placed a foley catheter.
他解尿困難，因此醫師幫他放置了導尿管。

2. The chairman's opinion _____ if the plan should be carried out or not.
主席的意見決定計畫是否繼續進行。

3. Due to over- _____ , lots of children suffer from obesity.
因為營養過剩，很多孩童都有肥胖的問題。

4. The wind _____ our experiment. Therefore, we postponed our plans.
風力干擾了我們的實驗，因此我們延後計畫。

5. These medications can _____ the growth of cancer cells.
這些藥物可以抑制癌細胞的生長。

◉ Simplify Nursing Notes

1. The patient didn't experience any headaches.

   We will keep _____

2. The patient has been bleeding over her thigh.

   We will keep _____

3. The patient complained of feeling nauseous.（改寫成另一句型）

   _____

4. The patient complained of a stomachache.（改寫成另一句型）

   _____

5. The patient complained of restlessness.（改寫成另一句型）

   _____

◉ Translation

1. 血糖可藉由飲食、運動及藥物治療來控制。

   _____

2. 為了控制血糖，你必須少量多餐。

   _____

3. 你記得應該如何控制血糖嗎？

   _____

4. 你必須規律地服藥並且回診追蹤檢查。

   _____

5. 你應該要避免受傷。因為高血糖會讓你容易受到感染。

   _____

Infectious Disease Unit
感染科

Learning Goals 學習目標

1. Assessing patients with fever
2. Collecting information about potential sources of infection
3. Explaining the natural course of cellu-litis to patients
4. Providing health education to patients

Outline 本章大綱

- Infectious Diseases and the Immune System
  感染性疾病與免疫系統
- Case Information: Cellulitis
  個案資訊：蜂窩性組織炎
- Admission Assessment　入院評估
- Hospitalization　住院療護
- Discharge Instructions　出院衛教

Medical English for Healthcare Professionals

Infectious Diseases and the Immune System 感染性疾病與免疫系統

24

Tens of thousands of pathogens exist in the environment we live in today. Therefore, it is impossible for anyone to avoid contacting diseases. The human body has an intricate defense mechanism protecting us from being harmed by these pathogens. We call this the immune system.

The immune system is divided into three parts. The first part is made up of our skin, mucosa and the appendages of those components. Their integrity determines if pathogens can invade our body. The second part is our innate immunity, which consists of **neutrophils**[1], **monocytes**[2] and **dendritic cells**[3]. These cells recognize pathogens with low specificity. However, they can fight against most pathogens immediately after invasion. The third part is our adaptive immunity, comprising of T and B **lympho-cytes**[4]. These cells recognize pathogens at an astonishing specificity. Their reaction is slow but much more powerful than our innate immunity.

When certain pathogens invade our body or we are wounded, the most common reaction observed is *inflammation*. This is a condition cha-racterized by five essential components: *redness*, *swelling*, *heat*, *pain* and *loss of function*.

成千上萬的病原體存在於今日我們居住的環境，因此沒有人能夠避免與它們接觸。人體有一個精巧的防禦系統保護我們免於受到病原體的傷害，我們稱為免疫系統。

免疫系統分為三部分。第一部分是皮膚、黏膜及其附屬器官。它們的完整度決定病原體是否可入侵體內。第二部分是由嗜中性球、單核球及樹突細胞組成的先天性免疫。它們雖以低特異性的方式辨識病原體，但幾乎能夠在其入侵後立即展開對抗。第三部分是由 T 與 B 淋巴球組成的適應性免疫。它們以驚人的特異性辨識病原體。雖然反應速度較慢，卻比先天免疫性更有力量。

當人體被病原體侵入或受傷時都會有的反應是一炎症反應。這是一種由紅、腫、熱、痛及功能損失五種特徵組成的狀況。

Terminology 術語

1. neutrophil [ˈnjutrəfɪl] 嗜中性球
2. monocyte [ˈmɑnəsaɪt] 單核球
3. dendritic cell [dɛnˈdrɪtɪk sɛl] 樹突細胞
4. lymphocyte [ˈlɪmfosaɪt] 淋巴球

Case Information 個案資訊

Cellulitis [ˌsɛljəˈlaɪtɪs] **蜂窩性組織炎**

1. **Causes**: Bacterial infection, mostly *Staphylococcus aureus*.
2. **Symptoms & Signs**: Localized pain/tenderness, swelling, lymphadenopathy, erythema, and local heat.

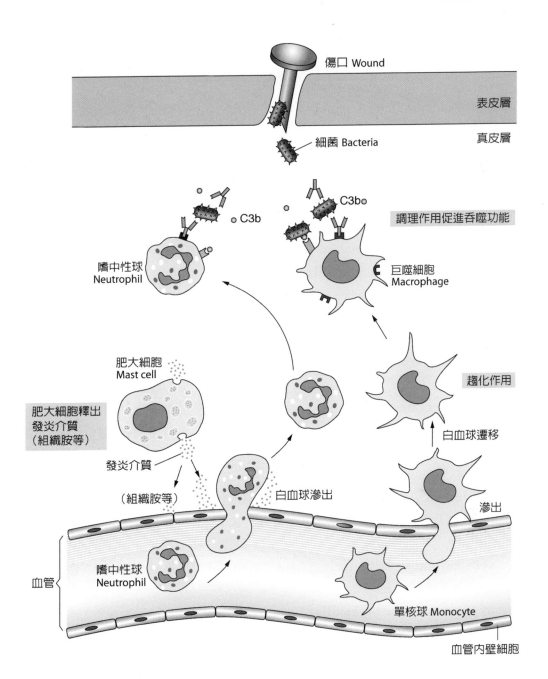

傷口 Wound

表皮層

細菌 Bacteria

真皮層

C3b

C3b

調理作用促進吞噬功能

嗜中性球
Neutrophil

巨噬細胞
Macrophage

肥大細胞
Mast cell

趨化作用

肥大細胞釋出
發炎介質
（組織胺等）

白血球遷移

發炎介質

白血球滲出

（組織胺等）

滲出

血管

嗜中性球
Neutrophil

白血球滲出

單核球 Monocyte

血管內壁細胞

Case Information 個案資訊

3. **Care**:

(1) Monitor the progress of inflammation, including redness, swelling, heat and pain.

(2) Give antibiotic treatment.

(3) Keep the wound clean.

(4) Return for follow-up exams regularly.

Admission Assessment　入院評估

25

Ms. Lin, a 20-year-old woman, suffered from fever.

N: Nurse　**P:** Patient

N: Good morning, Ms. Lin. How long have you had a fever? What's your temperature been?

P: I've had a fever for about 5 days. It's been 38 degree Celsius (℃), but sometimes risen to 40℃.

N: When you had the fever How did you feel?

P: I felt feverish with occasional **chills**[1] and **shivers**[2].

N: Did you do anything to relieve the fever?

P: Yes, I took some medicine. But my temperature didn't **revert**[3] back to normal.

N: Have you had a **runny nose**[4], **sore throat**[5] or **diarrhea**?

P: No, I haven't had these problems.

N: What about abdominal pain, or pain during **urination**[6]?

P: No, none of these either.

N: OK. Now tell me, what did you do this weekend?

P: I went to class and followed my normal daily routine.

N: Are you currently still feeling any kind of discomfort?

P: Yes, my hand is a little bit **swollen**[7] and painful.

N: Did you injure your hand, like cut it with a knife?

P: Hmm… my cat bit me one week ago. 2 days later, my left hand started swelling.

N: Have you been in contact with anyone with a fever or **infectious**[8] disease, or have you travelled abroad recently?

P: No.

N: OK. Please make yourself comfortable. The doctor will come by to see you in a bit. You can press the call button if you need any help.

林小姐，20 歲女性，患有發燒。

林小姐早安。你發燒多久了？會燒到幾度？

發燒約 5 天了。體溫 38℃，但有時升到 40℃。

發燒時你的感覺如何？

發燒時我偶有打冷顫及顫抖。

你有做些什麼來退燒嗎？

我有吃一些藥，但體溫並沒有回復到正常值。

你有流鼻水、喉嚨痛或腹瀉的情形嗎？

沒有，我沒有這些問題。

那是否有腹痛，或者排尿時有疼痛的情形呢？

都沒有。

好的，那你這週末做過什麼？

我去上課，且如往常般地生活。

你最近還有其他不舒服的地方嗎？

有，我的手有一點點腫痛。

手有受過傷嗎？譬如被刀切到？

嗯，一週前我的貓咬我一口。兩天後我的左手就開始腫起來了。

你最近曾經與發燒或感染性疾病患者接觸，或者出國過嗎？

沒有。

好的，請休息一下。醫師會稍微過來察看。若你需要協助，可以按叫人鈴。

P: I will. Thank you.

我會的，謝謝你。

Nursing Notes 護理記錄

C/O fever for 5 days. Has not been abroad or been in contact with people having contagious disease recently. Has tiny wound on the left hand, bitten by a cat one week ago.

主訴發燒 5 天。近日未曾出國或接觸過感染性疾病患者。左手小傷口是一週前被貓咬傷的。

Vocabulary and Sentence Examples 字彙與例句

1. chill [tʃɪl]
   (adj.) 冷的
   (v.) 打寒顫

   Malaria can cause fevers and chills.
   瘧疾會引起發燒及打寒顫。

2. shiver [ˈʃɪvə]
   (v./n.) 顫抖

   When her body temperature rose to 41℃, she began shivering a lot.　她發燒到 41℃ 時顫抖得很厲害。

3. runny nose [ˈrʌnɪ noz]
   流鼻水

   I started having a runny nose since last night.
   我從昨晚開始流鼻水。

4. sore throat [ˈsor θrot]
   喉嚨痛

   He has a sore throat.
   他喉嚨痛。

5. urination [jurəˈneʃən]
   (n.) 解尿

   If you feel pain during urination, you need to see a doctor.
   若你解尿時感到疼痛，需要去找醫師就診。

6. revert [rɪˈvɜt]
   (v.) 回復

   After the war, the lives of these citizens gradually reverted back its normal, peaceful self again.
   戰爭過後，居民逐漸回復到平靜的生活。

7. swollen [ˈswolən]
   (adj.) 腫脹的

   Her right hand is swollen.
   她的右手腫脹。

8. infectious [ɪnˈfɛkʃəs]
   (adj.) 具感染性的

   Blood collected from patients with AIDS may be very infectious.　採集自愛滋病患者的血液可能很具傳染性。

Terminology 術語

1. diarrhea [ˌdaɪəˈriə] 腹瀉

Hospitalization　住院療護

26

The nurse checked Ms. Lin's condition.	護理師正在檢查林小姐的情況。
N: How do you feel now, Ms. Lin?	林小姐，你現在覺得如何？
P: My fever has **subsided**[1], but my left hand still feels a little bit painful and swollen.	發燒已經退了，但我的手還有些疼痛和腫脹。
N: Let me check it. *(After observing the wound)* It's better than before.	讓我檢查一下。（視診傷口後）已比先前好多了。
P: I'm worried if my hand will ever return to normal again.	我擔心我的手是否能回復正常。
N: Don't worry. According to your condition, the **inflammation**[2] can be **temporarily**[3] controlled by **antibiotics**[4]. However, the damage in your left hand by the **bacteria** usually takes a little while to **recover**[5]. It should take 7~11 days.	別擔心。根據你的情形來看，炎症反應暫時被抗生素控制住了。然而細菌對左手造成的傷害通常需要一些時間復原，約7~11 天左右。
P: Then my hand will be normal after that?	那我的手會在那之後康復囉？
N: Sure. Cellulitis is a sort of local infection. As long as we **detect**[6] and control it early, there're **seldom**[7] functional **impairments**[8] left behind.	當然。蜂窩性組織炎為局部感染，只要及早察覺與控制，很少會帶來功能上的損害的。
P: Great! It's so good to hear this news.	太好了，很高興聽到這消息。
N: Just keep taking the antibiotics for about one week. The result of your treatment will determine if the course will need to be prolonged.	現在只要持續服用約一週的抗生素。不過治療結果會決定療程是否要延長。
P: I understand, thanks for your explanation.	我了解了，謝謝你的說明。
N: You're welcome.	不客氣。

Nursing Notes　護理記錄

Redness, swelling and tenderness in the left hand. Worried about functional impairment. Told the natural course and prognosis of cellulitis. Will keep observing wound in left hand for pus discharge or gangrene.

在左手有紅腫和壓痛情形。病人擔心有功能上的損害。告知蜂窩性組織炎的自然病程與預後。將持續觀察左手傷口是否有膿性分泌物或壞疽情形。

Tips on Writing

1. 主訴身體不適之處：若是全身不適，可用 from head to toe 或 all over；僅某處不適則用 **in**＋不適部位。例：
C/O discomfort **in** the right leg.

2. 將要觀察某處病況的寫法：可寫成 Will keep observing **A** for **B**。**A** 為觀察處，**B** 為要觀察發生的狀況。例：
Will keep observing **wound** on the hand for **pus discharge**.

Vocabulary and Sentence Examples 字彙與例句

1. subside [səbˊsaɪd]
(v.)減緩；消失

He was transferred to the general ward because his symptoms had subsided.
因為症狀減緩，他被轉進一般病房。

2. inflammation [ˏɪnfləˊmeʃən]
(n.) 發炎

Various pathogens can elicit inflammation where they invade our bodies.
各種病原體會在它們侵入我們身體之處引起發炎。

3. temporarily [ˊtɛmpəˏrɛrəlɪ]
(adv.) 暫時地

The typhoon will temporarily stop at this island and then quickly go away afterwards.
颱風會在小島暫時停留接著迅速離開。

4. antibiotic (n.) 抗生素 [ˏæntɪbaɪˊɑtɪk]

Antibiotics can inhibit the growth of bacteriae or kill them.
抗生素能抑制細菌的生長或是殺死它們。

5. recover [rɪˊkʌvə]
(v.) 復原

It will take half a year for your fracture to heal and recover.
你的骨折要花半年時間才能癒合及復原。

6. detect [dɪˊtɛkt]
(v.) 察覺；偵測

I detect sadness in your voice.
我察覺到你話語中的悲傷。

7. seldom [ˊsɛldəm]
(adv.) 偶爾；很少

He seldom drinks, so he became drunk after drinking only one glass of beer.
他很少喝酒，因此在喝完一杯啤酒後就醉倒了。

8. impairment (n.) 損傷 [ɪmˊpɛrmənt]

After a stroke, there may be some neurological impairments.
中風後可能會有神經學上的損傷。

Terminology 術語

1. bacteria [ˏbækˊtɪrɪə] 細菌

Discharge Instructions 出院衛教 27

This is the sixth day of Ms. Lin's hospitalization.

N: Good morning, Ms. Lin. This is the last of your antibiotic **injections**[1]. The doctor said you can go home after this.

P: Thanks, I feel much better these days. Oh, I almost forgot. Where can I get a **diagnosis certificate**? It's required by my school to prove I was sick during my **absence**[2] this week.

N: OK, I'll tell the doctor. How many certificates do you need?

P: Two, thanks.

N: You're welcome. After leaving our hospital, please remember to **maintain**[3] good **hygiene**[4] and clean your wound to avoid infections.

P: OK, I'll remember that.

N: If you get hurt, be sure to treat the wound right away. Clean it with water or **normal saline**, and apply some **disinfectant**[5] like **povidone-iodine**.

P: Do I need to place a bandage on it?

N: Yes. Also, keep it away from dirt.

P: I'll be sure to do that right away if I get hurt.

N: Maintain a regular lifestyle and a balanced diet. It will be good for your recovery.

P: I will. Is there anything else I have to remember?

N: Take oral antibiotics for 3 more days after discharge and come back for a follow-up exam next week.

P: Sure, thanks.

林小姐住院第 6 天。

林小姐早安。這是最後一劑的抗生素注射。醫師說打完後你就回家了。

謝謝。這幾天我確實感到好多了。噢，我差點忘了。我要去哪裡拿診斷證明書呢？我需要它證明這週在學校的缺席原因。

好的，我稍候會告訴醫師，請問你要幾份診斷證明書呢？

兩份，謝謝。

不客氣。在出院之後，請記得維持良好的衛生及清潔傷口，以避免受到感染。

好的，我會記得的。

如果受傷了，務必立刻處理傷口。用清水或生理食鹽水清潔它，並塗上一些消毒劑－優碘。

我需要用繃帶包紮嗎？

是的，而且，別讓它碰到髒污。

我若受傷，便立刻這麼做。

要過規律的生活，吃得均衡，這對你的復原很有幫助。

我會的。我還要記住什麼呢？

出院後你必須服用 3 天的口服抗生素，並且在下週回診追蹤檢查。

我會謹記在心。謝謝。

Nursing Notes 護理記錄

No redness, swelling, or tenderness in the wound. Fever subsided. Wound care instructions given. Will be discharged this afternoon. Told to take oral antibiotics for 3 days and return for follow-up.

傷口沒有發紅、腫脹或者壓痛。發燒已退。給予傷口照護衛教。今天下午將要出院。告知出院後要口服 3 天抗生素並回診追蹤。

Vocabulary and Sentence Examples 字彙與例句

1. injection [ɪn'dʒɛkʃən]
   (n.) 注射

   This medicine is designed only for intramuscular infection.
   這種藥物只設計為肌肉注射的方式。

2. absence ['æbsn̩s]
   (n.) 缺席；缺乏

   His absence affected the election results.
   他的缺席影響了投票的結果。

3. maintain [men'ten]
   (v.) 維持

   Maintaining a normal, regular life is good for one's health.
   維持生活規律對健康有益。

4. hygiene ['haɪdʒin]
   (n.) 衛生

   Oral hygiene is so important for preventing dental caries.
   口腔衛生對齲齒防治來說十分重要。

5. disinfectant [ˌdɪsɪn'fɛktənt]
   (n.) 消毒劑

   Use some disinfectant to clean the clothes because there're some blood spots on them.
   用一些消毒劑清洗衣服，因為上面有一些血漬。

Terminology 術語

1. diagnosis certificate [ˌdaɪəg'nosɪs sə'tɪfəkɪt] 診斷證明書
2. normal saline ['nɔrml̩ 'selɪn] 生理食鹽水
3. povidone-iodine ['povədon 'aɪədaɪn] 優碘

More Information

1. **發燒的問診重點**：詢問發燒持續的時間跟溫度、病人的主觀感覺、各個器官系統可能感染之常見症狀。

   (1) How long have you had a fever?
   你發燒多久了？

   (2) How high was your temperature?
   體溫多高？

   (3) How did you feel when this happened?
   發生時有何感覺？

   (4) Have you had a runny nose, sore throat, cough, or difficulty breathing?
   你有流鼻水、喉嚨痛、咳嗽或呼吸困難呢？

   (5) Have you had abdominal distension, abdominal cramps, or diarrhea?
   你有腹脹、腹絞痛或腹瀉嗎？

   (6) Have you had any pain in your extremities? Have you had any painful swellings in your neck, axilla or inguinal region?
   你的四肢會感到疼痛嗎？在頸部、腋下或鼠蹊部有腫脹情形嗎？

   (7) Have you been in contact with anyone with a contagious disease?
   你曾接觸過具有接觸感染性疾病的人嗎？

   (8) Have you been abroad within the last 3 months?
   近 3 個月來你有出國過嗎？

   (9) Have you had any medications given by injections?
   你有使用針劑嗎？

2. **施予藥物的路徑**
   PO＝per os＝by mouth　口服
   IM＝intramuscular [ˌɪntrəˋmʌskjələ] 肌內的
   IV＝intravenous [ˌɪntrəˋvinəs] 靜脈內的
   SC＝subcutaneous [ˌsʌbkjuˋtenɪəs] 皮下的
   SL＝sublingual [sʌbˋlɪŋgwəl] 舌下的

Exercise 小試身手

● Choose the Correct Answer

( ) 1. Use this _____ to clean the toilet. (A)infectant (B)wiper (C)disinfectant (D)cleaner 用這瓶消毒劑清潔廁所。

( ) 2. The tide _____ , and the island appears. (A)subsided (B)went (C)showed (D)flowed 潮水退了，島嶼也浮現出來。

( ) 3. _____ is the body's reaction to outside stimulus. (A)Fraction (B)Inflammation (C)Auction (D)Contraction
發炎是一種身體內對外來刺激的反應。

( ) 4. The landscape never _____ back to its original condition after the earthquake. (A)converted (B)replayed (C)diverted (D)reverted
可怕的地震過後，被破壞的地貌永遠無法復原了。

( ) 5. This cabin was built and will be here _____ . It will be removed in the autumn. (A)temporarily (B)occasionally (C)permanently (D)quickly
這座木造房屋只是暫時建造的，等到秋天就會拆除。

● Fill in the Blanks

1. He has _____ from pneumonia. 他遭受肺炎所苦。

2. Be cautious if you are _____ _____ _____ strangers.
當你與陌生人接觸時請務必小心。

3. _____ _____ is highly important for one's health.
個人衛生和健康息息相關。

4. _____ a habit of regular _____ can lower the risk of developing coronary artery disease. 維持規律的運動習慣可以減低冠狀動脈疾病的風險。

5. Because of his constant work in a noisy environment, he has some _____ _____ . 因為長期處於充滿噪音的工作環境，他的聽力有了損傷。

◎ Simplify Nursing Notes

1. 病人表示他的右腳不舒服。

   _____

2. 病人腹部有壓痛。

   _____

3. 將持續觀察傷口可能的出血。

   _____

4. 持續觀察發燒情形。

   _____

5. 將觀察血糖是否降低。

   _____

◎ Translation

1. 你發燒多久了？會燒到幾度？

   _____

2. 你有流鼻水、喉嚨痛或腹瀉的情形嗎？

   _____

3. 你最近曾經與發燒或感染性疾病患者接觸，或者出國過嗎？

   _____

4. 炎症反應暫時被抗生素控制住了。

   _____

5. 請問你要幾份診斷證明書呢？

   _____

Oncology Unit
腫瘤科

Learning Goals 學習目標

1. Assessing patients complaining about frequent bruising
2. Assessing hematology status
3. Clarifying which part of the hemato-logic system is being affected
4. Providing health education to patients

Outline 本章大綱

- The Elements of Blood
  血液的構成元素
- Case Information: Leukemia
  個案資訊：白血病
- Admission Assessment　入院評估
- Hospitalization　住院療護
- Discharge Instructions　出院衛教

Medical English for Healthcare Professionals

The Elements of Blood 血液的構成元素 28

The cellular components of blood include **erythrocytes**[1] (red blood cells, RBC), **leukocytes**[2] (white blood cells, WBC) and **platelets**[3] (PLT). These are all produced by stem cells within the bone marrow.

RBCs make up the major component of blood cells, with 4~6 million cells/mm^3. RBCs possess the ability to carry oxygen.

The WBC, may be considered the most important component of the immune system. It can be further divided into several subtypes using different methods, such as staining. WBC types include **neutrophils**[4], **eosinophils**[5], **basophils**[6], **monocytes**[7] and **lymphocytes**[8].

Platelets, important for blood clotting, have the ability to facilitate the coagulation process.

血液的構成元素包括紅血球(RBC)、白血球(WBC)及血小板(PLT)。它們是由骨髓裡的血液幹細胞製造的。

紅血球佔了血球細胞的絕大部分，約有 4~6 百萬個／立方釐米，也具備攜氧能力。

白血球是免疫系統中最重要的組成，可依據其染色結果的不同，進一步區分成嗜中性球、嗜酸性球、嗜鹼性球、單核球及淋巴球。

血小板是凝血作用的主力之一，可促進凝血反應。

Terminology 術語

1. erythrocyte [ɪˈrɪθrəˌsaɪt] 紅血球
2. leukocyte [ˈlukəsaɪt] 白血球
3. platelet [ˈpletlɪt] 血小板
4. neutrophil [ˈnjutrəfɪl] 嗜中性球
5. eosinophil [ˌiəˈsɪnəˌfɪl] 嗜酸性球
6. basophil [ˈbesəfɪl] 嗜鹼性球
7. monocyte [ˈmanəsaɪt] 單核球
8. lymphocyte [ˈlɪmfosaɪt] 淋巴球

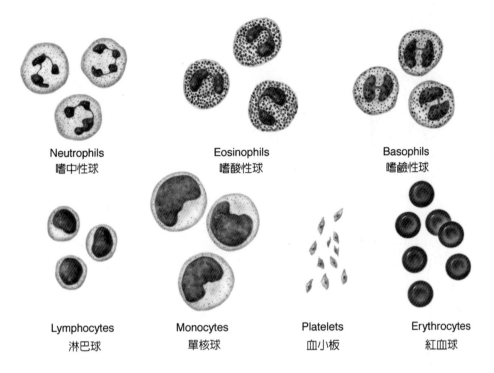

Neutrophils 嗜中性球	Eosinophils 嗜酸性球	Basophils 嗜鹼性球

Lymphocytes 淋巴球	Monocytes 單核球	Platelets 血小板	Erythrocytes 紅血球

Case Information 個案資訊

Leukemia [luˊkimɪə] 白血病

1. **Causes**: Chromosome mutation or exposure to irradiation.
2. **Symptoms & Signs**: RBC and PLT insufficiency, dysfunctional WBCs.
   (1) Fever, chills, night sweats.
   (2) Other flu-like symptoms.
   (3) Frequent infection.
   (4) Swollen tonsils.
   (5) Enlarged liver and spleen.
   (6) Pallor, dizziness, weakness and fatigue.
   (7) Nausea.
   (8) Bone pain and joint pain.
   (9) Unintentional weight loss.
3. **Care**:
   (1) Chemotherapy.
   (2) Symptomatic treatment by treating fever and discomfort.
   (3) Maintain a balanced diet.
   (4) Avoid eating raw foods.
   (5) Prevent infections.

Admission Assessment　入院評估

 29

Mrs. Hwang, a 57-year-old woman, has been bruising more frequently.

黃女士，57 歲女性，因時常瘀傷感到困擾。

N: Nurse　**P:** Patient

N: Good morning, Mrs. Hwang. Oh, there seems to be a lot of **bruises**[1] on your arms and legs.

黃女士早安。噢，你的腿和手臂上似乎有好多瘀傷。

P: Bruises are common in dancers, but I haven't danced in 3 months. I can't understand why I bruised so easily. Sometimes all I do is gently bump into a desk, and I get bruised!

瘀傷對舞者來說很常見。但我三個月前就沒在跳舞了，我很納悶為何那麼容易瘀傷。有時只是輕輕撞到桌子就瘀青了！

N: How long does it take for bruises to appear after you bump into something?

這些瘀傷都在你撞到東西後多久出現呢？

P: I don't know, maybe a few minutes after injury. I think they just appear automatically.

我沒注意，大約受傷後幾分鐘吧。我覺得它們是自動出現的。

N: Well, let me see your arms. Please open your mouth. *(Using a **penlight**[2] to **illuminate**[3])* There're tiny red **spots**[4] on your arms and within your mouth.

讓我看看你的手臂並請你張開嘴巴。（用筆燈照明）你的手臂和口腔內都有一些出血點。

N: I'd like to check your conjunctiva. *(Pulls her lower eyelid down)* It looks very pale. How has your **appetite**[5] been within the last 3 months? It seems like you're very thin.

我要檢查你的結膜。（將她的下眼瞼往下拉）。看起來很蒼白，你最近三個月胃口好嗎？你看起來似乎很瘦。

P: My appetite has been poor but I've recently tried to eat more of my favorite things.

最近的食慾不太好，即使我試著吃很多愛吃的東西。

N: Have you been catching colds recently?

你最近經常感冒嗎？

P: Yes, more than before.

是的，比以前更容易感冒。

N: You're so **prone**[6] to getting bruises, but this is not normal. You also have a poor appetite. The doctor has arranged to examine your blood cells and bleeding time. You may also need a **bone marrow biopsy**.

好的，易受感染、容易瘀傷及食慾差是不尋常的。醫師已安排你做血球細胞檢查和出血時間檢查。或許也需要做骨髓活體切片檢查。

P: Do you think it's leukemia? My mother died of this. I'm really worried I have leukemia.

會是白血病嗎？我母親就是因此病逝的。我非常擔心。

N: Well, we can't **jump to any conclusions**[7] yet without any evidence.

嗯，我們在沒有證據前不能妄下結論。

P: Alright, I hope it won't be bad news. | 好吧，希望不要是壞消息。

Nursing Notes 護理記錄

Many bruises and petechia on extremities. Conjunctiva is pale. C/O loss of appetite and susceptible to cold. Mother died of leukemia. Arranged for **CBC/DC**, bleeding time and bone marrow biopsy.

四肢有大量瘀傷和出血點。結膜蒼白。主訴食慾減低及容易感冒。母親死於白血病。已安排完全血球計數／分類計數檢查、出血時間檢查及骨髓活體切片檢查。

Vocabulary and Sentence Examples 字彙與例句

1. bruise [bruz]
   (n.) 瘀傷

   After the car accident, she just had a few bruises. 她在車禍後只有一些瘀傷。

2. penlight [ˈpɛnlaɪt]
   (n.) 筆燈；小手電筒

   The doctor used a penlight to check his pupillary light reflex. 醫師用筆燈檢查他的瞳孔光反射。

3. illuminate [ɪˈlumənet]
   (v.) 照亮

   The shadowless lamp illuminated the whole operation room. 無影燈照亮了整個手術室。

4. spot [spat]
   (n.) 斑點

   The doctor's white coat was marked with blood spots. 醫師的白袍上有一些血漬。

5. appetite [ˈæpəˌtaɪt]
   (n.) 食慾；胃口

   My appetite has gradually decreased over the last year. 最近一年內我的食慾下降了。

6. prone [pron]
   (adj.) 有…傾向的

   AIDS patients are more prone to opportunistic infections.
   後天免疫不全症候群的病人較容易有伺機性感染的傾向。

7. jump to any conclusions [dʒʌmp tu ˈɛnɪ kənˈkluʒənz] 妄下定論

   Don't jump to any conclusions until you get the clear picture. 把事情釐清之前不要妄下結論。

Terminology 術語

1. bone marrow biopsy [bon ˈmæro baɪˈapsɪ] 骨髓活體切片檢查
2. CBC/DC = complete blood count/differential count 完全血球計數／分類計數
   [kəmˈplit blʌd kaʊnt] [ˌdɪfəˈrɛnʃəl kaʊnt]

Hospitalization 住院療護

Mrs. Hwang received a second course of chemotherapy at the hospital to treat her leukemia.	黃女士因罹患白血病而前來醫院接受第二次化學治療。
N: Good morning, Mrs. Hwang. How are you going?	黃女士早安。你覺得如何？
P: A little bit tired.	有點累而已。
N: How was the first course of chemotherapy?	第一次化學治療的感覺如何？
P: Well, it was a very bad **experience**[1].	嗯，那真是一個不好的經驗。
N: Do you want to talk about it?	你願意談談嗎？
P: These medications made me **nauseous**[2] everyday. I **vomited**[3], even when I didn't eat anything.	這些藥物讓我每天感到噁心，儘管不吃東西我依舊會嘔吐。
N: Nausea and vomiting are very common side effects for patients receiving chemotherapy. I'll tell the doctor to prescribe some **antiemetics** for you. In addition, eating light meals may help.	這的確是令人不適且常見於化療患者的副作用。我會告知醫師開一些止吐劑來緩解。此外，清淡飲食亦有助益。
P: I'm grateful for this. Vomiting makes me afraid of eating anything. Also, my hair is falling out everyday.	我會很感激的。嘔吐讓我害怕吃任何東西。另外，我的頭髮每天都一直掉落。
N: **Chemotherapeutic agents** are **toxic**[4] not only to cancer cells but also to normal cells, like the cells in hair follicles or the cells in the digestive tract.	化療藥物不僅對癌細胞有毒性，對正常細胞也有。譬如説毛囊細胞或消化道的細胞。
P: Am I going to become **bald**[5]? I'll be **ugly**[6]!	我會變成禿頭嗎？那樣很醜！
N: If you don't mind, I would **recommend**[7] you wear a **wig**[8] during your treatment period. After treatments are finished, your hair will grow back again.	如果你不介意的話，我會建議你在治療期間戴假髮。等療程結束後，你的頭髮會再長回來的。
P: So is this only temporary?	所以這是暫時的了？
N: Of course.	當然。
P: Thanks for the information. This makes me feel much better.	謝謝你的説明。我感覺好多了。
N: You are welcome.	不客氣。

Nursing Notes 護理記錄

Felt nauseous after the first course. Antiemetics given with the second chemotherapy as instructed. Afraid of being bald. Explained the side effects and suggested wearing a wig. Well accepted.

病人在第一次療程時感覺噁心。遵照醫囑於第二次療程時同時給予止吐劑。病人擔心變成禿頭，在解釋副作用並建議戴假髮後，病人可接受。

Vocabulary and Sentence Examples 字彙與例句

1. experience (n.) 經驗 [ɪk'spɪrɪəns]	The doctor has lots of experience in performing this surgery. 這位醫師對此手術十分有經驗。
2. nauseous ['nɔʒəs] (adj.) 反胃的；噁心的	The bad smell in the house made everyone nauseous. 屋子裡不好的氣味讓眾人都感到反胃。
3. vomit ['vamɪt] (v.) 嘔吐	He began to vomit after getting off the roller coaster. 他一下雲霄飛車就開始嘔吐。
4. toxic ['taksɪk] (adj.) 對…有毒的	The insecticide is toxic not only to the insects but also to human beings. 殺蟲劑不僅對昆蟲有毒性，對人類也有。
5. bald [bɔld] (adj.) 禿頭的	He became bald early in his life. 他年輕時就禿頭了。
6. ugly ['ʌglɪ] (adj.) 醜陋的	Most people think that toads look ugly. 大多數人認為蟾蜍看起來很醜。
7. recommend (v.) 建議 [ˌrɛkə'mɛnd]	I recommend you study hard for this class, or else you'll fail the final exam. 我建議你認真學習這門課，否則期末考將會不及格。
8. wig [wɪg] (n.) 假髮	It's convenient to wear a wig to keep up with the latest fashion. 戴假髮跟上流行是一件很方便的事情。

Terminology 術語

1. antiemetic [ˌæntɪə'mɛtɪk] 止吐劑
2. chemotherapeutic agent [ˌkiməˌθɛrə'pjutɪk 'edʒənt] 化學治療藥劑

Discharge Instructions　出院衛教

31

Mrs. Hwang finished her second course of chemotherapy.

N: Good morning, how do you feel now?

P: Much better now than after the first time. I didn't **throw up**[1] much, and my appetite remained good.

N: Sounds like the antiemetics were quite effective.

P: Yeah, I think so.

N: Because your **nutritional status**[2] partially **deter-mines**[3] your condition and recovery, I suggest you have frequent and small meals.

P: I know, I must have enough energy to fight off the leukemia cells.

N: Good, remember not to eat **uncooked**[4] foods because you're not healthy enough to **tolerate**[5] any form of infection.

P: I'll keep this in mind.

N: Try not to go to public areas after you're discharged from the hospital.

P: What's wrong with going to public areas?

N: Well, the chemotherapy kills off cancer cells but also decreases your immunity. Therefore you're more prone to infections.

P: I see. I'll be more **cautious**[6].

N: Beware of people with colds or upper respiratory tract infections.

P: Got it, but if I become infected, how can I detect this on my own?

N: Usually you'll catch a fever, so if your body temperature increases, please return to see your doctor.

P: Thank you. I'll take a note and try to remember that.

黃女士已完成第二次化療。

早安，你現在覺得如何？

比之前好很多。我嘔吐不多，而且我的食慾仍舊不錯。

聽起來止吐藥十分有效。

我想也是。

由於你的營養狀態部分決定了你的身體狀況和復原速度，因此建議你少量多餐進食。

我知道，我也必須有足夠的能量來抵抗白血病細胞（癌細胞）。

很好。記得不要吃生食，因為你的健康狀態無法忍受任何感染。

我會留心的。

出院後盡可能不要到公共場所去。

到公共場所有什麼問題嗎？

嗯，化療殺死癌細胞，同時也降低你的免疫力。因此很容易被感染。

我明白了，我會更加小心的。

留意那些感冒和上呼吸道感染的人。

知道啦。對了，如果我被感染了，如何自行察覺呢？

通常你會發燒。因此如果你的體溫變得太高，請回診就醫。

謝謝。我會寫備忘錄並且試著記起來。

Nursing Notes 護理記錄

Feels better than the first time. Vomits less. Has better appetite. Suggested having frequent, small meals. Told not to eat raw food and not to go to public areas. Taught how to monitor body temperature. Well accepted.

病人較第一次療程感覺為佳。較少嘔吐，食慾也變好。建議她少量多餐。告知不可吃生食與出入公共場所。教導如何測量體溫。病人可接受。

Tips on Writing

1. 建議病人做某件事的寫法：可用 Someone suggested to the patient that he/she V. 或省略地寫成 suggest V-ing，例：
   The doctor suggested the patient receive an X-ray checkup.→Suggested receiving an X-ray checkup.
2. 護理記錄中時態的選用：病人的症狀與不適視為「事實」，故多用「現在式」；而醫護人員已執行的醫療措施則視同「已經發生的事」，故多用「過去式」。

   例：病人的抱怨用 feels/complains/concerns/regards/looks
   　　醫護人員已執行的事項用 told/suggested/informed/(was) given/(was) started

Vocabulary and Sentence Examples 字彙與例句

1. throw up [ˈθro ʌp]
   嘔吐

   As soon as the door opened, I threw up because of the rotten smell of apples.　門打開時，我因為爛蘋果的氣味而嘔吐了。

2. nutritional status [njuˈtrɪʃənḷ ˈstetəs]
   營養狀態

   Serum albumin levels can help us measure one's nutritional status.　血清白蛋白值可估量出營養狀態。

3. determine [dɪˈtɝmɪn]
   (v.) 決定

   If he has already determined his decision, no one can change his opinion.　如果他已做了決定，沒人能改變他的意見。

4. uncooked [ʌnˈkʊkt]
   (adj.) 未煮的；生的

   If you eat uncooked foods, you may suffer from acute enteritis.　如果你吃生食，可能會罹患急性腸炎。

5. tolerate [ˈtɑlə͵ret]
   (v.) 忍受

   I can't tolerate what she has done!
   我無法忍受她所做的任何事！

6. cautious [ˈkɔʃəs]
   (adj.) 小心翼翼的

   Be cautious when you cross the street by yourself.
   當你獨自穿越路口時要小心謹慎。

More Information

1. 腫瘤病人的問診重點

   (1) *Weight loss*: Have you lost more than 5 kg within the last 3 months?
   體重減輕：近 3 個月來是否體重減輕超過 5 公斤？

   (2) *Night sweat*: Have you ever sweated at night or in your sleep?
   夜間盜汗：你曾在睡眠期間或夜間流汗嗎？

   (3) *Fever*: Have you ever had a fever for a long duration?
   發燒：你曾長期發燒嗎？

2. 血液腫瘤病人的問診重點

   (1) *Bleeding tendency*: Easily bruised, massive bleeding after minor cuts, or bleeding after brushing teeth.
   出血傾向：易瘀血、在輕傷後大量出血，或者是刷牙後牙齦出血。

   (2) *Anemia*: Pale looking, palpitation, dizziness, exertional dyspnea.
   貧血：臉色蒼白、心悸、眩暈、運動性呼吸困難。

   (3) *Impaired immunity*: Susceptible to infection, infections at unusual sites.
   免疫受損：易受感染、異常區域感染。

   (4) *Systemic problems*: Fever of unknown origin, weight loss, night sweats.
   系統問題：不明原因發燒、體重減輕、夜間盜汗。

3. 對化療病人應該留意的事項

   (1) Nausea [ˈnɔzɪə]　噁心

   (2) Vomiting [ˈvamɪtɪŋ]　嘔吐

   (3) Diarrhea [ˌdaɪəˈrɪə]　腹瀉

   (4) Hair loss [hɛr lɔs]　掉髮

   (5) Malaise [məˈlez] / fatigue [fəˈtig]　疲倦

   (6) Susceptible to infections　易受感染

   (7) Specific toxicity to medications (depending on type of medication)
   藥物的特定毒性（視藥物種類而定）

Exercise 小試身手

● Choose the Correct Answer

( ) 1. The penlight wasn't bright enough to _____ the whole cavern.
(A)flash (B)illuminate (C)darken (D)illusion
一支小手電筒無法照亮整個洞穴。

( ) 2. He is getting weaker _____ cancer. (A)because of (B)and
(C)despite of (D)although 由於癌症，他變得越來越虛弱。

( ) 3. He's rather _____ to catching a cold. (A)suspicious (B)susceptible
(C)suspended (D)sustainable 他容易感冒。

( ) 4. I'm fine, with only a few cuts and _____ . (A)bruits (B)bruises
(C)brumes (D)hurts 我還好，僅有幾處割傷和瘀傷。

( ) 5. There're tiny red _____ on his arms and within his mouth. (A)spots
(B)sports (C)tickles (D)circles 他的口腔和手臂有許多細小的出血點。

● Fill in the Blanks

1. I'll refer you to the _____ _____ at the _____ _____ .
我會幫你轉診到醫學中心的血液科門診。

2. If you catch a _____ _____ , this might indicate that your _____ has
become weaker. 如果你經常感冒，那可能意謂是免疫力變差了。

3. What happened? There're so many _____ on your _____ and _____ .
發生什麼事？你的手臂和腿上有好多瘀傷。

4. Please apply pressure at the _____ site. 請用力按住出血處。

5. We cannot _____ _____ _____ _____ until the results from the
bone marrow examination _____ .
在骨髓檢查的結果出來之前，我們不能妄下結論。

● Simplify Nursing Notes

1. 我們建議病人接受化學治療。（使用簡略寫法即可）

_____

2. 醫師建議病人接受手術治療。（使用簡略寫法即可）

_____

3. 營養師建議病人多吃高蛋白食物。（使用簡略寫法即可）

_____

4. 護士替病人裝上靜脈點滴注射。（使用簡略寫法並留意常用之時態）

_____

5. 病人抱怨小腿浮腫。（使用簡略寫法並留意常用之時態）

_____

● Translation

1. 我要檢查你的結膜。

_____

2. 你最近三個月胃口好嗎？你看起來似乎很瘦。

_____

3. 你易受感染、容易瘀傷及食慾差是不尋常的。

_____

4. 化療藥物不僅對癌細胞有毒性，對正常細胞也有。

_____

5. 出院後盡可能不要到公共場所去。

_____

解答

Renal Unit
腎臟科

Learning Goals 學習目標

1. Assessing dialysis patients
2. Assessing patient's renal function
3. Assessing patients with arteriovenous fistula
4. Providng health education to patients

Outline 本章大綱

- About the Kidneys　關於腎臟
- Case Information: End Stage Renal Disease (ESRD)　個案資訊：末期腎疾病
- Admission Assessment　入院評估
- Hospitalization　住院療護
- Discharge Instructions　出院衛教

Medical English for Healthcare Professionals

About the Kidneys　關於腎臟

32

The **kidneys**[1] are like garbage factories that excrete many metabolic by-products and maintain the body's homeostasis. Most people have two kidneys, which consist of approximately one million **nephrons**[2]. The nephron is the basic unit of a kidney, which filtrates the **plasma**[3], absorbs and secretes various solutes in the filtrate and eventually produces urine.

The nephron can be divided into several parts. The first part is called the **glomerulus**[4], the site for plasma filtration. Most solutes, with the exception of albumin, are filtrated within the **renal tubules**[5]. The renal tubular cells adjust the constituents of urine by reabsorption or secretion according to the homeostatic status. The urine formed by these complex processes enters the **minor calyx**[6], **major**[7] **calyx** and **renal pelvis**[8]. Urine is then excreted via the urinary tract.

腎臟像是排除體內廢物的工廠，將許多代謝的副產物排出體外，並且維持體內恆定。絕大多數人有兩顆腎臟，其內各有約 1 百萬個腎元。腎元是腎臟功能的基本單位，可過濾血漿、吸收或分泌各種溶質並且在最後製造出尿液。

腎元可以被分割成數個部分。第一個部分叫作腎絲球，是過濾血漿之處。多數的溶質（白蛋白除外），幾乎都被過濾到腎小管的管腔。腎小管細胞依據體內恆定狀況，藉由分泌和再吸收作用調整尿液中的組成。經由這些複雜過程被製造出來的尿液進入小腎盞、大腎盞及腎盂。然後接著從泌尿道被排出。

Terminology 術語

1. kidney [ˈkɪdnɪ] 腎臟
2. nephron [ˈnɛfran] 腎元
3. plasma [ˈplæzmə] 血漿
4. glomerulus [gləˈmɛrjuləs] 腎絲球

5. renal tubule [ˈrinl̩ ˈt(j)ubjəl] 腎小管
6. minor calyx [maɪnə ˈkelɪks] 小腎盞
7. major calyx [ˈmedʒə ˈkelɪks] 大腎盞
8. renal pelvis [ˈrinl̩ ˈpɛlvɪs] 腎盂

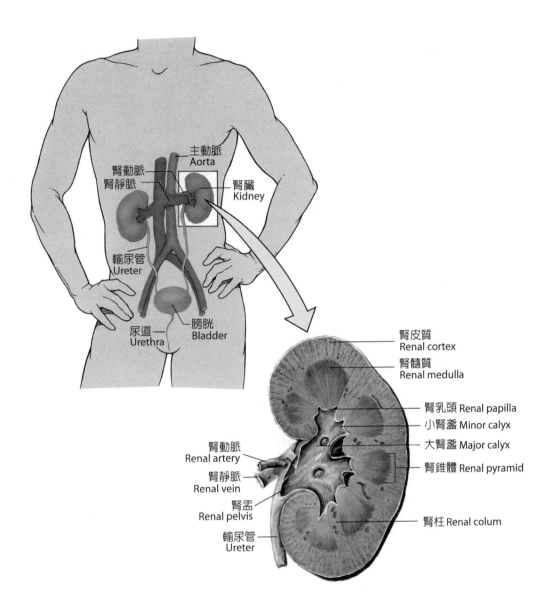

主動脈
Aorta

腎動脈
腎靜脈

腎臟
Kidney

輸尿管
Ureter

尿道
Urethra

膀胱
Bladder

腎皮質
Renal cortex

腎髓質
Renal medulla

腎乳頭 Renal papilla
小腎盞 Minor calyx
大腎盞 Major calyx

腎錐體 Renal pyramid

腎動脈
Renal artery

腎靜脈
Renal vein

腎盂
Renal pelvis

輸尿管
Ureter

腎柱 Renal colum

Case Information 個案資訊

End Stage Renal Disease (ESRD) [ɛnd stedʒ ˈrinl dɪˈziz] 末期腎疾病

1. **Causes**: DM, hypertension or adverse effect from medication, etc.
2. **Symptoms & Signs**: Pitting edema at the dependent extremities, dyspnea, electrolyte imbalance and disturbances in consciousness.
3. **Care**: Monitor vital signs, renal replacement therapy and care for the arterio-venous fistula.

Admission Assessment   入院評估

33

Mrs. Wu was admitted into the ward.

N: Nurse   **P:** Patient

N: How are you feeling, Mrs. Wu?

P: I'm really tired and feeling uncomfortable throughout my body.

N: May I ask why you came to our hospital today?

P: I felt dizzy and fell down last night. My son sent me to the ER immediately. The doctor saw my labwork and told me I needed **emergency[1] dialysis**.

N: Have you had this happen to you before?

P: No, but my family doctor told me that my kidney function is not very good.

N: Have you ever had difficulty urinating, pain during urination or recent pain in the **flanks[2]**?

P: No, I only caught a cold 3 days ago.

N: Did you take any medications to treat your cold?

P: Yes, I went to the pharmacy nearby and got some **NSAIDs**.

N: How many tablets did you take?

P: Well, about ten tablets.

N: Do you currently have hypertension or diabetes?

P: I've had hypertension for a long time. It's been controlled by medications though.

N: OK. Now let me check your blood pressure and respiratory sounds.

P: Go ahead.

N: Your systolic blood pressure is 160 mmHg while your diastolic pressure is 100 mmHg. You also have some signs of **mild[3] pulmonary edema**.

吳女士住進病房。

吳女士，你現在覺得如何？

我覺得好累，而且全身不舒服。

請問你為何會來醫院呢？

我昨晚因頭暈而跌倒。我兒子立刻送我到急診室。醫師看過我的檢驗報告後告訴我要接受緊急洗腎處置。

你曾經有類似的情況嗎？

沒有。但我的家庭醫師告訴我我的腎功能並不是非常好。

最近你有沒有感覺排尿困難，排尿疼痛或者腰側疼痛呢？

沒有，我只有感冒 3 天左右。

你有服用藥物來治療感冒嗎？

有的，我去附近藥房買了一些非類固醇抗發炎止痛劑。

你服用了多少顆呢？

嗯，10 顆左右。

你有高血壓或糖尿病嗎？

我有高血壓很久了。現在藉由藥物控制著。

好的，那麼現在我將檢查你的血壓和呼吸音。

請便吧。

你的收縮壓是 160 mmHg 而舒張壓是 100 mmHg。你也有輕微肺水腫的徵兆。

P: This sounds serious.

N: We'll try our best to control your symptoms. If you have any **shortness of breath**[4], please call us for help right away.

P: OK, thank you very much.

聽起來有點嚴重。

我們會盡全力控制症狀。如果你感到呼吸短促，請立刻找我們幫忙。

好的，非常謝謝你。

 Nursing Notes　護理記錄

Sent to the ER because of dizziness and falling. Caught a cold 3 days ago and took NSAIDs. C/O drowsiness. Vital signs: PR 120 bpm, RR 28/min, BT 37℃. Lab work showed electrolyte imbalance. Emergent dialysis done.

病人因為頭暈和跌倒被送至急診室。在 3 天前曾感冒並服用 NSAID。主訴感到困倦。生命徵象顯示：脈搏每分鐘 120 下，呼吸速率每分鐘 28 次，體溫 37℃。實驗室檢查顯示電解質不平衡。已施予緊急洗腎。

 Vocabulary and Sentence Examples　字彙與例句

1. emergency [ɪˋmɝdʒənt]
   (adj.) 緊急的

   Electrolyte imbalance can cause several emergency medical situations.　電解質不平衡能造成數種緊急醫療處境。

2. flank [ˋflæŋk]
   (n.) 腰側；脅腹

   I feel pain in my flanks.
   我感到腰側疼痛。

3. mild [maɪld]
   (adj.) 輕微的

   I caught a mild cold.
   我有輕微的感冒。

4. shortness of breath
   [ˋʃɔrtnɪs əv brɛθ]
   呼吸短促

   Shortness of breath is a common symptom for patients with heart disease.
   呼吸急促是心臟病患者的常見症狀。

Terminology 術語

1. dialysis [daɪˋælɪsɪs] 透析
2. NSAID＝non-steroidal anti-inflammatory drug 非類固醇抗發炎止痛劑
   [nan ˋstɛrɔɪdl̩ æntɪ ɪnˋflæmə͵torɪ drʌg]
3. pulmonary edema [ˋpʌlmə͵nɛrɪ iˋdimə] 肺水腫

Hospitalization 住院療護

34

Mrs. Wu is in the process of deciding which dialytic therapy to choose.

吳女士將決定她的洗腎方式。

N: Why do you look nervous?

為何你看起來這麼緊張？

P: The doctor told me that my kidney is damaged, and therefore, its function has almost been lost. I have to live with dialysis for the rest of my life.

醫師告訴我我的腎受損，因此幾乎喪失功能了，我必須靠洗腎來度過餘生。

N: I see, because your kidney function can no longer help **sustain**[1] your life, dialysis therapy is what you really need.

我了解。因為腎功能已經無法再維持你的生命，洗腎治療的確是你所需要的。

P: Is there any other form of treatment, like taking any medications or **undergoing**[2] any surgeries?

還有其他治療方式嗎？譬如說吃藥或者開刀？

N: In your situation, medications are not very effective. The only way to **restore**[3] your kidney function is to undergo a **transplantation**.

根據你的情況，藥物治療成效不大。唯一可以恢復腎臟功能的方式是進行移植手術。

P: Can I do that?

我可以接受移植嗎？

N: Well, it will take a long time to find a suitable kidney for you. At this moment, dialysis is the best way to keep you alive.

嗯，要找到一顆適合的腎臟十分耗時。此時，洗腎是讓你活下來最急迫以及最佳的選擇。

P: Alright. My doctor told me that there're two dialysis methods. One is via my blood vessels while the other is via my **peritoneum**. Which one do you think is better?

好吧。我的醫師告訴我有兩種洗腎方式。一種是經由血管的方式，另一種是經由腹部的方式，你認為哪一種比較好呢？

N: Well, if you choose **hemodialysis**, dialysis via your blood vessels, you must come to the dialysis center 3 times a week. The medical staff over there will take good care of you.

嗯，如果你選擇經由血管的方式來洗腎－血液透析，你必須每週來洗腎中心三次。那兒的醫療人員會好好地照顧你。

P: What about dialysis via my peritoneum?

那麼經由腹部來洗腎呢？

N: If you choose **peritoneal dialysis**, you will have to do this on your own. However, you will have more free time to yourself.

若選擇腹膜透析，你必須自己進行透析療程，但你會有較多的空閒時間。

P: Hmmm, this is a difficult decision.

嗯，這的確很難決定。

N: Your condition will also determine which dialysis method to choose. I'll arrange for you to visit the different dialysis centers, and then you can discuss your decision with the doctor.

P: OK, thank you.

洗腎方式也要視你的身體狀況而定。我會安排你去參觀不同的洗腎中心，你再和醫師討論你的決定。

好的，謝謝你。

Nursing Notes 護理記錄

Informed need for permanent dialysis. Provided related information about hemodialysis and peritoneal dialysis. Arranged to visit dialysis centers.

告知需永久接受透析治療。提供血液透析和腹膜透析的相關資訊。安排至洗腎中心參觀。

Vocabulary and Sentence Examples 字彙與例句

1. sustain [sə'sten]
   (v.) 維持

   The earth needs energy from the sunlight to sustain life.
   地球需要依靠陽光的能量維持生命。

2. undergo ['ʌndə·go]
   (v.) 進行

   I will undergo a physical examination next week.
   下週我要進行體格檢查。

3. restore [rɪ'stor]
   (v.) 修復；恢復

   We need to replace some broken parts in order to restore the computer. 電腦修復需要更新一些壞掉的零件。

Terminology 術語

1. transplantation [ˌtrænsplæn'teʃən] 移植
2. peritoneum [ˌpɛrətə'nɪəm] 腹膜
3. hemodialysis [ˌhimədaɪ'ælɪsɪs] 血液透析
4. peritoneal dialysis [ˌpɛrətə'nɪəl daɪ'ælɪsɪs] 腹膜透析

Discharge Instructions　出院衛教

35

Mrs. Wu underwent an operation creating an **arteriovenous fistula** *for hemodialysis.*	吳女士因血液透析進行了動靜脈瘻管術。
N: Mrs. Wu, how are you feeling today?	吳女士，你今天覺得如何？
P: Pretty good.	很好。
N: How is your wound after surgery?	術後傷口如何？
P: It stopped bleeding.	它停止出血了。
N: Good. Remember to keep the wound clean to prevent any infections.	很好。記得維持傷口的清潔以避免感染。
P: OK, I won't forget it.	好的，我不會忘記的。
N: Let me check the fistula with my stethoscope to see if your blood is still flowing smoothly.	讓我用聽診器來檢查動靜脈瘻管的血流是否通暢。
P: Is the fistula OK?	瘻管情形良好嗎？
N: Yes, you can touch it and feel the blood flow. This means the operation was quite successful. It's time to teach you how to care for your fistula.	是的，你可以碰觸並感覺到血流，表示手術很成功。該是教導你如何照顧瘻管的時候了。
P: What should I do?	我應該怎麼做呢？
N: First of all, you must do forearm exercises so that your hemodialysis can work.	首先，你必須做前臂運動，才能進行血液透析。
P: When should I start these exercises? And how do I do them?	我何時開始做這些運動？要怎麼做呢？
N: 24 hours after surgery, squeeze a **rubber**[1] ball with your hand on the side of the fistula. After several seconds, open your hand. Repeat this cycle 500 times every-day for about 2 months.	在術後 24 小時開始做，用瘻管側的手按握橡皮球，3 秒後放開。重複循環這動作，每天 500 次，持續約 2 個月。
P: OK, I'll keep this in mind.	好的，我會謹記在心的。
N: By the way, you need to protect your A-V fistula as well. Don't wear tight clothing or have your blood pressure taken or draw blood from the fistula because this will **impede**[2] your blood flow. Meanwhile, don't lift heavy objects or allow anything to press against it.	對了，你也需要保護動靜脈瘻管。勿穿過緊的衣服、勿於瘻管側的手測量血壓或抽血。因為那會阻礙血流。同時別提重物或讓任何東西壓迫它。

P: I see. Thanks for the **instructions**[3].

N: You're welcome. Here is a **booklet**[4] explaining everything about hemodialysis. If you have any questions, please feel free to ask us.

P: Great! This is all very helpful.

我明白。謝謝指導。

不客氣,這裡有一本小手冊解釋血液透析的資訊。如果你有任何問題,請向我們提問。

太好了,它可幫了我大忙。

Nursing Notes　護理記錄

Found **thrill** and **bruit** from A-V fistula. Will keep observing post-op wound for pain, bleeding or infection. Told to do forearm exercises 24 hours post-op. Instructed on how to self-care for A-V fistula.

動靜脈瘻管處有震顫感和嘈音。將持續觀察術後傷口是否出現疼痛、出血和感染情形。告知在術後 24 小時後開始進行前臂運動。教導動靜脈瘻管自我照顧事宜。

Tips on Writing

1. If 子句的使用
   (1) **If 子句之主詞和主要子句相同時可省略**,例:
   The patient complained of stomachache after eating spicy foods.→ Complained of stomachache after eating spicy foods.
   (2) **If 子句之主詞和主要子句不同需保留 If 子句之主詞**,例:
   The nurse told the patient to come back if *he* had severe pain.→Told to come back if he /the patient had severe pain.
2. 描述特定部位的發現:Find something＋in/on/over/near＋部位。例:
   Found lack of blood flow in the A-V fistula.
   Found malodorous discharge near the incision.

Vocabulary and Sentence Examples　字彙與例句

1. rubber [ˈrʌbɚ] 　(a.) 橡膠製的	Please tie a rubber band around your long hair. 請用橡皮筋把你的長髮紮起。
2. impede [ɪmˈpid] 　(v.) 阻礙	The car accident impeded the traffic flow. 這場車禍阻礙了交通(車流)。

3. instruction [ɪnˈstrʌkʃən]　　　They built this park by following his instructions.
　　(n.) 指導；講授　　　　　他們依照他的指導建造出這座公園。

4. booklet [ˈbʊklɪt]　　　　　You can get this booklet at the information counter.
　　(n.) 小手冊　　　　　　你可以在服務台取得這本小手冊。

Terminology 術語

1. arteriovenous fistula [ɑr،tɪrɪəvinəs ˈfɪstjʊlə] 動靜脈瘻管(A-V fistula)
2. thrill [θrɪl] 震顫感
3. bruit [brut] 嘈音

More Information

1. 向病人解釋透析治療－血液透析
   (1) If you want to receive hemodialysis, you must receive an operation to create an artificial vessel/A-V fistula.
      如果你採血液透析的話，必須進行手術以建立動靜脈瘻管。
   (2) You must come to the hospital/dialysis center 3 times a week and stay in the dialysis room 4 hours each time.
      你必須一週到院（或洗腎中心）3 次，每次留置在透析室 4 小時。

2. 向病人解釋透析治療－腹膜透析
   (1) You must insert a catheter into the abdomen for the administration of dialytic fluid.
      你必須從腹部插入導管以利透析液的注入。
   (2) You must learn how to keep the area around the dialytic catheter sterile.
      你必須學會如何讓透析導管保持無菌狀態。
   (3) You can have more free time if you choose peritoneal dialysis.
      如果你選擇腹膜透析的話，較能有空暇時間。

Exercise 小試身手

◉ Choose the Correct Answer

( ) 1. Severe hyperkalemia is an _____ condition which can be reversed by dialysis. (A)emergence (B)emergent (C)surgeon (D)stable
嚴重的高血鉀症是一種可經由透析逆反的緊急情況。

( ) 2. We cannot _____ our lives without water. (A)contain (B)obtain (C)sustain (D)retain 沒有水我們將無法維持生命。

( ) 3. The doctor suggested that I _____ a physical examination next week. (A)undergo (B)underestimate (C)understand (D)undermine
醫師建議我下週進行體格檢查。

( ) 4. The operation is aimed to _____ his cardiac function. (A)represent (B)record (C)request (D)restore 手術的目的是重建他的心臟功能。

( ) 5. We're searching for a _____ donor to donate a liver to her. (A)suitable (B)suicide (C)superb (D)superstitious
我們正在尋找一位合適的捐贈者捐肝給她。

◉ Fill in the Blanks

1. The doctor found crackles in his left _____ by using his _____ .
醫師藉由聽診器發現了他的左肺有爆裂音。

2. If you have _____ in breath, please call for help right away.
如果你感到呼吸急促,要立即求援。

3. The car is _____ our route, therefore we need to choose another road.
這輛車阻礙了我們的路,因此我們只好繞道。

4. You can get this _____ at the _____ center.
你可以在服務台取得這本觀光小手冊。

5. There are two types of dialysis: _____ and _____ _____ .
透析的方式有兩種－血液透析和腹膜透析。

● Simplify Nursing Notes

1. 護理師告訴病人如果傷口發炎就必須回診。

   _____

2. 醫師提醒病人如果感到急劇胸痛要立即至急診就醫。

   _____

3. 病人陳述如果他運動過於劇烈就會腰痛。

   _____

4. 護理師發現病人左腿的傷口流膿。

   _____

5. 病人發現自己的左邊腋下有腫塊。

   _____

● Translation

1. 最近你有沒有感覺排尿困難，排尿疼痛或者腰側疼痛呢？

   _____

2. 如果你感到呼吸短促，請立刻找我們幫忙。

   _____

3. 唯一可以恢復腎臟功能的方式是進行移植手術。

   _____

4. 洗腎是讓你活下來最急迫以及最佳的選擇。

   _____

5. 記得維持傷口的清潔以避免感染。

   _____

Urology Unit
泌尿科

*Medical English for
Healthcare Professionals*

Learning Goals 學習目標

1. Assessing patients with difficulty urin-ating
2. Collecting information about the features of urine
3. Teaching patients to practice self-care after the operation
4. Providing health education to patients

Outline 本章大綱

- The Components of the Urinary Tract
  泌尿道的組成
- Case Information: Benign Prostatic Hyperplasia (BPH)
  個案資訊：良性前列腺肥大
- Admission Assessment　入院評估
- Hospitalization　住院療護
- Discharge Instructions　出院衛教

The Components of the Urinary Tract　泌尿道的組成

36

The urinary tract consists of the renal pelvis, ureter, urinary bladder and urethra. Urine produced by numerous nephrons is collected by the renal pelvis. The **ureter**[1] is a long, muscular conduit for urine from the kidney to the **urinary bladder**[2], which acts as a reservoir for urine. The bladder can store several hundred milliliters of urine until we voluntarily excrete it through the **urethra**[3].

In the male urinary tract, the urethra is longer than that in the female, and divided into the **prostatic urethra**[4], **membranous urethra**[5], and finally the **penile urethra**[6]. The prostatic urethra is surrounded by the **prostate gland**[7]. In elderly males, the prostate usually enlarges and compresses the lumen of the prostatic urethra.

泌尿道由腎盂、輸尿管、膀胱及尿道組成。由無數的腎元製造的尿液被收集到腎盂。輸尿管是一條狹長的肌肉管路，它把尿液由腎臟輸送到尿液貯存槽－膀胱中。膀胱能夠貯存數百毫升的尿液直到我們自發地經由尿道排出。

在男性泌尿道中，尿道是比女性長的，又可以分成前列腺部尿道、膜部尿道及陰莖部尿道。前列腺部尿道由前列腺環繞著。在年老男性族群中，前列腺常常會肥大並且壓迫到前列腺部尿道的管腔。

Terminology 術語

1. ureter [juˋritə] 輸尿管
2. urinary bladder [ˋjʊrəˏnɛrɪ ˋblædə] 膀胱
3. urethra [juˋriθrə] 尿道
4. prostatic urethra [prasˋtætɪk juˋriθrə] 前列腺部尿道

5. membranous urethra 膜部尿道 [ˋmɛmbrənəs juˋriθrə]
6. penile urethra 陰莖部尿道 [ˋpɪnaɪl juˋriθrə]
7. prostate gland [ˋprastet glænd] 前列腺

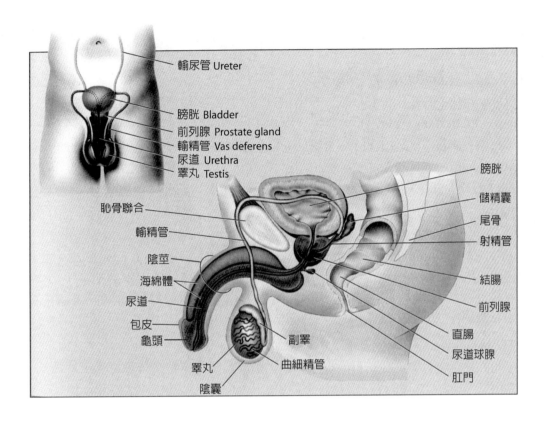

輸尿管 Ureter
膀胱 Bladder
前列腺 Prostate gland
輸精管 Vas deferens
尿道 Urethra
睪丸 Testis

恥骨聯合
輸精管
陰莖
海綿體
尿道
包皮
龜頭
睪丸
陰囊
副睪
曲細精管

膀胱
儲精囊
尾骨
射精管
結腸
前列腺
直腸
尿道球腺
肛門

Case Information 個案資訊

Benign Prostatic Hyperplasia (BPH) 良性前列腺肥大
[bɪˊnaɪn prasˊtætɪk ˌhaɪpəˊplezɪə]

1. **Causes**: Excessive androgen stimulation on prostatic tissue.
2. **Symptoms & Signs**: Hesitancy, frequency, urgency, nocturia, poor stream of the urine, urinary retention, and urinary tract infection.
3. **Care**:
   (1) Take medications as insructed.
   (2) Monitor the color and amount of urine.
   (3) Surgical treatment.
   (4) Avoid riding, lifting heavy objects and intense exercises after surgery.
   (5) Eat more fruit and vegetables and avoid stimulating beverages.

Admission Assessment　入院評估

37

Mr. Lu, a 60-year-old man, complained about difficulty urinating.

盧先生，60 歲男性，抱怨排尿困難。

N: Nurse　**P:** Patient

N: Good afternoon, Mr. Lu. May I ask, what is your major concern today?

早安，盧先生。請問你今天主要是為什麼來呢？

P: I feel like I can't fully empty my bladder when I urinate.

我覺得自己無法排光膀胱裡的尿液。

N: How many times a day do you go to the toilet?

你一天去上幾次廁所呢？

P: About 12~15 times a day. I feel like water is **dripping**[1] when I urinate.

一天大概 12~15 次。當我排尿時我感覺像水在滴。

N: Do you ever feel a sense of urgency or **hesitancy**[2] to **urinate**[3]?

你有急尿或排尿開始困難的情形嗎？

P: Yes I do.

我有。

N: Do you wake up in the middle of the night to urinate?

你會在午夜醒來上廁所嗎？

P: Yes, about twice a night.

會的，大概一晚 2 次。

N: How long have you had these symptoms?

你有這些症狀多久了？

P: About 3 months. It's kind of annoying.

3 個月左右。這實在很擾人。

N: OK. Has the doctor already explained that you have an **enlarged**[4] prostate gland?

好的，那醫師已經向你解釋前列腺變大的狀況了嗎？

P: Yes, he said it's a common problem in the elder population. He also did an anal examination to check the size of my prostate.

是的，他說這是老人常見的問題。他也做了肛診以檢查前列腺的大小。

N: Because of these symptoms, the doctor will **perform**[5] an operation on you at 10 a.m. tomorrow. Therefore, don't eat or drink anything after midnight.

由於上述症狀之故，醫師將在明早 10 點為你動手術。因此自午夜開始禁食。

P: Can I drink water?

我可以喝水嗎？

N: No, you cannot have anything by mouth starting at midnight. We'll give you water and electrolyte **supplements**[6] so you won't you feel too thirsty.

不行，午夜開始不能經口進食任何東西。我們會給你補充水分和電解質以使你不會感到口渴。

N: Please change into the operation gown and take off your underwear at tomorrow morning. If you have false teeth, necklace, ring, contact lens, or anything like that, please take it off.

明天早上請換上手術衣，並且把內衣褲都脫掉，如果有活動假牙、項鍊、戒指、隱形眼鏡等物品，請拿下來。

P: Alright, I'll keep that in mind.

好，我會謹記在心的。

Nursing Notes 護理記錄

Admitted for dysuria and nocturia. BPH diagnosed. Explained information about BPH. Surgery arranged at 10 a.m. tomorrow. Told to be NPO from midnight.

病人因排尿困難和夜尿而入院。診斷出患有良性前列腺肥大。已解釋前列腺肥大的資訊。手術安排於明早 10 點。告知午夜開始禁食。

Tips on Writing

表達住院或求診的原因：came to clinic (OPD)/admitted/hospitalized due to (for) ＋原因，例：
Came to clinic due to abdominal mass.
Came to OPD for pain during urination.
Admitted for sharp chest pain.

Vocabulary and Sentence Examples 字彙與例句

1. drip [drɪp]
   (v.) 滴水
   The lead pipe is dripping with something stinky.
   鉛管正在滴出一些有臭味的東西。

2. hesitancy [ˈhɛzətənsɪ]
   (n.) 猶豫；躊躇
   Urinary hesitancy is a common symptom in BPH patients.
   排尿躊躇（無法順利啟始排尿）是良性前列腺肥大患者常見的症狀。

3. urinate [ˈjʊrəˌnet]
   (v.) 排尿
   Do you experience pain during urination?
   你在排尿時會感到疼痛嗎？

4. enlarged [ɪnˈlardʒd]
   (adj.) 增大
   His enlarged thyroid gland makes it difficult for him to breathe. 增大的甲狀腺讓他呼吸困難。

5. perform [pəˈfɔrm]
   (v.) 執行；做
   The doctor is performing the operation now.
   醫師正在進行手術。

6. supplement [ˈsʌpləmənt]
   (n.) 補充
   The nutritional supplement is necessary for a growing child. 營養補充品對正在長大的孩子是必須的。

Hospitalization 住院療護

38

The operation was finished and everything went smoothly. Mr. Lu has returned to the ward.

手術完成且過程很順利，盧先生已回到病房。

N: Mr. Lu, we have inserted a **catheter** to **drain**[1] urine from your bladder.

盧先生，我們放置一條導尿管以便從膀胱引流尿液。

P: Why do I need this catheter?

我為什麼需要導尿管呢？

N: It will allow your surgical wound to heal. In addition, it will serve as a **route**[2] for normal saline **irrigation**[3].

這有助於你手術傷口的癒合。此外，也提供讓我們用生理食鹽水灌洗的路徑。

P: What is the purpose of this irrigation?

灌洗的目的是什麼呢？

N: Irrigation will help prevent blood clots from forming that might obstruct your urinary tract.

灌洗可防止血塊的形成，避免阻塞泌尿道。

P: Oh, I see.

我知道了。

N: You should stay in bed until the catheter is removed. Remember, don't remove it by yourself, or you'll hurt yourself.

在導尿管拔除之前你要盡量臥床休息。記得不要自己拔除它，這會傷害到你自己。

P: Alright, I'll remember that.

好的，我會記住的。

N: I'll check the flow and color of your urine every time I come by. However, you'll also have to check it on your own.

我每次過來時都會檢查你的尿液顏色和流動情形。不過，你也要自己檢查。

P: But I don't know what is normal or abnormal.

但我不知道情形是否正常。

N: First, pay attention to the color of your urine. If it turns red and **thick**[4], please call us immediately. This may **implicate**[5] the possibility of bleeding.

首先，注意尿液顏色。若變成紅色或黏稠的，請立刻告訴我們。這意味著可能有出血。

P: I see, and then?

我了解，然後呢？

N: Second, your blood flow should run smoothly. If it isn't, there may be an **obstruction**[6] somewhere along the urinary tract, including at the catheter site.

第二，血液流動要順暢。如果它不順暢，泌尿道和導尿管中一定有阻塞之處。

P: OK, I will pay attention to this.

好的，我會注意的。

N: The operation didn't affect your bowel functions, so you can start eating again.

手術未影響到腸道功能，所以你可以再次開始進食。

P: Is there anything else I should take note of?

我還要注意其他什麼事嗎？

N: Drink more water. It will help with the flow of your urine.

多喝水可幫助尿液的流動。

P: Got it. Thanks for your explanation.

我了解了，謝謝你的説明。

Nursing Notes   護理記錄

Operation finished at 12 p.m.. Catheter inserted. Will keep observing the urine for bleeding or pus. Taught to recognize the signs of bleeding or infection.

手術於中午 12 點結束。已放置導尿管。將持續觀察尿液中是否有血或膿。教導病人識別出血或感染的徵兆。

Vocabulary and Sentence Examples   字彙與例句

1. drain [dren] (v.) 排出；引流	A urinary catheter can help drain urine from the bladder. 導尿管能引流膀胱的尿液。
2. route [rut] (n.) 路徑	An intramuscular injection can be a route for administering medication.　肌肉注射可作為給藥的路徑之一。
3. irrigation [ˌɪrəˈgeʃən] (n.) 灌洗；沖洗	This irrigation process can prevent blood clots from forming.　灌洗可防止血塊形成。
4. thick [θɪk] (adj.) 黏稠的；濃的	If the color of your urine turns red and thick, this may implicate that you are bleeding somewhere. 尿液變為紅色且黏稠時，意味著可能有出血。
5. implicate [ˈɪmplɪˌket] (v.) 意味著	According to the X-ray, the shadow on the right lung implicates there's something wrong with it. 根據 X 光來看，右肺上的陰影意味著它發生問題了
6. obstruction (n.) 阻塞 [əbˈstrʌkʃən]	The roads have been obstructed and could take several days to clear.　道路路阻塞可能要花費數天時間才能清除乾淨。

Terminology 術語

1. catheter [ˈkæθɪtə] 導尿管；導管

Discharge Instructions　出院衛教

39

Mr. Lu prepared for discharge while the nurse gave him instructions to follow.	盧先生要出院了，護理人員正在告訴他需要注意的事情。
N: Mr. Lu, how are you feeling now?	盧先生，你今天覺得如何？
P: Pretty well, but sometimes I'm in a little pain when I urinate.	很不錯，不過有時我排尿時會感到一點點疼痛。
N: Over the next few days, you will probably feel some pain and a sense of urgency to urinate, but this will disappear soon afterwards.	這幾天你可能會感到疼痛以及有急尿感，但之後很快就會消失的。
P: That means I don't have to worry about this. When should I come back for a follow-up exam?	那表示我不用擔心這件事。我什麼時候要回診檢查？
N: A week later.	1 週後。
P: Is there anything I should take note of?	我需注意什麼呢？
N: First, take your medicines **on time**[1]. Then check and make a record of the color of your urine everyday.	首先，要準時服藥。接著，每天察看並記錄尿液的顏色。
P: Is the **amount**[2] I urinate also important?	尿液量也很重要嗎？
N: Of course. And remember if your urine becomes red and thick, you must return right away.	當然，然後記得如果尿液變紅或黏稠，你得馬上回診。
P: OK. What else?	好的，還有呢？
N: If you catch a fever or have difficulty urinating, you should return to see your doctor.	如果你有發燒或是再度難以排尿的情形，也要回診就醫。
P: I will. Can I exercise at home?	我會的。我在家可以運動嗎？
N: Light sports are allowed. But you have to avoid riding, **lifting**[3] heavy objects, **straining**[4] the muscle in your lower abdomen and participating in any **strenuous**[5] exercises. Sexual activity can be resumed after 6~8 weeks.	輕度運動是可以的。但是你得避免騎車、提重物、使用下腹肌肉，以及參與任何劇烈運動。6~8 週內也要避免性行為。
P: I think I'll be bored over the next few weeks.	看來我接下來幾週會很無聊。
N: Rest will allow your wounds to heal. Also, your doctor prescribed some **laxatives**[6] so you won't become **constipated**[7]. In addition, please eat more vegetables and fruits to increase your bowel movements.	休息有助於傷口癒合。醫師也有開一些輕瀉劑給你以避免便祕。此外，務必多吃蔬菜和水果，以促進腸道蠕動。
P: I see. Is coffee or tea allowed?	我了解。可以喝咖啡或茶嗎？

N: Drinks with caffeine should be avoided. They can impair the flow of your urine.

含有咖啡因的飲料都必須避免。它們會影響排尿。

P: Thank you. I'll remember all of these instructions.

謝謝你，我會記得這些指導事項。

Nursing Notes　護理記錄

Will be discharged. Told to recognize and handle abnormal findings of the wound. Told to take medicines punctually and to avoid strenuous exercise. Diet restrictions given.

將准予出院。告知如何辨認與處理傷口的異常發現。告知按時服藥與避免劇烈運動。給予術後的飲食限制之衛教。

Tips on Writing

表達各種衛教或替病人安排的句型：衛教／安排＋過去分詞

例：Discharge plan given.　　　　　　　Instructed on self-care of the wound.

　　Dietary instructions provided.　　　Ultrasonography arranged.

Vocabulary and Sentence Examples　字彙與例句

1. on time [an taɪm]
   準時

   Please arrive at the airport on time, or else you'll miss your flight.　請準時到達機場，否則你可能會錯過班機。

2. amount [əˋmaʊnt]
   (n.) 量

   The total amount of blood loss was around 400c.c..
   總失血量大約是 400 毫升。

3. lift [lɪft]
   (v.) 舉起；提起

   He lifted the baggage with his right arm.
   他用右手提起行李。

4. strain [stren]
   (v.) （肌肉）用力

   When you defecate, you must contract your abdominal muscles.　當你排便時，腹部肌肉必須用力。

5. strenuous [ˋstrɛnjʊəs]
   (adj.) 劇烈的；費力的

   Basketball is a strenuous sport.　籃球是一種劇烈運動。

6. laxative [ˋlæksətɪv]
   (n.) 輕瀉劑

   The doctor prescribed some laxatives for you.
   醫師有開一些輕瀉劑給你。

7. constipate (v.) 便祕
   [ˋkanstə͵pet]

   Being constipated frequently is not good for one's health.
   經常便祕有損健康。

More Information

1. 尿液特徵的問診重點

    (1) What color is your urine?
        你的尿液是什麼顏色？

    (2) Is it light red or bloody?
        它是淺紅色或是血紅色的？

    (3) Is it tea-colored?
        它是茶色的嗎？

    (4) What was the amount of urine you excreted yesterday?
        你昨日的排尿量是多少？

    (5) Is your urine foamy?　你的尿液有泡沫嗎？

2. 排尿狀況的問診重點

    (1) How often do you go to the toilet in the middle of the night?
        你夜間去上幾次廁所？

    (2) How many times do you urinate everyday?
        你每天排尿幾次？

    (3) Do you find the caliber of you urine flow reduced?
        你有發現尿流直徑變小了嗎？

    (4) Do you urinate in small amounts at a time?
        你一次的尿量都很少嗎？

    (5) Do you feel a quick urgency to urinate after you just urinated?
        你排完尿後很快又有尿意感了嗎？

    (6) Have you ever experienced pain or a burning sensation during urination?
        你排尿時曾感到疼痛或燒灼感嗎？

Exercise 小試身手

Choose the Correct Answer

( ) 1. He woke up in the middle of the night to _____ . (A)defecate (B)urinate (C)urination (D)urine 他晚上起床小解。

( ) 2. The _____ ventricle worsened the symptoms of the patient. (A)enlarged (B)large (C)shrink (D)shrinkage 增大的心室使病人的症狀惡化。

( ) 3. Folic acid _____ should be given to all pregnant women. (A)supplement (B)contribute (C)supper (D)sustenance 孕婦都應該補充葉酸。

( ) 4. He _____ the ID card into the card reader and turned on the computer. (A)input (B)put (C)placed (D)inserted 他插入身分辨識卡並且打開了電腦。

( ) 5. You should take another _____ in order to save time. (A)street (B)route (C)role (D)method 你應該選另一條路以便節省時間。

Fill in the Blanks

1. The intern used _____ _____ to _____ the patient's _____ _____ . 實習醫師使用生理食鹽水灌洗病人的引流管。

2. He _____ at the hotel _____ _____ , but the former customer had not left yet. 他準時到達旅館，但前一位客人尚未離開。

3. Observe the _____ , _____ and _____ of urine. 觀察尿液的顏色、氣味及量。

4. He can _____ objects as _____ as his own weight. 他能夠舉起和他一樣重的東西。

5. Basketball is a _____ sport. 籃球是一種劇烈運動。

● Simplify Nursing Notes

1. 病人因為劇烈腹痛來到急診。

_____

2. 病人因為肝臟有腫瘤前來住院。

_____

3. 病人因為輕微發燒來到門診。

_____

4. 為病人安排了糖尿病衛教課程。

_____

5. 給予病人傷口照護的方式。

_____

● Translation

1. 你有急尿或排尿開始困難的情形嗎？

_____

2. 我們會給你補充水分和電解質以使你不會感到口渴。

_____

3. 我們放置一條導尿管以便從膀胱引流尿液。

_____

4. 灌洗可防止血塊的形成，避免阻塞泌尿道。

_____

5. 你得避免騎車、提重物、使用下腹肌肉，以及參與任何劇烈運動。

_____

解答

Proctology Unit
直肛科

Medical English for
Healthcare Professionals

About the Lower Gastrointestinal Tract 關於下胃腸道

40

The lower gastrointestinal tract (lower **GI** in abbreviation) begins at the ligament of Treitz and is composed of the **jejunum¹**, **ileum²**, **ascending colon³**, **transverse colon⁴**, **descending colon⁵**, **sigmoid colon⁶**, **rectum⁷** and **anal canal⁸**.

The lower GI tract is where various substances, such as water and nutrients are absorbed. Although the small intestine (jejunum and ileum in the lower GI tract) is rather sterile, there're many bacteria that live within the colon and are capable of producing various vitamins, such as vitamin B and K.

下胃腸道（下消化道）從 Treitz 韌帶開始，由一部分的空腸、與全部的迴腸、升結腸、橫結腸、降結腸、乙狀結腸、直腸及肛管組成。

下消化道是人體主要吸收物質之處，譬如水分和營養。雖然小腸是無菌的（空腸與迴腸位於下胃腸道），但有許多細菌存於大腸，他們能製造一些維生素，譬如維生素 B 和 K。

Terminology 術語

1. GI＝gastrointestinal [ˌgæstraɪnˈtɛstənəl] 胃腸的
2. jejunum [ʤɪˈʤunəm] 空腸
3. ileum [ˈɪlɪəm] 迴腸
4. ascending colon [əˈsɛndɪŋ ˈkolən] 升結腸
5. transverse colon [trænsˈvɜs ˈkolən] 橫結腸
6. descending colon [dɪˈsɛndɪŋ ˈkolən] 降結腸
7. sigmoid colon [ˈsɪgmɔɪd ˈkolən] 乙狀結腸
8. rectum [ˈrɛktəm] 直腸
9. anal canal [ˈenḷ kəˈnæl] 肛管

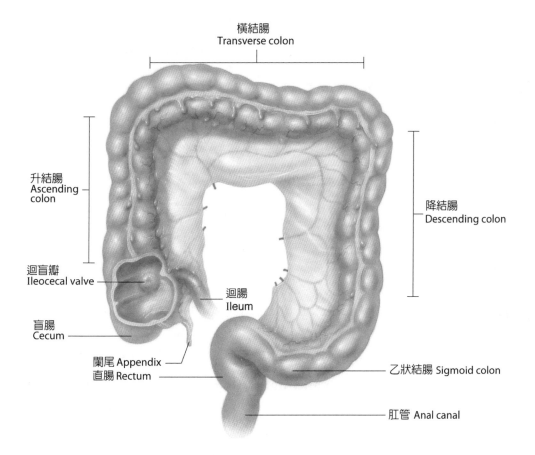

橫結腸
Transverse colon

升結腸
Ascending colon

降結腸
Descending colon

迴盲瓣
Ileocecal valve

迴腸
Ileum

盲腸
Cecum

闌尾 Appendix
直腸 Rectum

乙狀結腸 Sigmoid colon

肛管 Anal canal

Case Information 個案資訊

Colon Cancer [ˈkolən ˈkænsɚ] **結腸癌**

1. **Causes**: Diet high in fat and low in fiber, genetic mutation.
2. **Symptoms & Signs**: Change in bowel habits, alteration in the caliber of stool, bloody stool and stool with bloody streaks or occult blood.
3. **Care**:
   (1) Care after endoscopy.
   (2) Change dressings of wound post-op.
   (3) Consume low-residue diet for the first 3 weeks post-op.
   (4) Care after colostomy.

Admission Assessment　入院評估

41

Mr. Ho, was admitted to the ward because of suspected colon cancer.

何先生因為疑似罹患有結腸癌而住進病房。

N: Nurse　**P:** Patient

N: Good morning, Mr. Ho. May I ask what is the purpose of your hospital visit today?

何先生早安，請問你今天為何會來醫院？

P: For the last 6 months, I have been passing stools with bloody streaks.

我便中帶有血絲，持續大概半年了。

N: What is the color of your stool?

你的糞便是什麼顏色呢？

P: It's almost black.

幾乎是黑色的。

N: Have you ever seen any changes in the caliber of your stool?

你曾經發現糞便直徑有所改變嗎？

P: I haven't noticed any changes.

我沒注意到任何變化。

N: Have you felt any pain before or after **defecating**[1]?

你在排便前後有感到疼痛嗎？

P: No.

沒有。

N: Have you ever had a **hemorrhoid**?

你有痔瘡嗎？

P: Never.

我沒有痔瘡。

N: Has anyone in your family ever had similar symptoms?

你的任一位家人中和你有類似的症狀嗎？

P: No, but my grandfather and my uncle both **died of**[2] colon cancer.

沒有，但我的祖父和叔叔都死於結腸癌。

N: OK. The doctor has arranged an endoscopy of your rectum and colon tomorrow morning. Therefore, you must be NPO starting at midnight. NPO means you can't eat or drink anything.

好的。醫師已為你安排明天早上接受直腸結腸的內視鏡檢查。因此從午夜開始必須禁食。禁食意指你不能進食或飲用任何東西。

P: I see. What should I do if I feel thirsty?

我了解。那我口渴時怎麼辦？

N: You can take a cotton swab, dab it in water and **moisten**[3] your lips.

你可以用棉棒沾水來溼潤你的嘴唇。

P: Alright, thanks a lot.

好的，非常感謝。

Nursing Notes　護理記錄

Admitted due to suspected colon cancer. Has suffered stool with bloody streaks for half a year. Colonoscopy arranged. Told to be NPO starting at midnight.

病人因為疑似結腸癌而住院。苦於便中帶有血絲的狀況已有半年。已安排結腸鏡檢查。告知午夜開始禁食。

Tips on Writing

arrange, perform, check 的用法：如用於被動通常表示某種事務被執行；如用於主動，主詞非 nurse 時不可省略，要清楚標出執行者。例：
Digital rectal examination performed.
Brain CT arranged.
The doctor performed the operation for colon cancer.

Vocabulary and Sentence Examples　字彙與例句

1. defecate [ˈdɛfəˌket] 　(v.) 排便	What's wrong when you defecate? 你排便時有什麼問題嗎？
2. die of [ˈdaɪ əv] 　死於……	His uncle died of colon cancer.　他叔叔死於結腸癌。
3. moisten [ˈmɔɪsn̩] 　(v.) 溼潤	When you're NPO, you can take a cotton swab, dab it in water and moisten your lips. 禁食時，你可使用棉棒沾水來溼潤你的嘴唇。

Terminology 術語

1. hemorrhoid [ˈhɛmərɔɪd] 痔瘡

Hospitalization　住院療護

42

The nurse explained the surgical plan.

N: You're **scheduled**[1] to receive an operation at 10 a.m. tomorrow.

P: Yes, I know.

N: You look very **nervous**[2]. What's the problem?

P: The doctor told me that he will create an opening in my abdomen for a temporary fecal **passage**[3] way. This sounds **horrible**[4].

N: I can understand. However, this operation can help improve your health. **Furthermore**[5], the opening will be closed after the whole operation is done. Don't worry too much.

P: I see. I'll try my best to relax.

N: You've already been on a **clear liquid diet** for two days. For the operation, you should be NPO starting at midnight.

P: Just like when I received endoscopy?

N: That's right. And we will give you a **cleansing enema** in the evening.

P: What's that for?

N: We will inject a cleansing solution into your anus to clean the operation site. This may make you feel uncomfortable but will help ensure your safety during your operation.

P: I see. Thanks for the explanation.

N: You're welcome. Just call us if you need any help.

護理師正在解釋手術計畫。

你的手術預定於明早 10 點進行。

我知道。

你看起來很緊張。怎麼了？

醫師告訴我他要在我的腹部上創建一個開口以作為暫時的糞便通道之用。我覺得很可怕！

我能理解。不過這手術有助於增進你的健康。再者，這個開口在手術完成後就會關閉的。別太擔心了。

我知道。我會試著放輕鬆的。

因為即將動手術的緣故，目前為止你已經採清流質飲食 2 天了，午夜之後你也將要禁食。

就像我之前做內視鏡檢查那樣？

是的。我們還會在傍晚時給你做清潔灌腸。

它的用途是什麼？

我們將於你的肛門內注入清潔液以清潔要動手術的腸道。可能會讓你有一些不舒服，但是能確保明天動手術時的安全。

我明白，謝謝說明。

不客氣。如果需要任何幫忙就通知我們。

Nursing Notes　護理記錄

Told operation scheduled at 10 a.m. tomorrow. Explained surgical plan and colostomy. Told to be NPO starting at midnight.

告知病人明早 10 點動手術。解釋手術計畫和結腸造口。告知病人午夜開始禁食。

Tips on Writing

表達衛教內容的寫法

Told to V：告訴病人「要去做」→Told to avoid eating greasy foods.

Told how to V：教導病人「如何做」→Told how to avoid eating greasy foods.

Told may V：告訴病人「可以<u>選擇</u>這樣做」→Told may eat light foods.

Vocabulary and Sentence Examples　字彙與例句

1. schedule [ˈskɛdʒʊl]
   (v.) 預定
   (n.) 計劃表

   You're scheduled to undergo a check-up next Monday.
   你的體檢預定於下星期一進行。

2. nervous [ˈnɜvəs]
   (adj.) 神經質的；
   緊張的

   She is nervous because the deadline for her assignment is approaching.
   因為作業的繳交期限要到了，她顯得非常緊張。

3. passage [ˈpæsɪdʒ]
   (n.) 通道

   I found a new passage way to the basement parking lot.
   我找到通往地下室停車場的新通道。

4. horrible [ˈhɔrəbl]
   (adj.) 可怕的；糟透的

   It's horrible to have nightmares.　做惡夢很可怕。

5. furthermore [ˈfɜðəˌmor]
   (adv.) 而且；再者

   The house is too old. Furthermore, it's too far from the company.　這間房子太老舊，而且離公司太遠了。

Terminology 術語

1. clear liquid diet [klɪr ˈlɪkwɪd ˈdaɪət] 清流質飲食
2. cleansing enema [ˈklɛnzɪŋ ˈɛnəmə] 清潔灌腸

Discharge Instructions 出院衛教

43

The nurse checked the stoma on Mr. Ho's abdomen.

N: Good afternoon, Mr. Ho. May I check your stoma?

P: Go ahead.

N: Have you passed anything since yesterday?

P: Just gas and some liquid.

N: Let me see the liquid you have passed.

P: Is it normal?

N: Yes, It's quite clear with no blood. This is bowel secretion. There's no apparent bleeding of the intestines. Please check the passage and the color of the stoma everyday.

P: I did feel **slight**[1] pain around the stoma, and it smelled bad.

N: I think there's a bit of **breakdown**[2] surrounding your skin. The **collection pouch** isn't connecting well either. Let me **replace**[3] it with a new one.

P: Thank you very much.

N: You're welcome. Now I'm going to apply some povidone-iodine at the breakdown site.

P: The stoma makes me nervous and uncomfortable.

N: Take it easy. Don't forget that the stoma is just temporary?

P: I remember, but I'm still **afraid**[4] of the smell and the terrible look of the stoma.

N: I understand. We'll help you **get used to**[5] it during this period.

P: Thanks again.

護理師檢查何先生腹部的造口。

何先生午安，我可以看看你的造口嗎？

請便。

從昨天開始你有排出東西嗎？

只有有氣體和一些液體。

讓我看看你排出的液體。

它正常嗎？

是的，它很清澈且沒有血液混雜。這是腸道分泌物，表示目前為止沒有明顯的腸道出血。請每天檢查通道及造口顏色。

我覺得造口附近有輕微疼痛，而且有難聞的味道。

我想是造口旁的皮膚有小小的破裂。但造口袋的連接並不適當。讓我更換成新的。

非常謝謝你。

不客氣，現在我要塗抹一些優碘在你皮膚破裂的地方。

這個造口讓我覺得很緊張，也很不舒服。

放輕鬆囉。你忘記這個造口只是暫時性的嗎？

我記得。但我仍然很害怕造口的氣味及可怕的外觀。

我能理解。在這段時間裡，我們會協助你適應它的。

再次謝謝你。

Nursing Notes 護理記錄

Colostomy appears red, warm and soft on the left abdomen. Will keep observing the amount and color of stool. Found tiny skin **abrasion** near the pouch and povidone-iodine applied. Pouch replaced. Taught how to change the pouch.

結腸造口位於左腹部，外觀呈紅色，溫度溫暖，觸感柔軟。將持續觀察糞便的量和顏色。造口袋附近有微小的皮膚磨損，施予優碘消毒並更換造口袋。教導病人更換結腸造口袋。

Tips on Writing

「依醫囑」的寫法：根據某位醫師的醫囑可用以下句型

(1) Do something per Dr. XX's order → order 作為名詞，意指「醫囑」。例：
Antibiotics administered per Dr. Hwang's order.

(2) Do something as Dr. XX ordered → order 作為動詞，使用過去式。例：
IV drip given as Dr. Lin ordered.

Vocabulary and Sentence Examples 字彙與例句

1. slight [slaɪt]
   (adj.) 輕微的

   He felt slight pain in his abdomen.
   他感到輕微的肚子痛。

2. breakdown [ˈbrek͵daʊn]
   (n.) 破裂

   There's a little skin breakdown around the ear.
   耳朵附近有一個小小的皮膚破裂。

3. replace [rɪˈples]
   (v.) 更換

   I'd like to replace this pencil with a pen.
   我想把這支鉛筆換成一隻原子筆。

4. afraid [əˈfred]
   (adj.) 害怕

   He is afraid of being on stage.
   他害怕站在舞台上表演。

5. get used to [gɛt jusd tʊ]
   習慣於……

   I get used to getting up early.
   我習慣早起。

6. abrasion [əˈbreʒən]
   (n.) 磨損；擦傷

   A skin abrasion is a breakdown of skin.
   皮膚擦傷是指皮膚上有破裂的情形。

Terminology 術語

1. collection pouch [kəˈlɛkʃən paʊtʃ] 造口袋

More Information

1. 排便習慣的問診重點

   (1) How many times do you defecate (in a day)?

   你（一天）排便幾次？

   (2) Do you feel abdominal pain or a stomachache before/during defecation?

   你在排便前（時）會感到疼痛（胃痛）嗎？

   (3) Do you feel pain around the anus during defecation?

   你在排便時肛門附近會感到疼痛嗎？

   (4) Have you had constipation before?

   你先前曾有便祕情形嗎？

   (5) Do you usually feel like you can't completely pass stool right after defecation?

   在排完便後，你會經常有沒排乾淨的感覺嗎？

2. 糞便特徵的問診重點

   (1) Have you passed bloody/black/tarry stool?

   你排出血便／黑便／瀝青便嗎？

   (2) Is your stool accompanied with bloody streaks?

   你的糞便帶有血絲嗎？

   (3) Have you ever found any changes in the caliber of your stool?

   你曾發現糞便直徑的任何變化嗎？

   (4) Has your stool gotten looser or softer within the last 6 months?

   近半年來，你的糞便有變得鬆軟嗎？

Exercise 小試身手

● Choose the Correct Answer

( ) 1. He has pain upon _____ because of his bothersome hemorrhoid.
(A)urination (B)breathing (C)defecation (D)suffocation
他因為擾人的痔瘡造成排便疼痛。

( ) 2. His grandfather _____ _____ lung cancer. (A)died of (B)died
from (C)died at (D)died with 他的祖父死於肺癌。

( ) 3. The young lady became _____ at the sight of the dog barking.
(A)neurosis (B)nerve (C)nervousness (D)nervous
這位年輕小姐一看到狂吠的狗就變得很緊張。

( ) 4. He _____ a fantastic wonderland on the little island. (A)creature
(B)structure (C)built (D)created 他在一座小島上創造了一個樂園。

( ) 5. The iron is a solid object in room temperature but is in _____ form at
thousands of degrees. (A)gas (B)solution (C)liquid (D)mixture
鐵在室溫下是一種固體，但在數千度之下則變成液體。

● Fill in the Blanks

1. Before the _____ involving the _____ tract, patients routinely receive
a _____ _____ . 在胃腸手術之前，病人都常規地接受清潔灌腸。

2. He had a car _____ . Fortunately, he only had a _____ abrasion.
他發生車禍了，所幸只有輕微擦傷。

3. There's a little skin _____ around the ear. 耳朵附近有一個小小的皮膚破裂。

4. His position was _____ by Mr. Lin. 他的職務被林先生取代了。

5. She is _____ of encountering any _____ things.
她很害怕再次遇到恐怖的事物。

○ Simplify Nursing Notes

1. 根據吳醫師的醫囑給予硝化甘油錠。

2. 5% glucose water given under Dr. Wu's orders. （改寫成 as……ordered）

3. 護理師教導病人如何照顧傷口。

4. 護理師告知病人不可以運動。

5. 醫師執行了直腸癌手術。

○ Translation

1. 你的糞便是什麼顏色呢？

2. 醫師已為你安排明天早上接受直腸結腸的內視鏡檢查。

3. 你可以用棉棒沾水來溼潤你的嘴唇。

4. 我們會在傍晚時給你做清潔灌腸。

5. 從昨天開始你有從造口排出東西嗎？

Neurology Unit
神經科

Learning Goals 學習目標

1. Assessing patients with neurological deficits
2. Assessing patient's level of conscious and muscle strength
3. Providing health education to patients

Outline 本章大綱

- The Components of the Central Nervous System　中樞神經系統的組成
- Case Information: Cerebrovascular Accident (CVA)
  個案資訊：腦血管意外（腦中風）
- Admission Assessment　入院評估
- Hospitalization　住院療護
- Discharge Instructions　出院衛教

Medical English for Healthcare Professionals

The Components of the Central Nervous System 中樞神經系統的組成

44

The central nervous system perceives stimuli from the environment or body and then responds to them. It integrates information, creates thoughts, commends actions and functions as the master of our body.

The central nervous system can be roughly divided into two parts: the **brain**[1] and the **spinal cord**[2]. The brain and the spinal cord are divided into **gray matter**[3], which consists of many neurons, and **white matter**[4], which consists of numerous axons bridging these neurons.

The brain has four lobes: the **frontal lobe**[5], which controls many cognitive and motor functions; the **parietal lobe**[6], which has a sensory dominant function; the **temporal lobe**[7], which controls auditory sensations and engages in memory storage; and finally the **occipital lobe**[8], which plays an important part in visual sensation. The spinal cord, acts as a pathway to relay information around.

中樞神經系統從環境或體內感受刺激從而應對。它整合訊息、創造思想、號令行動，如同身體的主宰一般作用著。

中樞神經系統粗分為兩部分－腦與脊髓。腦與脊髓皆可區分成灰質和白質，前者由許多神經元組成，後者由無數個用以連結神經元的軸突組成。

大腦有四葉，分別是：額葉控制認知和運動；頂葉主管感覺，顳葉與聽覺和記憶有關；枕葉則在視覺扮演重要角色。另一方面，脊髓則作為訊息傳遞的中繼站。

Terminology 術語

1. brain [bren] 腦
2. spinal cord [ˈspaɪn̩ ˌkɔrd] 脊髓
3. gray matter [gre ˈmetə] 灰質
4. white matter [hwaɪt ˈmetə] 白質
5. frontal lobe [ˈfrʌnt̩ lob] 額葉
6. parietal lobe [pəˈraɪətḷ lob] 頂葉
7. temporal lobe [ˈtɛmpərəl lob] 顳葉
8. occipital lobe [akˈsɪpətḷ lob] 枕葉

Case Information 個案資訊

Cerebrovascular Accident 腦血管意外（腦中風）(CVA)

[ˌsɛrəbrəˈvæskjələ ˈæksədənt]

1. **Causes**: Hypertension, DM, or cardiac arrhythmia.
2. **Symptoms & Signs**:
   (1) Weakness of unilateral extremities
   (2) Facial palsy
   (3) Slurred speech
   (4) Deviation of the eye
   (5) Deviation of the corner of the mouth
   (6) Disturbance of the conscious
   (7) Headache
   (8) Dizziness

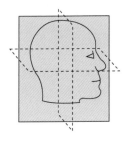

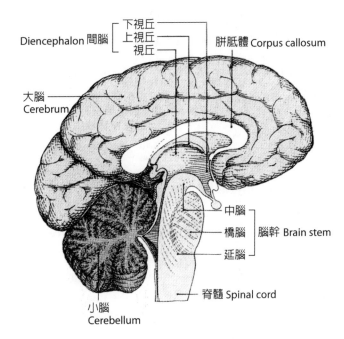

Diencephalon 間腦 ─ 下視丘 / 上視丘 / 視丘

胼胝體 Corpus callosum

大腦 Cerebrum

中腦 / 橋腦 / 延腦 — 腦幹 Brain stem

脊髓 Spinal cord

小腦 Cerebellum

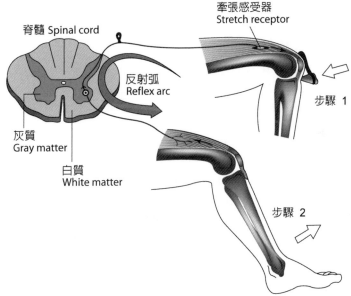

脊髓 Spinal cord

牽張感受器 Stretch receptor

反射弧 Reflex arc

步驟 1

灰質 Gray matter

白質 White matter

步驟 2

Case Information 個案資訊

3. **Care**:

(1) Monitor vital signs.

(2) Maintain cerebral perfusion.

(3) Check GCS.

(4) Encourage early rehabilitation.

(5) Take medications on time.

(6) Eat a low salt and fat diet.

Admission Assessment 入院評估

45

*Mr. Liao was admitted because of left **hemiparesis** and dizziness.*

廖先生因為左側無力與頭暈而住院。

N: Nurse   **P:** Patient

N: Good afternoon, Mr. Liao. Are you feeling better these days?

廖先生你好，你這幾天覺得好一點了嗎？

P: No, I can't lift my left arm and left leg. My muscles are also weak.

並不好，我現在無法舉起左臂和左腿。肌肉也沒什麼力氣。

N: Do you remember what happened when you experienced weakness in your left **extremities**[1]?

你還記得當你感到左側肢體無力時發生什麼事了嗎？

P: I got up in the morning and suddenly felt weak in my arm and then my leg.

我早上起床後，突然感覺左臂和左腿很無力。

N: At that time, could you speak **fluently**[2]?

當時你能夠流利地說話嗎？

P: Yes, I could.

我可以的。

N: After coming to the hospital, did you feel like your **strength**[3] improved?

到醫院以後，你覺得力氣有好些嗎？

P: A little bit, but it was not enough to go on with my daily activities.

一點點啦。但是還不夠應付日常活動。

N: OK. Let me take your blood pressure.

好的。現在我要量血壓了。

P: Please, go ahead.

請便吧。

N: Your blood pressure is 160/100 mmHg. This is high, but it is helping to maintain blood **perfusion**[4] to your brain.

你的血壓是 160/100 mmHg。血壓稍高，但如此方可維持腦部的血液循環。

P: Oh! That really sounds concerning, but it makes plenty of sense with your explanation.

哇，嚇了我一跳。不過經過你的解釋，我就能理解了。

N: In addition to feeling weak, are there any other problems bothering you?

除了無力之外，還有什麼困擾你的症狀嗎？

P: Well, I feel a little dizzy.

嗯，我有一點頭暈。

N: I'll tell your doctor. He has prescribed some intravenous medications to help deal with your weakness. He will arrange for some **rehabilitation**[5] therapy after your condition becomes more stable.

我會通知你的醫師。此外，他開了一些靜脈輸注的藥物以處理肌肉無力的問題。他也會在情況較穩定後為你安排復健。

P: I see. In the meantime, what should I do for now?

我明白。那我現在該做什麼？

N: You only need to rest in bed for the next days.

你只需要臥床休息幾天即可。

P: I will. Thank you.

我會的。謝謝你。

Nursing Notes　護理記錄

Sent to the ER because had left hemiparesis, corner of the mouth deviated to the left. **CT** and **MRI** showed stroke in the right brainstem. Vital signs stable. BP controlled at 160/100 mmHg. Feels weak and dizzy now. Told to rest in the bed.

因左側偏癱與嘴角左偏被送至急診室。電腦斷層攝影及核磁共振攝影顯示右側腦幹中風。生命徵象穩定，血壓控制在 160/110 mmHg。病人目前感覺無力及頭暈。告知於床上休息。

Tips on Writing

帶有原因的子句用法：如以 because 帶頭的子句主詞與主要子句相同，則主詞可被省略；倘若不同，則應保留以使句意明顯。例：
The patient didn't return for follow-up because he felt there was no problem to deal with.→Didn't return for follow-up because felt no problem to deal with.

Vocabulary and Sentence Examples　字彙與例句

1. extremity [ɪkˈstrɛmətɪ] (n.) 肢體	Extremities include hands and feet.　肢體包括手和腳。
2. fluently [ˈfluəntlɪ] (adv.) 流利地	After years of hard work, she can now speak Spanish fluently.　經過數年苦修，她現在可以流利地講西班牙語。
3. strength [strɛŋθ] (n.) 力量	She has quite a bit of strength in her arm. 她的手臂十分有力。
4. perfusion [pɚˈfjuʒən] (n.) 灌流	Because of vascular stenosis, perfusion to the lower extremities is poor. 因為血管狹窄之故，下肢的血液灌流十分貧乏。
5. rehabilitation (n.) 復健 [ˌrihəˌbɪləˈteʃən]	Patients who suffer from stroke must receive rehabilitation therapy afterwards.　中風的病人往後都必須接受復健治療。

Terminology 術語

1. hemiparesis [ˌhɛmɪˈpærəsɪs] 偏癱；半癱
2. CT＝computerized tomography [kəmˈpjutɚˌraɪzd təˈmagrəfɪ] 電腦斷層攝影
3. MRI＝magnetic resonance imaging [mægˈnɛtɪk ˈrɛzənəns ˈɪmɪdʒɪŋ] 核磁共振攝影

Hospitalization 住院療護

46

The nurse assessed the improvement in Mr. Liao's condition.

護理師正在評估廖先生的進步狀況。

N: Do you feel like the strength of your muscles have improved?

你覺得肌肉力量有進步嗎？

P: Well, I don't think it is **significant**[1].

嗯，我不覺得有顯著的進步耶。

N: Let me test your muscle strength. Please push my hand with yours. *(Later)* Good. Then raise your leg against my hand. *(Later)* Good.

讓我測試你的肌力。請用你的手推我的手，很好。請把腳抬起來抵抗我的手，很好。

P: What do you think?

你覺得如何？

N: Well, as you've **mentioned**[2], there's been little improvement.

嗯，和你提及的類似。有小幅度的進步。

P: *(Sighing)* I feel so **frustrated**[3].

唉，我好沮喪。

N: Don't discourage yourself. You just started rehabilitation 2 days ago.

別洩氣，你才剛開始復健兩天而已。

P: Will it take a long time to make some progress?

要花很長的時間才會有進步嗎？

N: It depends on how much **effort**[4] you put into this.

這取決於你願意付出多少努力。

P: I don't feel confident going on.

我沒有信心繼續下去。

N: Oh, come on. Don't you want to be able to do things on your own just like you used to?

別這樣嘛。難道你不想像以前那樣凡事都能靠自己嗎？

P: Of course I do.

我當然想。

N: The difficulty of rehabilitation often **exceeds**[5] our patient's **tolerance**[6]. If you overcome this, you'll set a good example! You can do it.

復健運動的困難往往超出病人的耐受度，你如果可以克服它，將會是最佳典範的。你做得到的。

P: Alright. Thanks for the encouragement. I'll try to do my best. It's time for today's rehabilitation session. Let's go!

好的。謝謝鼓勵。我會盡我所能。今天的復健時間到了，我們走吧！

 ## Nursing Notes 護理記錄

GCS: E4V5M6. Pupil size: 4+/4+. Muscle power: upper and lower left limb 3, upper and lower right limb 4-5. Feels frustrated about rehabilitaiton progress. Encouraged to increase efforts. Went to rehabilitation center around 1 p.m..

格拉斯高昏迷量表：睜眼反應 4 分／語言反應 5 分／運動反應 6 分。瞳孔大小：兩側皆為 4 mm 且對光有反應。肌力測試：左側上下肢 3 分，右側上下肢 4~5 分。病人對復健的進步程度感到挫折。鼓勵他多努力。約下午 1 點至復健中心進行復健。

Tips on Writing

1. GCS 評估項目：E (Eye opening)，睜眼反應；V Verbal response)，語言反應；M (Motor response)，運動反應。

2. 主動句的改寫：主動句可以改寫為被動句，其中的動詞應修改為 be＋過去分詞之被動式。而 be＋過去分詞的句子又可省略 be 動詞。例：
   The nurse suggested a regular exercise routine. → Regular exercise suggested.

Vocabulary and Sentence Examples 　字彙與例句

1. significant
   [sɪgˊnɪfəkənt]
   (adj.) 顯著的

   The effect of this medication is not significant.
   藥物的效果並不顯著。

2. mention [ˊmɛnʃən]
   (v.) 提及

   As I mentioned, he is gifted in mathematics.
   如同我提及的，他在數學方面非常有天賦。

3. frustrated [ˊfrʌstretɪd]
   (adj.) 沮喪的

   After losing the contest, she felt very frustrated.
   輸掉比賽後她感到非常沮喪。

4. effort [ˊɛfət]
   (n.) 努力

   Let's try one more time but with more effort this time.
   我們再試一次，這一次更努力些吧。

5. exceed [ɪkˊsid]
   (v.) 超越

   If you use your creativity, you will exceed your expectations.
   如果你能運用創造力，你將會超越預期的表現。

6. tolerance [ˊtalərəns]
   (n.) 耐受度

   His tolerance to morphine increased after several doses.
   在數次劑量後，他對嗎啡類止痛劑的耐受度會增加。

Terminology 術語

1. GCS＝Glasgow Coma Scale [ˊglæsgo ˊkomə skel] 格拉斯高昏迷量表

Discharge Instructions　出院衛教

47

Mr. Liao has been in the hospital for 2 weeks and is ready to go home.

N: You look good today.

廖先生已經在醫院待了 2 週，他準備要回家了。

你今天看起來氣色很好。

P: Do I? *(Laughing)* The doctor said I can go home today, since I've made good progress.

真的嗎？（大笑）因為醫師說我進步非常多，所以今天可以回家了。

N: Congratulations! I just need to remind you of a few things. First, take your medications **on schedule**[1]. This will prevent another stroke from happening in the future.

恭喜你，我有幾件事要提醒你。首先，要按時服藥。這可以避免下一次中風的發生。

P: I see. What if I miss a dose? Should I take a double dose next time?

我明白。萬一我忘記吃了怎麼辦？那下次要吃兩倍劑量嗎？

N: No, you should only take one dose, but please remember not to miss any doses.

不，你只需要吃一劑。但請記得不要漏吃任何一劑。

P: OK, I'll keep this in mind.

好的，我會謹記在心。

N: Second, monitor your blood pressure everyday.

第二，每天監測你的血壓。

P: OK. But what should I do if my blood pressure rises?

好的。那如果我的血壓變高時怎麼辦？

N: If it **fluctuates**[2] or rises too much, you should come back.

如果血壓變動得太厲害，或者升得很高，你應該回來就診。

P: I will.

我會的。

N: Keep yourself away from greasy and salty foods. They can **do harm**[3] to your health.

遠離油膩或高鹽食物，它們會危害你的健康。

P: Wow, it may be difficult for me to keep away from such delicious foods.

哇，要遠離那些美食對我來說有點困難。

N: Well, just give it a try.

嗯，就試試看吧。

P: Alright. I will eat a low salt and fat diet.

好啦，我會採少鹽少油的飲食。

N: Good luck. I hope the strength of your muscles returns in a short period of time.

祝你好運，希望你的肌力可以儘早完全恢復。

P: Thanks for your care.

謝謝妳的照顧。

N: You're welcome.

不客氣。

Nursing Notes　護理記錄

Instructed to take medicine regularly, monitor BP daily and avoid greasy and salty foods. Precisely states the correct and healthy dietary concept. Wheelchair lent. Left hospital at 10 a.m..

衛教病人需定時服藥、每天監測血壓，並避免油膩及高鹽食物。病人能夠詳細地陳述正確的與健康的飲食觀念。借出輪椅。早上 10 點出院。

Tips on Writing

記錄衛教成果：給予衛教時，病人可以正確地陳述衛教內容是較為有效的。在護理記錄上可以記錄其測試結果。例：
Told to keep balanced diet. 此句為護理師衛教內容。→ (The patient) precisely replied the food he should avoid. 此句測試病人是否了解衛教內容的結果。

Vocabulary and Sentence Examples　字彙與例句

1. on schedule
   [an ˈskɛdʒul] 準時

   The flight is on schedule. Let's get on the plane.
   飛機準時到達，咱們趕快上去吧。

2. fluctuate [ˈflʌktʃuᴗet]
   (v.) 變動

   The tide fluctuated a lot and made the boat unstable.
   潮汐變動很大，讓船隻變得不穩。

3. do harm [du harm]
   造成傷害；對⋯不利

   Those fried foods can do harm to your health.
   那些油炸食物對你的健康不利。

More Information

1. 了解病人是否具有**中風的危險因子**

   (1) Do you have hypertension?

   你有高血壓嗎？

   How was your blood pressure?

   你的血壓多少？

   Are you controlling it properly?

   血壓是否控制得宜？

   What medications are you taking to treat this?

   你吃什麼降血壓藥？

   (2) Do you have diabetes?

   你有糖尿病嗎？

   How was your blood sugar level before meals?

   你的飯前血糖是多少？

   (3) Do you have coronary artery disease/cardiac arrhythmia?

   你有冠狀動脈疾病／心律不整嗎？

   (4) Are you regularly taking the anticoagulants as instructed?

   你有依醫囑規律服用抗凝血劑嗎？

2. 詢問家屬關於病人的中風狀態

   (1) When was the last time he/she walked around normally?

   他／她最後一次正常走路是何時？

   (2) When was the last time you heard him/her speak fluently?

   你上次聽到他／她流利地説話是何時？

   (3) What did you see when he/she had a CVA?

   他／她中風時你看到什麼？

   (4) Which side did he/she feel weak?

   他／她感覺哪一側較無力？

   Did the corner of his/her mouth or eye deviate to one side?

   他／她的眼球和嘴角有歪向一邊嗎？

   (5) Did he/she speak fluently?

   他／她口齒清晰嗎？

Exercise 小試身手

● Choose the Correct Answer

( ) 1. Don't _____ him. Try to say something helpful instead. (A)courage (B)discourage (C)encourage (D)frustrated
別讓他洩氣，嘗試說些有幫助的話吧。

( ) 2. The velocity of this car _____ the speed limit. (A)exceeded (B)surmounted (C)jumped (D)succeeded 這輛車的速度超過速限了。

( ) 3. Make an _____ to defeat the opponent. (A)effect (B)affect (C)effort (D)inflict 努力一下並且擊敗對手。

( ) 4. You should take this medicine with caution and look out for possible side _____ . (A)endurance (B)effects (C)tolerance (D)defense
你應該小心服藥並注意可能會發生的副作用。

( ) 5. I'd like to hear your _____ . (A)anger (B)agreement (C)optimism (D)opinion 我想聽聽你的意見。

● Fill in the Blanks

1. You have to respect the thoughts of your patient and not let her feel _____ .
你必須尊重病人的想法，不要讓她感到沮喪。

2. The chairman _____ that we have to speak English _____ .
董事長提到，國際會議時我們必須使用流利的英文。

3. I request that the meeting be held _____ _____ . Otherwise we may _____ _____ to the prestige of our company.
我要求會議準時開始，否則將會傷害我們公司的名譽。

4. Since this is a major operation, we should _____ the patient's vital signs _____ to prevent any major fluctuations.
由於這是一項重大手術，我們必須持續地監測病人的生命徵象並避免它波動。

5. _____ _____ to restore his muscle _____ , he received _____ therapy to help his recovery after his _____ .
為了恢復肌肉力量，他在骨折復原後進行了復健治療。

⊙ Simplify Nursing Notes

1. 因為疼痛減輕所以他沒有回診追蹤。

   _____

2. 因為效果不佳，他自行停藥。

   _____

3. The patient was sent to the ER because he had intractable abdominal pain in the right lower quadrant.

   _____

4. The patient received a t-PA infusion and his condition was stabilized.

   _____

5. He was told to eat a low salt and fat diet. （請改以病人覆述的角度寫出衛教成果）

   _____

⊙ Translation

1. 你覺得肌肉力量有進步嗎？

   _____

2. 讓我測試你的肌力。請用你的手推我的手。

   _____

3. 要按時服藥。這可以避免下一次中風的發生。

   _____

4. 如果血壓變動得太厲害，或者升得很高，你應該回來就診。

   _____

5. 遠離油膩或高鹽食物，它們會危害你的健康。

   _____

General Surgery Unit
一般外科

Learning Goals 學習目標

1. Assessing patients with breast problems
2. Preparnig patients for breast surgery
3. Providing health education to patients

Outline 本章大綱

- About the Breasts　關於乳房
- Case Information: Breast Cancer
  個案資訊：乳癌
- Admission Assessment　入院評估
- Pre-Operative Care　術前照護
- Post-Operative Care　術後照護

Medical English for Healthcare Professionals

About the Breasts 關於乳房

48

The breasts are a part of the reproductive system, especially in women, from which babies feed on their breasts. Women's breasts begin to develop during puberty when they grow in size and mature. Men's breasts don't develop due to their lack of **estrogen**[1] stimulation.

Histologically, a breast consists of **dense connective tissue**[2], **adipose tissue**[3] and a ductal and lobular system which produces milk. The beginning of the ductal and lobular systems consists of clusters of **acini**[4] (which together form **lobules**[5]) that are responsible for the production of milk. They connect to numerous **ductules**[6], which aid in the transportation of milk. The ductules then converge into larger ducts, which eventually combine to form **lactiferous sinuses**[7] and ducts that connect out to the nipple.

At the surface, the breast is divided into four quadrants: UIQ, LIQ, UOQ, LOQ. Using these quadrants is a simple and convenient way to describe any **lesions**[8] or symptoms within the breast.

乳房對女性來説，是生殖系統的一部分，可哺育嬰兒。女性乳房在青春期開始發育，乳房的大小及其內在結構皆會成熟。因為缺乏雌激素的刺激，男性乳房並不發達。

組織學上來看，乳房包含了緻密結締組織、脂肪組織和能生產乳汁的管道和小葉系統。這些管道和小葉系統始於一群群負責生產乳汁的腺泡，進入無數負責運輸乳汁的小管道。這些小管道匯集成為更大的管道，最後合併起來形成輸乳竇和輸乳管並開口於乳頭。

從表面上來看，乳房可以分成內上、內下、外上及外下象限。是一種用於描述乳房病灶或症狀的簡便方式。

Terminology 術語

1. estrogen [ˈɛstrədʒən] 雌激素
2. dense connective tissue 緻密結締組織
   [ˌdɛns kəˈnɛktɪv ˈtɪʃu]
3. adipose tissue [ˈædəpos ˈtɪʃu] 脂肪組織
4. acini [ˈæsɪnaɪ] 腺泡（複數）
   （acinus 單數）
5. lobule [ˈlabjul] 小葉
6. ductule [ˈdʌktul] 小管
7. lactiferous sinus 輸乳竇
   [lækˈtɪfərəs ˈsaɪnəs]
8. lesion [ˈliʒən] 病灶

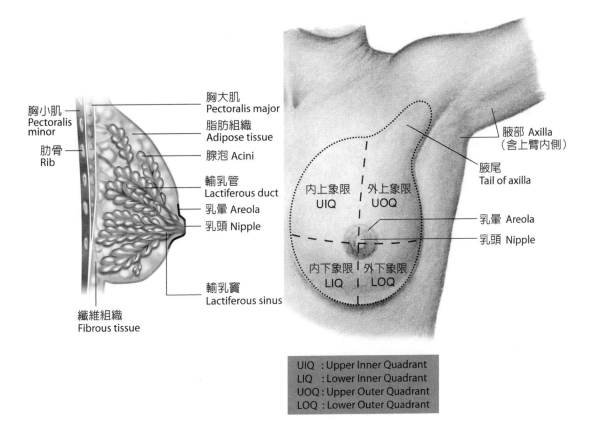

內上象限 UIQ
外上象限 UOQ
內下象限 LIQ
外下象限 LOQ

胸小肌 Pectoralis minor
肋骨 Rib
胸大肌 Pectoralis major
脂肪組織 Adipose tissue
腺泡 Acini
輸乳管 Lactiferous duct
乳暈 Areola
乳頭 Nipple
輸乳竇 Lactiferous sinus
纖維組織 Fibrous tissue
腋部 Axilla（含上臂內側）
腋尾 Tail of axilla
乳暈 Areola
乳頭 Nipple

UIQ : Upper Inner Quadrant
LIQ : Lower Inner Quadrant
UOQ : Upper Outer Quadrant
LOQ : Lower Outer Quadrant

Case Information 個案資訊

Breast Cancer [brɛst ˈkænsɚ] 乳癌

1. **Causes**: Excessive estrogen stimulation to breast tissue or genetic mutation.

2. **Signs & Symptoms**: Breast lump/mass, abnormal discharge from the nipple or skin and lymphadenopathy in the axillary region.

3. **Care**:

   (1) Surgery and chemotherapy.

   (2) Provide psychological support.

   (3) Treat areas of discomfort.

   (4) Drain the post-op wound.

   (5) Avoid lifting heavy objects on the affected side.

   (6) Massage the affected side to prevent lymphatic edema.

   (7) Return for follow-up exams.

Admission Assessment　入院評估

49

Ms. Kao visited the hospital to have her breast tumor examined.

高小姐因為乳房腫塊前來醫院診治。

N: Nurse　**P:** Patient

N: Good morning, Ms. Kao. What is your major concern today?

高小姐早安。今天你最主要的問題是什麼呢？

P: I have a **mass**[1] on my right breast.

我右側的乳房有腫塊。

N: Does it feel **elastic**[2] or firm?

是很有彈性的還是堅實的呢？

P: I think it feels a little bit firm.

我想它有一點堅實。

N: Are there distinct **margins**[3] surrounding the mass?

腫塊周圍的邊緣清楚嗎？

P: No, but I can feel where it is most **prominent**[4].

不，但我能感受到最凸出之處。

N: OK. Does it increase in size during your menstrual period?

好的。它會隨著你的月經週期而增大嗎？

P: No, it doesn't.

不會。

N: Is it painful?

會感到疼痛嗎？

P: No, my entire breast just feels painful during my period.

沒有，我只有在月經週期時會感覺整個乳房都在痛。

N: Have you seen any **discharge**[5] from the nipple?

你有看見乳頭的分泌物嗎？

P: Yes, sometimes.

有時候有。

N: Have you noticed what the discharge looks like? Is it bloody or milky?

你有留意那是怎樣的分泌物嗎？是血紅色的還是乳白色的呢？

P: It's a little bit pinkish.

它有一點粉紅色。

N: How long have you noticed this mass?

你留意到這個腫塊有多久了？

P: About half a year. Initially, it was small but later grew in size within the last month.

大約半年吧，起初它很小，之後在上個月變得比較大。

N: OK, have you ever taken oral **contraceptives**?

好的，你有服用口服避孕藥嗎？

P: Yes, I have taken them for about 2 years.

有的，我大約服用了 2 年。

N: Has anyone from your family ever had breast cancer?

你有家人罹患乳癌嗎？

P: Yes, my grandmother died of breast cancer.

有的，我的祖母死於乳癌。

N: Alright. The doctor will be in to see you in a bit and arrange any **necessary**[6] examinations.

好的。醫師會進來看你並且幫你安排必要的檢查。

P: I see. Thanks a lot.

我明白。多謝。

Nursing Notes　護理記錄

C/O right breast mass. No pain or apparent discharge from the nipple. Family history of breast cancer. Waiting for doctor's examination.

主訴右側乳房有腫塊，無察覺疼痛或乳頭有明顯分泌物。有乳癌家族史。等待醫師診察。

Vocabulary and Sentence Examples　字彙與例句

1. mass [mæs]
   (n.) 腫塊

   He felt a mass around his inguinal region.
   他在他的鼠蹊部感覺到腫塊。

2. elastic [ɪˈlæstɪk]
   (adj.) 有彈性的

   Rubber is an elastic substance.
   橡膠是一種有彈性的物質。

3. margin [ˈmardʒɪn]
   (n.) 邊緣

   Watch out for the sharp margins of the desk, or you'll get a bruise.　小心桌子尖銳的邊緣，否則你將會瘀傷。

4. prominent [ˈpramənənt]
   (adj.) 明顯的

   The mountain is most prominent when viewed from the plains.　當你從平原眺望時，這座山是最為明顯的。

5. discharge [dɪsˈtʃardʒ]
   (n.) 分泌物

   There must be something wrong if you can see discharge coming from your ears.
   如果耳朵有分泌物流出來，那一定有什麼不對勁。

6. necessary [ˈnɛsəˌsɛrɪ]
   (adj.) 必要的

   Air and water are necessary substances to sustain life.
   空氣和水分是維持生命的必要物質。

Terminology 術語

1. contraceptive [ˌkantrəˈsɛptɪv] 避孕藥

Pre-Operative Care　術前照護

50

The resulst from the breast mass biopsy showed a cancer leison on the right breast. This operation worried Ms. Kao.

乳房腫塊活體切片檢查的結果顯示右側乳房有乳癌病灶，高小姐對於手術十分擔心。

N: Good afternoon, Ms. Kao. Are you feeling OK?

高小姐午安。你還好嗎？

P: No. The doctor told me that I have breast cancer and must receive an operation for treatment.

我不好。醫師說我罹患乳癌，而且要動手術來治療。

N: This is bad news. However, since we detected it early, we're more likely to cure it.

的確是個壞消息。不過由於早期發現，所以治癒率相當高。

P: I understand, but I'm still very worried.

我了解。但我還是很擔心。

N: Can you tell me what your major concern is?

P: First, I'm worried about how this will affect my physical appearance. I don't want my breasts to become **asymmetrical**. This would be ugly.

N: In addition to your tumor **resection**[1], the **plastic**[2] **surgeon**[3] will **reconstruct**[4] your breast.

P: Oh, the doctor mentioned this as well. I'm just so nervous. I forgot he told me this already.

N: It's OK. Do you have any other concerns about your treatment?

P: Yeah. I don't understand why I have to receive chemotherapy after the operation.

N: Well, even though your breast cancer is in its early stages, it is **recommend**[5] by doctors that patients receive chemotherapy to reduce the recurrence rate.

P: I see. Should I take note of anything before the operation?

N: Now, I will remind you something that you should aware before your surgery.

P: OK. That's what I want to know.

N: Firstly, the doctor may order a preoperative shower. You may take a shower on the night before the surgery.

P: OK. That sounds good.

N: Secondly, an enema may be ordered. It is able to clear your bowel to make the surgery goes smoothly.

P: Will an enema be uncomfortable?

N: May be or maybe not. An enema will make your bowel move, just like to go to the toilet.

P: Oh, I see.

可以告訴我你在擔心什麼嗎？

首先，我擔心它對外觀的影響。我不想乳房變得不對稱，這樣很醜。

除了腫瘤切除術之外，整形外科醫師會幫你重建乳房。

噢，醫師也講過。我太緊張了。忘記他已經跟我講過了。

沒關係。你對治療還有任何疑問嗎？

有的，我不懂為何在手術之後要接受化療。

嗯，即使是早期乳癌，醫師們會建議病人接受化療以降低復發的機會。

我懂了。那我在手術之前要注意什麼？

現在，我來跟你說明一下手術前需要注意的事項。

好，那正是我想知道的。

首先，醫生也許會囑咐術前需要洗澡，在手術的前一晚，你需要洗個澡。

好，聽起來不錯。

再來，灌腸可能也是需要的，這會讓你的腸子清乾淨，讓手術更順利。

灌腸會不舒服嗎？

也許會，也許不會，灌腸是讓你的腸子蠕動，就像要去上廁所一樣。

喔！我知道了

N: In addition, you will need to follow food and fluid restrictions. That means have nothing by mouth starting at midnight on the night before surgery.	除此之外，你也會有食物及水分的限制，那表示手術的前一晚，午夜之後不能吃任何東西。
P: OK. It is not difficult for me.	這對我來講不難。
N: Finally, you need to take off all of your accessories, including, rings, neckless, watch etc.	最後，你需要拿掉所有的飾品，包括：戒指、項鍊、手錶等等。
P: That's no problem. I already take them off except watch. I will take it off before the surgery.	沒問題，除了手錶以外，我已經把它們拿下了，我會在手術前把手錶拿下來。
N: That's all I want to tell you. Do you have any questions?	這就是我要說的，你有任何問題嗎？
P: No, Thanks a lot. By the way, please remind me again nothing by mouth starting at midnight, I am afraid that I forget.	沒有，非常感謝，喔，對了，請你午夜前再提醒我一次不要吃東西，我怕我會忘記。
N: No problem, I will.	沒問題，我會的。

Nursing Notes 護理記錄

Right breast cancer lesion found. Patient was educated about **mastectomy**. Well accepted. Mastectomy arranged **CM**. Told to be NPO starting at midnight.

發現右側乳房的癌症病灶。衛教病人乳房切除術相關事項。乳房切除術安排於明晨。告知病人午夜開始禁食。

Vocabulary and Sentence Examples 字彙與例句

1. resection [rɪˈsɛkʃən] (n.) 切除術	Resection is a type of surgical procedure. 切除術是外科手術的一種。
2. plastic [ˈplæstɪk] (adj.) 整形的	Plastic surgery can be used for restructional and cosmetic purposes. 整形手術可被用於重建及美容的目的。
3. surgeon [ˈsɜdʒən] (n.) 外科醫師	The surgeon removed his stomach tumor. 外科醫師摘除他的胃腫瘤。
4. reconstruct [ˌrikənˈstrʌkt] (v.) 重建	They reconstructed their hometown after the terrible earth-quake. 他們在可怕的地震後重建家園。
5. recommend [ˌrɛkəˈmɛnd] (v.) 建議；推薦	The doctor did not recommend this operation for you. 醫師建議你不要接受手術。

Terminology 術語

1. asymmetrical [ˌesɪˈmɛtrɪkḷ] 不對稱的
2. mastectomy [mæsˈtɛktəmɪ] 乳房切除術
3. CM　明晨（*cras mane*，意指 coming morning）

Post-Operative Care　術後照護

51

Ms. Kao returned to the general ward after the operation.

N: How are you feeling so far?

P: The wound is a bit painful and over the last hour I have felt nauseous and almost vomited twice.

N: Take it easy. These must be side effects from your analgesic. Here are your pain killer pills, they are able to relieve your pain. Also, the antiemetic tablets will help to relieve uncomfortable symptoms.

P: That's great. Thank you so much.

N: The draining tube will drain the fluid around your wound. Your wound should be clean without pus and feel no heat. In addition, the drainage may be red within the next few days but will turn clear. If the wound or the drainage becomes pus-like or thick, please notify us right away.

P: Alright, I'll observe these changes. How long will I stay in the hospital?

N: You can go home after 4~5 days and then come back for a follow-up exam next week. The doctor will assess if the wound has healed and figure out a chemotherapy schedule for you.

P: I see. Can I begin to eat now?

N: Do you have already passed the flatus (air)?

P: Yes, I did about 20 minutes ago.

N: In that case, of course you can. Frequent and small meals will help decrease your nausea. Also, you should eat foods with plenty of vitamin C and

高小姐於術後回到一般病房。

到目前為止你感覺如何？

傷口有一點痛。而且我在 1 小時內有兩次感到噁心及嘔吐。

放輕鬆。這是止痛劑的副作用。這是你的止痛藥，它會讓你的疼痛好一點，還有，這是你的止吐藥會讓你不舒服的症狀好一些。

太好了，非常感謝。

引流管將從傷口附近把液體引流出來。你的傷口應該要是乾淨的、沒有膿、沒有感到灼熱，除此之外，引流液在頭幾天會有點紅，之後會變清澈。若變得濃稠或有膿狀物，請立刻告知我們。

好的，我會觀察引流液的變化。對了，我大概要在醫院待多久？

4~5 天後你就可以回家，然後在下週回診追蹤。醫師會評估傷口是否癒合並安排你的化療時間表。

我明白。我現在能吃東西了嗎？

你已經排氣了嗎？

是的，大概 20 分鐘前。

如果是這樣的話，你可以吃東西。少量多餐能協助你減少噁心感。此外，攝取富含維生素 C 和蛋白質的食物以幫助傷口

protein to help your wound heal, like vegetables, fruits, soybeans and dairy products.

P: That sounds good.

N: And don't carry heavy objects with your right arm. This can **exacerbate**[1] the wound and cause fluid to **accumulate**[2], preventing the wound from healing.

P: Thanks for the instructions. I'll keep this in mind.

N: You're welcome. Let me show you how to massaging your right arm. Start from the distal end and make your way to the proximal site, like from the hand to the forearm and then to the arm. Let's start by massaging your right arm now to prevent edema from forming.

P: Thanks for your **demonstration**[3]. I'll try to do this myself.

N: In addition, after surgery, be sure to follow the recommendations to protect against surgical site infection.

P: What do I need to be aware?

N: These are:

1. Ask your doctors or nurses to clean their hands before they examine you or check your wound.

2. Do not allow visitors to touch the surgical wound or drainage.

3. Ask family and friends to clean their hands before and after visiting you.

4. Make sure you understand how to care for your wound before you leave the hospital. I will show you how to do it tomorrow.

5. Always clean your hands before and after caring for your wound.

6. If you have any symptoms of an infection, such as redness and pain at the surgery site, drainage, or fever, contact your doctor immediately.

癒合。譬如說，蔬菜、水果、大豆及乳製品。

聽起來不錯。

而且不要用右手提取重物。這會加劇傷口液體的堆積，影響傷口癒合。

謝謝指導，我會謹記在心的。

不客氣，讓我來示範如何按摩你的右手臂。先從遠端朝近端的方向，譬如說，從手開始，到前臂，然後是上臂。那我們現在就來按摩你的右手臂，避免水腫的發生。

謝謝示範。我會照著做的。

除此之外，手術後請遵循下列的建議，保護不要受到感染。

我應該要注意什麼呢？

有下列幾項：

1. 要求你的醫生、護理師在檢查的傷口前先洗手。

2. 不要讓訪客碰你的傷口或引流管。

3. 要求你的家人和朋友在探訪你之前洗手。

4. 在離開醫院前，確定你知道如何處理你的傷口，我明天會告訴你如何做。

5. 照顧你的傷口前、後一定要洗手。

6. 如果有任何感染的徵象，例如：在手術部位。或引流管發紅或疼痛，或者發燒，立刻聯絡你的醫師。

P: Thank you very much for your advice.　非常感謝你的建議。

N: You're welcome.　不客氣。

Nursing Notes　護理記錄

Drainage: redness, small amount. Feels nauseous. Antiemetic given. Taught to massage right upper extremity and avoid lifting heavy objects with right arm.

引流液：紅色，少量。病人感到噁心，給予止吐劑。教導病人按摩右側上肢並避免用右臂提重物。

Tips on Writing

病人狀況的描述法：形容詞(adj.)與名詞(n.)的轉換使用

nauseous→nausea

dizzy→dizziness

full→fullness

例：病人感到頭暈　→　(The patient) Feels dizzy.＝(The patient) Has dizziness.

Vocabulary and Sentence Examples　字彙與例句

1. exacerbate (v.) 使加劇　Smoking exacerbates asthmatic attack.
   [ɪgˋzæsəˌbet]　吸菸會加劇氣喘發作。

2. accumulate (v.) 累積　Learning is a process of accumlating and integrating
   [əˋkjumjəˌlet]　knowledge.　學習是一種知識積累和整合的過程。

3. demonstration (n.) 示範　This exercise demonstration is for the elders.
   [ˌdɛmənˋstreʃən]　這項運動示範是為了老年人而做的。

Terminology 術語

1. analgesic [ˌænælˋdʒizɪk] 止痛劑

2. drainage [ˋdrenɪdʒ] 引流液

3. distal [ˋdɪstḷ] 遠端的

4. proximal [ˋprɑksəmḷ] 近端的

More Information

1. 問診的常用句子

(1) Are you feelling pain here?
你會感到乳房疼痛嗎？

(2) Can you localize the site of maximal pain?
你能指出最痛的位置嗎？

(3) Does the level of pain change during your menstrual period?
疼痛程度的變化有隨月經週期而波動嗎？

(4) Does the pain become more severe when you apply pressure or touch it?
按壓乳房時疼痛有否加劇？

(5) Where is the mass you've palpated?
你摸到的腫塊在哪裡？

(6) Does the size of the lump alter between your period?
腫塊大小會隨月經週期改變嗎？
Is it firm or elastic?
硬塊是硬的還是有彈性的？
How long have you noticed this lump?
你留意到乳房腫塊多久了？

(7) What does the discharge from your nipple look like?
乳頭分泌物的特徵是什麼？
What about the color of your nipple discharge?
乳頭分泌物的顏色是什麼？
How does it smell?
（分泌物）聞起來的氣味如何？
What does it look like?
（分泌物）看起來像什麼？

(8) Has the mass/lump grown in size over the last month?
一個月內，腫塊有增大嗎？

(9) Have any of your relatives had breast cancer, in particular your mother or sister?　你有親戚罹患乳癌嗎？尤其是你的母親或姐妹。

(10) Have you used oral contraceptives before?
你以前有服用過口服避孕藥嗎？
How long have you taken them?
服用（口服避孕藥）多久了？

Exercise 小試身手

● Choose the Correct Answer

( ) 1. There was a big _____ on his liver. (A)mass (B)mess (C)muss (D)miss 他的肝臟有個大腫塊。

( ) 2. Rubber is a kind of _____ product. (A)reluctance (B)elastic (C)plastic (D)compliance 橡膠是一種有彈性的物質。

( ) 3. The tree was very _____ within the plains. (A)prominent (B)dominant (C)dormant (D)protestant 這棵樹在平原中特別醒目。

( ) 4. Oxygen is _____ for human beings. (A)exposure (B)essential (C)element (D)factorial 氧氣對人類來說是不可或缺的。

( ) 5. The _____ was good at investigating. (A)protective (B)additive (C)constructive (D)detective 這位偵探善於抽絲剝繭。

● Fill in the Blanks

1. Because of _____ _____ , she paid a large amount of money to the _____ _____ . 由於美容因素，她花大錢找整形外科醫師幫忙。

2. Because this building is quite _____ , the architect _____ to _____ it. 因為這棟建築物十分不對稱，建築師決定重建它。

3. Whenever you feel _____ , I _____ you take some _____. 當你感到噁心時，我建議你服用止吐劑。

4. Strenuous _____ will _____ your _____ _____ . 劇烈運動會使你胸痛加劇。

5. _____ _____ in the lower _____ of patients with congestive _____ _____ . 鬱血性心衰竭患者的下肢有液體堆積。

● Simplify Nursing Notes

1. Feels painful in the abdomen.（改寫成名詞主訴）

   _____

2. Had backache.（改寫成形容詞句型）

   _____

3. Feels distended in the abdomen.（改寫成名詞主訴）

   _____

4. Has nausea.（改寫成形容詞句型）

   _____

5. Feels edematous in the legs.（改寫成名詞主訴）

   _____

● Translation

1. 腫塊是堅實的還是很有彈性的呢？

   _____

2. 你有看見乳頭的分泌物嗎？

   _____

3. 即使是早期乳癌，醫師們會建議病人接受化療以降低復發的機會。

   _____

4. 這是止痛劑的副作用。

   _____

5. 不要用右手提取重物。這會加劇傷口液體的堆積，影響傷口癒合。

   _____

Gynecology Unit
婦 科

Learning Goals 學習目標

1. Assessing female patients with abdo-minal pain
2. Collecting information about patient's menstrual cycle
3. Instructing the use of patient control-led analgesia (PCA)
4. Providing health education to patients

Outline 本章大綱

- The Components of the Female Repro-ductive System　女性生殖系統的組成
- Case Information: Ovarian Cancer
  個案資訊：卵巢癌
- Admission Assessment　入院評估
- Hospitalization　住院療護
- Discharge Instructions　出院衛教

Medical English for
Healthcare Professionals

The Components of the Female Reproductive System 女性生殖系統的組成

Several organs make up the female reproductive system, including the **uterus**[1], where the **fetus**[2] develops and grows; the ovary, where the **ovum**[3] is produced and matures; the **fallopian tube**[4], where the ovum meets the **sperm**[5]; the **vagina**[6], through which the fetus is delivered. These are all very important for maintaining pregnancy in women. Their function and structures are highly dependent on the levels of serum estrogen.

The **uterine**[7] structure changes during every menstrual cycle. Its **endometrium**[8] grows in the **follicular phase**[9] of the menstrual cycle and further becomes mature in the **luteal phase**[10] for the conception of a fertilized egg. If there's no fertilized ovum, the thickened endometrium will breakdown and will be eliminated through the vagina. The menstrual cycle occurs every month starting from puberty until the age of forty or fifty. As one ages, the number of available ova decreases. Menopause then occurs, ending the menstrual cycles.

幾個器官構成女性生殖系統，包含胎兒生長發育之處的子宮、卵子產生和成熟之處的卵巢、精子和卵子相遇處的輸卵管、以及胎兒出生時所經過的陰道。這些器官對女性的孕程都很重要，而其功能和構造受到血清中的雌激素濃度而影響。

子宮結構隨月經週期改變，子宮內膜在濾泡期生長並且在黃體期成熟以便接受受精卵。如果沒有受精卵，增厚的子宮內膜便會剝落並從陰道排出。月經週期每月循環始於青春期，結束於 40 或 50 歲左右。年齡愈增，卵巢內可用的卵子量愈減。更年期來臨時，月經就不再來潮。

Terminology 術語

1. uterus [ˈjutərəs] 子宮
2. fetus [ˈfitəs] 胎兒
3. ovum [ˈovəm] 卵子
4. fallopian tube [fəˈlopɪən tjub] 輸卵管
5. sperm [spɜm] 精子
6. vagina [vəˈdʒaɪnə] 陰道
7. uterine [ˈjutərɪn] 子宮的
8. endometrium [ˌɛndəˈmitrɪəm] 子宮內膜
9. follicular phase [fəˈlɪkjulə fez] 濾泡期
10. luteal phase [ˈlutɪəl fez] 黃體期

Case Information 個案資訊

Ovarian cancer [oˈvɛrɪən ˈkænsə] 卵巢癌

1. **Causes**: Excessive ovulation, or genetic mutation.
2. **Symptoms & Signs**:
   (1) Abnormal vaginal bleeding or post-menopausal bleeding
   (2) Abdominal distension
   (3) Abdominal pain
   (4) GI discomfort
   (5) Difficulty urinating

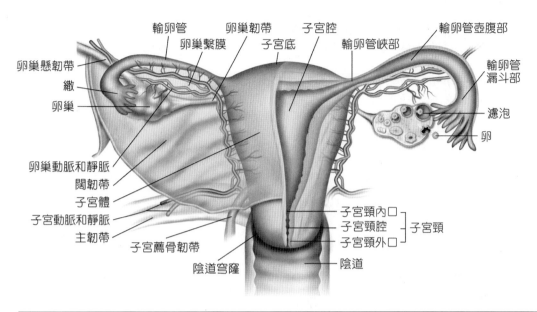

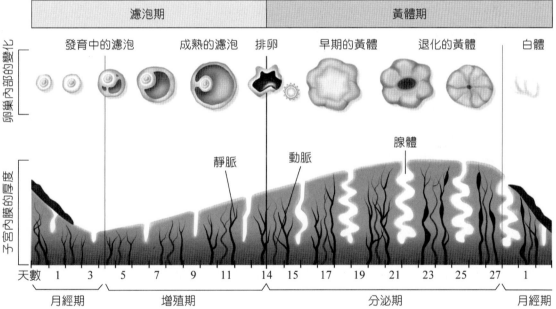

Case Information 個案資訊

3. **Care**:
   (1) Surgery and chemotherapy.
   (2) Provide psychological support.
   (3) Treat any discomfort.
   (4) Drain the post-op wound.
   (5) High calcium diet post-op.
   (6) Avoid strenuous exercise within the first 3 months after the operation.
   (7) Teach patients how to care for the port-A catheter.

Ms. Wang was admitted because of sustained abdominal pain.

王小姐因持續腹痛而入院。

N: Nurse　**P:** Patient

N: Good morning, Ms. Wang. What brought you to the hospital today?

王小姐早安。今天你為何會到醫院來呢？

P: I've been having abdominal pain that's been really **bothering**[1] me.

我一直有相當困擾我的腹痛。

N: How long has it been?

它持續多久了？

P: Since 2 months ago. In the beginning, I felt dullness and fullness around my **navel**[2]. I initially thought it was caused by poor **digestion**[3], so I took some antacids for it.

持續 2 個月了。起初只是肚臍周圍的悶脹感。我剛開始以為是消化不良引起的，所以我服用了一些制酸劑。

N: Did you feel better afterwards?

服用之後有改善嗎？

P: No, the discomfort continued and became worse. I went to the clinic and then was referred to the **gynecologist** here.

沒有，不舒服的感覺持續而且變嚴重，我去診所就醫然後被轉診給這裡的婦科醫師。

N: OK. Has your **menstrual period** been regular recently?

好的。近來你的月經週期規則嗎？

P: Yes, it has been regular recently.

是的，近來都規則。

N: Well, did the doctor tell you the results from the **ultrasound** examination?

嗯，醫師有告訴你超音波檢查的結果嗎？

P: Yes. There's a tumor in my right ovary. He suggested that I receive an operation.

是的。我右側卵巢有個腫瘤。他建議我接受手術。

N: Yes. The operation will remove the tumor and the department of **pathology** can identify whether it is **benign**[4] or **malignant**[5].

是的。手術將會取出腫瘤然後由病理科鑑別它是良性的或是惡性的。

P: Got it. What time will the operation be?

我明白了。何時要動手術呢？

N: It is scheduled at 11 a.m. tomorrow, so don't eat and drink anything after midnight.

預定於明早 11 點進行。你午夜後必須禁食。

P: I see. Thank you.

我知道。謝謝你。

Nursing Notes 護理記錄

C/O abdominal fullness and discomfort. Symptoms worsened to abdominal pain over the last 3 months. No change in the interval or amount of menses. Ultrasound showed right ovarian tumor. Operation arranged at 11 a.m. tomorrow. Told to be NPO after midnight.

病人主訴腹脹和不適。症狀在最近三個月惡化為腹痛。月經的週期和量都沒有改變。超音波顯示右側卵巢腫瘤。手術安排在明早 11 點。告知病人午夜後禁食。

Tips on Writing

1. 否定句的連接詞：以 or 來連接，例：The patient had no change in her menstrual period. / The patient has not had sex within the last 6 months.
併為：Has no change in her menstrual period **or** had no sex within the last 6 months.

2. 描述檢查或病史的陰性反應：Have/Has no＋symptoms 或 Without＋symptoms，例：The patient has no cough, sputum production or sore throat.
→Has no cough, sputum production, or sore throat. 或 Without cough, sputum production or sore throat.

Vocabulary and Sentence Examples 字彙與例句

1. bother [ˈbɑðɚ] (v.) 使擾人、困擾	The noise is really bothering me. 噪音十分擾人。
2. navel [ˈnevl̩] (n.) 肚臍	Navel is the more common term for *umbilicus*. "Navel"是"umbilicus"（肚臍）的一般用詞。
3. digestion [daɪˈʤɛstʃən] (n.) 消化	He has poor digestion. 他患有消化不良。
4. benign [bɪˈnaɪn] (adj.) 良性的	Uterine myoma is a benign tumor. 子宮肌瘤是良性腫瘤。
5. malignant [məˈlɪgnənt] (adj.) 惡性的	Colon cancer is quite malignant. 結腸癌相當惡性。

Terminology 術語

1. gynecologist [ˌgaɪnəˈkɑləʤɪst] 婦科醫師
2. menstrual period 月經週期 [ˈmɛnstruəl ˈpɪrɪəd]
3. ultrasound [ˈʌltrəˌsaʊnd] 超音波
4. pathology [pəˈθɑləʤɪ] 病理學

Hospitalization 住院療護

Ms. Wang's operation was completed, and she was returned to the ward from the **recovery**[1] *room.*

手術結束,王小姐從恢復室被送回到病房。

N: The operation was performed and went quite smoothly. Your tumor was **excised**[2] with your ovaries, fallopian tubes and uterus.

手術進行得十分順利,腫瘤跟你的雙側卵巢、輸卵管及子宮一併切除了。

P: I know. What are these tubes for?

我知道。這些管子是做什麼用的?

N: They aid in draining the discharge from your wound. The nurse **on duty**[3] will change the drainage bag every 8 hours.

它們協助引流出來自傷口的分泌物。值班護理師每 8 小時會更換一次引流袋。

P: When will you take them out?

你們何時會把它們拔除?

N: We'll take them out when the drainage is less than 50 c.c. per day. Meanwhile, the color of the fluid should be clear without pus or blood.

當引流液每天少於 50 毫升且顏色清澈,不含膿或血時,我們就會拔除它們。

P: I see. What is this tube for?

我了解。這條管子是做什麼用的?

N: Since we removed your **pelvic**[4] organs, your bladder function will temporarily be affected. That urinary catheter will help you urinate. We'll remove it when your bladder function returns to normal. It will take 2~3 days.

因為移除骨盆器官會暫時影響膀胱功能,導尿管能協助你排尿。我們會在你的膀胱功能恢復時移除它。這需要 2~3 天的時間。

P: Got it. Thanks for the explanation.

我明白了,謝謝說明。

N: You're welcome. During the next few days, please stay in bed. Try to breathe deeply to **improve** your lung function.

不客氣。這幾天請務必臥床休息。你可以嘗試深呼吸來增進肺部功能。

P: But it hurts when I take a deep breath.

但當我深呼吸時便會感到疼痛。

N: This machine, called a **PCA**, will give you pain-killers whenever you press this button.

這台機器叫做病人自控式止痛器,當你按下按鈕,它會給你止痛劑。

N: Now, try to take a deep breath. Are you still feeling pain?

現在再嘗試深呼吸。你還感覺痛嗎?

P: Not at all. This is a great design for people like me.

不痛了。對我們而言真是極佳的設計。

N: That's right. If you still feel any discomfort, or your drainage becomes bloody, please call us for help.

P: I will, thank you very much.

沒錯。如果你仍感不適，或者引流液變成血色，請找我們協助。

我會的，非常謝謝你。

Nursing Notes　護理記錄

Returned to the ward from the recovery room at 4:00 p.m. Draining tube patent. Drainage light yellow. 50 c.c. in the left draining bag. Foley catheter inserted. IV drip with fluid supplement given as Dr. Wu instructed.

於下午 4 點從恢復室回到病房。引流管暢通，引流液淡黃色。左側引流袋有 50 毫升引流液。導尿管已放置。依照吳醫師的醫囑給予靜脈滴注輸液。

Vocabulary and Sentence Examples　字彙與例句

1. recovery [rɪˈkʌvərɪ]
   (n.) 復原

   Recovery from his leg fracture was quite fast.
   他的大腿骨折復原得很快。

2. excise [ɪkˈsaɪz]
   (v.) 切除

   The skin tag was excised by the dermatologist.
   皮膚贅物被皮膚科醫師切除了。

3. on duty [an djutɪ]
   值班

   I go on duty starting 9 a.m. everyday.
   我每天早上 9 點值班。

4. pelvic [ˈpɛlvɪk]
   (adj.) 骨盆的

   The pelvic organs include the uterus, ovary, fallopian tube, vagina, ureter, bladder, urethra and rectum.　骨盆器官包括子宮、卵巢、輸卵管、陰道、輸尿管、膀胱、尿道及直腸。

Terminology 術語

1. PCA ＝ patient-controlled analgesia　病人自控式止痛器
   [ˈpeʃənt kənˈtrold ænælˈʤiziə]

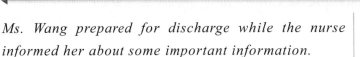

Ms. Wang prepared for discharge while the nurse informed her about some important information.

王小姐將要出院了。護理師告訴她一些重要的事情。

N: You can go home after we remove these tubes. Congratulations!

我們移除這些管子之後你就可以出院了。恭喜！

P: Thanks for all your care.

謝謝你們的照顧。

N: You're welcome. The **port-A catheter** was inserted around your right shoulder. You will receive **chemotherapy** via this route.

不客氣。port-A 導管裝設在你的右肩，你將從這管路接受化學治療。

P: When should I come back for a follow-up exam?

我何時要回診追蹤呢？

N: Next Wednesday. The first dose of chemotherapy will be **administered**[1] at the same time.

下週三。第一次化學治療也會同時給予。

P: I see. Anything else?

我知道了。還有嗎？

N: Due to[2] the operation, you no longer have **endogenous**[3] estrogen to prevent the loss of calcium from your body. For this reason, you have to eat foods higher in calcium.

由於手術之故，你已經沒有內生性的雌激素來預防體內的鈣質流失。因此你要攝取富含鈣質的食物。

P: What kind of foods should I eat?

我應吃什麼食物呢？

N: In addition to **dairy products**[4], you should eat tofu, Chinese cabbage, and drink soybean milk.

除了乳製品以外，你還可以吃豆腐、大白菜和喝豆漿。

P: What kind of exercises can I do?

那我可以做什麼樣的運動？

N: All strenuous sports should be avoided for the next 3 months, including jogging, jumping and riding bikes or scooters. Mild exercise is **permissible**[5]. For example, speed walking.

3 個月內你必須避免所有的劇烈運動，包括慢跑、跳躍、騎腳踏車、騎機車等。溫和的運動是可以的，例如快步走。

P: I'll try to remember this. Anything else?

我會記住的。還有其他的嗎？

N: Avoid having sex for the next 6 weeks.

6 週內不要有性行為。

P: OK, I'll keep this in mind.

好的，我會謹記在心。

Nursing Notes　護理記錄

Draining tube removed. Will be discharged per Dr. Wu's order. Suggested no strenuous exercise. Reminded to return for follow-up as well as chemotherapy.

引流管已移除。將依據吳醫師的醫囑讓病人出院。建議避免劇烈運動。提醒回診追蹤和化學治療。

Vocabulary and Sentence Examples　字彙與例句

1. administer [əd'mɪnəstə] (v.) 給予；提供	The nurse administered the medication to the patient as instructed.　護理師依醫囑給予病人藥物。
2. due to ['dju tʊ] 由於	Her fatigue is due to her cold. 她會覺得累是因為她感冒了。
3. endogenous [ɛn'dɑdʒənəs] (adj.) 內生的	There are several kinds of endogenous analgesics in our brain.　我們的大腦中有數種內生性的止痛劑。
4. dairy product ['dɛrɪ 'prɑdəkt] 乳製品	Dairy products include milk powder, milk, yogurt, ice cream and chocolate. 乳製品包括奶粉、牛奶、優酪乳、冰淇淋及巧克力。
5. permissible [pə'mɪsəbl̩] (adj.) 可允許的	Walking around after the operation was permissible to help strengthen her muscles and prevent her from falling.　術後走動對她而言是被允許的，因為可以強化她的肌力並預防跌倒。

Terminology 術語

1. port-A catheter [port e 'kæθɪtə]　port-A 導管
2. chemotherapy [ˌkimə'θɛrəpɪ]　化學治療

More Information

1. 病史的問診要點

(1) Have you had shortened/lengthened intervals of bleeding between periods?
你月經週期的出血曾有縮短或延長嗎？

(2) Have you used pads or tampons within the last 24 hours?
你在 24 小時內使用過護墊或衛生棉嗎？

(3) Have you found blood clots within your menses?
在經血中你曾發現血塊嗎？

(4) Do you regularly take contraceptives?
你有規律地服用避孕藥嗎？

(5) Do you have abdominal pain?
你有腹痛嗎？
What's the timing, location, duration of the pain?
疼痛何時發生？在何處？持續多久？

(6) What's the color/amount/odor of your vaginal discharge?
你的陰道分泌物的顏色／量／氣味如何？

(7) At what age did your first begin to menstruate?
你初經是幾歲來？

(8) When was your last normal menstrual period?
你最後一次正常的月經是何時？

Exercise 小試身手

● Choose the Correct Answer

(　) 1. The air pollution around the highway is really ＿＿＿＿＿＿ .
(A)bothersome　(B)disgust　(C)ugly　(D)bad
高速公路附近的空氣污染實在很擾人。

(　) 2. The stomach is the major organ responsible for ＿＿＿＿ .　(A)disgusting
(B)digestion　(C)diagnosis　(D)diffusion　胃是我們體內主要的消化場所。

(　) 3. The concert is ＿＿＿＿＿ on next Monday.　(A)schooled　(B)scholar
(C)schedule　(D)scheduled　音樂會預定在下週一。

(　) 4. This is a rather ＿＿＿＿＿ disease and not worth worrying about.
(A)beware　(B)benign　(C)best　(D)beast
這是一種相當良性的疾病，不值得擔心。

(　) 5. The economy is only ＿＿＿＿＿ undergoing depression due to the
shortage of oil.　(A)slightly　(B)shortly　(C)temporarily　(D)inevitably
經濟只是由於石油短缺而暫時不景氣。

● Fill in the Blanks

1. The doctor ＿＿＿＿＿ an operation on him to ＿＿＿＿＿ the ＿＿＿＿＿ from
his liver.　醫師為他進行手術以切除肝臟的腫瘤。

2. His ＿＿＿＿＿ from ＿＿＿＿＿ injuries will take a long time and may leave
＿＿＿＿＿ impairments.
燒傷的傷口復原需要花很多時間，而且還會留下功能性缺損。

3. We should be more ＿＿＿＿＿ to those ＿＿＿＿＿ or ＿＿＿＿＿ .
對待受傷或生病的人應該要更體貼。

4. The split of large molecules into smaller ones is a ＿＿＿＿＿ process for
＿＿＿＿＿ of ＿＿＿＿＿ .　將大分子分解為小分子是吸收營養的必要步驟。

5. What's the amount of your vaginal ＿＿＿＿＿ ?　你陰道分泌物的量如何？

● Simplify Nursing Notes

1. The patient didn't have a fever.
   The patient didn't have a sore throat.

   _____

2. The patient had no abnormal heart rhythms.
   The patient had no cardiac murmurs.

   _____

3. The patient didn't have difficulty urinating.
   The patient didn't have pain during urination.

   _____

4. The patient didn't have ocular deviation.
   The patient didn't have dilated pupils.

   _____

5. The patient hasn't had any irregular menstrual periods.
   The patient hasn't had sex recently.

   _____

● Translation

1. 近來你的月經週期規則嗎？

   _____

2. 導尿管能協助你排尿。

   _____

3. 你可以嘗試深呼吸來增進肺部功能。

   _____

4. 這台機器叫做病人自控式止痛器，當你按下按鈕，它會給你止痛劑。

   _____

5. port-A 導管裝設在你的右肩，你將從這管路接受化學治療。

   _____

解答

Obstetrics Unit
產　科

Learning Goals 學習目標

1. Approaching pregnant patients
2. Assessing the condition of pregnant women ready for delivery
3. Providing health education to patients

Outline 本章大綱

- The Fetal Development and Delivery
  胎兒成長與分娩
- Case Information: Normal Spontaneous Delivery (NSD)　個案資訊：正常自然生產
- Admission Assessment　入院評估
- Hospitalization　住院療護
- Discharge Instructions　出院衛教

Medical English for
Healthcare Professionals

The Fetal Development and Delivery 胎兒成長與分娩

56

The fertilization process begins when a sperm encounters and joins the ovum within the **ampulla**[1] of the fallopian tube. This process results in the formation of a new cell called a "fertilized egg."

After fertilization, the fertilized egg moves from the fallopian tube to the uterus, where it fuses with the endometrium, the wall of the uterus, and begins to grow in size. The interface between the fetus and uterus is formed and called the **placenta**[2]. This serves as an exchange platform between the fetus and the mother. While the fetus receives oxygen and nutrients from the mother, it also eliminates waste and carbon dioxide through the mother's circulation.

The mother gives birth to her baby by contracting her uretus. This process is called a **normal spontaneous delivery (NSD)**[7]. Delivery by incision of the abdominal wall and uterus is called a **cesarean section (C/S)**[8]. After delivery, the doctor or nurse will cut the **umbilical cord**[9] to separate the baby from the mother. The mother will then have a second uterine contraction to eliminate the remnants of the placenta. Upon completion of the delivery, the enlarged uterus will contract itself and gradually become reduced in size.

「受精」開始於精子與卵子於輸卵管壺腹部相遇，而受精過程形成的新細胞稱為「受精卵」。

受精後，受精卵從輸卵管往子宮移動，當它與子宮接觸時，會開始和子宮內膜融合並快速成長。子宮和受精卵的交界稱為胎盤，是胎兒與母體交換的平台。胎兒從母體的循環接收氧氣和營養並且排除二氧化碳和廢物。

母親可擠壓寶寶從陰道產出（稱為自然生產），或者藉由剖腹產產出（稱為剖腹生產）。生產後，醫師或護理師將會剪斷臍帶使寶寶與母體分離。母親會有第二波的子宮收縮以排除胎盤的殘留物。生產完成時，擴大的子宮會開始自動收縮並且逐漸縮小其體積。

Terminology 術語

1. ampulla [æmˊpʌlə] 壺腹部
2. placenta [pləˊsɛntə] 胎盤
3. normal spontaneous delivery (NSD) [ˊnɔrmḷ spanˊtenɪəs dɪˊlɪvərɪ] 自然生產
4. cesarean section (C/S) 剖腹生產 [sɪˊzɛrɪən ˊsɛkʃən]
5. umbilical cord [ʌmˊbɪlɪkḷ kɔrd] 臍帶

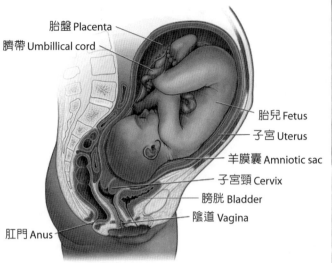

胎盤 Placenta
臍帶 Umbillical cord
胎兒 Fetus
子宮 Uterus
羊膜囊 Amniotic sac
子宮頸 Cervix
膀胱 Bladder
陰道 Vagina
肛門 Anus

Case Information 個案資訊

Normal Spontaneous Delivery (NSD) 自然生產
[ˈnɔrml̩ spanˈtenɪəs dɪˈlɪvərɪ]

1. **Causes**: Delivery of the baby from the mother's vagina by using only her own effort.
2. **Symptoms & Signs**: Regular uterine contractions accompanied by pain, bloody show, cervical dilatation, and sometimes rupture of the membranes.
3. **Care**:
   (1) Monitor symptoms and signs of delivery.
   (2) Provide psychological support.
   (3) Provide wound care.
   (4) Observe the recovery process after delivery.
   (5) Teach patients how to massage their uterus, breast-feed and take care of their breasts.

Admission Assessment　入院評估

*Mrs. Wu, a 29-year-old expectant mother, had a complaint about **labor pain** and **bloody show**.*	吳女士是一位 29 歲的待產婦女，主訴陣痛和現血。
N: Nurse　**P:** Patient	
N: Will this be your first baby?	這是你的第一胎嗎？
P: No, This will be my second one.	不，這是我的第二胎。
N: Is this your second **pregnancy**[1]?	這是你第二次懷孕嗎？
P: No, This is my third pregnancy. I had an **abortion**[2] previously.	不，這是第三次懷孕。我之前曾經有一次流產。
N: When is the **due date** of your baby supposed to be?	預產期是什麼時候呢？
P: Well, today.	嗯，是今天。
N: How frequently are you feeling pain?	你多久會疼痛一次？
P: About every 2~3 minutes.	大約 2~3 分鐘。
N: How long is the pain lasting?	每次大約痛多久呢？
P: About 1 minute.	大約痛 1 分鐘。
N: Have you **water broken** yet?	你破水了嗎？
P: Not yet.	還沒有。
N: I'd like to check the baby's heartbeat.	我將要檢查胎兒的心跳。
P: Does it sound normal?	心跳正常嗎？
N: Yes, it sounds regular and strong. Now we'll check your cervical opening.	是的，聽起來十分規律且強大。現在要檢查子宮頸開口情形。
P: "Ah---".	啊～
N: It's 8 centimeters (cm). It's time to go to the delivery room. Let's go!	已開 8 公分。該進產房了。走吧！

Nursing Notes 護理記錄

$G_3P_2SA_1$, EDC: June 16th, GA: 39+2 weeks. FHB: 150/min, UC: 45"/3'-5', Cx os: 5 cm, Eff: moderate, Station: 0, ROM: (+). Emergency preparation for admission.

產婦懷孕 3 次，生產 2 次，有 1 次自然流產記錄，預產期為 6/16，妊娠期為 39 週又 2 天。胎兒心搏速率：150／分，子宮收縮：3~5 分鐘一次，每次 45 秒，子宮頸開口 5 公分，子宮頸軟化程度：中等，胎兒高度：0，破水：(+)。緊急準備入院。

Tips on Writing

重要的縮寫

(1) $G_xP_ySA_zAA_n$：x 次懷孕，y 次生產，z 次自然流產，n 次人工流產
(2) EDC：Expected date of confinement，預產期
(3) GA：Gestational age，妊娠期
(4) FHB：Fetal heartbeat，胎兒心搏速率
(5) UC：Uterine contraction，子宮收縮
(6) Cx os：Cervical opening，子宮頸開口
(7) Eff：Effacement，子宮頸軟化程度
(8) ROM：Rupture of membranes，羊膜破裂、破水

Vocabulary and Sentence Examples 字彙與例句

1. pregnancy [ˈprɛgnənsɪ] | She is a mother who has had several pregnancies.
   (n.) 懷孕 | 她是一位曾經有多次懷孕的母親。
2. abortion [əˈbɔrʃən] | She had an abortion because of a car accident.
   (n.) 流產；墮胎 | 由於車禍之故，她流產了。

Terminology 術語

1. labor pain [ˈlebə pen] 陣痛
2. bloody show [ˈblʌdɪ ʃo] 現血
3. due date [dju det] 預產期
4. water break [ˈwɔtə brek] 破水

Hospitalization 住院療護

58

*Mrs. Wu gave birth to a baby boy. The nurse assessed her recovery **post-partum**[1].*

N: Good morning, Mrs. Wu, how are you feeling?

P: Quite well.

N: Are you satisfied with the PCA?

P: Yes, I barely feel any pain, and I'm sleeping well.

N: Are you massaging your lower abdomen?

P: Yes, pretty often.

N: I'll check if your uterus is **contracting**[2] down to its normal size now. *(Palpates the lower abdomen corresponding to the uterus)* This feels very good. You'll feel your uterus becoming smaller by about one finger's **width**[3] everyday. It will completely **descend**[4] into your pelvis in about 10 days.

P: Can I stop massaging my abdomen after I can't feel it anymore?

N: Sure. Now let's check your **incision**[5] site. Does it hurt?

P: Not anymore. I only felt a little pain after the first day of delivery.

N: Your incision has healed well. There's no redness, swelling or bleeding. Keep up with the **sitz bath,** and it will help with the healing process.

P: That's good. I'll keep repeating the baths.

N: Are you going to **breast-feed**[6] your baby?

P: I decided I'd like to. I heard breast-feeding is beneficial for my baby's health and my own health.

N: Great, I'll teach you how to feed your baby. I'll also give you a booklet with more information.

P: OK, thanks a lot.

吳女士生了一名小男嬰,護理師正在評估她的產後復原狀況。

吳女士早安,你現在感覺如何?

還不錯。

你對病人自控式止痛器滿意嗎?

很滿意,我幾乎感覺不到疼痛,同時也睡得很好。

你有按摩下腹部嗎?

有,我常常做。

讓我來檢查一下你的子宮是否收縮到正常狀態。(觸摸對應到子宮的下腹部)感覺非常好,你可以感覺到它每天大概下降一指寬,大約 10 天左右就會完全下降到骨盆了。

那我能感覺不到它收縮後停止按摩腹部嗎?

當然,來檢查你的傷口吧。會痛嗎?

不再痛了。我只在產後第一天感到疼痛。

傷口的縫合線癒合得很好,沒有發紅、腫脹或出血。繼續坐浴有益於癒合過程。

太好了!我會繼續這麼做的。

你要哺餵母乳嗎?

我決定哺餵母乳,聽說哺餵母乳有益於我與寶寶的健康。

很好,我會教你如何哺餵寶寶,也會給你一本小冊子,內含更多的資訊。

好的,非常謝謝你。

Nursing Notes 護理記錄

1st day of NSD, active uterine contractions, fundus: 1 finger width above umbilicus. Wound: clean with a little discharge, no redness, swelling or bleeding. Good postpartum recovery. Massaged uterus. Gave postpartum sitz bath.

自然產後第一天，子宮有主動收縮，子宮底高度位於臍上一指寬，傷口乾淨，有少許分泌物，但無紅腫或出血。產後復原良好，能夠自己執行子宮按摩，已完成產後坐浴。

Vocabulary and Sentence Examples 字彙與例句

1. post-partum [post ´partəm]
   (n.) 產後的

   Post-partum hemorrhage is an obstetric emergency which requires immediate management.
   產後出血是一種產科急症，需要立即處置。

2. contract [kən´trækt]
   (v.) 收縮

   Her uterus is contracting well. 她的子宮收縮良好。

3. width [wɪdθ] (n.) 寬度

   The road is 10 meters in width. 這條路有 10 公尺寬。

4. descend [dɪ´sɛnd]
   (v.) 下降

   The cable car descended from the top of the mountain.
   這座纜車從山頂下降。

5. incision [ɪn´sɪʒən]
   (n.) 傷口；切口

   Let me check the incision from your left foot.
   讓我檢查你左腳的傷口。

6. breast-feed [´brɛst fid]
   哺餵母乳

   All mothers should breast-feed their babies, since this is beneficial for their health.
   為了他們的健康著想，媽媽們應哺餵母乳。

Terminology 術語

1. sitz bath [´sɪts ˌbæθ] 坐浴

Discharge Instructions　出院衛教

59

After the fourth day of delivery, the baby and mother continued to do well. Mrs. Wu prepared for discharge.

N: Your uterus is contracting well. Please continue to check its **position**[1] and size everyday.

產後第四天，嬰兒和母親的狀況都很好，吳女士準備要出院了。

你的子宮收縮良好。請繼續每天確認它的收縮大小和位置。

P: How long should I continue to do this?

我要持續這個動作多久呢？

N: About one week. After that, you shouldn't feel your uterus anymore.

大約 1 週，在那之後你就不會再感覺到子宮收縮了。

P: What about the amount of discharge? Will it decrease as well?

那分泌物的量呢？它也會減少嗎？

N: Yes, the amount of discharge will decrease, and the color will become lighter. If you see an increase in discharge or the color turns red, lie down and massage your uterus to help it to contract.

當然，量會減少，顏色也會變淡。如果量變多或者顏色轉紅，你就必須躺下並且按摩你的子宮以幫助子宮收縮。

P: I'll keep that in mind.

我會謹記在心的。

N: Remember to return immediately if your condition worsens.

記得，萬一情況沒有變好，請立即回診。

P: All right, I understand.

好的，我曉得。

N: Keep your **perineal** area clean and dry. If you catch a fever, this may mean you have an infection, so please come back here if you're not feeling well.

保持會陰部清潔和乾燥，如果你發燒了，可能是受到感染，若你感到不適，請回診就醫。

P: I understand. Will I be able to exercise at home?

我知道。我在家能做運動嗎？

N: Yes. **Appropriate**[2] exercise can help with your recovery, decrease any post-partum discomfort, and help with weight loss. You can read about more **details**[3] from the booklet I gave you. If you have any more questions, please fell free to call us.

可以的，適當的運動可以幫助你恢復、減輕產後不適及減重。更多細節請查閱我先前給你的小冊子。如果你有任何問題，請通知我們。

P: I will. Thanks a lot.

我知道了，多謝你。

Nursing Notes 護理記錄

4th day of NSD, active uterine contraction, fundus: 3 finger width below umbilicus. Wound: dry and clean without discharge, redness, swelling or bleeding. Breast-feed with prominent engorgement.

自然產後第四天，子宮有主動收縮，子宮底位於臍下三指寬。傷口清潔且乾燥，無分泌物、紅腫或出血現象。餵哺母乳，有明顯漲奶情形。

Vocabulary and Sentence Examples 字彙與例句

1. position [pəˈzɪʃən]
   (n.) 位置

   Please check the position of all your components to ensure the safety of your tourists.
   請檢查所有零件的位置以確保遊客的安全。

2. appropriate [əˈproprɪˌet]
   (adj.) 適當的

   Appropriate exercise can help with your recovery.
   適當的運動可以幫助你恢復。

3. detail [ˈditel]
   (n.) 細節；詳情

   Please tell me more details about this therapy.
   請告知我更多關於治療的細節。

Terminology 術語

1. perineal [ˌpɛrəˈniəl] 會陰的

More Information

哺餵母乳的順序

(1) Touch the corner of the baby's mouth with your finger.
以手指觸碰嬰兒嘴角。

(2) Put the baby's face next to your breast.
將嬰兒的臉置於乳房一側。

(3) Gently stroke the baby's lip with your nipple.
以乳頭輕觸嬰兒嘴唇。

(4) Begin the feeding.
開始哺餵。

(5) Stop feeding and pat the baby's back to eliminate air from his/her stomach.
停止哺餵，並輕拍嬰兒背部以排出胃中空氣。

Exercise 小試身手

● Choose the Correct Answer

( ) 1. She received an _____ . (A)abortion (B)adaptation (C)adoption (D)addition 她接受人工流產。

( ) 2. _____ of your legs muscles will result in movement of your limbs. (A)constriction (B)continuation (C)contraction (D)congestion 足夠的肌肉收縮帶來我們肢體的動作。

( ) 3. She mended her _____ very carefully. (A)inclusion (B)wound (C)intuition (D)immersion 她細心照料傷口。

( ) 4. Please check the _____ of the lead pipe. (A)position (B)playground (C)place (D)plateau 請確認鉛管的位置。

( ) 5. The board is 2 meters in _____ . (A)wide (B)weight (C)board (D)width 這塊板子寬兩公尺。

● Fill in the Blanks

1. Because this was her second _____ , she was already familiar with the _____ from _____ and her _____ _____ .
由於這是她的第二次懷孕，她很了解陣痛和破水的意義。

2. By carefully with _____ the uretus after delivery, the _____ will _____ _____ .
經過細心按摩，生產後的子宮會漸漸下降。

3. _____ _____ has a number of benefits to both mother and baby.
哺餵母乳對母親及寶寶有許多好處。

4. The baby was _____ one month _____ its _____ _____ .
寶寶在預產期前一個月就出生了。

5. A _____ _____ will help the wound in your _____ heal.
坐浴對於會陰傷口很有幫助。

Simplify Nursing Notes

產婦懷孕 4 次，生產 2 次，無自然流產記錄，有 1 次人工流產。

預產期 9 月 30 日，懷孕 38 週又 5 天。

胎兒心跳：140 次／分，子宮收縮：3 分鐘一次，每次 60 秒，子宮頸擴張 3 公分，子宮頸外翻程度：中等，胎兒高度：0，未破水。給予入院準備。

_____

_____

_____

_____

Translation

1. 吳女士是一位 29 歲的待產婦女，主訴陣痛和現血。

_____

2. 預產期是什麼時候呢？

_____

3. 讓我來檢查一下你的子宮是否收縮到正常狀態。

_____

4. 保持會陰部清潔和乾燥，如果你發燒了，可能是受到感染。

_____

5. 適當的運動可以幫助你恢復、減輕產後不適及減重。

_____

解答

Pediatric Unit
小兒科

Learning Goals 學習目標

1. Approaching pediatric patients
2. Explaining care instructions to parents
3. Providng health education to patients

Outline 本章大綱

- About the Pediatric Department
  關於小兒科
- Case Information: Croup
  個案資訊：哮吼
- Admission Assessment　入院評估
- Hospitalization　住院療護
- Discharge Instructions　出院衛教

Medical English for
Healthcare Professionals

About the Pediatric Department 關於小兒科

60

The **Pediatric¹** department is a special medical facility that serves children. There is a famous saying, "A child is not a small adult. A baby is not a small child". **Pediatricians²** have to learn about the unique **pathophysiology³** of babies and children. In addition, they must memorize different dosages of medications for pediatric patients.

There are many stages within child development (based on age), including the fetal stage (before birth), **infancy⁴** (birth to 12 months old), early childhood (1~4 years old), late childhood (5~10 years old), and **adolescence⁵** (11~18 years old). People around 19 years of age can be viewed as being in a transitional period, in which they develop in different physiological and psychological aspects.

小兒科是服務孩童的醫學專業領域。「孩童並非體型小的大人，而嬰兒也並非更小的小孩。」這句名言讓兒科醫師必須學習嬰兒和孩童與大人不同的病理生理學並記住不同的藥物劑量。

孩童的發展階段包括：胎兒期（出生前）、嬰兒期（出生到周歲）、幼兒早期（1~4 歲）、幼兒晚期（5~10 歲）及青少年期（11~18 歲）。19 歲的人們可歸類在轉型期，其生理及心理方面會有不同的發展。

Terminology 術語

1. pediatric [ˌpidɪˈætrɪk] 小兒科的
2. pediatrician [ˌpidɪəˈtrɪʃən] 小兒科專科醫師
3. pathophysiology 病理生理學 [ˌpæθəˌfɪzɪˈɑlədʒɪ]
4. infancy [ˈɪnfənsɪ] 嬰兒期
5. adolescence [ˌædlˈɛsn̩s] 青少年期

青少年期
Adolescence

胎兒期
Fetal stage

孩童的發展階段
Stage of child development

幼兒晚期
Late childhood

嬰兒期
Infancy

幼兒早期
Early childhood

Case Information 個案資訊

Croup [krup] 哮吼

1. **Causes**: Viral (most) or bacterial infection in the upper airway.
2. **Symptoms & Signs**: Stridor, barking cough, suprasternal retraction, intercostal retraction, hoarseness, and difficulty breathing.
3. **Care**:
   (1) Monitor TPR.
   (2) Maintain adequate ventilation.
   (3) Provide aerosol treatment.
   (4) Bed-rest and drink an adequate amount of water.
   (5) Educate patients on disease transmission.
   (6) Teach patients how to perform chest percussion.
   (7) If symptoms and signs of croup are present, see a doctor right away.

Admission Assessment 入院評估

61

*Bob, a 2-year-old boy, presented to the hospital for 2 days of coughing. His voice was **hoarse**[1] and he had difficulty breathing.*

鮑柏是個已經咳嗽兩天的 2 歲男孩，聲音沙啞且呼吸困難。

D: Doctor　**N:** Nurse　**P:** Patient　**M:** Mother

N: Hello, Bob.

哈囉，鮑柏。

P: Hi.

嗨。

N: I'd like to check Bob's **height**[2], **weight**[3] and body temperature. Please place him on the exam table.

我要檢查鮑柏的身高、體重及體溫。請把他放到檢查桌上。

M: OK.

好的。

N: He is 80 centimeters tall and weighs 13 kilograms. His body temperature is 38.5℃. Please wait a few minutes. The doctor will be in shortly.

他有 80 公分高，13 公斤重。體溫是 38.5℃。請稍等一會兒，醫師稍後會到。

(Five minutes later, the doctor comes in …)

（5 分鐘後醫師進來了。）

D: Hello, Bob. What's up?

哈囉，鮑柏。你怎麼啦？

P: *(In a hoarse voice)* I'm not feeling well.

（沙啞的聲音）我不舒服。

M: He has a fever. He has also been coughing severely and sometimes has difficulty breathing.

他有發燒、嚴重的咳嗽及呼吸困難的情形。

D: How long has he had these symptoms?

這樣的情況持續多久了呢？

M: Uh, about 2 days.

呃，大約 2 天。

D: How's his appetite?

他的食慾如何？

M: He doesn't want to eat anything. I forced him to drink some milk but he threw it up right afterwards.

他不想吃任何東西。我強迫他喝牛奶但他隨後吐了出來。

D: Has he coughed up any sputum?

他有咳出任何痰液嗎？

M: Yes, but not very much, when he coughs, it sounds like he's **barking**[4].

不多，但當他咳嗽時，那聲音很像狗的吠叫聲。

D: I see. Bob, let me listen to your breathing and heart beats. Please pull up your shirt.

我了解。鮑柏，讓我檢查你的呼吸和心跳，請把衣服拉起來。

(The mother helps pull his shirt up.)

（母親幫忙拉起鮑柏的衣服。）

D: Then open your mouth and say "ahhhhh".

接著張開嘴巴並且說「啊～」

P: "Ahhhhh---".

「啊～」

D: *(Turns to the mother.)* It seems like he has a lot of sputum, and his throat is swollen. He has a common upper respiratory infection, called croup. We need to admit him to our hospital for treatment.

（轉向母親）看來他有很多痰而且喉嚨紅腫，這是常見的上呼吸道感染－哮吼。我們需要讓他住院並且接受治療。

M: Alright. Thank you very much.

好的，非常謝謝你。

Nursing Notes 護理記錄

Came to **OPD** due to severe cough. Height: 80 cm. Weight: 13 kg. Conscious: alert, irritable. TPR: 38.5℃, 110/min, 30/min. Has mild **subcostal** and **supraclavicular retraction**. Use of accessory respiratory muscles observed.

因為嚴重咳嗽前來門診。身高 80 公分,體重 13 公斤。意識:清醒但躁動。體溫 38.5℃,脈搏每分鐘 100 下,呼吸每分鐘 30 次。有肋下和鎖骨上回縮情形。

Tips on Writing

1. **OPD**＝outpatient department 門診(部)
2. 描寫症狀的嚴重程度
   (1) 輕微:mild, minor, slight, a little
   (2) 嚴重:major, severe, serious, profound, a lot
      例:Has mild fever.
         Has severe abdominal pain.

Vocabulary and Sentence Examples 字彙與例句

1. hoarse [hɔrs]
   (adj.) 沙啞的
   His voice was hoarse from yelling too much.
   他因為常常吼叫,造成聲音沙啞。

2. height [haɪt]
   (n.) 身高
   The girl's height is 100 centimeters.
   這女孩的身高是 100 公分。

3. weight [wet]
   (n.) 體重
   What is your weight?
   你的體重多少?

4. bark [bark]
   (v.) 吠叫
   The dog barked at the strangers standing in front of the door.
   這條狗對站在門前的陌生人們吠叫著。

Terminology 術語

1. subcostal [sʌbˈkastəl] 肋骨下方的
2. supraclavicular [ˌsuprəkləˈvɪkjələ] 鎖骨上方的
3. retraction [rɪˈtrækʃən] 回縮

Hospitalization 住院療護

*The nurse explained the **therapeutic**[1] method to Bob's mother.*	護理師正在向鮑柏的母親解釋他的治療方式。
N: Bob has a swollen throat and needs **aerosol therapy** to relieve his discomfort.	鮑柏的喉嚨紅腫，需要氣霧治療以緩解不適。
M: I see. What can I do for him?	我了解。我能為他做什麼呢？
N: Since this therapy uses **steam**[2] containing medicine, we need him to **cooperate**[3] with us. You can help by telling him to **inhale**[4] the steam.	由於氣霧治療使用含有藥物的蒸汽，因此我們需要他的配合。你可以幫我告知他吸入這些蒸汽。
M: No problem.	沒問題。
N: Bob, please sit on your mother's lap.	鮑柏，請坐到媽媽的膝上。
P: OK.	好的。
(15 minutes later)	（15 分鐘後）
N: Your therapy is done. What a good boy you are, Bob.	氣霧治療結束了。鮑柏，你真是個乖男孩。
P: *(Smiling)* Thank you.	（微笑著）謝謝。
M: How soon will it take for him to recover?	他要多久才會康復呢？
N: He may need 2~3 days to fully recover. During the next few days, we'll provide him with some oxygen containing a higher **humidity**[5]. This will improve his condition and breathing.	大約需要 2~3 天才能完全康復。在這段期間，我們會先給予他高溼度的氧氣。如此可以改善他的呼吸情況。
M: Thank you.	謝謝。
N: You're welcome. We'll also keep him under observation for any signs of airway obstruction, such as shortness of breath or **cyanosis**, which is more severe.	不客氣。我們也會密切觀察他是否有出現呼吸道阻塞的徵象。譬如說，呼吸短促或者嚴重變成發紺現象。
M: I understand. What can I do for him?	我了解。我能為他做什麼呢？
N: Let him rest and encourage him to eat. This will make him stronger so that he can fight off his illness.	讓他歇息並且鼓勵他多吃一些。這會讓他更強壯以便對抗疾病。
M: Anything else?	還有呢？
N: Encourage him to drink more water as well.	鼓勵他多喝水。
M: Got it. Thanks a lot.	我明白了，多謝。

Nursing Notes 護理記錄

Stridor detected. Aerosol therapy given stat as instructed. Will keep observing patient's HR and RR. 30% Oxygen via nasal cannula given as instructed.

檢查到哮鳴音。依醫囑立即給予氣霧治療。將持續觀察病人的心跳和呼吸速率。依醫囑給予經鼻套管之 30%氧氣。

Vocabulary and Sentence Examples 字彙與例句

1. therapeutic [ˌθɛrəˈpjutɪk] (adj.) 治療的	The type of therapeutic approach to treat his disease has not been decided yet. 此疾病的治療方式尚未決定。
2. steam [stim] (n.) 蒸汽	The hot water produced a lot of steam, causing the kettle to boil over. 水被煮開了，水壺中有很多蒸汽跑出來。
3. cooperate [koˈɑpəˌret] (v.) 合作	Our company hopes to cooperate with you to create an innovative product. 我們公司希望與你合作創造出創新的產品。
4. inhale [ɪnˈhel] (v.) 吸入	Hold your breath! Don't inhale the air. It's toxic! 憋住呼吸！不要吸入空氣，因為裡面有毒！
5. humidity [hjuˈmɪdətɪ] (n.) 溼度（氣）	The room is filled with humidity. 這間房間充滿了溼氣。

Terminology 術語

1. aerosol therapy [ˌeəˈrasɔl ˈθɛrəpɪ] 氣霧治療
2. cyanosis [ˌsaɪəˈnosɪs] 發紺
3. stridor [ˈstraɪdə] 哮鳴音

Discharge Instructions　出院衛教　　63

Bob's condition stabilized and he prepared to go home.	鮑柏的情況變穩定，他準備要回家了。
N: Hi, Bob. You're ready to leave the hospital.	嗨，鮑柏，你將要離開醫院了。
P: Thanks. I can't wait to go home!	謝謝。我等不及要回家了！
N: Congratulations! *(Turns to his mother)* He can go home today. Please give him **acetaminophen** syrup every 6 hours to relieve his fever.	恭喜！（轉向母親）今天他可以回家了，請你每 6 小時給他普拿疼糖漿以緩解發燒症狀。
M: How much should I give him?	我要給他多少糖漿呢？
N: 6 c.c. each time.	一次給 6 毫升。
M: OK, I'll do that.	好的，我會記得。
N: The **medicon syrup** is for his cough. Give him 6 c.c. after each meal and before he sleeps.	咳嗽糖漿是止咳用的，每餐飯後及睡前各給他 6 毫升。
M: Should I limit his water intake?	我要限制他的攝水量嗎？
N: Not really. Encourage him to drink more fluids. Juice, milk and water are all suitable.	不用，鼓勵他多攝取水分，果汁、牛奶及開水都很適合。
M: What kind of food should he eats if he has a poor appetite?	如果他的食慾很差，我應該給他吃什麼東西呢？
N: You can try giving him light, frequent meals. In addition, **refrigerated**[1] foods such as pudding or yogurt can help relieve his sore throat.	你可以讓他少量多餐進食。此外，布丁或優格這一類冷藏過的食物可以緩解他喉嚨痛的症狀。
M: I see. Umm, is he **contagious**[2]?	嗯，他的疾病會傳染嗎？
N: Definitely. He has a kind of viral infection that can be transmitted through aerosols. Please do not go to public places like the park.	當然，這是一種病毒感染，會藉由飛沫傳染。請勿至公共場所，譬如說公園。
M: He has a little brother at home. What should I do to prevent him from **spreading**[3] this disease?	他有一個弟弟，我應該做什麼來預防傳染呢？
N: Have him wear a **mask**[4]. This will help prevent him from transmitting the disease. Also, you should pat his back to help him cough sputum out.	讓他戴上口罩，可以避免大多數的傳染。對了，你可以拍他的背來協助他把痰咳出來。
M: Oh, thank you very much.	好，非常感謝你。

Nursing Notes 護理記錄

Vital signs stable. 98% **Saturation** without oxygen supplementation. Told mother to give patient a mask and encourage him to drink more water. Told not to go to public areas. Suggested to give light, frequent meals to improve appetite.

生命徵象穩定，無給氧情況下，氧氣飽和度為 98%。教導母親讓他戴口罩及多喝水。告知勿出入公共場所。建議給予少量多餐以增進病人之食慾。

Tips on Writing

對家屬的衛教寫法：Instructed/Told/Taught＋somebody＋to have/make/help ＋patient＋V，例：
Told mother to give patient medications after meals.
Taught father how to clean the wound of the patient.
Instructed mother to have patient measure blood sugar before and after meals.

Vocabulary and Sentence Examples 字彙與例句

1. refrigerated
   [rɪˈfrɪdʒəˌretɪd]
   (adj.) 被冷藏過的

   The food should be refrigerated in order to keep it fresh.
   食物應該冷藏以保持新鮮。

2. contagious [kənˈtedʒəs]
   (adj.) 接觸感染性的

   Have you been in contact with anyone with a contagious disease? 你有接觸接觸感染性疾病的人嗎？

3. spread [sprɛd]
   (v.) 散播

   He spread the seeds over the soil.
   他將種子往土壤裡散播。

4. mask [mæsk]
   (n.) 口罩

   Wear a mask when you go to the hospital.
   到醫院去時請穿戴口罩。

Terminology 術語

1. acetaminophen [æsətæˈmɪnəfən] 普拿疼
2. medicon syrup [ˈmɛdɪkən ˈsɪrəp] 咳嗽藥水
3. saturation [ˌsætʃəˈreʃən] 飽和度

More Information

1. 小兒常見疾病

   (1) Cold [kold] 普通感冒

   (2) Flu [flu] 流行性感冒

   (3) Ear infection (acute/chronic otitis media) 耳部感染（急／慢性中耳炎）
   [ir ɪnˋfɛkʃən]

   (4) Respiratory tract infections 呼吸道感染
   [rɪˋspaɪrəˏtorɪ trækt ɪnˋfɛkʃən]

   (5) Allergies (rhinitis, asthma, dermatitis) 過敏（鼻炎、氣喘、皮膚炎）
   [ˋælədʒɪz] [raɪˋnaɪtɪs ˋæzmə ˏdɜməˋtaɪtɪs]

   (6) Infectious diarrhea (bacterial or viral) 傳染性腹瀉（細菌性或病毒性）
   [ɪnˋfɛkʃəs daɪəˋriə] [bækˋtɪrɪəl] [ˋvaɪrəl]

   (7) Measles [ˋmizļz] 麻疹

   (8) Chickenpox [ˋtʃɪkənˏpaks] 水痘

2. 描寫病人罹病經過的主題句

   (1) Someone has come down with the cold for two days. 某人已感冒 2 天。

   (2) Since 8/4, someone had the flu. 某人自 8 月 4 日罹患流行性感冒。

   (3) Someone has suffered from a runny nose. 某人有流鼻水的症狀。

   (4) Someone has diarrhea. 某人有腹瀉的症狀。

   (5) Someone has been infected with *Staphylococcus*. 某人受到葡萄球菌的感染。

Exercise 小試身手

◉ Choose the Correct Answer

( ) 1. His voice is _____ from speaking too much. (A)harness (B)hoarse (C)horse (D)horm 他因為說太多話而聲音沙啞。

( ) 2. The dog _____ very loudly everyday. (A)barks (B)balks (C)breaks (D)blacks 這隻狗每天吠叫得很大聲。

( ) 3. The _____ spurt from the smokestack of the train. (A)smoke (B)smog (C)fog (D)steam 蒸汽從火車煙囪中激射而出。

( ) 4. Keep this plant in the room that has a higher _____ level. (A)humanity (B)humidity (C)humid (D)dry 將這株植物養在潮溼的房間。

( ) 5. Keep the fruit _____ , or else it'll quickly become rotten. (A)ice (B)cool (C)cold (D)refrigerated 將這些水果冷藏，否則它們很快就會爛掉。

◉ Fill in the Blanks

1. His _____ is 180 centimeters and his _____ is 100 kilograms. 他的身高 180 公分，體重 100 公斤重。

2. In order to prevent _____ from _____ , patients with a cold should wear a _____ . 為了避免傳播病毒，感冒的人應該戴上口罩。

3. The man is _____ because he cannot _____ enough _____ . 這個人因為無法吸入足夠的氧氣而呈現發紺。

4. We need children to _____ . Otherwise, we won't be able to provide _____ _____ . 我們需要小孩合作，否則無法進行氣霧治療。

5. His throat is _____ . We suspect that he has been _____ with _____ . 他的喉嚨紅腫，我們懷疑他被細菌感染了。

● Simplify Nursing Notes

1. 病人的傷口有嚴重出血。
_____

2. 病人的右手腕輕微疼痛。
_____

3. 告知母親避免讓病人暴露在陽光下。
_____

4. 告知父親讓病人按時服藥。
_____

5. 教導母親使用支氣管擴張劑。
_____

● Translation

1. 我要檢查鮑柏的身高、體重及體溫。請把他放到檢查桌上。
_____

2. 他有發燒、嚴重的咳嗽及呼吸困難的情形。
_____

3. 鮑柏的喉嚨紅腫，需要氣霧治療以緩解不適。
_____

4. 我們需要他的配合。你可以幫我告知他吸入這些蒸汽。
_____

5. 咳嗽糖漿是止咳用的，每餐飯後及睡前各給他 6 毫升。
_____

解答

Ophthalmology Unit
眼　科

Learning Goals 學習目標

1. Assessing patients with visual impair-ments
2. Preparing the patient for eye surgery
3. Providing health education to patients

Outline 本章大綱

- About the Eyes　關於眼睛
- Case Information: Cataract
  個案資訊：白內障
- Admission Assessment　入院評估
- Pre-Operative Care　術前照護
- Post-Operative Care　術後照護

Medical English for Healthcare Professionals

About the Eyes　關於眼睛

64

The eyes are one of the most important organs which we use to perceive the environment, to observe changes from our surroundings, and to see many different objects in the world. Anatomically, the eye is divided into three layers: the sclera, the uvea and the retina.

The outermost layer is called the **sclera**[1], which is composed of dense connective tissue forming a relatively strong architecture of the eye. In the anterior side of the eye, the sclera continues to the **cornea**[2], a transparent layer with a high refractive power that can magnify objects.

The intermediate layer of the eye is called the **uvea**[3], in which many small vessels pass through. This layer consists of the **choroid**[4], **ciliary body**[5] and **iris**[6]. Pigments within the intermediate layer absorb light and help sharpen images we see.

The innermost layer is called the **retina**[7], which perceives light and transforms it into electrical signals sent to our brain. The brain processes these signals and interprets them. The **lens**[8], another structure with magnifying power, resides between the **pupil**[9] and the **vitreous body**[10]. The ciliary muscles adjust the shape of the lens and alter the magnifying power. The vitreous body makes up a major component of the eyeball. It is transparent and allows light to go through without significant obstacles.

眼睛是身體最重要的器官之一。我們藉它感知環境、觀察周遭的變化,並且察看世界上許多不同的事物。眼睛的解剖構造分成鞏膜、葡萄膜及視網膜。

鞏膜位於最外層,它由結締組織組成,構成眼睛相對強韌的結構。眼睛前面的部分,鞏膜與透明的角膜相連,角膜有很強的折射力,能夠放大我們看到的物體。

葡萄膜位於中間層,有許多小血管通過,此層含有脈絡膜、睫狀體及虹膜。光刺激會被此層吸收,進而使我們的視覺更為清晰銳利。

視網膜位於最內層,它能夠感知外界來的光線刺激並將之轉換為電訊號傳至大腦。大腦接受這些訊號並解讀它。水晶體亦有放大能力,它位於瞳孔和玻璃體之間,睫狀肌控制水晶體的形狀並藉此改變它的放大能力。玻璃體是眼球中最主要的成分,光線能夠在最小阻礙的情況下通過它。

Terminology 術語

1. sclera [ˈsklɪrə] 鞏膜
2. cornea [ˈkɔrnɪə] 角膜
3. uvea [ˈjuvɪə] 葡萄膜
4. choroid [ˈkorɔɪd] 脈絡膜
5. ciliary body [ˈsɪlɪˌɛrɪ badɪ] 睫狀體
6. iris [ˈaɪrɪs] 虹膜

7. retina [ˈrɛtɪnə] 視網膜

8. lens [lɛnz] 水晶體

9. pupil [ˈpjupl̩] 瞳孔

10. vitreous body [ˈvɪtrɪəs bɑdɪ]
玻璃體

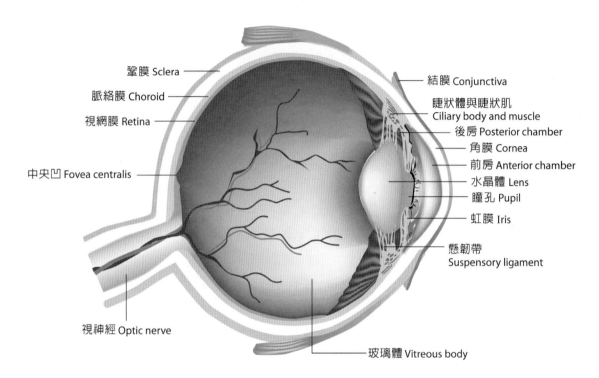

鞏膜 Sclera
脈絡膜 Choroid
視網膜 Retina
中央凹 Fovea centralis
視神經 Optic nerve
結膜 Conjunctiva
睫狀體與睫狀肌 Ciliary body and muscle
後房 Posterior chamber
角膜 Cornea
前房 Anterior chamber
水晶體 Lens
瞳孔 Pupil
虹膜 Iris
懸韌帶 Suspensory ligament
玻璃體 Vitreous body

Case Information 個案資訊

Cataract [ˈkætəˌrækt] 白內障

1. **Causes**: Aging, working with radiations or exposure to strong light, DM.
2. **Symptoms & Signs**:
   (1) Near-sightedness
   (2) Decrease perception of blue color
   (3) Blindness (if untreated)
3. **Care**:
   (1) Check visual acuity and field.
   (2) Surgery for treatment.
   (3) Monitor changes in visual acuity and intraocular pressure.
   (4) Clean secretions, avoid light and rubbing-eye after operation.
   (5) Told patients to wear an eye patch and take medications regularly after operation.
   (6) Return for follow-up exams as instructed.

Admission Assessment　入院評估

65

*Mrs. Shen, a 50-year-old woman, visited the hospital due to **blurred**[1] vision.*

沈女士，50 歲女生，因為視力模糊而來到醫院。

N: Nurse　**P:** Patient

N: Hello, Mrs. Shen, what's the matter with your eyes?

哈囉，沈女士。你的眼睛怎麼啦？

P: I have been having problems seeing things recently.

我最近有視物的問題。

N: Can you describe your blurred vision in more detail? For example, can you read the newspaper?

你對視力模糊能否描述詳細些？譬如說，你能讀報紙嗎？

P: No, I can't. I can't even see traffic lights.

不能。我甚至無法看清楚紅綠燈。

N: Do you have double vision, meaning you see 2 **objects**[2] instead 1?

你會將一個物體看成兩個嗎？

P: Not exactly. But I feel as if my vision is **foggy**[3].

不會，但我覺得霧霧的。

N: Does the fogginess affect your eyes to the same extent on both sides?

這些霧氣對你的雙眼影響程度是否相同呢？

P: Well, my right eye is better than the left.

嗯，右眼的狀況比左眼好一些。

N: Is it affecting your daily life or work?

會影響你的日常生活或工作嗎？

P: At first it didn't affect me too much, but lately I think it's really affected my ability to shop by myself.

起初影響不大。但最近我覺得有影響到我獨自出門購物。

N: What's your current occupation?

你的職業是什麼呢？

P: I was a cashier in the shopping mall, but I retired 2 years ago.

我是購物中心的收銀員，但我兩年前退休了。

N: Now I need to evaluate your **visual acuity** and **visual field**, please come with me.

現在我需要檢查你的視力和視野，請跟我來。

(The nurse leads Mrs. Shen to the examination room.)

（護理師帶著沈女士至檢查室。）

N: OK, the doctor will examine your retina as well as your lens. After that, he will make a diagnosis and discuss a treatment plan with you.

好的，醫生等會兒會檢查你的視網膜和水晶體，之後，他會下診，並且和你討論治療計畫。

P: Thank you very much.

非常謝謝你。

N: You're welcome.

不客氣。

Nursing Notes 護理記錄

Complained of blurred vision. Feels as if fog is covering eyes. OS worse. Visual acuity and visual field examination done. The doctor admitted her for eye treatment. Admission completed.

主訴視力模糊，感覺有霧氣籠罩眼睛。左眼較嚴重。視力和視野檢查已完成。入院手續完成。

Tips on Writing

1. 描寫症狀：Feel like/Feel as if＋N. 感覺（症狀）像什麼東西

   例：Feels like vision is foggy.   Feels as if I've been bitten/burned/pushed.

   Feels like needles stabbing my back.   Feels as if ants are crawling over my hands and feet.

2. 眼睛的縮寫

   OD＝right eye　右眼　　　OS＝left eye　左眼　　　OU＝both eyes　雙眼

Vocabulary and Sentence Examples 字彙與例句

1. blurred [blɝd]
   (adj.) 模糊的

   Your vision is blurred because you have cataracts.
   視力模糊乃因白內障所致。

2. object [ˈabdʒɪkt]
   (n.) 物體

   Beware of hitting that object. You may get into a serious car accident if you bump into it!
   小心那個物體。萬一你撞到它你可能會出嚴重的車禍！

3. foggy [ˈfagɪ]
   (adj.) 多霧的

   It's dangerous to drive in foggy weather.
   在多霧天氣裡開車很危險。

Terminology 術語

1. visual acuity [ˈvɪʒuəl əˈkjuətɪ] 視力
2. visual field [ˈvɪʒuəl fild] 視野

Pre-Operative Care　術前照護

66

Mrs. Shen was diagnosed with a cataract in her left eye. She decided to have surgery.

N: Mrs. Shen, I'm going to help you prepare for surgery.

P: OK. Thank you.

N: First, I'll give you some **eye drops** to **dilate**[1] your pupils. This will allow the doctor to operate on your lens.

P: Please, go ahead. How long will the operation take?

N: Usually less than one hour.

P: Will it hurt? I'm really worried it will be painful.

N: Don't worry, it's practically painless.

P: Will I be conscious during the operation?

N: It's up to you. Most of the doctors recommend that their patients remain **conscious**[2] during surgery.

P: So I'd like to stay awake but will I feel any pain during the one hour operation?

N: Yes. We'll give you a local anesthetic. This will make you less likely to feel any pain.

P: Will I have to remain in the hospital afterwards? My neighbor said she got to leave the hospital right after her operation.

N: You can leave here soon after the operation, but your left eye must be covered by an **eye patch**[3] to prevent it from being damaged. I would suggest your family pick you up. Some patients are not used to seeing with only one eye.

P: Oh, I understand. My husband will come pick me up later then.

N: OK. Just call us if you need any assistance.

沈女士左眼患有白內障。她決定接受手術。

沈女士，我現在要協助你完成手術前的準備。

好的，謝謝你。

首先，我會給你點一些眼藥水，以使瞳孔擴大，利於醫師進行手術。

請便。這項手術會花多少時間呢？

通常一小時之內就會結束了。

會痛嗎？我還蠻怕痛的。

別擔心，這手術幾乎不會疼痛。

手術過程中我是清醒的嗎？

這取決於你。大多數的醫師建議病人在手術時保持清醒。

所以接下來一小時中我的神智清晰，那會感覺到痛嗎？

會的，我們會給你局部麻醉劑，使你幾乎不會感覺到痛。

之後我需要住院嗎？我的鄰居說她手術後不久就離開醫院回家去了。

你可以在術後很快回家，但你的左眼必須用眼罩遮蓋著以避免傷害。我也建議你的家人前來接你，很多病人並不習慣用一隻眼睛行動。

噢，我了解。我的先生稍後會過來接我。

好的，需要幫忙時請告知我們。

Nursing Notes 護理記錄

Vital signs stable. Eye drops given to dilate left pupil. Education on pre-op and operation methods, choice of anesthsia. Well accepted.

生命徵象穩定，給予左眼散瞳眼藥水。術前衛教手術方式及麻醉選擇。病人充分接受。

Vocabulary and Sentence Examples 字彙與例句

1. dilate [daɪˊlet]
   (v.) 擴張；擴大

   The cat dilated its eyes to focus on its prey.
   貓瞪大牠的眼睛，瞄準牠的獵物。

2. conscious [ˋkanʃəs]
   (adj.) 神智清醒的

   He may become conscious an hour after his operation.
   她可能在手術 1 小時後會清醒。

3. eye patch [ˊaɪ ˏpætʃ]
   眼罩

   You can wear an eye patch when you take a nap during the afternoon. 當你下午小睡片刻時，可戴上眼罩。

Terminology 術語

1. eye drop [ˊaɪ drap] 眼藥水

Post-Operative Care　術後照護

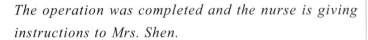

67

The operation was completed and the nurse is giving instructions to Mrs. Shen.

N: Hello, how are you feeling now?

P: A little bit **itchy**[1] and uncomfortable.

N: That's quite common right after surgery.

P: I also have some discharge from my eye. Can I clean it?

N: Well, the discharge is also common. You can clean your eye, but try not to touch or press your left eye too much. Your eye will be more **sensitive**[2] to light and **mechanical**[3] pressure.

P: OK. I'll keep this in mind.

N: From now on, you must wear an eye patch all the time. This will prevent your eye from being **rubbed**[4] and touched. It will also protect it from bright lights.

P: Can I take it off when I sleep?

N: I'm afraid you can't. Don't take it off until your next follow-up exam.

P: I see. Thanks for your explanation.

N: Here's your medication. Use these eye drops 3 times a day.

P: How about this one?

N: The ointment should be used once only before you go to bed.

P: Can I continue doing housework as before?

N: Yes, just don't lift any heavy objects or bend down past your waist.

P: I'll try to remember. Is there anything else I should take note of?

手術完成，護理師正在指導沈女士一些事項。

哈囉，你現在感覺如何呀？

有一點癢和不舒服。

這在術後是很常見的。

眼睛還有一些分泌物，我可以清理它們嗎？

嗯，分泌物也是很常見的現象。你可以清理眼睛，但請別太常接觸或按壓到眼睛。因為它們會對光線和機械壓力較敏感。

好的，我會謹記在心的。

從現在開始你必須時時戴眼罩，它可以保護眼睛免於搓揉、按壓，同時也能避開強光的刺激。

我睡覺時可以拿起來嗎？

恐怕不行。直到你下次回來追蹤之前都不要脫下眼罩。

好，謝謝你的說明。

這是你的藥物，每天點三次眼藥水。

那這一個呢？

眼藥膏只在你睡前使用一次。

我能像以前一樣繼續做家事嗎？

可以的，只要別提重物或者彎腰就可以了。

我會記住的。還有什麼事情是我要注意的？

N: Yes, you should come back for follow-up exams regularly. The doctor will monitor the progress in your visual ability.

有的，你必須按時回診追蹤檢查。醫師會監測你視力的進步情況。

P: I understand. Thanks a lot.

我了解，多謝！

Nursing Notes　護理記錄

Post-Op Instructions: May have itchy sensation, discharge, hypersensitivity to light, and slight discomfort. Told to avoid rubbing or touching eye. Taught to wear an eye patch. Use eye drops and ointment regularly as instructed.

術後衛教：手術眼可能有癢感、分泌物、對光敏感及輕微不適。告知需避免接觸光線或揉眼睛。教導戴眼罩和規律地依醫囑使用眼藥水及眼藥膏。

Vocabulary and Sentence Examples　字彙與例句

1. itchy [ˈɪtʃɪ]
   (adj.) 發癢的

   I felt itchy where the mosquito bit me.
   我感覺蚊子叮咬處發癢。

2. sensitive [ˈsɛnsətɪv]
   (adj.) 敏感的；易受傷的

   Newborns are very sensitive to injuries.
   新生兒對於傷害是很敏感的。

3. mechanical [məˈkænɪkl̩]
   (n.) 機械的

   The doctor used a mechanical ventilator to support the boy's ventilation.
   醫師使用機械式呼吸器維持男孩的呼吸。

4. rub [rʌb]
   (v.) 揉搓

   If something gets into your eyes, please don't rub them. It can hurt your cornea.
   有東西跑進眼睛時不要揉搓眼睛，因為會傷害你的角膜。

More Information

1. 問診的常用句子
   (1) Do you have blurred vision?
       你有視力模糊的情形嗎？
   (2) When you look at objects, do you ever have double vision?
       往一邊看時，你會把一個物體看成兩個嗎？
   (3) Do you feel like there is something in your eyes?
       你眼睛有異物感嗎？
   (4) Are you afraid of bright sunlight?
       你畏光嗎？
   (5) Do your eyes have a lot of discharge?
       你的眼睛有很多分泌物嗎？
   (6) Do your eyes feel sore?
       你會感到眼睛痠痛嗎？
   (7) Do your eyes hurt?
       你的眼睛會痛嗎？
   (8) Do your eyes feel inflamed?
       眼睛有發炎嗎？

2. 檢查時的常用句子
   (1) Please look at the light.
       請看著光源。
   (2) Please move your eyes according to the light.
       眼睛請隨光源移動。
   (3) Please look into the lens.
       看著水晶體。
   (4) Tell me which of my fingers are moving.
       告訴我哪一隻手指頭正在移動。
   (5) Look straight ahead at my ear.
       直視我的耳朵。
   (6) Please start reading the lines from the top row. What letter of the alphabet do you see?
       請從最上一排開始讀起。你看到的字母是什麼？
   (7) Which line is more clear?　　哪一條線較清晰？
   (8) Please cover your left eye.　　請遮住你的左眼。

Exercise 小試身手

◉ Choose the Correct Answer

( ) 1. Wearing dirty eyeglasses can make objects appear _____ . (A)blue (B)blurred (C)blink (D)blank 眼鏡髒了可能造成視力模糊。

( ) 2. This machine can _____ light energy into electromeganetic energy. (A)transfer (B)transduce (C)transit (D)transform 這台機器可以將光能轉換成電磁能。

( ) 3. There's heavy _____ in the mountains. (A)fog (B)figure (C)fix (D)fork 山區大霧瀰漫。

( ) 4. A human's pupils will _____ after death. (A)dilute (B)diplopia (C)dilate (D)diverge 人死亡後瞳孔會放大。

( ) 5. Was the driver _____ during that time? (A)comfortable (B)conscientious (C)conscious (D)confluent 司機在當時是神智清醒的嗎？

◉ Fill in the Blanks

1. If you feel an _____ _____ , then your _____ is _____ . 傷口會癢的感覺意味著正在癒合。

2. Eyes are _____ to ultraviolet light. 紫外線容易使眼睛脆弱。

3. Let me check your _____ _____ and _____ _____ . 我檢查一下你的視力和視野吧。

4. Apply two _____ of this _____ _____ medication before going to bed. 睡前點兩滴眼藥水。

5. Because of his _____ , he cannot see _____ in front of him _____ . 因為白內障，他無法清晰地看到前方的物體。

● Simplify Nursing Notes

1. 感覺眼前一片黑。

2. 感覺腹痛如刀割。

3. 感覺雙腳像穿了襪子。

4. 教導病人不要直視太陽。

5. 告知病人不可揉眼睛。

● Translation

1. 你對視力模糊能否描述詳細些？

2. 現在我需要檢查你的視力和視野，請跟我來。

3. 我會給你點一些眼藥水，以使瞳孔擴大，利於醫師進行手術。

4. 你可以在術後很快回家，但你的左眼必須用眼罩遮蓋著以避免傷害。

5. 你可以清理眼睛，但請別太常接觸或按壓到眼睛。

解答

Ear, Nose, and Throat (ENT) Unit

耳鼻喉科

Learning Goals 學習目標

1. Approaching patients complaining about ear discharge or hearing impairment
2. Assessing the postoperative condition of patients receiving tympanoplasty
3. Providing health education to patients

Outline 本章大綱

- About ENT　關於耳鼻喉
- Case Information: Chronic Otitis Media (COM)
  個案資訊：慢性中耳炎
- Admission Assessment　入院評估
- Hospitalization　住院療護
- Discharge Instructions　出院衛教

Medical English for Healthcare Professionals

About ENT　關於耳鼻喉

68

ENT is the abbreviation for "Ear, Nose, and Throat". The ear is divided into three parts, the outer ear, the middle ear and the inner ear. The outer ear contains the **external auditory canal**[1] and the **auricle**[2], both of which help to collect sounds from the environment. The middle ear has structures amplifying sounds. These include the **tympanic membrane**[3], **malleus**[4], **incus**[5] and **stapes**[6]. The inner ear also contains structures for listening and maintaining equilibrium, the **cochlear**[7] system and **vestibular**[8] system.

The nose is composed of an external structure and an inner architecture which includes the nasal cavity and the **sinuses**[9]. Because of the close connection of the nose and the environment, various kinds of infections are common. The most common is sinusitis.

The throat is a component of the airway and the phonation structure, vocal cords. The throat also resides near the common pathway of the respiratory and alimentary system. Therefore, foreign bodies (food) can often get lodged in the throat and require ENT doctors to perform emergency surgeries. Infections and neoplasm are other problems that can also occur.

ENT 是耳鼻喉三字的縮寫。耳朵分成三部分,分別是外耳、中耳和內耳。外耳包含外耳道和耳殼,兩者都能幫助收集環境的聲音。中耳有放大聲音的結構,包含了鼓膜、槌骨、砧骨、鐙骨。內耳包含了聽覺和平衡的構造,即耳蝸和前庭系統。

鼻部包含了鼻腔和鼻竇等外在及內在的構造。因為鼻部與環境有著密切的接觸,因此容易得到各種感染,最常見的有鼻竇炎。

喉嚨包含呼吸道和發聲的聲帶組成,它們位於呼吸道和消化道的共同通道附近。因此在急診室,耳鼻喉科醫師常常需要幫病人夾出一些異物。這些構造也可能發生各種感染症和腫瘤。

Terminology 術語

1. external auditory canal 外耳道
   [ɪkˋstɜnl ˋɔdəˏtorɪ kəˋnæl]
2. auricle [ˋɔrɪkl̩] 耳殼
3. tympanic membrane 鼓膜
   [tɪmˋpænɪk ˋmɛmbren]
4. malleus [ˋmælɪəs] 鎚骨
5. incus [ˋɪŋkəs] 砧骨
6. stapes [ˋstepiz] 鐙骨
7. cochlear [ˋkɑklɪə] 耳蝸的
8. vestibular [vəsˋtɪbjələ] 前庭的
9. sinus [ˋsaɪnəs] 鼻竇
   (全稱為 perinasal sinus)

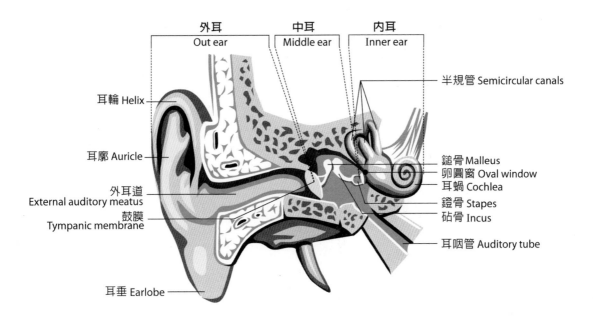

外耳 Out ear　中耳 Middle ear　內耳 Inner ear

半規管 Semicircular canals
耳輪 Helix
耳廓 Auricle
鎚骨 Malleus
卵圓窗 Oval window
耳蝸 Cochlea
外耳道 External auditory meatus
鐙骨 Stapes
砧骨 Incus
鼓膜 Tympanic membrane
耳咽管 Auditory tube
耳垂 Earlobe

Case Information 個案資訊

Chronic Otitis Media (COM) 慢性中耳炎

[ˈkrɑnɪk əˈtaɪtɪs ˈmidɪə]

1. **Causes**: Chronic bacterial infection.
2. **Symptoms & Signs**: Ear pain, ear discharge, headache and hearing impairment.
3. **Care**:
   (1) Assessment of symptoms and hearing ability.
   (2) Surgical therapy.
   (3) Post-operative care: Cold compressions and pain management. Avoid spicy or tough to chew foods. Manage secretions and bleeding.
   (4) Return for follow-up exams as instructed.

Admission Assessment　入院評估

Mr. Chen, a 20-year-old man, has suffered from chronic otitis media for one year.	陳先生是 20 歲男性，一年來為慢性中耳炎所苦。
N: Nurse　**P:** Patient	
N: Mr. Chen, how are you feeling today?	陳先生，你今天覺得如何？
P: Not bad, but within the last month, there has been an increase in discharge from my ear.	不會太糟，但是最近一個月我的耳朵分泌物更多了。
N: Have you had an ear ache or headache?	你有耳朵痛或頭痛的情形嗎？
P: No, I have just had some discomfort around my left ear.	不會，只有左耳附近有點兒不舒服。
N: Have you had a fever during this period?	你在這段期間有發燒嗎？
P: No.	沒有。
N: How about your ability to hear? Do you feel as if sounds are coming from your right side?	你的聽力如何？你會覺得聽聲音都從右邊來嗎？
P: Yes. I can't hear voices from my left side very well.	是的，我左耳無法聽到聲音。
N: Have you had **tinnitus**[1] or **vertigo**[2]?	你有耳鳴或者眩暈的情形嗎？
P: I have tinnitus, but it rarely bothers me.	我會耳鳴，但不常造成困擾。
N: Do you have a **stuffy nose**[3] or runny nose especially around dusty or cold weather?	你接觸到灰塵或冷天氣時會容易鼻塞或者流鼻水嗎？
P: Yes, always.	是的，我總是如此。
N: How long have you had these symptoms?	你有這些症狀多久啦？
P: About one year. My doctor told me that I have chronic otitis media.	大約一年。我的醫師告訴我這是慢性中耳炎。
N: Your tympanic membrane isn't **intact**[4], probably due to your otitis media. The doctor will perform **tympanoplasty** to restore your tympanic membrane tomorrow.	而且你的鼓膜也因為中耳炎破裂了。醫師明天會為你進行鼓室成形術以重建之。
P: Will I undergo **general anesthesia**?	我需要接受全身麻醉嗎？
N: Definitely, so you must be NPO after midnight.	當然，因此午夜之後要禁食。
P: Alright, I'll be sure to do that.	好的，我會遵守。

Nursing Notes 護理記錄

Hx of chronic otitis media. Admitted for left ear tympanoplasty. Admission completed. Operation scheduled CM. Told to be NPO after midnight.

病人有慢性中耳炎的病史。因接受左耳鼓室成形術而住院。住院手續已完成。手術安排在明日早上，已告知午夜後要禁食。

 Tips on Writing

1. Hx＝history　病史

2. 病人入院的寫法
   Admitted for/due to＋原因：表示為了什麼原因而住院。
   Admission completed：表示住院手續已經完成。

3. Progress 的用法
   (1) Progress＝is making progress (in)→在……上有所進步（改善）
   The patient's condition progressed.　病人的狀況**進步**（改善）了。
   The patient is making progress in her lung function.　病人的肺功能**進步**了。
   (2) Progress to＋新的狀況→進展為……
   The patient's illness has now progressed to hepatic failure.
   病人**進展**為肝衰竭。

 Vocabulary and Sentence Examples 字彙與例句

1. tinnitus [tɪˈnaɪtəs] 　(n.) 耳鳴	Tinnitus is a symptom from which you hear noises inside your ears.　耳鳴是一種會從耳朵裡聽到噪音的症狀。
2. vertigo [ˈvɜtɪgo] 　(n.) 眩暈	When you are attacked by vertigo, you may feel as if your surroundings are spinning around you. 當你發生眩暈時，你可能會感覺周遭環境繞著你旋轉。
3. stuffy nose [ˈstʌfɪ noz] 鼻塞	Having a stuffy nose is a very common symptom of the flu. 鼻塞是流行性感冒常見的症狀。
4. intact [ɪnˈtækt] 　(adj.) 完整無損的	The package arrived intact.　包裹完整無損地運達。

Terminology 術語

1. general anesthesia [ˈdʒɛnərəl ˌænəsˈθiʒə] 全身麻醉
2. tympanoplasty [ˌtɪmpənəˈplæstɪ] 鼓室成形術

The operation was completed. Mr. Chen was returned to the ward for post-operative care.

手術完成了，陳先生回到病房接受術後照護。

N: Mr. Chen, I'm going to place an **ice pack**[1] over your neck and ear to relieve your pain.

陳先生，我會在你的頸部和耳朵附近放置冰袋以減輕疼痛。

P: Thanks. Can I only use it when I feel painful?

謝謝。可以只在疼痛時使用嗎？

N: Yes, but don't use it for more than 20 minutes. Otherwise, you will hurt your skin.

當然，但是別超過 20 分鐘，否則可能會傷及你的皮膚。

P: OK, I understand.

好的，我了解了。

N: If you still feel pain, please call us and we can get you some painkillers.

如果你還覺得疼痛，請告知我們，我們會給你一些止痛藥。

P: I see. When can I eat? I've been NPO for almost a day now.

我了解。我可以進食了嗎？我幾乎一整天沒吃東西了。

N: You can eat right now. Just be careful not to **choke**[2].

你現在就可以吃東西，但是要注意別嗆到了。

P: I understand. Are there any restrictions for what I can eat?

我了解。有任何飲食上的限制嗎？

N: No restrictions except for spicy foods and foods difficult to chew.

別吃太辣及難以咀嚼的食物，除此之外別無限制。

P: OK. Do you have any other advice?

好的。還有其他建議嗎？

N: Yes. Keep the wounds on your ear and neck away from water over the next two days. You must be **cautious**[3] not to let anything get into your ear canal.

當然，耳朵和頸部的傷口兩天內要保持乾燥不碰水，你必須小心別讓任何東西進到你的耳道內。

P: I'll be careful. What if I see any discharge or bleeding from my ear?

我會注意的。那如果我耳朵有分泌物或出血怎麼辦呢？

N: Please call us immediately. Your wound is quite tiny. Any **perceivable**[4] discharge or bleeding should catch your attention.

請立即告訴我們。這個傷口很小，所以任何可察覺的分泌物或出血應該都能吸引你的注意。

P: OK, I'll look out for this.

好的，我會特別注意。

N: Please rest for now. The doctor will be in to see you in a bit.

那麼現在你可以休息了，醫師很快就會來看你。

P: Thanks a lot.

多謝。

Nursing Notes 護理記錄

Vital signs stable. TPR: 36.5℃, 65/min. 10/min. Ice pack being placed over **post-auricular** area and neck. On diet. Will keep observing wound for discharge and bleeding.

病人的生命徵象穩定，體溫 36.5℃，脈搏每分鐘 65 下，呼吸速率每分鐘 10 次。耳後及頸部冰敷中，已開始飲食。將持續觀察是否有分泌物和出血。

Vocabulary and Sentence Examples 字彙與例句

1. ice pack [ˈaɪs pæk]
   (n.) 冰袋

   If you have an acute sport injury, please use an ice pack to relieve any pain and swelling.
   當你發生急性運動傷害時，請用冰袋緩解疼痛和腫脹。

2. choke [tʃok]
   (v./n.) 嗆到；窒息

   The elderly are prone to choking because of degeneration in their ability to swallow.
   因為吞嚥功能退化，老年人很容易嗆到。

3. cautious [ˈkɔʃəs]
   (adj.) 留意；小心

   The doctor was very cautious while performing the operation. 這位醫師很小心地進行這項手術。

4. perceivable [pəˈsivəbḷ]
   (adj.) 可察覺的

   The change in surrounding is quite perceivable.
   周遭環境的改變相當容易被察覺。

Terminology 術語

1. post-auricular [postəˈrɪkjələ] 耳後的

Discharge Instructions 出院衛教

71

Mr. Chen prepared for discharge.

N: I don't see any discharge or bleeding from your ear canal. You don't have a fever either. The doctor has **permitted**[1] you to be discharged from the hospital.

P: That is great news to me. I wonder what I need to be careful about at home.

N: Keep away from foods that are **tough**[2] to chew for 2 weeks. **Straining**[3] your **masticatory** muscles may impair your wounds from healing.

P: Got it. How about ice cream?

N: Ice cream is okay. Also, you have to monitor any discharge or bleeding from the wound.

P: If I have any of them, what can I do?

N: Come back to the ER for help.

P: I'll remember to do that.

N: Here's your ointment. Use a little to cover your wound every night before your sleep. This can prevent infections and help your wound heal. In addition, don't take out the cotton ball in your auditory canal until you return for a follow-up.

N: One more thing, your hearing ability has not completely been restored. When you return for follow-up next week, the doctor will arrange rehabilitation therapy for you in the following 2~3 months.

P: I'll keep that in mind. Can I exercise?

N: Yes, but please avoid strenuous exercises the first week after the operation. For example, jogging or going to the gym are not allowed.

P: I see. Is there anything else?

陳先生正準備出院。

你的耳道沒有分泌物或出血情形，也沒有發燒，醫師准許你出院了。

真是太好了。我想知道在家時有哪些注意事項。

2 週內避免難以咀嚼的食物，過度拉扯咀嚼肌可能會妨礙傷口癒合。

我了解。那可以吃冰淇淋嗎？

可以。你也必須監測傷口是否有分泌物和出血的情形。

如果我有其中一種，該怎麼做？

前來急診求助。

我會記住的。

每天晚上睡前使用一些藥膏覆蓋你的傷口，以免細菌感染並且幫助傷口癒合。此外，在你回診追蹤前不要取出耳道內的棉球。

還有一件事，你的聽力尚未完全恢復。當你下週回診時，醫師會安排你在接下來的 2~3 個月裡進行復健治療。

我會謹記在心。那我能運動嗎？

可以的，但在術後第一週請避免劇烈的運動。譬如說，慢跑或者到健身房健身。

我明白。還有要注意的事嗎？

N: No. Please let me know if you still have any questions.

沒有了。如果你還有任何問題請告知我。

P: No more. Thanks a lot!

沒有問題了，多謝！

Nursing Notes 護理記錄

Wound clear. Discharge instructions given. Told to avoid foods difficult to chew. Instructions for using ointment given. Next follow-up exam arranged.

病人的傷口乾淨。已給予出院衛教，告知避免堅韌的食物。指導藥膏的使用方式。已安排下次回診追蹤時間。

Vocabulary and Sentence Examples 字彙與例句

1. permit [pəˊmɪt] 　(v.) 允許	Harvard University has permitted him to enter the campus. 哈佛大學已經允許他入學。
2. tough [tʌf] 　(adj.) 堅韌的；咬不動的	The steak is too tough to chew. 這塊牛排太老了以致於我咬不動。
3. strain [stren] 　(v.) 拉傷	Joe strained his calf muscles during the competition. 喬在比賽中拉傷了他的小腿。

Terminology 術語

1. masticatory [ˊmæstəkəˌtorɪ] 咀嚼的

More Information

1. 問診的常用句子

   (1) Have you had a cough, runny nose or sore throat?
   你有咳嗽、流鼻水或喉嚨痛嗎？

   (2) How long have you had these symptoms?
   你有這些症狀多久了？

   (3) Are you coughing up blood?
   你咳嗽帶血嗎？

   (4) Do you have an ear ache or any discharge from the ear?
   你有耳痛或耳朵有分泌物嗎？

   (5) Do you have pain around your ears or neck?
   你的耳朵或頸部附近會痛嗎？

   (6) Have you had a nose bleed?
   你有流鼻血嗎？

   (7) Do you feel like there is a foreign body within your throat?
   你喉嚨有異物感嗎？

   (8) Do you have an oral ulcer that is healing very slowly?
   你有難以痊癒的口腔潰瘍嗎？

2. 檢查時的常用句子

   (1) Please open your mouth and continue to keep it open.
   請張口並保持著這個姿勢。

   (2) Please hold your breath.
   請摒住呼吸。

   (3) Please open your mouth and say "Ah---".
   請張口說「啊」。

   (4) Please turn your head to the right.
   請將頭向右轉。

   (5) I'm going to use a swab to touch your pharynx. You may feel a little discomfort.
   我將用棉棒觸碰你的咽部，你可能會有些微的不適感。

Exercise 小試身手

● Choose the Correct Answer

(   ) 1. Can you _____ what I'm saying?   (A)hear   (B)hate   (C)hair   (D)heel
你有聽到我說的話嗎？

(   ) 2. Use care while eating to prevent yourself from _____ .   (A)drink
(B)choking   (C)inhale   (D)aspirate   請小心以避免嗆到。

(   ) 3. When you come home at night, please be _____ .   (A)caution
(B)care   (C)cautious   (D)careless   當你晚上回家時，請務必小心留意。

(   ) 4. The sound is too soft to be _____ .   (A)prepare   (B)perceived
(C)precipitate   (D)preserve   這聲音太小以致於無法察覺。

(   ) 5. He _____ his muscle from jogging.   (A)sprained   (B)strained
(C)stained   (D)stretched   他因為慢跑造成肌肉拉傷。

● Fill in the Blanks

1. During your periods of _____ _____ , do you have _____ or
_____ ?   在你聽力減損的期間，你有眩暈或耳鳴的症狀嗎？

2. This operation does not require you to have _____ _____ . In contrast,
it only requires you to have _____ _____ .
這項手術不需要全身麻醉，相反的，它只需要局部麻醉就可以了。

3. Do you have a _____ _____ , _____ _____ ,
or _____ _____ ?   你有喉嚨痛、鼻塞或流鼻水的情形嗎？

4. Because of the surgery, you need to receive _____ therapy for your
_____ muscles, which are responsible for _____ .
由於手術的關係，你需要接受具有咀嚼功能的咀嚼肌的復健治療。

5. Without my _____ , no one is allowed to step near this room.
沒有我的許可，任何人都不可以接近那個房間。

● Simplify Nursing Notes

1. 病人的肝功能指數進步了。

_____

2. 病人的心臟功能惡化到功能性第四類。

_____

3. 病人的肌肉力量進展為五分。

_____

4. 病人因為疝氣手術而住院。

_____

5. 病人住院手續已經完成。

_____

● Translation

1. 你有耳朵痛或頭痛的情形嗎？

_____

2. 你有耳鳴或者眩暈的情形嗎？

_____

3. 我會在你的頸部和耳朵附近放置冰袋以減輕疼痛。

_____

4. 耳朵和頸部的傷口兩天內要保持乾燥不碰水。

_____

5. 過度拉扯咀嚼肌可能會妨礙傷口癒合。

_____

General Dentistry Unit

一般牙科

Learning Goals 學習目標

1. Assessing patients with dental caries
2. Preparing patients for dental treatment
3. Giving oral health instructions (OHI) to patients

Outline 本章大綱

- About the Teeth　關於牙齒
- Case Information: Dental Caries
  個案資訊：齲齒
- Dental Examination　牙科診察
- Dental Treatment　牙科治療
- Dental Care Education　牙科衛教

Medical English for Healthcare Professionals

About the Teeth 關於牙齒

72

The tooth is composed of **enamel**[1], **dentin**[2], **cementum**[3] and **pulp**[4]. Pulp is a soft tissue containing many blood vessels, nerve endings and various connective tissue cells. It supplies teeth with blood and nutrition. Other tissues are hard and responsible for the shape and strength of the teeth.

Most people have two sets of teeth throughout their lives, deciduous dentition and permanent dentition. Deciduous teeth include 2 **incisors**[5], 1 **canine**[6] and 2 **molars**[7]. Permanent teeth include 2 **premolars**[8] and 1 additional molar to that contained in deciduous dentition from each quadrant. In total, there are 20 teeth in the deciduous dentition and 32 in the permanent dentition. Generally, the permanent teeth will gradually replace deciduous ones within ages 6 through 12.

牙齒由牙釉質（琺瑯質）、牙本質（象牙質）、牙骨質及牙髓所組成。牙髓是由許多血管、神經末梢及各種結締組織細胞構成的軟組織，供應牙齒血流及養分。其餘皆為硬組織，負責構成牙齒的型態及強度。

大多數的人一生有兩套牙齒，分別為乳齒列及恆齒列。前者（乳齒列）每一象限有 2 顆乳門齒、1 顆乳犬齒及 2 顆乳臼齒；後者（恆齒列）比乳齒列於每一象限多出 2 顆小臼齒及 1 顆大臼齒。總言之，乳齒列有 20 顆牙齒，恆齒列則有 32 顆牙齒。通常恆齒會在 6~12 歲陸續取代乳齒。

Terminology 術語

1. enamel [əˈnaml̩] 牙釉質（琺瑯質）
2. dentin [ˈdɛntɪn] 牙本質（象牙質）
3. cementum [səˈmɛntəm] 牙骨質
4. pulp [pʌlp] 牙髓
5. incisor [ɪnˈsaɪzə] 門齒
6. canine [ˈkenaɪn] 犬齒
7. molar [ˈmolə] 大臼齒
8. premolar [prɪˈmolə] 小臼齒；前臼齒

Case Information 個案資訊

Dental Caries [ˈdɛntl̩ ˈkɛriz] 齲齒（俗稱蛀牙）

1. **Causes**: Bacteria in the oral cavity consume sugars as "food", generating acidic substances that produce decalcification and decay on the surfaces of teeth.
2. **Symptoms & Signs**: Cavity, white decalcified patch and toothache.

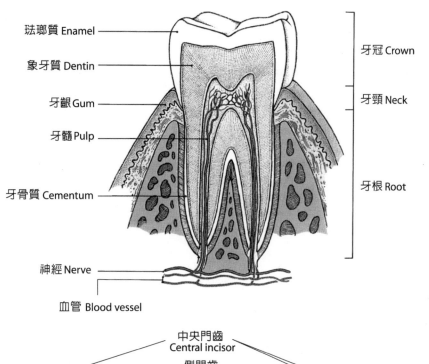

牙冠 Crown
牙頸 Neck
牙根 Root

珐瑯質 Enamel
象牙質 Dentin
牙齦 Gum
牙髓 Pulp
牙骨質 Cementum
神經 Nerve
血管 Blood vessel

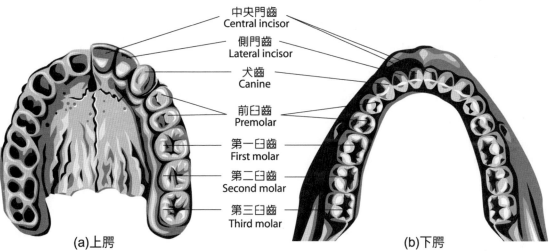

中央門齒
Central incisor
側門齒
Lateral incisor
犬齒
Canine
前臼齒
Premolar
第一臼齒
First molar
第二臼齒
Second molar
第三臼齒
Third molar

(a)上腭　　　　　　　　　　　　　　　(b)下腭

Case Information 個案資訊

3. **Care**:
   (1) Brush teeth correctly.
   (2) Use dental floss to clean inter-dental spaces.
   (3) Avoid cavity-causing foods, i.e. candies, sodas and cookies containing sugar.
   (4) Do not chew betel nut or smoke.
   (5) Have routine oral examinations regularly.

Dental Examination　牙科診察

73

Mr. Hu visited the OPD because of a toothache.

N: Nurse　**D:** Doctor　**P:** Patient

N: Good morning, Mr. Hu. Sorry to have kept you waiting.

P: That's all right.

N: For medical records, would you mind if I ask you a few questions?

P: No, please go ahead.

N: Have you had any systemic diseases?

P: No, I've been pretty healthy.

N: Are you **allergic**[1] to any types of food or medications?

P: No, not at all.

N: OK. What is the problem with your teeth?

P: Last night, I started having a really bad toothache.

N: Can you identify the tooth that hurts?

P: I'm not sure. It seems to be one of my left lower posterior teeth.

N: We need to do some examinations to locate it then.

P: I see. *(Opening his mouth)*

N: OK, I can see a large **cavity**[2] on the last molar on the lower, left side.

P: Is it bad? Do I need to have it **pulled out**[3]?

N: It depends on the severity. Would you mind getting an X-ray?

(After a while, the X-ray was taken)

D: Well, the X-ray showed the cavity involved some dentin, which is why you are sensitive to hot and cold drinks. Therefore, we'll arrange an appointment to remove the infected part of your tooth, and **restore**[4] it.

胡先生因牙痛來到門診（部）。

早安，胡先生。抱歉讓你久等了。

沒關係。

醫療程序之故，介意我請問你一些問題嗎？

我不介意，請問吧。

你有任何系統性的疾病嗎？

沒有，我挺健康的。

你會對任何食物或藥物過敏嗎？

一點也不會。

好的。你的牙齒有什麼問題呢？

昨晚我的牙齒痛得非常厲害。

你能夠指出是哪顆牙在痛嗎？

我不確定。好像是左下方後面的其中一顆牙齒。

那麼我們需要做一些檢查來確認是哪顆牙齒會痛。

我知道了。（張開嘴巴）

好的，我看到在左下排最後一顆臼齒上有個大的蛀洞。

情況很糟嗎？需要拔掉嗎？

這得視蛀牙的嚴重程度而定，介意照張X光片嗎？

（過了一會兒，X光片照好了）

嗯，X光片顯示，蛀洞已經擴及到牙本質，這就是你會對冷熱飲敏感的原因。我們將為你安排一次約診，以清除受到感染的齒質並將牙齒復形。

N: Mr. Hu, let's see when will you be available for an appointment?

P: Thursday will be OK.

胡先生，請問你什麼時候方便回診呢？

星期四好了。

Nursing Notes　護理記錄

C/O toothache. Decay on last molar of left posterior region seen on X-ray. Suggested undergoing restoration. Next visit would be this Thursday.

主訴牙痛。X 光檢查發現左下排最後一顆臼齒為齲齒。建議進行修補術。病人將於星期四回診。

Vocabulary and Sentence Examples　字彙與例句

1. allergic [əˈlɚʤik]
   (adj.) 過敏性的

   I am allergic to penicillin.　我對盤尼西林過敏。

2. cavity [ˈkævətɪ]
   (n.) （牙齒的）蛀洞

   Dental cavities are caused by bacteria.
   牙齒的蛀洞是由細菌引起的。

3. pull out [pʊl aʊt]
   拔除（牙齒）

   I had a bad tooth pulled out last night.
   我昨晚拔除一顆蛀牙。

4. restore [rɪˈstɔr]
   (v.) 修補（蛀牙）

   I wonder if my tooth decay will be able to be restored.
   我想知道我的蛀牙是否可以修補好。

Dental Treatment 牙科治療

74

Mr. Hu returned to the dental OPD on Thursday.

胡先生於星期四至牙科門診部。

N: Good morning, Mr. Hu. How are you feeling today?

早安，胡先生。你今天好嗎？

P: The toothache has gotten worse over the last few days. I'm pretty worried about today's treatment. Will it hurt?

牙痛在這幾天越來越嚴重了。我滿擔心今天的治療，會很痛嗎？

N: Well, you will **inevitably**[1] feel some pain or discomfort. Would you like a local anesthetic?

嗯，難免會有不舒服的感覺，你需要局部麻醉嗎？

P: Yes, I think I would.

好的，我想是需要的。

N: Today we have to remove your infected dental tissue. After that, we'll recommend the most suitable restorative material for you.

今天我們會幫你把蛀牙的部分移除，之後，我們會在補牙材料上的選擇給你一些建議。

P: What are my choices?

我有哪些選擇？

N: The most applied materials are **resin**[2] and **amalgam**[3].

最常使用的是樹脂和銀粉。

P: What's the differences between the two?

兩者有什麼差別嗎？

N: Resin provides a better-looking **appearance**[4]. However, its stability is poor. On the other hand, the stability of amalgam is better than resin, but the silver color really is not favored by many patients.

樹脂在外觀上比較好看，但材料穩定度較差；另一方面，銀粉材料穩定度優於樹脂，不過很多人不喜歡它銀色的外觀。

P: I see. Thanks for the explanation.

我明白了。謝謝說明。

N: You're welcome.

不客氣。

(After the treatment)

（治療之後）

D: Judging from the structure of your remaining tooth, we suggest that you choose amalgam as the restorative material. What do you say?

根據你剩餘的齒質來評估，我們建議你選擇銀粉來填補牙齒，如何？

P: But I'm very concerned about the appearance of my smile…

但是我很在乎笑起來的樣子…

D: In that case, you should choose resin. Since the stability of resin is poor, you will need to come back for follow-ups twice a year.

這樣的話，你最好選擇樹脂。不過，由於它的穩定度比較差，所以你每半年需要回診追蹤一次。

P: I will, thank you.

我會的，謝謝你。

Nursing Notes 護理記錄

C/O aggravating toothache. The doctor removed the carious tissue and restored the tooth with resin. Told to return for a follow-up exam after 6 months. Patient cooperated.

主訴牙痛加劇。醫師已移除蛀牙部分並以樹脂填補。已告知病人半年後回診追蹤。病人同意配合。

Vocabulary and Sentence Examples 字彙與例句

1. inevitably [ɪnˈɛvətəblɪ]
   (adv.) 必然地

   He inevitably failed the exam, because he didn't study hard enough.　因為他不夠用功，考試當然不及格。

2. resin [ˈrɛzɪn]
   (n.) 樹脂（補牙材料）

   It is made from the resin.　它是用樹脂做成的。

3. amalgam [əˈmælgəm]
   (n.) 銀粉（補牙材料）

   A report showed that amalgam can be harmful to one's health.　有報導指出補牙用的銀粉對身體健康有害。

4. appearance (n.) 外觀
   [əˈpɪrəns]

   The appearance of the museum changed.
   博物館的外觀改變了。

Dental Care Education　牙科衛教　75

6 months later, Mr. Hu returned to the dental OPD for a follow-up exam.	6 個月以後，胡先生至牙科門診回診。
D: How are you feelling today?	今天感覺如何呢？
P: Pretty good.	挺好的。
D: You have a routine dental check-up today.	好的，今天是例行性的牙科檢查。
P: OK, I'm ready. *(Opening his mouth)*	好的，我準備好了。（打開嘴巴）
(After the check-up)	（檢查結束後）
N: The doctor said the previous restoration seems to be doing well. However, we found some **decalcification** on it.	醫師表示，先前的補綴物看起來狀況還不錯。然而，我們發現牙齒有些脫鈣的情形。
P: Does that mean I have to undergo another treatment again?	意思是說我還要再接受另一次的治療嗎？
N: Not to worry. Decalcification does not mean you have tooth **decay**[1]. Decalcification precedes tooth decay and is caused by poor oral hygiene.	別緊張。脫鈣並不是指蛀牙，而是由於口腔衛生不好所產生的蛀牙前兆。
P: How can I prevent it from getting worse?	我如何防止情況更加惡化呢？
N: The best way to prevent it from getting worse is to improve your oral **hygiene**[2] by brushing your teeth correctly and using **dental floss**[3] and an **interdental brush**[4].	最佳方式是改善口腔衛生，正確刷牙及使用牙線與牙間刷。
P: How often should I brush my teeth? Is twice a day enough?	我要多久刷一次牙呢？一天兩次夠嗎？
N: Remember to brush your teeth after every meal.	切記在每餐飯後刷牙。
P: How about **mouth rinse**[5] or sugar-free gum? I've heard this can help clean teeth.	那漱口水和無糖口香糖呢？聽說這些能協助清潔牙齒。
N: Only brushing your teeth correctly, using dental floss and avoiding foods that can cause cavities will maintain your oral health.	唯有正確刷牙、使用牙線與牙間刷及避免致齲食物才能保有良好的口腔健康。
P: What are cavity-causing foods?	哪些是致齲食物呢？
N: These are foods rich in surgar, like soda, candy, sweet cookies or cakes.	富含糖分的食物，像是汽水、糖果、甜的餅乾或糕點等。
P: I see, thanks a lot.	我知道了，多謝。

Nursing Notes 護理記錄

Decalcification was found on premolars. Oral health instructions given. Well accepted.

前臼齒有脫鈣情形。給予口腔健康衛教。病人可接受。

Vocabulary and Sentence Examples 字彙與例句

1. decay [dɪˋke]
   (v.) 蛀蝕
   (n.) 蛀牙

   Sweets can cause tooth decay. 甜食會蛀蝕牙齒。

2. hygiene [ˋhaɪdʒin]
   (n.) 衛生、清潔

   Oral hygiene is of high importance.
   口腔衛生是非常重要的。

3. dental floss
   [ˋdɛntl̩ flɔs]
   (n.) 牙線

   The correct use of dental floss and a tooth brush are highly recommended by dentists. 牙醫師建議，除了正確刷牙之外最好還能使用牙線來清潔牙齒。

4. interdental brush
   [ˏɪntəˋdɛntl̩ brʌʃ]
   (n.) 牙間刷

   Interdental brushing is useful for patients wearing braces.
   牙間刷對於接受矯正治療的患者來說相當實用。

5. mouth rinse
   [mauθ rɪns]
   (n.) 漱口水

   Mouth rinse helps maintain our oral hygiene.
   漱口水可以協助我們維持良好的口腔衛生。

Terminology 術語

1. decalcification [diˏkælsəfəˋkeʃən] （蛀牙形成過程初期的）脫鈣

Exercise 小試身手

● Choose the Correct Answer

( ) 1. I can see a large _____ on your last molar. (A)case (B)care (C)cavity (D)hole 我在你的最後一顆臼齒上看到一個很大的蛀洞。

( ) 2. We will _____ your tooth after this treatment. (A)restore (B)reuse (C)rebuild (D)regain 在治療後，我們會將你的牙齒復形。

( ) 3. She has been _____ from a backache since last night. (A)suffering (B)referring (C)preferring (D)transferring 她從昨晚開始感到背部不適。

( ) 4. _____ is the preceding sign for dental caries. (A)Calibration (B)Recalcification (C)Calculation (D)Decalcification
脫鈣是牙齒即將形成蛀牙的前兆。

( ) 5. Oral _____ is of high importance. (A)habit (B)hygiene (C)hobby (D)hydration 口腔衛生是非常重要的。

● Fill in the Blanks

1. Most people have two sets of teeth throughout their lives. These two sets of teeth are called _____ dentition and _____ dentition.
大多數人終其一生擁有兩套牙齒。這兩套牙齒稱為乳齒列及恆齒列。

2. Every tooth is composed of 4 parts- _____ , _____ , cementum and _____ .
每顆牙齒皆由四個部分所構成－牙釉質、牙本質、牙骨質及牙髓。

3. I had a bad tooth _____ _____ last night. 我昨晚拔了一顆蛀牙。

4. _____ _____ , a.k.a. tooth decay, is one of the most common oral diseases. 齲齒（蛀牙）是最常見的口腔疾病之一。

5. The use of _____ _____ , an _____ _____ , and a tooth brush is recommended by dentists.
牙醫師建議除了正確刷牙之外最好還能使用牙線來清潔牙齒。

◉ Translation

1. 我看到在左下排最後一顆臼齒上有個大的蛀洞。

———————————————————————————————

2. 蛀洞已經擴及到牙本質，這就是你會對冷熱飲敏感的原因。

———————————————————————————————

3. 今天我們會幫你把蛀牙的部分移除。

———————————————————————————————

4. 我們發現牙齒有些脫鈣的情形。

———————————————————————————————

5. 最佳預防蛀牙的方式是正確刷牙及使用牙線與牙間刷。

———————————————————————————————

Psychiatry

精神醫學

Medical English for
Healthcare Professionals

Psychiatry is a medical science about the study and treatment of mental disorders. These mental disorders include various **affective**[1], behavioural, **perceptual**[2], **cognitive**[3] and drive abnormalities which reflect the dysfunction of our brain.

Our brain is so well protected by the skull, as well as the blood-brain barrier. Its structure and function is also much more complicated than other organs. So, there still exist great difficulties in discovering the true mechanism behind almost all mental disorders.

The other difficulty is about golden **criteria**[4] for diagnosis. Hypertension can be diagnosed by measuring the blood pressure, so is blood sugar for diabetes mellitus. For depression or any other mental disorders, there exist no objective, simple measures for a clear-cut diagnosis. Mental disorders need to be diagnosed in accordance with the criteria listed in diagnostic manuals such as the widely used *Diagnostic and Statistical Manual of Mental Disorders* (DSM), published by the American Psychiatric Association, and the *International Classification of Diseases* (ICD), edited and used by the World Health Organization.

Psychiatric assessment typically starts with a mental status examination and the compilation of a case history. Psychological tests and physical examinations may be conducted, including on occasion the use of neuroimaging or other neuro-physiological techniques.

Psychiatric treatment applies a variety of modalities, including psychoactive medication, psychotherapy, and other techniques such as electroconvulsive treatment, or transcranial magnetic stimulation.

　　精神醫學是一門研究與治療精神疾病的科學，這些精神疾病包括各種不同的情感、行為、知覺、認知與驅力上的異常，這些是源自腦部功能的異常。

　　我們的腦部受到頭骨及血腦障壁的嚴密保護。它的結構與功能，相較於其他器官，複雜了很多，所以要了解精神疾病的致病機轉就存在很大的困難。

　　另外一個困難則是在診斷上缺乏黃金標準，像是血壓可以用來做出高血壓的診斷，血糖過高就是糖尿病。但是像是憂鬱症或任何其他精神疾患，並沒有一個客觀簡單的方法來做出明確的診斷。精神疾患的診斷目前必須依靠診斷手冊中的準則，現在廣泛使用的診斷手冊有兩種，一是美國精神醫學學會的精神疾患診斷與統計手冊（縮寫為 DSM），第二種則是世界衛生組織的國際疾病分類系統。

　　精神醫學的評估一開始是心智狀態檢查及詳細病史，接下來可進行心理測驗及理學檢查，有時也需要做神經影像或其他神經生理學檢測。

　　精神醫學治療包括幾種不同類別，包括精神藥物、心理治療、電痙攣療法，或經頭骨電磁刺激等。

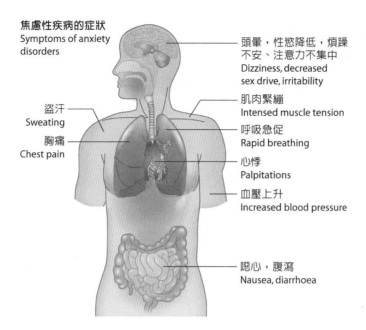

焦慮性疾病的症狀
Symptoms of anxiety disorders

頭暈，性慾降低，煩躁不安、注意力不集中
Dizziness, decreased sex drive, irritability

肌肉緊繃
Intensed muscle tension

盜汗
Sweating

呼吸急促
Rapid breathing

胸痛
Chest pain

心悸
Palpitations

血壓上升
Increased blood pressure

噁心，腹瀉
Nausea, diarrhoea

Terminology 術語

1. affective [əˈfɛktɪv] 感動的；感情的（在精神醫學中用以形容一個人的情感表現或情緒狀態）
2. perceptual [pəˈsɛptʃuəl] 知覺的；知覺力的
3. cognitive [ˈkɑgnətɪv] 認知的（指思考、想法、判斷）
4. criterion [kraɪˈtɪrɪən] 標準；準則（複數為 criteria）

Case Information 個案資訊

Panic Attack [ˈpænɪk əˈtæk] 恐慌發作

1. **Causes**: Panic attacks can happen at any time and any place without warning. Many people with panic disorder develop intense anxiety between episodes.

2. **Symptoms & Signs**: Extreme and unreasoning anxiety and fear, often accompanied by disturbed breathing, increased heart activity, vasomotor changes, sweating, and a feeling of dread.

3. **Care**:
   (1) Take a deep breathe and slow down.
   (2) Take a small break, such as walk, read a book or do something that they like to do.
   (3) Try to find out what is causing your panic attacks.
   (4) Learn to get rid of your negative thoughts.

Ms. Lee, a 45-year-old married female, was admitted due to very frequent panic attacks in these 7 days.

N: Nurse   **P:** Patient

N: Can you describe what happened to you in the first place?

P: It was an especially **stressful**[1] time at work. All week my heart would race and I'd have a pain in my chest. By the time weekend rolled around, when sitting watching TV, I broke into a cold sweat ... and then my throat seem choked. I just cannot breathe and felt that I am going to die. Everything seem so unreal and out of control.

N: It happened 7 days ago, right? And what happened after?

P: I was brought into ER by my husband. My blood was drawn and tested. They also ran ECG. But they just cannot find anything wrong, except the carbon dioxide level is low in my blood. They gave me a shot, some kind of tranquilizer I think. They also gave me several pink tablets for the next possible attacks.

N: Did you sleep well recently?

P: In these couple of years, I had difficult falling into sleep. The sleep quality was also very poor, **superficial**[2] and easily interrupted.

N: Do you feel sad? Lack of interest? Or, even have the ideation of ending your life?

李小姐，45 歲已婚女性，因為最近 7 天中發生了許多次恐慌發作而住院。

可以請你形容一下第一次發生的情形嗎？

那一陣子我的工作很忙，整個禮拜我都覺得心跳很快，也有點胸痛。到了週末的時候，當我看著電視，突然冒冷汗，然後喉嚨就好像被塞住了。我無法呼吸，並且覺得自己快要死掉了。周遭的事情都變得不真實，整個也都失去了控制。

這是七天前發生的事對嗎？然後呢？

我被我先生送到急診室，抽了血送驗，也做了心電圖。但是除了血液中二氧化碳濃度偏低外，並沒有甚麼異常的結果。他們幫我打了一針，我想應該是鎮定劑吧！他們也給了我一種粉紅色的藥片，讓我在發作時可以服用。

你最近睡得好嗎？

這兩年來，我有入睡困難，而且睡眠品質也不好，睡得很淺、容易中斷。

你覺得心情不好嗎？對事物缺乏興趣，甚至有想結束生命的想法？

P: Of course I am not in a good mood to do anything. But it is due to the fear of another attack. And I have no **intention**[3] at all to end my own life.

N: Thanks for providing so much information. If you felt panic again, please let us know right away.

當然我沒有心情去做任何事情，但這是因為擔心恐慌會再發作，不過我並沒有想死的念頭。

謝謝你提供我們這麼多的資訊，假如你覺得恐慌就要發作，請立刻通知我們。

 Nursing Notes 護理記錄

Clear **consciousness**[4]. Good attention and very cooperative.

Mood: Anxious with some **dysphoria**.

Speech: **Relevant**[5] and **coherent**[6].

Thought: Worries and fears about panic attack. She wants to be sure that there is no serious physical problem. No **delusion**, formal thought disorders. No **suicidal ideation**.

意識清楚，注意力良好，也很配合。

情緒：焦慮、也有些心情不好。

說話：適切且完整。

思考：擔心並害怕恐慌發作，想確定身體狀況確實沒問題。沒有妄想或思考障礙，沒有自殺意念。

Vocabulary and Sentence Examples　字彙與例句

1. stressful [ˈstrɛsfəl]
   (adj.) 有壓力的，緊張的

   Have a test is very stressful.　考試是很有壓力的。

2. superficial [ˌsupəˈfɪʃəl]
   (adj.) 膚淺的，淺薄的

   A superficial wound means that the individual has a wound that is on or near the surface of the skin.
   淺層傷口表示個體的傷口位於皮膚的表面或附近。

3. intention [ɪnˈtɛnʃən]
   (n.) 意向；意圖，目的；打算

   My good intentions were repaid by good results.
   我的善意得到了善報。

4. consciousness [ˈkanʃəsnɪs]
   (n.) 意識；知覺

   The patient lost consciousness.　病人失去了知覺。

5. relevant [ˈrələvənt]
   (adj.) 有關的；適當的，貼切的

   His gender isn't relevant to whether he is a good nurse.
   他的性別跟他是不是一個好護理師不相關。

6. coherent [koˈhɪrənt]
   (adj.) 有條理的，首尾一貫的；一致的

   This coherent speech was interrupted by protester.
   抗議者中斷了這場有條理的演說。

Terminology 術語

1. dysphoria [dɪsˈfərɪə] 憂鬱情緒；煩躁不安
2. delusion [dɪˈluʒən] 妄想
3. suicidal ideation [ˌsuəˈsaɪdl̩ ˌaɪdɪˈeʃən] 自殺意念

More Information

DSM-5　Diagnostic Criteria for Panic Attack　恐慌發作診斷準則

A discrete period of intense fear or discomfort, in which four (or more) of the following symptoms developed abruptly and reached a peak within minutes:
一段特定時期的強烈害怕或不適，必須在下列症狀中至少有四個或以上症狀的突然發生，並在幾分鐘之內變得極為嚴重：

- Palpitations, and/or accelerated heart rate　心悸或／和心跳加速
- Sweating　冒汗
- Trembling or shaking　顫抖或發抖
- Sensations of shortness of breath or being smothered　呼吸短促或透不過氣來
- Feeling of choking　窒息感
- Chest pain or discomfort　胸痛或不舒服
- Nausea or abdominal distress　噁心或腸胃不適
- Feeling dizzy, unsteady, lightheaded, or faint　頭暈、感覺不穩、頭重腳輕，或暈倒
- Chills or hot flashes　冷顫或發熱
- Paresthesias (numbness or tingling sensations)　感覺異常，麻木或震顫感覺
- De-realization (feelings of unreality) or depersonalization (being detached from oneself)　失真感或覺得不是自己的感覺
- Fear of losing control or going insane　害怕失去控制或發瘋
- Sense of impending death　發冷或發熱

Hospitalization 住院療護

*After examinations, including 24 hours' ECG, EEG, thyroid function, no abnormality was **detected**[1]. A couple of panic attacks happened in the week after examination, but **responded**[2] very well after the use of Alprazolam, a short-acting **anxiolytics**.*

N: Did Doctor Huang discuss with you about the diagnosis?

P: Yes, I was told that everything looks fine with my body. It should be panic disorder which could be related to my life stress and emotion management. Are you sure that there is nothing wrong with my heart or endocrine?

P: In this moment, all the examination done revealed no **evidence**[3] of physical problem. The only possible explanation should be a mental disorder. Some dysfunction happened in your brain which resulted in autonomic dysfunction and fearful mood. From the good response to an anxiolytics during the attack also favor the **diagnosis**[4].

P: Doctor told me that I need to take **antidepressant** for several months. Is it true? I do not feel blue or want to commit suicide. Why I need to take antidepressant?

N: Several studies found that antidepressants turned out to be the most effective treatment for panic attacks. Anxiolytics can only **alleviate**[5] the symptoms of panic attack, but unable to prevent it. However, it will take several months for antidepressants' full **efficacy**[6].

住院之後做了一些檢查,包括 24 小時心電圖、腦波、甲狀腺功能,都沒有發現異常。第一週的住院發生了兩次恐慌,使用短效抗焦慮藥物 Alprazolam 後,症狀很快就解除。

黃醫師已經跟你就診斷部分做討論了嗎?

是的,我被告知身體健康的部分沒有問題,應該是恐慌症,和我生活中壓力與情緒的處理有關。你確定我的心臟和內分泌系統都沒有問題嗎?

目前所有的檢查結果都很正常,唯一的可能應該是精神疾患。你腦中某種功能出現異常,進而造成自律神經異常和害怕的感覺,而且根據抗焦慮藥物對恐慌發作很好的治療效果,更證實了恐慌症這個診斷。

醫師說我必須吃幾個月抗憂鬱的藥物,真的得這樣嗎?我並沒有心情不好或想自殺,為何需要吃抗憂鬱的藥物呢?

有一些研究發現,服用抗憂鬱藥物對於控制恐慌發作是最好的治療。抗焦慮藥物可以幫忙立即解除恐慌發作的症狀,但無法預防未來再發作。但是抗憂鬱的藥物一般需要吃幾個月,這樣它的效果才能完全發揮。

Nursing Notes　護理記錄

Ms. Lee still had some doubt about the diagnosis. However, she is less fearful toward the panic attacks. It was noted that she quite easily got mad about her son and husband. In general, she seems anxious-prone and too tensed.

李小姐對於診斷仍然有些不確定，但是她對於恐慌發作已經沒有那麼害怕。病房中發現她容易對先生和兒子發脾氣，整體來說也容易焦慮和太緊繃。

Vocabulary and Sentence Examples　字彙與例句

1. detect [dɪˈtɛkt]
   (v.) 偵測；察覺

   I detected anger in her voice.
   我察覺出她說話聲裡含著憤怒。

2. respond [rɪˈspɑnd]
   (v.) 回應；反應

   The patient is responding well to treatment.
   病人對治療反應良好。

3. evidence [ˈɛvədəns]
   (n.) 跡象；痕跡；證據

   There are evidences that somebody has been living here.　有跡象顯示有人一直住在這裡。

4. diagnosis [ˌdaɪəgˈnosɪs]
   (n.) 診斷；病名

   The two doctors made different diagnoses of my disease.　兩位醫師對我的病下了不同的診斷結論。

5. alleviate [əˈlivɪˌet]
   (v.) 減輕（痛苦等）；緩和

   He take some medicine to alleviate cold symptoms.
   他服用了一些藥物來減輕感冒症狀。

6. efficacy [ˈɛfəkəsɪ]
   (n.) 效力；療效

   In pharmacology, efficacy refers to the maximum response achievable from a drug.
   在藥理學上，efficacy 指的是從藥物中獲得最大效果的效力。

Terminology 術語

1. anxiolytic [æŋˌzaɪəˈlɪtɪk] 抗焦慮藥物
2. antidepressant [ˌæntɪdiˈprɛsənt] 抗憂鬱藥物

Discharge Instructions　出院衛教

In the second weeks' admission, Ms. Lee only had mild chest tightness and dizziness twice. Discharge is arranged tomorrow.

P: Is it ok for me to use Alprazolam for my panic attacks? Is there any limitation of how many tablets I can take per day?

N: You can take Alprazolam as soon as you feel that the panic is going to happen. Under your current condition, you do not need to worry about taking too much anxiolytics. Some patients will use even 6 tablets per day. However, this means that they should have higher dose of antidepressants to control the frequency of attacks.

P: Anything else I need to pay attention to?

N: Do not have too much coffee, alcohol, or any **stimulants**[1]. Reduce your work load and stay away situations which will make feel angry or frustrated.

在第二週住院期間，李小姐只有兩次覺得輕微的胸悶和頭暈，準備明天出院。

當我恐慌發作時我都可以使用 Alprazolam 嗎？每天有限制說可以只吃幾顆嗎？

你只要覺得好像恐慌要開始發作就可以吃 Alprazolam 了，不用擔心你會吃太多，有些病人甚至每天吃到 6 顆。但如果是這樣，這可能代表說他們抗憂鬱藥物的劑量需要增加，這樣才能控制恐慌發作的頻率。

有其他我需要注意的事項嗎？

不要喝太多的咖啡、酒類，或其他提神的東西。減少你的工作負擔，避免會讓你生氣或挫折的情境。

 Nursing Notes　護理記錄

Ms. Lee has been instructed about how to use anxiolytics and antidepressants. However, cognitive-behavior therapy should be needed for her stress reduction and emotion management.

李小姐已經被告知如何使用抗焦慮與抗憂鬱藥物，但對於如何減少壓力及情緒管理，可以做認知行為治療。

 Vocabulary and Sentence Examples　字彙與例句

1. stimulant [ˈstɪmjələnt]
   (n.) 刺激物，興奮劑，酒

The lowering of interest rates will act as a stimulant to economic growth.　利率的下降將刺激經濟增長。

Exercise 小試身手

⊙ Choose the Correct Answer

( ) 1. When he got up he felt _____. (A)dizen (B)dizzy (C)dizzyingly (D)dizygotic 他站起來時覺得頭暈。

( ) 2. The child was almost _____ by the heavy smoke. (A)choked (B)chokedamp (C)choc (D)choir 這孩子幾乎被濃煙窒息了。

( ) 3. _____ _____ is a group of metabolic diseases in which a person has high blood sugar. (A)Heart disease (B)Panic attack (C)Diabetes mellitus (D)Renal failure 糖尿病是一種有高血糖的代謝性疾病。

( ) 4. _____ _____ are periods of intense fear or apprehension that are of sudden onset and of variable duration from minutes to hours. (A)Heart disease (B)Panic attack (C)Diabetes mellitus (D)Renal failure
恐慌發作時會突然間感覺強烈的恐懼或憂慮,時間變化會從幾分鐘到幾小時。

( ) 5. Tom was under the _____ that he saw many cockroachs in front of him. (A)delude (B)delusive (C)delusion (D)delubrum
湯姆懷有幻覺,他看到了很多蟑螂在他面前。

⊙ Fill in the Blanks

1. There was _____ on his forehead. 他額頭冒著汗。

2. _____ is a sensation of tingling, tickling, prickling and burning of a person's skin. 感覺異常是一種刺痛、發癢、刺痛或燒灼人皮膚的感覺。

3. _____ is an unusually or abnormally rapid or violent beating of the heart.
心悸是一種心臟不尋常或異常快速或猛烈的跳動。

4. Early pregnancy is often accompanied by _____. 懷孕初期常伴有噁心。

5. He _____ when he heard the news. 聽到這消息時,他暈了過去。

● Simplify Nursing Notes

1. 她有定期回醫院門診診療並服用藥物。

    _____

2. 她已有很長的時間無法安穩的睡覺。

    _____

3. 病人有很長的思覺失調症病史且從未接受治療。

    _____

4. 病人聽見聲音叫她去做「壞事」。

    _____

5. 病人對那聲音感到疲憊和害怕。

    _____

● Translation

1. 你覺得心情不好嗎？對事物缺乏興趣，甚至有想結束生命的想法？

    _____

2. 有一些研究發現，服用抗憂鬱藥物對於控制恐慌發作是最好的治療。

    _____

3. 抗焦慮藥物可以幫忙立即解除恐慌發作的症狀。

    _____

4. 你只要覺得好像恐慌要開始發作就可以吃 Alprazolam 了。

    _____

5. 不要喝太多的咖啡、酒類，或其他提神的東西。

    _____

參考書目 | References

于博芮、胡文郁、胡月娟、周守民、黃翠媛、吳韻淑、羅筱芬、簡淑慧、鄭春秋、柳秋芳、陳麗糸、劉向援、郭素娥、劉桂芬、鄭麗珠、王雪娥、凃秀妮、陳怡如、林金絲⋯李惠玲(2020)·*成人內外科護理*（上、下冊，八版）·華杏。

王桂芸、馮容芬、丘周萍、李玉秀、李惠玲、周桂如、徐淑芬、陳惠絹、陳麗華、歐嘉美、劉英妹、石光中、白玉珠、吳沁樺、尚忠菁、林麗華、胡麗霞、范淑芳⋯劉劍華(2021)·*新編內外科護理學*（六版）·永大。

中華民國解剖學學會(1998)·*解剖學辭彙：中英對照表*·力大。

李華寶、韋建華(2007)·*實用醫護英語*·專業全民英檢。

余金燕(2004)·*常見疾病字詞*（修訂版）·合記。

黃宣宜、陳瑞蘭、洪芬芳、張榮珍、李朝雄、湯美霞、江青桂、呂雀芬、陳美碧、金蓉蓉、林靜蘭、余靜雲、馬玉琴、陳淑姬、侯玟里、李姿瑩、黃一玲、吳佳珍、施燕華⋯王慈婷(2021)·*最新精神科護理學*（十版）·永大。

劉正義、袁瑞晃、楊菁華(2014)·*華杏醫學縮寫辭典*（四版）·華杏。

劉明德、蔡玟蕙、薛承君、甘宜弘、張銘峰、韓文蕙、徐玉珍、馮兆康、傅綢妹、王守玉、呂維倫、薛嘉元、蔣蓮娜、Seak, J. C. K. (2022)·*醫護英文用語*（六版）·新文京。

謝瀛華(2016)·*實用醫學縮寫辭典*（五版）·華格那。

蘇秀妹、石惠美、蔡素珍(2008)·*Nursing English for pre-professionals*（初版二刷）·希伯崙。

Guyton, A. G., & Hall, J. E. (2005)·*新編醫用生理學*（修訂版，林佑穗、袁宗凡譯）·合記。

Perry, J.、蔡碧華(2005)·*護理美語*（三版）·偉華。

Tony, G. (2007). *Oxford english for careers: Nursing 1*. Oxford University Press.

附錄 | Appendix

Common Abbreviation for Medical Personnel 醫護常用縮寫

簡寫符號與單位

Ⓛ	left 左側		mμ	millimicron 毫微米	
Ⓡ	right 右側		mμc	millimicrocurie(nanocurie) 毫微居里	
□, ♂	male 男性的；男性		mμg	millimicrogram(nanogram) 毫微克	
○, ♀	female 女性的；女性		μEq	microequivalent 微當量	

A

A-aO₂	alveolar-arterial oxygen gradient 肺泡及動脈氧量差
AAPMC	antibiotic-associated pseudomembranous colitis 抗生素性大腸偽膜性結腸炎
AAROM	active assisted range of motion 主動輔助式運動範圍
AAV	adeno-associated virus 腺性病毒
AB; Ab	antibody 抗體
A>B	air greater than bone (conduction) 空氣傳導大於骨性傳導
ABE	acute bacterial endocarditis 急性細菌性心內膜炎
ABG	arterial blood gas analysis 動脈血液氣體分析
ABx	antibiotics 抗生素
AC	air conduction 空氣傳導（聽力檢查）
	anterior chamber 前房
	anterior colporrhaphy 前側陰道縫合術
AC&BC	air and bone conduction 空氣及骨性傳導
AcCoA	acetyl coenzyme A 乙醯輔酶 A
accom.	accommodation (eye examination) 調節（眼科檢查）
ACE	angiotensin-converting enzyme 血管收縮素轉換酶
ACh; Ach	acetylcholine 乙醯膽鹼
AChE; AchE	acetylcholinesterase 乙醯膽鹼酯酶
ACI	acute coronary infarction 急性冠狀動脈梗塞
acid phos.; AP	acid phosphatase 酸性磷酸酶
ACTH	adrenocorticotropic hormone (corticotropin) 促腎上腺皮質激素
AD	atopic dermatitis 異位性皮膚炎
ADA	adenosine deaminase 腺苷酸脫胺酶
ADE	acute disseminated encephalitis 急性瀰漫性腦炎
ADEM	acute disseminating encephalomyelitis 急性瀰漫性腦脊髓炎

adenoca.	adenocarcinoma　腺癌
ADH	alcohol dehydrogenase　乙醇去氫酶
	antidiuretic hormone　抗利尿激素
ADHD	attention deficit hyperactivity disorder　注意力不足／過動症
ADPKD	autosomal dominant polycystic kidney disease　顯性染色體性多囊性腎病變
ADV	adenovirus　腺病毒
AED	antiepileptic drug　抗癲癇藥
	automated extermal defibrillator　體外自動去纖維顫動器
AEP	auditory evoked potential　聽覺誘發電位
AER	auditory evoked response　聽覺誘發反應
AF	atrial flutter　心房撲動
AFB	acid-fast bacillus　耐酸性桿菌
aff	afferent　傳入的
A fib	atrial fibrillation　心房纖維顫動
AFO	ankle-foot orthosis　踝足部整直法；踝足矯具
AFP	alpha-fetoprotein　α 胎兒蛋白
A/G; A/G ratio	albumin-globulin ratio　白蛋白與球蛋白比值
Ag; ag	antigen　抗原
AGA	appropriate for gestational age　胎兒大小合於妊娠週數
AGC	absolute granulocyte count　顆粒性白血球絕對計數
AGE	acute gastroenteritis　急性腸胃炎
AGN	acute glomerulonephritis　急性腎絲球腎炎
$AgNO_3$	silver nitrate　硝酸銀
A/G ratio	albumin/globulin ratio　白蛋白與球蛋白比值
AGT	antiglobulin test　抗球蛋白試驗
AGTT	abnormal glucose tolerance test　異常葡萄糖耐受性試驗
AICA	anterior inferior cerebellar artery　前下小腦動脈
AICD	automatic implantable cardioverter defibrillator　植入型心臟整流去顫器
AIDS	acquired immune deficiency syndrome　後天免疫缺乏症候群；愛滋病
AIDS-KS	acquired immunodeficiency syndrome with Kaposi's sarcoma　後天性免疫缺乏症候群併有卡波西氏肉瘤
AIHA	autoimmune hemolytic anemia　自體免疫溶血性貧血
AIHD	acquired immune hemolytic disease　後天性免疫溶血疾病
AIN	acute interstitial nephritis　急性間質性腎炎
AK; A/K	above knee　膝上的
AK amp	above-knee amputation　膝上截肢術
ALA	antilymphocyte antibody　抗淋巴球抗體
ALB; alb.	albumin　白蛋白

ALD	adrenoleukodystrophy 腎上腺腦白質營養不良
ALG	antilymphocytic globulin 抗淋巴球性球蛋白
ALP	alkaline phosphatase 鹼性磷酸酶
ALS	acute lateral sclerosis 急性脊髓側索硬化症
ALT	alanine aminotransferase 丙胺酸胺基轉移酶
AMA	anti-mitochondrial antibody 抗粒線體抗體
AMI	acute myocardial infarction 急性心肌梗塞
AML	acute myelogenous leukemia 急性骨髓性白血病
AN	anorexia nervosa 厭食症
ANC	absolute neutrophil count 嗜中性白血球絕對計數
ANF	atrial natriuretic factor 心房利尿鈉因子
anti HBc	anti-hepatitis B core antibody 抗 B 型肝炎核心抗原抗體
anti HBe	anti-hepatitis B envelope antibody 抗 B 型肝炎 e 抗原抗體
anti HBs	anti-hepatitis B surface antibody 抗 B 型肝炎表面抗原抗體
AO	abdominal aorta 腹主動脈
$A_2 < P_2$	second aortic sound is less than second pulmonary sound 主動脈瓣第二心音小於肺動脈瓣第二心音
$A_2 > P_2$	second aortic sound is greater than second pulmonary sound 主動脈瓣第二心音大於肺動脈瓣第二心音
APACHE	acute physiology and chronic health evaluation 急性生理和慢性健康評估
APE	acute pulmonary edema 急性肺水腫
APL	abductor pollicis longus 外展拇長肌
APN	acute pyelonephritis 急性腎盂腎炎
apo E	apolipoprotein E 脂蛋白本體 E
APR	abdominoperitoneal resection 腹膜切除術
APTT; aPTT	activated partial thromboplastin time 活化部分凝血酶原時間
AR	aortic regurgitation 主動脈逆流；主動脈瓣閉鎖不良
ARD	acute respiratory disease 急性呼吸道疾病
ARDS	acute respiratory distress syndrome 急性呼吸窘迫症候群
ARF	acute renal failure 急性腎衰竭
ARG; Arg	arginine 精胺酸
AROM	active range of motion 自主運動範圍
AS	aortic stenosis 主動脈瓣狹窄
ASA I	Healthy patient with localized pathological process 有局部病理變化的正常人
ASA II	A patient with mild to moderate systemic disease 有輕度至中度系統性疾病的病人

ASA III	A patient with a severe systemic disease that limits activity but is not incapacitating　有嚴重系統性疾病，但尚有部分活動能力的病人	
ASA IV	A patient with an incapacitating systemic disease　有嚴重疾病而無法活動的重病病人	
ASA V	moribund patient not expected to live　預期無救的重病病人	
ASLO	antistreptolysin - O titer　抗 O 型鏈球菌落血素效價	
AST	aspartate aminotransferase (GOT)　天門冬胺酸胺基轉移酶	
	aspartate transaminase　天門冬酸轉胺酶	
ATLV	adult T-cell leukemia virus　成人 T 細胞白血病病毒	
ATM	acute transverse myelopathy　急性橫貫性脊髓病	
ATN	acute tubular necrosis　急性腎小管壞死	
ATP	adenosine triphosphate　腺苷三磷酸	
ATPase	adenosine triphosphatase　腺苷三磷酸酶	
AUC	area under the curve　曲線下區域（藥物濃度）	
A-V	arteriovenous　動靜脈的	
AV/AF	anteverted/anteflexed　向前彎／前傾的	
AVB	atrioventricular block　房室傳導阻斷	
AVF	arteriovenous fistula　動靜脈瘻管	
aVF	augmented unipolar lead, left leg　左腿向量增加單極導線（心電圖）	
aVL	augmented unipolar lead, left arm　左臂向量增加單極導線（心電圖）	
AVM	arteriovenous malformation　動靜脈畸形	

B

B＞A	bone greater than air　骨性傳導大於空氣傳導	
Ba	barium　鋇	
BAL	bronchoalveolar lavage　支氣管肺泡灌洗	
BAND	band neutrophil　帶狀型嗜中性白血球（梭狀核球）	
Baso; baso.	basophil　嗜鹼性白血球	
BBO	bronchobronchiolitis obliterans　阻塞性支氣管及小支氣管炎	
B/C	blood urea nitrogen/creatinine ratio　血尿素氮與肌酸酐比值	
BCG	bacillus Calmette-Guerin (vaccine)　卡介苗	
Bil; bil	bilirubin　膽紅素	
BK	below knee　膝下的	
BKA	below knee amputation　膝下截肢術	
BMD	Becker muscular dystrophy　貝克型進行性肌肉萎縮症	
BMT	bone marrow transplantation　骨髓移植	
BOOP	bronchitis obliterans with organized pneumonia　閉鎖性支氣管炎併有器質性肺炎	
BPH	benign prostatic hypertrophy　良性前列腺肥大	

BSA	bovine serum albumin　牛血清白蛋白
BSO	bilateral salpingo-oophorectomy　兩側輸卵管卵巢切除術
BUN	blood urea nitrogen　血尿素氮

C

C_{cr}	creatinine clearance rate　肌酸酐廓清率
CAD	coronary artery disease　冠狀動脈疾病
CAH	congenital adrenal hyperplasia　先天性腎上腺增生
cAMP	cyclic adenosine monophosphate　環形腺苷單磷酸
Ca/P	calcium to phosphorus ratio　鈣磷比值
CBD	common bile duct　總膽管
CCK	cholecystokinin　膽囊收縮素
CDH	congenital diaphragmatic hernia　先天性橫膈膜疝氣
	congenital dislocation of the hip　先天性髖關節脫位
	congenital dysplasia of the hip　先天性髖關節發育不良
cDNA	complementary DNA　互補 DNA
CEA	carcino-embryonic antigen　癌胚抗原
CFU	colony-forming units　菌落形成單位
CGN	chronic glomerulonephritis　慢性腎絲球腎炎
CHD	common hepatic duct　總肝管
	congenital heart disease　先天性心臟病
CIN	cervical intra-epithelial neoplasia　子宮頸部上皮內贅瘤
CIS	carcinoma in situ　原位癌
CJD	Creutzfeldt-Jakob disease　庫賈氏病
CK	creatine kinase　肌胺酸激酶
CLL	chronic lymphocytic leukemia　慢性淋巴球性白血病
CML	chronic myelocytic leukemia　慢性骨髓細胞性白血病
CMV	cytomegalovirus　巨細胞病毒
CNS	central nervous system　中樞神經系統
CO	carbon monoxide　一氧化碳
C/O	chief complaint　主訴
COAD	chronic obstructive airway disease　慢性阻塞性呼吸道疾病
COLD	chronic obstructive lung disease　慢性阻塞性肺病（同 COPD）
COMT	catechol-O-methyl transferase　兒茶酚氧甲基轉移酶
COPD	chronic obstructive pulmonary disease　慢性阻塞性肺病（同 COLD 或 COAD）
CPAP	continuous positive airway pressure　持續性呼吸道正壓
CPB	cardiopulmonary bypass　心肺分流

CPN	chronic pyelonephritis	慢性腎盂腎炎
CPPV	continuous positive pressure ventilation	持續性正壓換氣
CPR	cardiopulmonary resuscitation	心肺復甦術
Cr	creatinine	肌酸酐
CRD	chronic renal disease	慢性腎病

CREST　calcinosis, Raynaud's phenomenon, esophageal dysfunction, sclerodactyly and teleangiectasis　鈣化、雷諾氏現象、食道功能不良、硬皮症及微血管擴張

CRF	chronic renal failure	慢性腎衰竭
CRP	C-reactive protein	C－反應質蛋白
CS; C/S	cesarean section	帝王切開術；剖腹生產術
CSF	cerebrospinal fluid	腦脊髓液
CT	computerized tomography	電腦斷層攝影

CTGA　complete transposition of the great arteries　完全性大動脈（血管）完全轉位症

CUC	chronic ulcerative colitis	慢性潰瘍性結腸炎
CV	cardiovascular	心臟血管的
CVA	cerebrovascular accident	腦血管意外；腦中風
CVS	cardiovascular surgery	心臟血管外科
CW	cardiac work	心臟作功
	continuous wave	連續波

D

D_L	maximal diffusing capacity	最大擴散能力
D_{50}	50% dextrose injection	50%葡萄糖注射
2-D	two-dimensional	平面
3-D	three-dimensional	三度空間；立體
DA	degenerative arthritis	退化性關節炎
	dopamine	多巴胺
DAD	delayed after depolarization	去極化後延遲
DAI	diffuse axonal injury	瀰漫性軸索損傷
dB	decibel	分貝
D&C	dilation and curettement	（子宮頸）擴張及（子宮內膜）刮除術
D/C	discontinued	中斷
DDX	differential diagnosis	鑑別診斷
DHA	decosahexaenoic acid	二十二碳六烯酸
DHEA	dehydroepiandrosterone	去氫表雄固酮
DHT	dihydrotestosterone	二氫睪固酮
DKA	diabetic ketoacidosis	糖尿病性酮酸血症

dL	deciliter 十分之一公升；公合；分升	
DLCO	Diffusing capacity of lung for carbon monoxide 肺部一氧化碳擴散量	
DM	diabetes mellitus 糖尿病	
DORV	double-outlet right ventricle 右心室雙出口症	
DPL	diagnostic peritoneal lavage 診斷性腹膜灌洗	
Dr; Dr.	doctor 醫師；博士	
DRE	digital rectal examination 直腸指診	
DRG	diagnosis-related group 診斷關聯群	
DT	delirium tremens 震顫性譫妄	
DTaP-Hib-IPV	白喉破傷風非細胞性百日咳、b型嗜血桿菌及不活化小兒麻痺五合一疫苗	
DTR	deep tendon reflex 深部肌腱反射	
DU	duodenal ulcer 十二指腸潰瘍	

E

EAD	early after depolarization 早期後去極化
EAE	experimental allergic encephalomyelitis 實驗型過敏性腦脊髓炎
EBM	evidence-based medicine 實證醫學
EBV	Epstein-Barr virus 艾伯斯坦－巴爾氏病毒
ECF	extracellular fluid 細胞外液
ECG	electrocardiogram 心電圖
ECHO virus	enterocytopathogenic human orphan virus 人類腸道細胞致病性孤獨病毒；埃可病毒
ECM	extracellular material 細胞外物質
ECMO	extracorporeal membrane oxygenation 體外黏膜氧合作用
E. coli	*Escherichia coli* 大腸桿菌
ECT	electric convulsive therapy 電痙治療
ECV	extracellular volume 細胞外液量
ED_{50}	expected death rate of 50% 預期50%致死率
EDH	epidural hematoma 硬腦膜外出血
EEG	electroencephalogram 腦電圖；腦液圖
	electroencephalography 腦電波描記法；腦電波圖
EGD	esophagogastroduodenoscopy 食道胃十二指腸鏡檢查
EKG	electrocardiogram 心電圖
EM	electron microscope 電子顯微鏡
	electron microscopy 電子顯微鏡檢查
EMB	ethambutol （抗結核用藥）
EMG	electromyogram 肌電圖
	electromyography 肌電流描記法

EMT	emergency medical technician 急診醫檢技術員
ENDO	endotracheal 氣管內的
EOM	extraocular movement 眼外肌運動
EPS	extrapyramidal syndrome 錐體外路徑症候群
EPSP	excitatory postsynaptic potential 興奮性突觸後電位
ER	emergency room 急診室
ESRD	end-stage renal disease 末期腎臟疾病
ETOH	ethyl alcohol 乙醇；酒精
EVS	endoscopic variceal sclerosis 靜脈曲張硬化內視鏡檢查

F

Fab	antigen binding fragment （抗體的）抗原結合部
5-FC	5-fluorocytosine （抗黴菌用藥）
5-FU	5-fluorouracil 五氟尿嘧啶（抗癌用藥）
FD_{50}	median fatal dose 半數致死劑量
FDA	Food and Drug Administration 食品藥物管理署
FEV_1	forced expiratory volume (in one second) 第一秒用力呼氣容積
FGN	focal glomerulonephritis 局部腎絲球腎炎
FHR	fetal heart rate 胎兒心跳速率
$FICO_2$	concentration of carbon dioxide in inspired gas 吸入氣體中的二氧化碳含量
FIGO	International Federation of Gynecology and Obstetrics 國際婦產科聯合協會
FIO_2	concentration of oxygen in inspired gas 吸入氣體中的氧含量
FiO_2	fraction of inspired oxygen 吸入氧氣分量
FNA	fine-needle aspiration 細針抽取
FNAB	fine-needle aspiration biopsy 細針抽取活體組織切片
FNAC	fine-needle aspiration cytology 細針抽取細胞學檢查
FNH	focal nodular hyperplasia 局部結節狀增生
FOB	fecal occult blood 糞便潛血
FOBT	fecal occult blood test 糞便潛血試驗
FOU	fever of unknown (origin) 不明熱
FPG	fasting plasma glucose 空腹血糖
FSGS	focal segmental glomerulosclerosis 局部及分節性腎絲球硬化症
FSH	follicle-stimulating hormone 濾泡刺激激素
FTA	fluorescent treponemal antibody 螢光螺旋體抗體
FTG	full thickness graft 全厚層皮膚移植
FUO	fever of unknown origin 不明熱

G

GA	gestational age	妊娠週數；胎齡
GABA	gamma-aminobutyric acid	γ 胺基丁酸
GBBS	group B beta-hemolytic streptococcus	B 群 β 溶血性鏈球菌
GBS	group B *Streptococci*	B 群鏈球菌
	Guillain-Barre' Syndrome	基林巴瑞氏症候群
GC/MS	gas chromatography/mass spectroscopy	氣相色層分析／質量光譜儀測定法
GCS	Glasgow coma score or scale	格拉斯哥氏昏迷指數
GDA	gastroduodenal artery	胃十二指腸動脈
GDM	gestational diabetes mellitus	妊娠糖尿病
GERD	gastroesophageal reflux disorder	胃食道逆流
GFR	glomerular filtration rate	腎絲球過濾率
GGT; GGTP	gamma-glutamyl transpeptidase	γ 麩胺醯轉胜肽酶
GH	growth hormone	生長激素
GI	gastrointestinal	胃腸的
GN	glomerulonephritis	腎絲球腎炎
GNB	Gram-negative bacillus	革蘭氏陰性桿菌
GNC	Gram-negative coccus	革蘭氏陰性球菌
GND	Gram-negative diplococcus	革蘭氏陰性雙球菌
GOT	Glutamic oxaloacetic transaminase	麩胺酸草醯乙酸胺基轉移酶
GPB	Gram-positive bacillus	革蘭氏陽性桿菌
GPC	Gram-positive coccus	革蘭氏陽性球菌
G-6-PD	glucose-6-phosphate dehydrogenase	葡萄糖六磷酸去氫酶缺乏症
GRH	growth hormone releasing hormoe	生長激素釋放激素
GTT	glucose tolerance test	葡萄糖耐量試驗
GU; gu	genitourinary	泌尿生殖器的
GVHD	graft-versus-host disease	移植物抗宿主症
GVHR	graft-versus-host reaction	移植物抗宿主反應

H

HAGG	hyperimmune antivariola gamma globulin	高免疫抗天花 γ 球蛋白
HAV	hepatitis A virus	A 型肝炎病毒
HB; Hb.	hemoglobin	血紅素
HBcAg	hepatitis B core antigen	B 型肝炎核心抗原
HBeAb	hepatitis B envelope antibody	B 型肝炎 e 抗體
HBeAg	hepatitis B envelope antigen	B 型肝炎 e 抗原
HBIG	hepatitis B immunoglobulin	B 型肝炎免疫球蛋白
HbO_2	oxygenated hemoglobin	氧化血紅素

HBsAg	hepatitis B surface antigen	B 型肝炎素面抗原
HBV	hepatitis B virus	B 型肝炎病毒
HCC	hepatocellular carcinoma	肝細胞癌
HCG	human chorionic gonadotropin	人類絨毛膜促性腺激素
HCO$_3$	bicarbonate	重碳酸鹽
Hct.; hct.	hematocrit	血比容
HD	hemodialysis	血液透析
HEENT	head, eyes, ears, nose, and throat	頭、眼、耳、鼻及喉
HELLP	hemolsis, elevated liver enzymes, and low platelet (count)	溶血、肝酵素增高及血小板（計數）低
HF	heart failure	心臟衰竭
Hg	*Hydrargyrus* (mercury)（拉）	汞
5-HIAA	5-hydroxyindoleacetic acid	羥基吲哚乙酸
HIB	*Hemophilus influenzae* type B	流行性感冒嗜血桿菌 B
HIDA	hepato-iminodiacetic acid	肝－亞胺基雙醋酸
HIV	human immunodeficiency virus	人類免疫缺乏病毒
HIV-I	human immunodeficiency virus-I	人類免疫缺乏病毒第一型
HIVD	herniated intervertebral disc	椎間盤突出
HLA	histocompatability locus antigen	組織相容性基因座抗原
HMG	hydroxymethylglutaryl coenzyme A	羥甲基戊二酸輔酶 A
H$_2$O	water	水
H$_2$O$_2$	hydrogen peroxide	雙氧水
HOCM	hypertrophic obstructive cardiomyopathy	肥大阻塞性心肌病變
HPA	hypothalamic-pituitary-adrenal	下視丘－腦下垂體－腎上腺
HPLC	high-performance liquid chromatography	高效能液相色層分析法
HPV	human papilloma virus	人類乳頭狀病毒
HR	heart rate	心跳速率
HSP	Henoch-Schonlein Purpura	漢蕭二氏紫斑症
5-HT	5-hydroxytryptamine (serotonin)	5－羥色胺（血胺素）
HTLV	human T-cell leukemia virus	人類 T 細胞白血病病毒
5-HTP	5-hydroxytryptophan	5－羥色胺酸
HUS	hemolytic-uremic syndrome	溶血性尿毒症症候群
Hx.	history	病史；病歷

I

I&A	irrigation and aspiration	沖洗及抽吸
IABC	intra-aortic balloon counterpulsation	主動脈內氣球抗心搏作用
IABP	intra-aortic balloon pumping	主動脈內氣球幫浦

IBD	inflammatory bowel disease	發炎性腸道疾病
IBS	irritable bowel syndrome	刺激性腸道症候群
ICF	intensive care facility	加護設備
	intracellular fluid	細胞內液
ICH	intracerebral hemorrhage	大腦內出血
	intracranial hemorrhage	顱內出血
ICP	intracranial pressure	顱內壓
ICT	insulin coma therapy	胰島素昏迷治療法
ID$_{50}$	median infective dose	半數致感染劑量
IDA	iron deficiency anemia	缺鐵性貧血
IDDM	insulin-dependent diabetes mellitus	胰島素依賴型糖尿病
I/E	inspiratory-expiratory (ratio)	吸氣與呼氣比值
IG; Ig	immunoglobulin	免疫球蛋白
IgA	immunoglobulin A	免疫球蛋白 A
IgD	immunoglobulin D	免疫球蛋白 D
IGDM	infant of gestational diabetic mother	妊娠糖尿病母親所產下的嬰兒
IgE	immunoglobulin E	免疫球蛋白 E
IgG	immunoglobulin G	免疫球蛋白 G
IGIV	immune globulin intravenous	靜脈注射用免疫球蛋白
IgM	immunoglobulin M	免疫球蛋白 M
IHA	immune hemolytic anemia	免疫溶血性貧血
IHD	ischemic heart disease	缺血性心臟疾病
IICP	increased intracranial pressure	顱內壓增高
ILD	interstitial lung disease	肺間質病變
I.M.	intramuscular (injection)	肌肉內的（注射）
IMIG	intramuscular immunoglobulin	肌肉內免疫球蛋白
I&O	in and out	出入
	intake and output	攝入及排出
IPPV	intermittent positive-pressure ventilation	間歇性正壓換氣
ISO	International Standards Organization	國際標準組織
ITP	idiopathic thrombocytopenic purpura	自發性血小板減少性紫斑病
IUD	intrauterine device	子宮內裝置（避孕器）
IUGR	intrauterine growth retardation	子宮內胎兒生長遲滯
IV	intravenously	靜脈內注射的
IVD	intervertebral disc	椎間盤
IVH	intraventricular hemorrhage	腦室內出血
IVIG	intravenous immunoglobulin	靜脈注射免疫球蛋白
IVP	intravenous pyelography	靜脈注射腎盂攝影術

J

JAMA	Journal of the American Medical Association	美國醫學會雜誌
JDM	juvenile diabetes mellitus	幼年型糖尿病
JGA	juxtaglomerular apparatus	近腎絲球器
JOMAC	judgement, orientation, memory, attention, and calculation	判斷力、定向感、記憶力、注意力及計算力

K

KAP	knowledge, attitude, and practice	知識、態度及實踐
KUB	kidney, ureter, and bladder	腎臟、輸尿管及膀胱（腹部 X 光攝影）

L

LASER	light amplification by stimulated emission of radiation	雷射
LBBB	left bundle branch block	心傳導束左支阻滯
LCIS	lobular carcinoma *in situ*	小葉原位癌
LD_{50}	median lethal dose	半數致死劑量
LDH	lactic dehydrogenase	乳酸去氫酶
L-dopa	levodopa	左旋多巴（藥名）
LGA	large for gestational age	胎兒大小大於妊娠週數
LGN	lateral geniculate nucleus	側膝狀體核
LIMA	left internal mammary artery (graft)	左內乳動脈（移植）
LLQ	left lower quadrant	左下象限
LMD	local medical doctor	地方開業醫師
LN	lupus nephritis	狼瘡性腎炎
Ln	lymph node	淋巴結
LND	lymph node dissection	淋巴結切除
LNMP	last normal menstrual period	最近一次正常經期
LOQ	lower outer quadrant	下外象限
Lp	lipoprotein	脂蛋白
LRQ	lower right quadrant	右下象限
LSO	left salpingo-oophorectomy	左側輸卵管卵巢切除術
LTB_4	leukotriene B_4	白三烯素 B_4
LUQ	left upper quadrant	左上象限
LV	left ventricle	左心室
LVAD	left ventricular assist device	左心室輔助器
LVEDP	left ventricular end-diastolic pressure	左心室舒張期末壓
LVEDV	left ventricular end-diastolic volume	左心室舒張期末容積
LVEF	left ventricular ejection fraction	左心室排血分量
LVH	left ventricular hypertrophy	左心室肥大

M

MABP	mean arterial blood pressure	平均動脈壓
MAC	minimum alveolar concentration	最小肺泡濃度
MAD	major affective disorder	重大情感障礙
MALT	mucosa-associated lymphoid tissue	黏膜相關性淋巴組織
MAOI	monoamine oxidase inhibitor	單胺氧化酶抑制物（劑）
MBD	may be discharged	許可出院
MBP	mean blood pressure	平均血壓
MCGH	mean corpuscular hemoglobin	平均紅血球血紅素
MCGN	minimal-change glomerular nephritis	極小變化之腎絲球腎炎
MCHC	mean corpuscular hemoglobin concentration	平均紅血球血紅素濃度
MCP	metacarpal phalangeal (joint)	掌骨與指骨間的（關節）
MCV	mean corpuscular volume	平均血球容積
MD	Doctor of Medicine	醫學博士
MG	myasthenia gravis	重症肌無力症
MGN	membranous glomerulonephritis	膜性腎絲球炎
MHC	major histocompatibility complex	主要組織相容性複合物
MI	myocardial infarction	心肌梗塞
MIC	minimum inhibitory concentration	最低抑制濃度
MMR	measles, mumps, rubella	麻疹、腮腺炎、德國麻疹
MMS	Mini-Mental State	迷你智能狀態表
MODY	maturity onset diabetes of youth	年輕人成年發作型糖尿病的
MPGN	membranoproliferative glomerulonephritis	膜增殖性腎絲球腎炎
MPH	Master of Public Health	公共衛生學碩士
MR	mitral regurgitation	二尖瓣回流
MRCP	magnetic resonance cholangiopancreatography	核磁共振膽胰管攝影術
MRI	magnetic resonance imaging	核磁共振攝影
MRSA	methicillin-resistant *Staphylococcus aureus*	二甲氧基苯青黴素抗性之金黃色葡萄球菌
MSE	mental status examination	心智狀態檢查
MTX	methotrexate	（抗腫瘤用藥及免疫抑制劑）
MVP	mitral valve prolapse	二尖瓣脫垂

N

NBTE	nonbacterial thrombotic endocarditis	非細菌性血栓性心內膜炎
NCS	nerve conduction studies	神經傳導檢查
NCV	nerve conduction velocity	神經傳導速度
NE	norepinephrine	正腎上腺素

NEC	necrotizing enterocolitis	壞死性腸炎
NEEP	negative end-expiratory pressure	呼氣末期負壓
NG	nasogastric	鼻胃的
NICU	neonatal intensive care unit	新生兒加護病房
NIDDM	non-insulin-dependent diabetes mellitus	非胰島素依賴型糖尿病
NIH	National Institutes of Health	國家衛生機構
NKHA	nonketotic hyperosmolar acidosis	非酮性高滲透性酸血症
NKHS	nonketotic hyperosmolar syndrome	非酮性高滲透性症候群
NM	neuromuscular	神經肌肉的
NMP	normal menstrual period	正常經期
NPH	neutral protamine Hagedorn (insulin)	中性魚精蛋白（中效胰島素）
NPO	*nulla per os*（拉）	禁食
N/S	normal saline	生理食鹽水
NSAID	nonsteroidal anti-inflammatory drug	非類固醇類消炎藥
NSD	normal spontaneous delivery	自然生產；順產
NTG	nitroglycerin	硝基甘油

O

OA	osteoarthritis	骨關節炎
OB	obstetrics	產科學
OBS	obstetrics	產科
OCD	obsessive-compulsive disorder	強迫症
OCHA	office for the Coordination of Humanitarian Affairs	到院前心（肺）功能停止
OD	*oculus dexter*（拉）	右眼
o.d.	*omni die*（拉）	每日
OGTT	oral glucose tolerance test	口服葡萄糖耐量試驗
OHA	oral hypoglycemic agents	口服降血糖藥
OL	*oculus laevus*（拉）	左眼
ON	optic nerve	視神經
OP; op	operation	手術
OPLL	ossification of posterior longitidinal ligament	後縱韌帶骨化
os	*oculus sinister*（拉）	左眼
OT	occupational therapist	職能治療師
	occupational therapy	職能治療
OU	*oculi unitas*（拉）	兩眼；雙眼
	oculus uterque（拉）	每一眼

P

P(AaDO$_2$)	alveolar-arterial oxygen tension difference	肺泡與動脈血氧壓力差
PaCO$_2$	arterial carbon dioxide pressure	動脈二氧化碳分壓
PAEDP	pulmonary artery end diastolic pressure	肺動脈舒張末期壓力
PAF	platelet activating factor	血小板活化因子
PAGE	polyacrylamide gel electrophoresis	聚合丙烯醯胺膠體電泳
PaO$_2$	arterial oxygen pressure	動脈氧分壓
PAOD	peripheral arterial occlusive disease	周邊動脈阻塞疾病
PAPVR	partial anomalous pulmonary venous return	肺靜脈部分異常性回流
PCA	patient-controlled analgesia	病人自控式止痛
PCKD	polycystic kidney disease	多囊性腎病
PCO$_2$	carbon dioxide pressure	二氧化碳分壓
PCP	phencyclidine HCl	（迷幻藥，俗稱「天使塵粒」）
PCWP	pulmonary capillary wedge pressure	肺微血管楔壓
PDA	patent ductus arteriosus	開放性動脈導管
PEEP	positive end expiratory pressure	呼氣末期正壓
PGI$_2$	prostaglandin I$_2$	前列腺素 I$_2$
PICU	pediatric intensive care unit	小兒科加護病房
PKU	phenylketonuria	苯酮尿症
PLT	platelet	血小板
PMN; PMNN	polymorphonuclear neutrophil	多形核嗜中性白血球
POEMS	plasma cell dyscrasia with polyneuropathy, organomegaly, endocrinopathy, monoclonal 單株漿細胞異常併有多病灶性神經病變、器官巨大、內分泌病變	
PPHN	persistent pulmonary hypertension of the newborn	新生兒持續性肺性高血壓
PPROM	preterm premature rupture of membranes	早產早期破水
PRBC	packed red blood cells	濃縮紅血球
p.r.n.	*pro re nata*（拉）	需要時
PSA	prostate-specific antigen	前列腺特異性抗原
PSGN	poststreptococcal glomerulonephritis	鏈球菌感染後腎絲球腎炎
PT	prothrombin time	凝血酶原時間
PTT	partial thromboplastin time	部分凝血活酶時間
PvO$_2$	partial pressure of venous oxygen	靜脈氧分壓

Q

QMI	Q wave myocardial infarction	心肌梗塞之 Q 波
q.o.d.	*quaque other die*（拉）	每隔一天
q.o.h	*quaque other hora*（拉）	每隔一小時

q.o.n.　　*quaque other nocte*（拉）　每隔一夜

qpm　　*quaque post meridiem*（拉）　每天晚上

qqh　　*quaque quarta hora*（拉）　每四小時

R

RBBB　　right bundle branch block　心傳導束右支阻斷

RCT　　randomized clinical trial　隨機臨床試驗

RDS　　respiratory distress syndrome　呼吸窘迫症候群

RDW　　red (cell) distribution width　紅血球細胞分佈寬度

RHD　　rheumatic heart disease　風溼性心臟病

RLQ　　right lower quadrant　右下象限

ROS　　review of systems　全身各系統檢查（病歷檢閱）

RPGN　　rapidly progressive glomerulonephritis　快速進行性腎絲球腎炎

RQ　　respiratory quotient　呼吸商數

RSO　　right salpingo-oophorectomy　右側輸卵管及卵巢切除術

RT　　radiation therapy or radiotherapy　放射線治療

RTA　　renal tubular acidosis　腎小管過酸症

RTN　　renal tubular necrosis　腎小管壞死

RV　　right ventricle　右心室

RVEDP　　right ventricular end-diastolic pressure　右心室舒張期末壓

RVEDV　　right ventricular end-diastolic volume　右心室舒張期末容積

S

SAH　　subarachnoid hemorrhage　蜘蛛膜下出血

SA node　　sino-atrial node　竇房結

SARS　　severe acute respiratory syndrome　嚴重急性呼吸道症候群

SCC　　squamous cell carcinoma　鱗狀細胞癌

SCID　　severe combined immunodeficiency disease　重度合併性免疫缺乏症

SDH　　subdural hematoma　硬膜下血腫

SGA　　small for gestational age　胎兒大小小於妊娠週數

SIADH　　serum inappropriate antidiuretic hormone　血清中抗利尿激素分泌不當

SIMV　　synchronized intermittent mandatory ventilation　同步間歇性強迫換氣

SJS　　Stevens-Johnson syndrome　史蒂芬強森症候群

SLE　　systemic lupus erythematosus　全身性紅斑狼瘡

SLRT　　straight leg raising test　腳伸直抬高試驗

SOAP　　subjective data, objective data, assessment, plan　主觀資料、客觀資料、
　　　　評估及計畫

SPECT　　single photon emission computery tomography　單一光子激發電腦斷層

SSP; SSPE　　subacute sclerosing panencephalitis　亞急性硬化性全腦炎

SSSS	staphylococcal scalded skin syndrome　葡萄球菌鱗狀皮膚症候群
STD	sexual transmitted disease　性傳染病；性病
STORCH	syphilis, toxoplasmosis, other agents, rubella, cytomegalovirus, and herpes　淋病、弓型蟲病、其他病原、德國麻疹、巨細胞病毒及疱疹
STS	serologic test for syphilis　梅毒血清學試驗

T

TAH	total abdominal hysterectomy　剖腹式子宮完全切除術
TAPVC	total anomalous pulmonary venous connection　肺靜脈連結完全異常
TAPVR	total anomalous pulmonary venous return　肺靜脈回流完全異常
TB	tuberculosis　結核病
TCA	tricyclic antidepressant　三環抑鬱劑
TD	tardive dyskinesia　遲發性運動困難
TEM	transmission electron microscopy　穿透型電子顯微鏡
TG	triglyceride　三酸甘油酯
TGA	transposition of the great arteries　大動脈轉位
TIBC	total iron-binding capacity　鐵結合總容量
TID; t.i.d	*ter in die*（拉）　一天三次
TKR	total knee replacement　全膝關節置換術
TMJ	temporomandibular joint　顳腭關節
TMP-SMZ	trimethoprim-sulfomethoxazole　（抗生素名）
TNM	tumor, nodes, metastases　腫瘤、淋巴結、轉移（癌症分期）
TOA	tubo-ovarian abscess　輸卵管卵巢膿瘍
TOF	Tetralogy of Fallot　法洛氏四重畸形
TORCH	toxoplasmosis, rubella, cytomegalovirus, herpes simplex virus　毒漿體病、麻疹、巨細胞病毒、單純疱疹病毒
TPHA	*Treponema pallidum* hemagglutination　梅毒螺旋體紅血球凝集
TPN	total parenteral nutrition　全靜脈營養法
TPO	thrombopoietin　血小板生成素
TPR	temperature, pulse, and respiration　體溫、脈搏及呼吸
TRH	thyrotropin-releasing hormone　甲狀腺激素釋放荷爾蒙
TRUS	transrectal ultrasound　經直腸超音波
TRUSP	transrectal ultrasound of the prostate　經直腸前列腺超音波
TSH	thyroid stimulating hormone　甲狀腺刺激激素
TUPR	transurethral prostatic resection　經尿道前列腺切除術
TURBN	transurethral resection bladder neck　經尿道膀胱頸切除術
TURP	transurethral resection of the prostate　經尿道前列腺切除術
TVH	total vaginal hysterectomy　全陰道子宮切除術

U

UC	ulcerative colitis	潰瘍性結腸炎
UIQ	upper inner quadrant	上內象限
UN	urea nitrogen	尿素氮
UPJ	ureteropelvic junction	輸卵管腎盂接連處
UV	ultraviolet	紫外線的
UVA	ultraviolet A light	紫外線 A
UVB	ultraviolet B light	紫外線 B

V

VATER	vertebral, anal, tracheal, esophageal and renal anomalies	脊椎、肛門、氣管、食道及腎臟異常
VDRL	Venereal Disease Research Laboratories	性病研究室（梅毒血清檢驗）
VF	ventricular fibrillation	心室纖維震顫
VLDL; VLDLP	very low-density lipoprotein	極低密度脂蛋白
Vt	tidal volume	潮氣容積
VUJ	vesicoureteral junction	膀胱輸尿管接連處
VUR	vesicoureteral reflux	膀胱輸尿管回流
VZIG	varicella-zoster immune globulin	水痘帶狀疱疹免疫球蛋白
VZV	varicella zoster virus	水痘帶狀疱疹病毒

W

WHO	World Health Organization	世界衛生組織
WPW	Wolff-Parkinson-White (syndrome)	渥帕懷三氏（症候群）

Diagnosis of Common Diseases 常見疾病診斷

A

Abdominal aortic aneurysm　腹主動脈瘤

Acquired immunodeficiency syndrome
　後天免疫缺乏症候群（愛滋病）

Acute cholangitis　急性膽道炎

Acute cholecystitis　急性膽囊炎

Acute gastroenteritis　急性腸胃炎

Acute myocardial infarction　急性心肌梗塞

Acute pyelonephritis　急性腎盂炎

Acute renal failure　急性腎衰竭

Angina pectoris　心絞痛

Anorexia nervosa　厭食症

Anxiety disorder　焦慮症

Appendicitis　闌尾炎

Arrhythmia　心律不整

Asthma　氣喘

Atrial fibrillation　心房顫動

Atrial septal defect　心房中隔缺損

Attention-deficit hyperactivity disorder
　注意力不足／過動症

Autism　自閉症

B

Benign prostatic hypertrophy/hyperplasia
　良性前列腺增生／肥大

Bipolar disorder　雙相情緒障礙

Brain tumor　腦瘤

Breast cancer　乳癌

Bulimia　暴食症

C

Cellulitis　蜂窩性組織炎

Cerebral infarction　腦梗塞

Cerebral vascular accident　腦血管意外

Cervical cancer　子宮頸癌

Chronic bronchitis　慢性支氣管炎

Chronic obstructive pulmonary disease
　慢性阻塞性肺病

Colon cancer　大腸癌

Congenital heart disease　先天性心臟病

Congestive heart failure　鬱血性心臟衰竭

Constipation　便祕

Coronary artery disease　冠狀動脈心臟病

Cystitis　膀胱炎

D

Dementia　失智症

Diabetes mellitus　糖尿病

Diabetic ketoacidosis　糖尿病酮酸中毒

Diarrhea　腹瀉

Diverticulitis　憩室炎

E

Emphysema　肺氣腫

Encephalitis　腦炎

Endometrial cancer　子宮內膜癌

Epilepsy　癲癇

Esophageal cancer　食道癌

F

Fecal incontinence　糞便失禁

Food poisoning　食物中毒

Fracture　骨折

G

Gastric cancer　胃癌

Gastritis　胃炎

Gastroesophageal reflux disease　胃－十二
　指腸逆流疾病

H

Hand-foot-mouth disease　手足口病

Hemorrhoids　痔瘡

Hepatitis　肝炎

Hepatoma　肝癌

Hydrocephalus　水腦症

Hypertension　高血壓

Hyperthyroidism　甲狀腺機能亢進

I

Ileus　腸阻塞

Inguinal hernia　腹股溝疝氣

Intussusception　腸套疊

L

Leukemia　白血病

Liver abscess　肝膿瘍

Liver cirrhosis　肝硬化

Lung abscess　肺膿瘍

Lung cancer　肺癌

Lymphoma　淋巴瘤

M

Major depression　重鬱症

Meningitis　腦膜炎

Meningoencephalitits　腦膜腦炎

Mitral regurgitation　二尖瓣逆流

Mitral stenosis　二尖瓣狹窄

Mitral valve prolapse　二尖瓣脫垂

Multiple sclerosis　多發性硬化症

Myasthenia gravis　重症肌無力

O

Ovarian cancer　卵巢癌

P

Pancreatic cancer　胰臟癌

Panic disorder　恐慌症

Parkinson's disease　巴金森氏病

Peptic ulcer　消化性潰瘍

Peripheral artery occlusive disease　周邊動脈阻塞性疾病

Peripheral neuropathy　周邊神經病變

Peritonitis　腹膜炎

Phobia　恐懼症

Pneumonia　肺炎

Pulmonary embolism　肺栓塞

Pulmonary tuberculosis　肺結核

R

Rheumatoid arthritis　類風濕性關節炎

S

Schizophrenia　思覺失調症

Spinal cord injury　脊髓損傷

Supraventricular tachycardia　上心室心搏過速

Systemic lupus erythematous　全身性紅斑性狼瘡

T

Tetralogy of Fallot　法洛氏四重症

U

Urethritis　尿道炎

Urinary incontinence　尿失禁

V

Varicose vein　靜脈曲張

Ventricular fibrillation　心室顫動

Ventricular septal defect　心室中隔缺損

Ventricular tachycardia　心室心搏過速

Volvulus　腸扭結

Vocabulary 各章字彙表

Chapter 1 呼吸胸腔科

字 彙

1. sputum [ˈspjutəm] (n.) 痰液
2. heartburn [ˈhɑrt.bɝn] (n.) 胃灼熱；心口灼熱
3. tiny [ˈtaɪnɪ] (adj.) 微（細）小的
4. bloody streak [ˈblʌdɪ strik] (n.) 血絲
5. stethoscope [ˈstɛθə.skop] (n.) 聽診器
6. occupation [ɑkjəˈpeʃən] (n.) 職業
7. reveal [rɪˈvil] (v.) 顯示
8. invasive [ɪnˈvesɪv] (adj.) 侵入性的
9. insert [ɪnˈsɝt] (v.) 插入；放置
10. quit [kwɪt] (v.) 戒除；停止
11. instruction [ɪnˈstrʌkʃən] (n.) 指示；說明
12. strictly [ˈstrɪktlɪ] (adv.) 嚴格地
13. prolong [prəˈlɔŋ] (v.) 延長
14. follow-up [ˈfalo ʌp] (n.) 追蹤
15. continuously [kənˈtɪnjuəslɪ] (adv.) 連續地
16. monitor [ˈmɑnətə] (v.) 監視；監控 (n.) 監測器
17. consultation [ˌkɑnsʌlˈteʃən] (n.) 諮詢
18. shortness of breath [ˈʃɔrt əv brɛθ] 呼吸急促
19. sore throat [sor θrot] (n.) 喉嚨痛
20. sputum [ˈspjutəm] (n.) 痰液
21. dry cough [draɪ kɔf] (n.) 乾咳
22. loss of smell [luz əv smel] 喪失嗅覺
23. vaccination [væksəˈneɪʃən] (n.) 接種疫苗
24. antiviral [ˌæntiˈvaɪrəl] (adj.) 抗病毒
25. side effect [ˈsaɪd ɪˌfekt] (n.) 副作用
26. altered [ˈɔltər] (adj.) 改變的
27. impaired [ɪmˈpɛrd] (adj.) 損傷；不全
28. isolation [ˌaɪsəlˈeʃən] (n.) 隔離
29. aware [əˈwɛr] (adj.) 察覺的；知道的
30. fingertip [ˈfɪŋɡəˌtɪp] (n.) 指尖
31. pulse oximeter [pʌls okˈsɪmɪtə] (n.) 脈搏血氧計
32. outpatient department [ˈaʊtˌpeʃənt dɪˈpartmənt] (n.) 門診
33. immune system [ɪˈmjun ˈsɪstəm] (n.) 免疫系統

術 語

1. nostril [ˈnɑstrɪl] 鼻孔
2. nasal cavity [ˈnezḷ ˈkævətɪ] 鼻腔
3. vibrissa [vaɪˈbrɪsə] 鼻毛
4. pharynx [ˈfærɪŋks] 咽
5. larynx [ˈlærɪŋks] 喉
6. trachea [ˈtrekɪə] 氣管
7. bronchi [ˈbrɑŋkaɪ] 支氣管（複數）（bronchus 單數）
8. alveoli [ælˈvialaɪ] 肺泡（複數）（alveolus 單數）
9. pulmonary tuberculosis [ˈpʌlməˌnɛrɪ t(j)uˌbɝkjə ˈlosɪs] 肺結核
10. bronchoscopy [brɑŋˈkɑskəpɪ] 支氣管鏡檢查
11. anesthetic [ˌænəsˈθɛtɪk] 麻醉劑
12. vital signs [ˌvaɪtḷ ˈsaɪns] 生命徵象
13. nasal cannula [ˈnezḷ ˈkænjələ] 鼻套管（供氧用）
14. pneumonia patch [njuˈmonjə pætʃ] 肺炎塊
15. blood oxygen concentration [blʌd ˈɑksədʒən ˌkɑnsɛnˈtreʃən] 血氧濃度
16. draw blood [drɔ blʌd] 抽血
17. RT-PCR (real-time polymerase chain reaction) [ˈriəl taɪm pəˈlɪməreɪs tʃeɪn riˈækʃən] 及時反轉錄聚合酶連鎖反應
18. Rapid Antigen Test [ˈræpɪd ˈæntədʒən tɛst] 快速抗原檢測

Chapter 2 心血管科

字 彙

1. concern [kən'sɜn] (n.) 關心的事
   (v.) 關係到
2. dull [dʌl] (adj.) 隱約的；模糊的
3. suffer from ['sʌfə fram] 罹患
4. call button [kɔl 'bʌtn̩] (n.) 叫人鈴
5. intake ['ɪn.tek] (n.) 攝入
6. output ['aut.put] (n.) 排出
7. greasy ['grizɪ] (adj.) 油膩的
8. salty ['sɔltɪ] (adj.) 鹹的
9. flavor [flevə] (n.) 調味料
10. miserable ['mɪzərəbl̩] (adj.) 痛苦的
11. tablet ['tæblɪt] (n.) 錠劑
12. tightness ['taɪtnɪs] (n.) 緊壓感
13. persist [pə'sɪst] (v.) 持續
14. store [stɔr] (v.) 貯藏；貯存
15. tightly ['taɪtlɪ] (adv.) 緊密地
16. bottle [batl̩] (n.) 瓶子
17. burning ['bɜnɪŋ] (adj.) 灼熱的
18. effective [ə'fɛktɪv] (adj.) 有效的

術 語

1. atrium ['etrɪəm] 心房
2. ventricle ['vɛntrɪkl̩] 心室
3. myocardium [.maɪə'kardɪəm] 心肌
4. aorta [e'ɔrtə] 主動脈
5. artery ['artərɪ] 動脈
6. venule ['vɛnjul] 小靜脈
7. vein [ven] 靜脈
8. vena cava ['vænə kevə] 腔靜脈
9. coronary artery ['kɔrə.nɛrɪ 'artərɪ] 冠狀動脈
10. anterior descending branch
    [æn'tɪrɪə dɪ'sɛndɪŋ bræntʃ] 前降枝
11. circumflex branch
    ['sɜkəm.flɛks bræntʃ] 迴旋枝

12. angina pectoris [æn'dʒaɪnə 'pɛktərɪs] 心絞痛
13. hypertension [haɪpə'tɛnʃən] 高血壓
14. diabetes [.daɪə'bitɪs] 糖尿病
15. myocardial infarction
    [.maɪə'kardɪəl ɪn'farkʃən] 心肌梗塞
16. electrocardiography [ɪ.lɛktrə.kardɪ'agrəfɪ] 心電圖(ECG/EKG)
17. nitroglycerin [.naɪtrə'glɪsərɪn] 硝化甘油(NTG)
18. catheterization [.kæθətərɪ'zeʃən] 心導管手術
19. ER = emergency room [ɪ'mɝdʒənsɪ rum] 急診室

Chapter 3 胃腸科

字 彙

1. suddenly ['sʌdn̩lɪ] (adv.) 忽然地
2. gradually ['grædʒuəlɪ] (adv.) 逐漸地
3. tearing ['tɛrɪŋ] (adj.) 撕裂的
4. cramp [kræmp] (v.) 抽筋；痙攣
5. pharmacy ['farməsɪ] (n.) 藥局
6. medication [mɛdɪ'keʃən] (n.) 藥物；藥物治療
7. ward [wɔrd] (n.) 病房
8. bowel movement ['bauəl muvmənt] 排便；腸蠕動
9. blood pressure [blʌd 'prɛʃə] 血壓
10. consent [kən'sɛnt] (n.) 同意；同意書
11. stable ['stebl̩] (adj.) 穩定的
12. faint [fent] (adj.) 昏厥的；即將暈倒的
13. prescribe [prɪ'skraɪb] (v.) 開（藥方）
14. lifestyle ['laɪf.staɪl] (n.) 生活型態
15. canned [kænd] (adj.) 罐裝的
16. preserved [prɪ'zɝvd] (adj.) 醃製的
17. painkiller ['pen.kɪlə] (n.) 止痛藥
18. congratulate [kən'grætʃə.let] (v.) 恭喜

術 語

1. esophagus [ɪˈsafəgəs] 食道
2. stomach [ˈstʌmək] 胃
3. small intestine [smɔl ɪnˈtɛstɪn] 小腸
4. large intestine [larʤ ɪnˈtɛstɪn] 大腸
5. rectum [ˈrɛktəm] 直腸
6. salivary glands [ˈsælə.vɛrɪ ˈglændz] 唾腺
7. saliva [səˈlaɪvə] 唾液
8. liver [ˈlɪvə] 肝臟
9. gallbladder [ˈgɔl.blædə] 膽囊
10. bile [baɪl] 膽汁
11. pancreas [ˈpænkrɪəs] 胰臟
12. mucosa [mjuˈkosə] 黏膜（層）
13. submucosa [.sʌbmjəˈkosə] 黏膜下層
14. muscular layer [ˈmʌskjələ ˈleə] 肌肉層
15. serosa [sɪˈrosə] 漿膜層
16. erosion [ɪˈroʒən] 糜爛
17. ulcer [ˈʌlsə] 潰瘍
18. peptic ulcer (PU) [ˈpɛptɪk ˈʌlsə] 消化性潰瘍
19. antacid [æntˈæsɪd] 制酸劑
20. Aspirin [ˈæspərɪn] 阿斯匹靈
21. hemoglobin [.himəˈglobɪn] 血紅素
22. intravenous drip [.ɪntrəˈvinəs drɪp] 靜脈點滴注射
23. blood transfusion [blʌd .trænsˈfjuʒən] 輸血
24. endoscopy [ɛnˈdaskəpɪ] 內視鏡檢查
25. NPO 禁食（ *nulla per os*，意指 nothing by mouth）
26. acid reducer [ˈæsɪd rɪˈdjusə] 制酸劑

Chapter 4 肝膽科

字 彙

1. fluid [ˈfluɪd] (n.) 液體
2. distend [dɪsˈtɛnd] (v.) 撐開；使…漲起
3. establish [əˈstæblɪʃ] (v.) 建立

4. satisfying [ˈsætɪs.faɪɪŋ] (adj.) 令人滿意的；符合要求的
5. solitary [ˈsalə.tɛrɪ] (adj.) 單獨的
6. pierce [pɪrs] (v.) 穿刺
7. destroy [dɪˈstrɔɪ] (v.) 摧毀
8. puncture [ˈpʌŋktʃə] (n.) 刺孔 (v.) 穿刺
9. thigh [θaɪ] (n.) 大腿
10. compress [kəmˈprɛs] (v.) 壓緊
11. absolutely [ˈæbsə.lutlɪ] (adv.) 絕對地
12. towel [taʊl] (n.) 毛巾；浴巾
13. chamber pot [ˈtʃembə pat] 便盆

術 語

1. insulin [ˈɪnsəlɪn] 胰島素
2. glycogen [ˈglaɪkəʤən] 肝醣
3. glucagon [ˈglukəgən] 升糖素
4. growth hormone [groθ ˈhɔrmon] 生長激素
5. anterior pituitary gland 腦下垂體前葉 [ænˈtɪrɪə pɪˈtjutærɪ glænd]
6. insulin-like growth factor [ˈɪnsəlɪn laɪk groθ ˈfæktə] 類胰島素生長因子
7. hepatocyte [ˈhɛpətosaɪt] 肝細胞
8. electrolyte [ɪˈlɛktrə.laɪt] 電解質
9. hepatocellular carcinoma (HCC) [.hɛpətəˈsɛljulə .karsɪˈnomə] 肝細胞癌
10. liver cancer [ˈlɪvə ˈkænsə] 肝癌
11. abdomen [ˈæbdomən] 腹部
12. tea-colored urine [tiˈkʌləd ˈjurɪn] 茶色尿
13. anti-viral agent [æntɪˈvaɪrəl ˈeʤənt] 抗病毒藥物
14. residual liver function [rɪˈzɪʤuəl lɪvə ˈfʌŋkʃən] 肝臟殘餘功能
15. liver transplantation [lɪvə .trænsplæn ˈteʃən] 肝臟移植
16. trans-arterial chemo-embolization [træns arˈtɪrɪəl kimə .ɛmbəlɪˈzeʃən]

經動脈化療栓塞術(TACE)

17. inguinal region [ˈɪŋgwɪn̩ ˈridʒən]
鼠蹊部

Chapter 5 內分泌科

字彙

1. health check-up [hɛlθ ˈtʃɛk ʌp] 健康檢查

2. toilet [ˈtɔɪlɪt] (n.) 廁所

3. approximately [əˈpraksəmɪtlɪ] (adv.)
大約地;概略地

4. post-meal [ˈpostˌmil] (adj.) 飯後的

5. sterilize [ˈstɛrəˌlaɪz] (v.) 消毒;無菌

6. administer [ədˈmɪnəstə] (v.) 給予(藥物)

7. diabetic [ˌdaɪəˈbɛtɪk] (adj.) 糖尿病的

8. urinate [ˈjʊrəˌnet] (v.) 排尿

9. determine [dɪˈtɜmɪn] (v.) 決定

10. severe [səˈvɪr] (adj.) 嚴重的;劇烈的

11. nutrition [njuˈtrɪʃən] (n.) 營養

12. refined [rɪˈfaɪnd] (adj.) 精製的;提煉的

13. nutritionist [njuˈtrɪʃənɪst] (n.) 營養師

14. suitable [ˈsjutəbl̩] (adj.) 適合的

15. disturb [dɪˈstɜb] (v.) 干擾;使…混亂

16. inhibit [ɪnˈhɪbɪt] (v.) 抑制

17. absorption [əbˈsɔrpʃən] (n.) 吸收

18. reduce [rɪˈdjus] (v.) 減少;降低

19. requirement [rɪˈkwaɪrmənt] (n.) 要求;需求

20. motivate [ˈmotəˌvet] (v.) 激發

21. prevent [prɪˈvɛnt] (v.) 避免

22. susceptible [səˈsɛptəbl̩] (adj.) 易感的

術語

1. hypothalamus [ˌhaɪpoˈθæləməs] 下視丘

2. pituitary gland [pɪˈtjuɪtærɪ glænd] 腦下垂體

3. thyroid gland [ˈθaɪrɔɪd glænd] 甲狀腺

4. adrenal gland [əˈdrinəl glænd] 腎上腺

5. testis [ˈtɛstɪs] 睪丸

6. ovary [ˈovərɪ] 卵巢

7. diabetes mellitus (DM)
[ˌdaɪə ˈbitiz ˈmɛlətəs] 糖尿病

8. hyperglycemia [ˌhaɪpəglaɪˈsimɪə] 高血糖

Chapter 6 感染科

字彙

1. chill [tʃɪl] (adj.) 冷的
(v.) 打寒顫

2. shiver [ˈʃɪvə] (v./n.) 顫抖

3. runny nose [ˈrʌnɪ noz] 流鼻水

4. sore throat [ˈsor θrot] 喉嚨痛

5. urination [jʊrəˈneʃən] (n.) 解尿

6. revert [rɪˈvɜt] (v.) 回復

7. swollen [ˈswolən] (adj.) 腫脹的

8. infectious [ɪnˈfɛkʃəs] (adj.) 具感染性的

9. subside [səbˈsaɪd] (v.) 減弱;消失

10. inflammation [ˌɪnfləˈmeʃən] (n.) 發炎

11. temporarily [ˈtɛmpəˌrɛrəlɪ] (adv.) 暫時地

12. antibiotic [ˌæntɪbaɪˈatɪk] (n.) 抗生素

13. recover [rɪˈkʌvə] (v.) 復原

14. detect [ˌdɪˈtɛkt] (v.) 察覺;偵測

15. seldom [ˈsɛldəm] (adv.) 偶爾;很少

16. impairment [ɪmˈpɛrmənt] (n.) 損傷

17. injection [ɪnˈdʒɛkʃən] (n.) 注射

18. absence [ˈæbsn̩s] (n.) 缺席;缺乏

19. maintain [menˈten] (v.) 維持

20. hygiene [ˈhaɪdʒin] (n.) 衛生

21. disinfectant [ˌdɪsɪnˈfɛktənt] (n.) 消毒劑

術語

1. neutrophil [ˈnjutrəfɪl] 嗜中性球

2. monocyte [ˈmanəsaɪt] 單核球

3. dendritic cell [dɛnˈdrɪtɪk sɛl] 樹突細胞

4. lymphocyte [ˈlɪmfosaɪt] 淋巴球

5. cellulitis [ˌsɛljəˈlaɪtɪs] 蜂窩性組織炎

6. diarrhea [ˌdaɪəˈriə] 腹瀉

7. diagnosis certificate [‚daɪəg′nosɪs sə′tɪfəkɪt] 診斷證明書

8. normal saline [′nɔrml̩ ′selɪn] 生理食鹽水

9. povidone-iodine [′povədon ′aɪədaɪn] 優碘

Chapter 7 腫瘤科

字　彙

1. bruise [bruz] (n.) 瘀傷

2. penlight [′pɛnlaɪt] (n.) 筆燈；小手電筒

3. illuminate [ɪ′lumə‚net] (v.) 照亮

4. spot [spat] (n.) 斑點

5. appetite [′æpə‚taɪt] (n.) 食慾；胃口

6. prone [pron] (adj.) 有⋯傾向的

7. jump to any conclusions [dʒʌmp tu ′ɛnɪ kən′kluʒənz] 妄下定論

8. experience [ɪk′spɪrɪəns] (n.) 經驗

9. nauseous [′nɔʒəs] (adj.) 反胃的；噁心的

10. vomit [′vamɪt] (v.) 嘔吐

11. toxic [′taksɪk] (adj.) 對⋯有毒的

12. bald [bɔld] (adj.) 禿頭的

13. ugly [′ʌglɪ] (adj.) 醜陋的

14. recommend [‚rɛkə′mɛnd] (v.) 建議

15. wig [wɪg] (n.) 假髮

16. throw up [′θro ʌp] 嘔吐

17. nutritional status [nju′trɪʃənl̩ ′stetəs] 營養狀態

18. determine [dɪ′tɜmɪn] (v.) 決定

19. uncooked [ʌn′kʊkt] (adj.) 未煮的；生的

20. tolerate [′talə‚ret] (v.) 忍受

21. cautious [′kɔʃəs] (adj.) 小心翼翼的

術　語

1. erythrocyte [ɪ′rɪθrə‚saɪt] 紅血球

2. leukocyte [′lukə‚saɪt] 白血球

3. platelet [′pletlɪt] 血小板

4. neutrophil [′njutrəfɪl] 嗜中性球

5. eosinophil [‚iə′sɪnə‚fɪl] 嗜酸性球

6. basophil [′besəfɪl] 嗜鹼性球

7. monocyte [′manə‚saɪt] 單核球

8. lymphocyte [′lɪmfosaɪt] 淋巴球

9. leukemia [lu′kimɪə] 白血病

10. bone marrow biopsy [bon ′mæro baɪ′apsɪ] 骨髓活體切片檢查

11. CBC/DC = complete blood count/ differential count [kəm′plit blʌd kaʊnt] [‚dɪfə′rɛnʃəl kaʊnt] 完全血球計數／分類計數

12. antiemetics [‚æntɪə′mɛtɪks] 止吐劑

13. chemotherapeutic agent [‚kimə‚θɛrə′pjutɪk ′edʒənt] 化學治療藥劑

Chapter 8 腎臟科

字　彙

1. emergent [ɪ′mɜdʒənt] (adj.) 緊急的

2. flank [′flæŋk] (n.) 腰側；脅腹

3. mild [maɪld] (adj.) 輕微的

4. shortness of breath [′ʃɔrtnɪs əv brɛθ] 呼吸短促

5. sustain [sə′sten] (v.) 維持

6. undergo [′ʌndə‚go] (v.) 進行

7. restore [rɪ′stɔr] (v.) 修復；恢復

8. unoccupied [ʌn′akjəpaɪd] (adj.) 空閒的；空著的

9. rubber [′rʌbə] (adj.) 橡膠製的

10. impede [ɪm′pid] (v.) 阻礙

11. instruction [ɪn′strʌkʃən] (n.) 指導；講授

12. booklet [′bʊklɪt] (n.) 小手冊

術　語

1. kidney [′kɪdnɪ] 腎臟

2. nephron [′nɛfran] 腎元

3. plasma [′plæzmə] 血漿

4. glomerulus [glə′mɛrjuləs] 腎絲球

5. renal tubule [′rinl̩ ′t(j)ubjəl] 腎小管

6. minor calyx [maɪnə ˈkelɪks] 小腎盞

7. major calyx [ˈmedʒə ˈkelɪks] 大腎盞

8. renal pelvis [ˈrinl̩ ˈpɛlvɪs] 腎盂

9. end stage renal disease (ESRD)
[ɛnd stedʒ ˈrinl̩ dɪˈziz] 末期腎疾病

10. dialysis [daɪˈælɪsɪs] 透析

11. NSAID = non-steroidal anti-inflammatory drug
[nan ˈstɛrɔɪdl̩ æntɪ ɪnˈflæmə͵torɪ drʌg]
非類固醇抗發炎止痛藥

12. pulmonary edema [ˈpʌlmə͵nɛrɪ iˈdimə]
肺水腫

13. transplantation [͵trænsplænˈteʃən] 移植

14. peritoneum [͵pɛrətəˈniəm] 腹膜

15. hemodialysis [͵himədaɪˈælɪsɪs] 血液透析

16. peritoneal dialysis [͵pɛrətəˈniəl daɪˈælɪsɪs]
腹膜透析

17. arteriovenous fistula [ar͵tɪrɪəvinəs ˈfɪstjulə]
動靜脈瘻管 (A-V fistula)

18. thrill [θrɪl] 震顫感

19. bruit [brut] 嘈音

Chapter 9 泌尿科

字 彙

1. drip [drɪp] (v.) 滴水

2. hesitancy [ˈhɛzətənsɪ] (n.) 猶豫；躊躇

3. urinate [ˈjurə͵net] (v.) 排尿

4. enlarged [ɪnˈlardʒd] (adj.) 增大

5. perform [pəˈfɔrm] (v.) 執行；做

6. supplement [ˈsʌpləmənt] (n.) 補充

7. drain [dren] (v.) 排出；引流

8. route [rut] (n.) 路徑

9. irrigation [͵ɪrəˈgeʃən] (n.) 灌洗；沖洗

10. thick [θɪk] (adj.) 黏稠的；濃的

11. implicate [ˈɪmplɪ͵ket] (v.) 意味著

12. obstruction [əbˈstrʌkʃən] (n.) 阻塞

13. on time [an taɪm] 準時

14. amount [əˈmaunt] (n.) 量

15. lift [lɪft] (v.) 舉起；提起

16. strain [stren] (v.) （肌肉）用力

17. strenuous [ˈstrɛnjuəs] (adj.) 劇烈的；費力的

18. laxative [ˈlæksətɪv] (n.) 輕瀉劑

19. constipate [ˈkanstə͵pet] (v.) 便祕

20. augment [ɔgˈmɛnt] (v.) 加強

術 語

1. ureter [juˈritə] 輸尿管

2. urinary bladder [ˈjurə͵nɛrɪ ˈblædə] 膀胱

3. urethra [juˈriθrə] 尿道

4. prostatic urethra [prasˈtætɪk juˈriθrə] 前列腺部尿道

5. membranous urethra [ˈmɛmbrənəs juˈriθrə] 膜部尿道

6. penile urethra [ˈpinaɪl juˈriθrə] 陰莖部尿道

7. prostate gland [ˈprastet glænd] 前列腺

8. benign prostatic hyperplasia (BPH)
[bɪˈnaɪn prasˈtætɪk ͵haɪpəˈpleziə] 良性前列腺肥大

9. catheter [ˈkæθɪtə] 導尿管；導管

Chapter 10 直腸科

字 彙

1. defecate [ˈdɛfə͵ket] (v.) 排便

2. die of [ˈdaɪ əv] 死於……

3. moisten [ˈmɔɪsn̩] (v.) 溼潤

4. schedule [ˈskɛdʒul] (v.) 預定
(n.) 計劃表

5. nervous [ˈnɝvəs] (adj.) 神經質的；緊張的

6. passage [ˈpæsɪdʒ] (n.) 通道

7. horrible [ˈhɔrəbl̩] (adj.) 可怕的；糟透的

8. furthermore [ˈfɝðə͵mor] (adv.) 而且；再者

9. slight [slaɪt] (adj.) 輕微的

10. breakdown [ˈbrek͵daun] (n.) 破裂

11. replace [rɪˈples] (v.) 更換

12. afraid [əˈfred] (adj.) 害怕

13. get used to [gɛt jusd tu] 習慣於……

14. abrasion [əˈbreʒən] (n.) 磨損；擦傷

術 語

1. GI = gastrointestinal [ˌgæstrəɪnˈtɛstənəl] 胃腸的

2. jejunum [dʒɪˈdʒunəm] 空腸

3. ileum [ˈɪlɪəm] 迴腸

4. ascending colon [əˈsɛndɪŋ ˈkolən] 升結腸

5. transverse colon [trænsˈvɜs ˈkolən] 橫結腸

6. descending colon [dɪˈsɛndɪŋ ˈkolən] 降結腸

7. sigmoid colon [ˈsɪgmɔɪd ˈkolən] 乙狀結腸

8. rectum [ˈrɛktəm] 直腸

9. anal canal [ˈenḷ kəˈnæl] 肛管

10. colon cancer [ˈkolən ˈkænsə] 結腸癌

11. hemorrhoid [ˈhɛmərɔɪd] 痔瘡

12. clear liquid diet [klɪr ˈlɪkwɪd ˈdaɪət] 清流質飲食

13. cleansing enema [ˈklɛnzɪŋ ˈɛnəmə] 清潔灌腸

14. collection pouch [kəˈlɛkʃən pautʃ] 造口袋

Chapter 11　神經科

字 彙

1. extremity [ɪkˈstrɛmətɪ] (n.) 肢體

2. fluently [ˈfluəntlɪ] (adv.) 流利地

3. strength [strɛŋθ] (n.) 力量

4. perfusion [pəˈfjuʒən] (n.) 灌流

5. rehabilitation [ˌrihəˌbɪləˈteʃən] (n.) 復健

6. significant [sɪgˈnɪfəkənt] (adj.) 顯著的

7. mention [ˈmɛnʃən] (v.) 提及

8. frustrated [ˈfrʌstretɪd] (adj.) 沮喪的

9. effort [ˈɛfət] (n.) 努力

10. exceed [ɪkˈsid] (v.) 超越

11. tolerance [ˈtalərəns] (n.) 耐受度

12. on schedule [an ˈskɛdʒul] 準時

13. fluctuate [ˈflʌktʃuˌet] (v.) 變動

14. do harm [du harm] 造成傷害；對…不利

術 語

1. brain [bren] 腦

2. spinal cord [ˈspaɪnḷ ˌkɔrd] 脊髓

3. gray matter [gre ˈmetə] 灰質

4. white matter [hwaɪt ˈmetə] 白質

5. frontal lobe [ˈfrʌntḷ lob] 額葉

6. parietal lobe [pəˈraɪətḷ lob] 頂葉

7. temporal lobe [ˈtɛmpərəl lob] 顳葉

8. occipital lobe [akˈsɪpətḷ lob] 枕葉

9. cerebrovascular accident (CVA) [ˌsɛrəbrəˈvæskjələ ˈæksədənt] 腦血管意外（腦中風）

10. hemiparesis [ˌhɛmɪˈpærəsɪs] 偏癱；半癱

11. CT = computerized tomography [kəmˈpjutəˌraɪzd təˈmagrəfɪ] 電腦斷層攝影

12. MRI = magnetic resonance imaging [mægˈnɛtɪk ˈrɛzənəns ˈɪmɪdʒɪŋ] 核磁共振攝影

13. GCS = Glasgow Coma Scale [ˈglæsgo ˈkomə skel] 格拉斯高昏迷量表

Chapter 12　一般外科

字 彙

1. mass [mæs] (n.) 腫塊

2. elastic [ɪˈlæstɪk] (adj.) 有彈性的

3. margin [ˈmardʒɪn] (n.) 邊緣

4. prominent [ˈpramənənt] (adj.) 明顯的

5. discharge [dɪsˈtʃardʒ] (n.) 分泌物

6. necessary [ˈnɛsəˌsɛrɪ] (adj.) 必要的

7. resection [rɪˈsɛkʃən] (n.) 切除術

8. plastic [ˈplæstɪk] (adj.) 整形的

9. surgeon [ˈsɜdʒən] (n.) 外科醫師

10. reconstruct [ˌrikənˈstrʌkt] (v.) 重建

11. recommend [ˌrɛkəˈmɛnd] (v.) 建議；推薦

12. exacerbate [ɪgˈzæsɚˌbet] (v.) 使加劇

13. accumulate [əˈkjumjəˌlet] (v.) 累積

14. demonstration [ˌdɛmənˈstreʃən] (n.) 示範

術 語

1. estrogen [ˈɛstrədʒən] 雌激素

2. dense connective tissue [ˌdɛns kəˈnɛktɪv ˈtɪʃu] 緻密結締組織

3. adipose tissue [ˈædəpos ˈtɪʃu] 脂肪組織

4. acini [ˈæsɪnaɪ] 腺泡（複數）（acinus 單數）

5. lobule [ˈlabjul] 小葉

6. ductule [ˈdʌktul] 小管

7. lactiferous sinus [lækˈtɪfərəs ˈsaɪnəs] 輸乳竇

8. lesion [ˈliʒən] 病灶

9. breast cancer [brɛst ˈkænsɚ] 乳癌

10. contraceptive [ˌkantrəˈsɛptɪv] 避孕藥

11. asymmetrical [ˌesɪˈmɛtrɪkl] 不對稱的

12. mastectomy [mæsˈtɛktəmɪ] 乳房切除術

13. CM 明晨（*cras mane*，意指 coming morning）

14. analgesic [ˌænælˈdʒizɪk] 止痛劑

15. drainage [ˈdrenɪdʒ] 引流液

16. distal [ˈdɪstl] 遠端的

17. proximal [ˈpraksəml] 近端的

Chapter 13 婦 科

字 彙

1. bothersome [ˈbaðəsəm] (adj.) 擾人的

2. navel [ˈnevl] (n.) 肚臍

3. digestion [daɪˈdʒɛstʃən] (n.) 消化

4. benign [bɪˈnaɪn] (adj.) 良性的

5. malignant [məˈlɪgnənt] (adj.) 惡性的

6. recovery [rɪˈkʌvərɪ] (n.) 復原

7. excise [ɪkˈsaɪz] (v.) 切除

8. on duty [an djutɪ] 值班

9. pelvic [ˈpɛlvɪk] (adj.) 骨盆的

10. administer [ədˈmɪnəstɚ] (v.) 給予；提供

11. due to [ˈdju tu] 由於

12. endogenous [ɛnˈdadʒənəs] (adj.) 內生的

13. dairy product [ˈdɛrɪ ˈpradəkt] 乳製品

14. permissible [pəˈmɪsəbl] (adj.) 可允許的

術 語

1. uterus [ˈjutərəs] 子宮

2. fetus [ˈfitəs] 胎兒

3. ovum [ˈovəm] 卵子

4. fallopian tube [fəˈlopɪən tjub] 輸卵管

5. sperm [spɝm] 精子

6. vagina [vəˈdʒaɪnə] 陰道

7. uterine [ˈjutərɪn] 子宮的

8. endometrium [ˌɛndəˈmitrɪəm] 子宮內膜

9. follicular phase [fəˈlɪkjulɚ fez] 濾泡期

10. luteal phase [ˈlutɪəl fez] 黃體期

11. ovarian cancer [oˈvɛrɪən ˈkænsɚ] 卵巢癌

12. gynecologist [ˌgaɪnəˈkalədʒɪst] 婦科醫師

13. menstrual period [ˈmɛnstruəl ˈpɪrɪəd] 月經週期

14. ultrasound [ˈʌltrəˌsaund] 超音波

15. pathology [pəˈθalədʒɪ] 病理學

16. PCA＝patient-controlled analgesia [ˈpeʃənt kənˈtrold ænælˈdʒizɪə] 病人自控式止痛器

17. port-A catheter [port e ˈkæθɪtɚ] Port-A 導管

18. chemotherapy [ˌkimoˈθɛrəpɪ] 化學治療

Chapter 14 產 科

字 彙

1. pregnancy [ˈprɛgnənsɪ] (n.) 懷孕

2. abortion [əˈbɔrʃən] (n.) 流產；墮胎

3. post-partum [post ˈpartəm] (n.) 產後的

4. contraction [kənˈtrækʃən] (n.) 收縮

5. width [wɪdθ] (n.) 寬度

6. descend [dɪˈsɛnd] (v.) 下降

7. incision [ɪnˋsɪʒən] (n.)　傷口；切口

8. breast-feed [ˋbrɛst fid]　哺餵母乳

9. position [pəˋzɪʃən] (n.)　位置

10. appropriate [əˋproprɪˏet] (adj.)　適當的

11. detail [ˋditel] (n.)　細節；詳情

術　語

1. ampulla [æmˋpʌlə]　壺腹部

2. placenta [pləˋsɛntə]　胎盤

3. normal spontaneous delivery (NSD)
[ˋnɔrmḷ spanˋtenɪəs dɪˋlɪvərɪ]　自然生產

4. cesarean section (C/S)
[sɪˋzɛrɪən ˋsɛkʃən]　剖腹生產

5. umbilical cord [ʌmˋbɪlɪkḷ kɔrd]　臍帶

6. labor pain [ˋlebɚ pen]　陣痛

7. bloody show [ˋblʌdɪ ʃo]　現血

8. due date [dju det]　預產期

9. water break [ˋwɔtɚ brek]　破水

10. sitz bath [ˋsɪts ˏbæθ]　坐浴

11. perineal [ˏpɛrəˋniəl]　會陰的

Chapter 15　小兒科

字　彙

1. hoarse [hɔrs] (adj.)　沙啞的

2. height [haɪt] (n.)　身高

3. weight [wet] (n.)　體重

4. bark [bark] (v.)　吠叫

5. therapeutic [ˏθɛrəˋpjutɪk] (adj.)　治療的

6. steam [stim] (n.)　蒸汽

7. cooperate [koˋapəˏret] (v.)　合作

8. inhale [ɪnˋhel] (v.)　吸入

9. humidity [hjuˋmɪdətɪ] (n.)　溼度（氣）

10. refrigerated [rɪˋfrɪdʒəˏretɪd] (adj.)
被冷藏過的

11. contagious [kənˋtedʒəs] (adj.)　接觸感染性的

12. spread [sprɛd] (v.)　散播

13. mask [mæsk] (n.)　口罩

術　語

1. pediatric [ˏpidɪˋætrɪk]　小兒科的

2. pediatrician [ˏpidɪəˋtrɪʃən]　小兒科專科醫師

3. pathophysiology [ˏpæθəˏfɪzɪˋalədʒɪ]
病理生理學

4. infancy [ˋɪnfənsɪ]　嬰兒期

5. adolescence [ˏædḷˋɛsṇs]　青少年期

6. croup [krup]　哮吼

7. aerosol therapy [ˏeəˋrasəl ˋθɛrəpɪ]　氣霧治療

8. cyanosis [ˏsaɪəˋnosɪs] (n.)　發紺

9. stridor [ˋstraɪdə]　哮鳴音

10. acetaminophen [æsətæˋmɪnəfən]　普拿疼

13. medicon syrup [ˋmɛdɪkənˋsɪrəp]　咳嗽藥水

14. saturation [ˏsætʃəˋreʃən]　飽和度

Chapter 16　眼　科

字　彙

1. blurred [blɜd] (adj.)　模糊的

2. object [ˋabdʒɪkt] (n.)　物體

3. foggy [ˋfagɪ] (adj.)　多霧的

4. dilate [daɪˋlet] (v.)　擴張；擴大

5. conscious [ˋkanʃəs] (adj.)　神智清醒的

6. eye patch [ˋaɪ ˏpætʃ]　眼罩

7. itchy [ˋɪtʃɪ] (adj.)　發癢的

8. sensitive [ˋsɛnsətɪv] (adj.)　敏感的；易受傷的

9. mechanical [məˋkænɪkḷ] (n.)　機械的

10. rub [rʌb] (v.)　揉搓

術　語

1. sclera [ˋsklɪrə]　鞏膜

2. cornea [ˋkɔrnɪə]　角膜

3. uvea [ˋjuvɪə]　葡萄膜

4. choroid [ˋkorɔɪd]　脈絡膜

5. ciliary body [ˋsɪlɪˏɛrɪ badɪ]　睫狀體

6. iris [ˋaɪrɪs]　虹膜

7. retina [ˋrɛtɪnə]　視網膜

8. lens [lɛnz]　水晶體

9. pupil [ˈpjupl̩] 瞳孔

10. vitreous body [ˈvɪtrɪəs badɪ] 玻璃體

11. cataract [ˈkætəˌrækt] 白內障

12. visual acuity [ˈvɪʒʊəl əˈkjuətɪ] 視力

13. visual field [ˈvɪʒʊəl fild] 視野

14. eye drop [ˈaɪ drap] 眼藥水

Chapter 17 耳鼻喉科

字 彙

1. tinnitus [tɪˈnaɪtəs] (n.) 耳鳴

2. vertigo [ˈvɜtɪgo] (n.) 眩暈

3. stuffy nose [ˈstʌfɪ noz] 鼻塞

4. intact [ɪnˈtækt] (adj.) 完整無損的

5. ice pack [ˈaɪs pæk] (n.) 冰袋

6. choke [tʃok] (v./n.) 嗆到；窒息

7. cautious [ˈkɔʃəs] (adj.) 留意；小心

8. perceivable [pəˈsivəbl̩] (adj.) 可察覺的

9. ice pack [ˈaɪs pæk] (n.) 冰袋

10. choke [tʃok] (v./n.) 嗆到；窒息

11. cautious [ˈkɔʃəs] (adj.) 留意；小心

12. perceivable [pəˈsivəbl̩] (adj.) 可察覺的

13. permit [pəˈmɪt] (v.) 允許

14. tough [tʌf] (adj.) 堅韌的；咬不動的

15. strain [stren] (v.) 拉傷

術 語

1. external auditory canal
[ɪkˈstɜnl̩ ˈɔdəˌtorɪ kəˈnæl] 外耳道

2. auricle [ˈɔrɪkl̩] 耳殼

3. tympanic membrane
[tɪmˈpænɪk ˈmɛmbren] 鼓膜

4. malleus [ˈmælɪəs] 鎚骨

5. incus [ˈɪŋkəs] 砧骨

6. stapes [ˈstepiz] 鐙骨

7. cochlear [ˈkaklɪə] 耳蝸的

8. vestibular [vəsˈtɪbjələ] 前庭的

9. sinus [ˈsaɪnəs] 鼻竇（全稱為 perinasal sinus）

10. chronic otitis media (COM)
[ˈkranɪk əˈtaɪtɪs ˈmidɪə] 慢性中耳炎

11. general anesthesia [ˈdʒɛnərəl ˌænəsˈθiʒə]
全身麻醉

12. tympanoplasty [ˌtɪmpənəˈplæstɪ] 鼓室成
形術

13. post-auricular [postəˈrɪkjələ] 耳後的

14. masticatory [ˈmæstəkəˌtori] 咀嚼的

Chapter 18 一般牙科

字 彙

1. allergic [əˈlədʒik] (adj.) 過敏性的

2. cavity [ˈkævətɪ] (n.) （牙齒的）蛀洞

3. pull out [pʊl aʊt] 拔除（牙齒）

4. restore [rɪˈstor] (v.) 修補（蛀牙）

5. inevitably [ɪnˈɛvətəblɪ] (adv.) 必然地

6. resin [ˈrɛzɪn] (n.) 樹脂（補牙材料）

7. amalgam [əˈmælgəm] (n.) 銀粉（補牙材料）

8. appearance [əˈpɪrəns] (n.) 外觀

9. decay [dɪˈke] (v.) 蛀蝕　(n.) 蛀牙

10. hygiene [ˈhaɪdʒin] (n.) 衛生、清潔

11. dental floss [ˈdɛntl̩ flɔs] (n.) 牙線

12. interdental brush [ˌɪntəˈdɛntl̩ brʌʃ] (n.)
牙間刷

13. mouth rinse [maʊθ rɪns] (n.) 漱口水

術 語

1. enamel [əˈnaml̩] 牙釉質（琺瑯質）

2. dentin [ˈdɛntɪn] 牙本質（象牙質）

3. cementum [səˈmɛntəm] 牙骨質

4. pulp [pʌlp] 牙髓

5. incisor [ɪnˈsaɪzə] 門齒

6. canine [ˈkenaɪn] 犬齒

7. molar [ˈmolə] 大臼齒

8. premolar [priˈmolə] 小臼齒；前臼齒

9. dental caries [ˈdɛntl̩ ˈkɛriz] 齲齒（俗稱蛀牙）

10. decalcification [diˌkælsəfəˈkeʃən]
（蛀牙形成過程初期的）脫鈣

Chapter 19 精神醫學

字 彙

1. stressful [ˈstrɛsfəl] (adj.) 有壓力的，緊張的

2. superficial [ˌsupəˈfɪʃəl] (adj.) 膚淺的，淺薄的

3. intention [ɪnˈtɛnʃən] (n.) 意向；意圖，目的；打算

4. consciousness [ˈkanʃəsnɪs] (n.) 意識；知覺

5. relevant [ˈrɛləvənt] (adj.) 有關的；適當的，貼切的

6. coherent [koˈhɪrənt] (adj.) 有條理的，首尾一貫的；一致的

7. detect [dɪˈtɛkt] (v.) 偵測；察覺

8. respond [rɪˈspand] (v.) 回應；反應

9. evidence [ˈɛvədəns] (n.) 跡象；，痕跡；證據

10. diagnosis [ˌdaɪəgˈnosɪs] (n.) 診斷；病名

11. alleviate [əˈlivɪˌet] (v.) 減輕（痛苦等）；緩和

12. efficacy [ˈɛfəkəsɪ] (n.) 效力；療效

13. stimulant [ˈstɪmjələnt] (n.) 刺激物，興奮劑，酒

術 語

1. affective [əˈfɛktɪv] 感動的；感情的
（在精神醫學中用以形容一個人的情感表現或情緒狀態）

2. perceptual [pəˈsɛptʃuəl] 知覺的；知覺力的

3. cognitive [ˈkagnətɪv] 認知的（指思考、想法、判斷）

4. criterion [kraɪˈtɪrɪən] 標準；準則（複數為 criteria）

5. dysphoria [dɪsˈfərɪə] 憂鬱情緒；煩躁不安

6. delusion [dɪˈluʒən] 妄想

7. suicidal ideation [ˌsuəˈsaɪdḷ ˌaɪdɪˈeʃən] 自殺意念

8. anxiolytic [æŋˌzaɪəˈlɪtɪk] 抗焦慮藥物

9. antidepressant [ˌæntɪdɪˈprɛsənt] 抗憂鬱藥物

MEMO

MEMO

國家圖書館出版品預行編目資料

醫護英文－醫療照護會話篇／劉明德，胡月娟，釋高上，蔡玫蕙，甘宜弘，薛承君，鄭群亮，黃偉俐，郭彥志，王惠芳，林郁婷，韓文蕙，馮兆康，張銘峰，Jonathan Chen-Ken Seak，Annie Li，呂維倫，王守玉，黃瑋婷，楊美華編著.－第四版.－新北市：新文京開發出版股份有限公司，2023.05

面；　公分

ISBN 978-986-430-926-9（平裝）

1.CST：英語　2.CST：醫學　3.CST：會話

805.188　　　　　　　　　　　　　　　　112007196

醫護英文－醫療照護會話篇（第四版）　（書號：B316e4）

審 訂 者	李燕晉	徐會棋	胡月娟	釋高上	林清華	鍾國彪
編 著 者	劉明德	胡月娟	釋高上	蔡玫蕙	甘宜弘	薛承君
	鄭群亮	黃偉俐	郭彥志	王惠芳	林郁婷	韓文蕙
	馮兆康	張銘峰	Jonathan Chen-Ken Seak		Annie Li	
	呂維倫	王守玉	黃瑋婷	楊美華		

出 版 者　新文京開發出版股份有限公司

地　　址　新北市中和區中山路二段 362 號 9 樓

電　　話　(02) 2244-8188（代表號）

Ｆ Ａ Ｘ　(02) 2244-8189

郵　　撥　1958730-2

初　　版　西元 2010 年 1 月 5 日

第 二 版　西元 2014 年 1 月 2 日

第 三 版　西元 2017 年 7 月 1 日

第 四 版　西元 2023 年 5 月 25 日

New Wun Ching Developmental Publishing Co., Ltd.

New Age · New Choice · The Best Selected Educational Publications — NEW WCDP

新文京開發出版股份有限公司

NEW
WCDP

新世紀・新視野・新文京 — 精選教科書・考試用書・專業參考書